"Like melt-in-your-mouth chocolate,
HARMONY is sinfully delicious from start to
finish. I absolutely loved this book!"
—Millie Criswell, author of *Desperate*

"OH GOD, EDWINA . . .
ONLY YOU."

She lifted her chin enough to look into Tom's face. Thank goodness, no lumps were rising on his forehead this time. Through his laughter, which now she had deemed overwrought delirium, she said on her behalf, "There wasn't any time to say 'Look out.'"

"Wouldn't have done any good if you had." The smile he gave her sent her pulse racing. She had no doubt he could have made even the most stodgy old maid fall into a fit of vapors.

Why did he have to be so . . . so . . . him? Why couldn't she have fallen onto a man who was bald and had a wart on his nose? Temptation would not be running amok in her brain if she had.

But it was. And at an alarming rate. If Tom so much as moved his mouth a fraction toward hers, she would let him kiss her. Again. She wanted him to. Desperately.

He knew. He knew what she wanted and he was going to do it.

Her heartbeat thrummed. She lowered her head. Slowly. He lifted his. Slowly. Her eyelids flitted closed . . . and she waited. . . .

"Like melt-in-your-mouth chocolate,
HARMONY
is sinfully delicious from start to finish.
I absolutely loved this book!"
—Millie Criswell, author of *Desperate*

PRAISE FOR
STEF ANN HOLM
AND HER WILD, WONDERFUL
WESTERN ROMANCE
FORGET ME NOT

"A cheery story . . . one endowed with Holm's fine sense of atmosphere, and an enjoyable heroine who changes and grows from a spunky, spoiled socialite to an independent woman."

—*Publishers Weekly*

"Ms. Holm transports the reader back to the Wild West. . . . Her characters come alive before your eyes in this delightful and highly entertaining story. A rollicking good time!"

—*Rendezvous*

"An engaging love story about a woman seeking to transform her life and gain independence. The secondary characters, J.D.'s irascible father and the cowboys, add to the underlying humor of Josephine's thoroughly Western adventure."

—Gerry Benninger, *Romantic Times*

"Stef Ann Holm takes us on a wonderful journey . . . filled with rich, historical detail. . . . She brings authentic characters to life, leaving the reader emotionally satisfied and eager for more."

—Robin La Fevers, Compuserve Romance Reviews

"A book that fans . . . will not forget any time soon. J.D. and Josephine make a charming pair and the secondary characters are all first rate. The Wyoming Territory is at its descriptive best in the hands of that master scribe, Stef Ann Holm."

—Harriet Klausner, *Amazon Books* (online)

"Stef Ann Holm has written a true 'forget-me-not' book. A real keeper. She gets better with each word she writes."
—Jan Robison, Waldenbooks

"Eastern gal meets western cowpoke and it's unforgettable! *Forget Me Not* is a surefire read from gifted storyteller Stef Ann Holm. Read it!"
—Suzanne Coleburn, *The Belles & Beaux of Romance*

"I truly enjoyed being in the West again with Jo and J.D. What an adventure. Just the right amount of romance, action, and history to spice up an afternoon of reading. Stef Ann can't be beat."
—Sharon Harbaugh, Munchkin Book Shop

"*Forget Me Not* highlights Stef Ann Holm's incredible talent. As a reader I walk with her memorable characters every step of the way."
—Elaine Galit, Blue Willow Books

"*Forget Me Not* will truly not be forgotten for years to come."
—Shelly Ryan, 1,001 Paperbacks

"*Forget Me Not* was a warm blending of relationships, reality, growth, humor, and love. Sweet as Jo's peach pies."
—Yvonne Zalinski, Paperback Outlet

"A not-to-be-missed reading experience that won't be easily forgotten. Fans of Americana, rejoice!"
—Sharon Walters, Paperback Place

"This story is so very heartwarming. It is like discovering a charming new treasure. The characters . . . are wonderful."
—Book Rack

Books by Stef Ann Holm

Harmony
Forget Me Not
Portraits
Crossings
Weeping Angel
Snowbird
King of the Pirates
Liberty Rose
Seasons of Gold

Published by POCKET BOOKS

Stef Ann Holm

Harmony

POCKET BOOKS

New York   London   Toronto   Sydney   Tokyo   Singapore

This book is a work of fiction. Names, characters, places and incidents are products of the author's imagination or are used fictiously. Any resemblance to actual events or locales or persons, living or dead, is entirely coincidental.

An *Original* Publication of POCKET BOOKS

POCKET BOOKS, a division of Simon & Schuster Inc.
1230 Avenue of the Americas, New York, NY 10020

ISBN: 0-671-00205-8

First Pocket Books printing December 1997

10 9 8 7 6 5 4 3 2 1

POCKET and colophon are registered trademarks of Simon & Schuster Inc.

Cover design by Jim Lebbad
Cover photo by Catherine Gehm, tip-in illustration by Ben Perini

Printed in the U.S.A.

For my husband, Barry,
who dragged me into the arms-and-tackle store
and showed me a whole new world.
You may be able to mountain-bike, skateboard,
surf, Rollerblade, and shoot a bow and arrow,
but just remember who whips your butt at gin rummy.

Harmony

❧ Prologue ❧

Murphy Magee was known for his humorous antics when he was three sheets to the wind—which was each evening from around six o'clock until whenever Lynell Pickering, the bartender at the Blue Flame Saloon, cut him off.

Because Murphy was a tinsmith by trade and a spendthrift by nature, the lint in his pocket stretched farther than his coin. So the group of men at the bar on this chilly autumn night found it curious that Murphy Magee would buy drinks for the house. But none questioned the good fortune of free liquor, and the generous rounds were accepted with devil-may-care grins.

When the hour neared midnight, Lynell told Murphy it was time to button up and be off to bed. Swilling down the last dram of whiskey from his tumbler, the wobbly Murphy allowed himself to be suited up for the elements by the barkeep.

Nudged through the door, Murphy stood on the boardwalk and recoiled as the wind blustered in his face. The gusts whistled through tree boughs, stirred up foliage, and ruffled the storefront awnings on Main.

Warding off a shiver, Murphy set out on a path down the middle of the street. He had the niggling feeling that he had done something twice, but he couldn't recall exactly what.

It had rained while he was in the Blue Flame, the air smelling like worms and musty wood. Large round puddles lay scattered before him like silver mirrors. He approached a shimmering pool, peered over scuffed boot toes, and gazed at his reflection. A fat white face rested on his shoulder.

Murphy quickly swung around, staggered, then searched the nearby shadows for a trace of the chap who was following him. No one stepped out to reveal himself. With a wry snort, Murphy meandered along until the next puddle came into view and that very same milky face hovered at his ear. As he turned around this time, he stepped backward. The wet splash at his feet caused him to look down once more.

In the rippling water, not only were his features distorted, but so were those of the man's face, whose features were as plump as pudding.

"Aye . . ." Murphy said with a broad grin at the reflection of the full moon that hung high in a dark sky. "I know who you be now, Mr. Man in the Moon. So you think to follow me, eh?" Then he purposefully jumped double-footed into the puddle with an uneven laugh. Blotches of cold, silty water marked the bottoms of his pants. He wavered as he watched his face and the moon above him settle on the puddle's surface once more.

Giving the moon a crude gesture with his middle finger, Murphy moved on. He tried to remember the people he'd spoken with today. . . . Lynell Pickering's voice was the most prominent, but a few others came to the surface.

A lopsided smile hitched the corner of his mouth. There had been that Miss Edwina Huntington. A pretty lady, but too prissy to suit his fancy. She'd been nice to him, though. She'd given him five hundred dollars. *Why . . . ?* He couldn't readily recollect. Then he believed he'd traded words with Tom Wolcott. Tom, he liked. The man was as red-blooded as they came.

For some reason, Murphy thought that his business with Miss Huntington in some way connected with Tom . . . but nothing came to mind.

Another puddle loomed, and Murphy hopped square into it, taking pleasure in the spray he sent onto the pavers. The road was torn up a bit here and there to make way for the sewers Harmony's Department of Public Roads had taken it into their fool brains the town needed.

Murphy ambled toward home with that great albino face in the sky floating after him. At every puddle, he took a leap dead center. It became a game of sorts as he met with each one. He paid no heed to the primitive fence and its sign of dim words that faded into the night. All he could see was the circumference of the biggest of all puddles—just behind the slates of wood.

Disregarding the barrier, Murphy let his legs spring him skyward. Only he didn't connect with the ground. His feet sliced into a giant void.

"Sweet Jaysus!" His lament echoed in his ears, and then was lost on the wind.

As Murphy plunged to a sure death, an ill-timed revelation sobered his brain. It was the queerest of moments to remember. But remember he did.

He knew now why Miss Huntington had given him five hundred dollars, and why Tom Wolcott had sought him out this evening at the Blue Flame.

Sweet Jesus. If the fall didn't kill him, surely the pair of them would once they found out what he'd done.

Chapter

❧ 1 ❧

As Tom Wolcott rode his piebald into Harmony, a party of six exhausted but satisfied men fell in behind him on plodding horses. Their duckcloth hunting suits, spanking new a week ago, now bore smatterings of mud, dung, and blood. But they'd gotten their great outdoors thrill in Montana, having bagged between them two elks, a cougar, and a half-dozen hares.

Cutting across Main Street toward Hess's Livery, Tom spied Shay Dufresne lounging in the sunlit double-wide doorway. Seeing his old friend and new partner, Tom sat taller in the saddle and his mood lightened. They'd known each other since boyhood, having grown up in the same Texas town. After turning eighteen, they'd traveled the western countryside together. They separated for a while, each trying their hand at different ventures, but now Tom had convinced Shay to come to Montana from Idaho. This would be the last time he had to take a group of greenhorn Easterners on a hunting trip. From now on, Shay would be in charge of the expeditions while Tom got his arms-and-tackle store off the ground.

"Hey, partner," Tom said in a greeting, reigning in and dismounting. He held onto the bridle leathers with one gloved hand while gripping his friend's hand in the other. "When'd you get in?"

"Three days ago." Shay gave him a warm smile, laugh lines etching creases at the corners of his eyes. His face was a bit angular, his nose a little too pointed; but he had a gaze that bespoke loyalty and trust.

Tom spoke around the cigarette in his mouth. "Max put you up?"

"As best he could." Shay withdrew his hand. "With all the crates and boxes you have stacked to the rafters, there's barely a free inch left to put up a cot."

Aside from stabling over two dozen riding and pack-horses with Max Hess, Tom had been using the livery as his warehouse and temporary business quarters.

"It'll all be moved out tomorrow." Over his piebald's rump, Tom called to the grin-happy city slickers. "Gentlemen, move those horses into the stables and Max will see to them. Unhitch your gear and trophies. There's a butcher on Hackberry Way who'll dress the meat, and if you want those horns mounted, I'm the man to see."

"By jinks, I want the whole head and neck on a lacquered wall plaque," came a jovial reply from the Bostonian banker.

"I can do that." Just as Tom tethered his horse on the branch of the only tree in front of the livery, a droopy looking bloodhound came trotting up. The dog shook off and shot his owner with Evergreen Creek water. "Dammit, Barkly, you could have done that elsewhere."

Barkly sat on his haunches; wet, loose skin hung in folds about his head and neck. His nose lifted toward Tom, and he made a grunting noise through his black nostrils.

"Don't tell me anything I don't know," Tom said off-handedly to the canine. "Shay, you think you can help them undo those diamond hitches? They're liable to take their knives to the ropes if they can't work the knots loose." With a flick of his wrist, Tom tossed his smoke on the ground and crushed the butt with the instep of his boot. "I need to make myself feel human again."

Tired and dirty, Tom longed to shed the navy lace-up-at-the-throat sweater that hugged his shoulders. Dust-coated Levi's and chaps encased his legs. His knee-high boots bore the nicks of twigs and pine needles. The stubble phase of a beard had lapsed into grubby; and he smelled like campfire smoke, game, and wet dog. He wanted nothing more than to soak in a hot sudsy tub, shave, then slip into a fresh set of clothes.

"Making yourself human will have to wait. A lawyer came by twice while you were gone. Last Tuesday he talked with Max, then yesterday I spoke with him." Shay slipped his hand into his pocket, produced a calling card, and read, "Alastair Stykem. You know him?"

"I've never met him, but I know he's got an office on Birch Avenue."

"He's real anxious to talk to you."

"About what?"

Handing Tom the card, Shay shrugged. "Hell if I know. I told him you were expected back today. He pressed me for a time, so I gave him one. You've got a two-o'clock appointment at his office."

Tom swore beneath his breath. "What time is it now?"

Shay took a watch out of his vest pocket. "Two-ten." Gazing up at Tom, he said, "I figured you'd be in by noon."

"We got that cougar just before lunch, and we had to pack it."

"You'd better get on over there. I'll handle things here."

Tom put a thumb to his hat brim and pushed back, then rubbed the grit off his brow. "Stykem didn't tell you what this was all about?"

"No. He just said he needed to talk to you. And that it was important."

Undoing the buckle of his gun belt, Tom looped the leather strap holstering his revolver over the saddle horn; he slung his chaps across the seat.

To the dog, Tom instructed, "Wait," then to Shay he said, "Whatever this is, it'd better not take long."

Leaving the livery behind, Tom walked down Main for a block, giving cursory glances to the post office, Storman's Feed and Fuel, and Buskala's Boarding House. He had become accustomed to the business buildings' being brick rather than the wood that was the norm where he and Shay hailed from. Nearly all were two stories and had canvas awnings of various shapes and heights that overhung the high board sidewalks. The corner supported the Blue Flame Saloon. A turn on Birch Avenue and he passed the barbershop, the druggist's, Treber's Men's Clothing store, and the Brooks House Hotel.

He'd rather have been going in the opposite direction so that he could take a look at the warehouse on Old Oak Road. A vacant lot away from the blacksmith's, but at least not across the railroad tracks by the lumberyard and flour mill, stood the building he'd bought from Murphy Magee. The interior measured a good size, comfortable enough to stock his merchandise and display his trophies and still have plenty of aisle room. For the past few months, he'd spent nearly all his income on sporting goods to fill his store. Tom had been taking men on hunting trips for the better part of a year. The trial period was over. His advertisements in eastern papers had proved to be successful in attracting suit-and-collar types out West for camping adventures they couldn't experience in the big cities.

Tom felt at ease in the woods, but the boisterous antics of dandies grated on him after the first day out. Being isolated with men sporting handlebar mustaches and rifles with superfine sights—front and rear—to guarantee a sure shot was not his idea of a challenge. Real gamesmen had to actually work at stalking their prey; not be so out of shape they were unable to hike up hills. Nor would they pine over the loss of forbidden flasks of brandy; Tom allowed no liquor in the campsites.

But now that Shay had arrived, Tom would stay behind in the store, letting the would-be hunters buy as many gadgets as they pleased while his partner took them out on the trail. Tom wasn't opposed to all the newfangled gadgets that helped a man bag his game with relative ease; he just preferred not to use them.

Grasping the handle of a door, Tom let himself inside a lobby that had the faint scent of ink. He crossed the granite floor tiles to a narrow stairwell on his right. At the top, a single hall featured two doors. In gold lettering, the first had ALASTAIR STYKEM, ATTORNEY AT LAW spelled out. Tom went in the office.

A young woman in a high-buttoned blouse sat behind a receiving desk, plucking at keys of a typewriter with one finger. On his intrusion, she looked up and down, then up again; then left and right as if she planned on fleeing. A pair of wire bow spectacles perched on her thin nose. Black ink smudged her forehead and chin. But it wasn't the ink that made him stare at her—it was the color of her hair. A vivid red-orange. Like Indian paintbrush petals.

"M-may I h-help you?" she stammered, not meeting his gaze while pushing her glasses farther up her nose. She left an ink smear across the freckled bridge.

"I have a two-o'clock appointment."

"M-Mr. W-Wolcott?"

His nod went ignored because she refused to lift her head. He had to resort to saying, "Yes."

"Th-they've been waiting for you."

They?

The woman stood, kept her gaze pinned to the carpet's cabbage rose pattern, and took a few steps to the paneled door. Knocking, she stuck her head through the crack she'd opened. "Mr. Wolcott is here," she announced in a clear, smooth voice.

"Good. Send him in." An exasperated breath punctuated the man's next words. "Crescencia, wipe that typewriter ink off your face."

"Yes, Papa."

Crescencia withdrew, then backed toward the desk so

9

Tom couldn't see her face—as if he hadn't already. Mumbling into the hankie she'd produced from a fold in her skirt, she said, "Y-you may go in, M-Mr. W-Wolcott."

Tom slipped by the desk and nudged the interior door the rest of the way open with his shoulder.

Alastair Stykem sat with his back to the window, sheer curtains deflecting the intensity of afternoon sun. Upon Tom's entrance, the lawyer rose from behind a massive oak desk and extended his hand. Tom had to step farther into the room to grasp it. After the formality, he felt a presence to his right and looked down at the occupant in the chair. A pair of pale, mint-colored eyes leveled on him. The woman had rich mahogany hair swept away from her oval face. Huge bows ran around the band of her hat, which sprouted a large blue chrysanthemum.

The lawyer's voice pulled Tom's gaze away. "Mr. Wolcott."

"Stykem," Tom said in acknowledgment.

"You know Miss Huntington?"

Unbidden, Tom's glance once again landed on the seated woman. "I've seen her around." But he had never inquired after her. There was an old-maidish air to the way she carried herself. He would have guessed her to be ten years older than him. But up this close, he could see he'd been mistaken. He had to have had her by at least five.

"Well then, please sit down, Mr. Wolcott."

Tom lowered himself onto one of the plump leather chairs, but he didn't feel at ease in the cushioned depths. Anxiousness made him reach for the half-pack of Richmonds in his front pants pocket, but he stopped himself midway when he saw the disapproval on Miss Huntington's face.

"I see no reason for preamble," Alastair continued. "Miss Huntington has known about the situation for a week, so I'll come right to the point." The lawyer steepled pudgy fingers against his paunch. "Murphy Magee is dead. He fell into a sewer hole last Monday night and sustained fatal injuries."

Tom regarded Alastair quizzically for a moment. Some sixth sense made him proceed with care. "I'm sorry to hear that. Murphy was a regular guy."

"Be that as it may, a problem has arisen that only Mr. Magee could have settled. Since he's not with us, the case has been brought to my attention by the county recorder's office in the hope that I can mediate a peaceful conclusion to this unfortunate situation."

The words *county recorder's office* cautioned Tom into silence. Resting his foot on a dusty knee, he pressed his back into the chair and depicted a comfort he didn't feel. Before he'd left Tuesday morning, he'd slipped the receipt Murphy had given him beneath the door to the county recorder's office so that he could pick up the deed when he got back into town. Obviously something had gone wrong. Maybe the clerk needed more information. Maybe Murphy hadn't written out the bill of sale correctly. The man had been drunk when they'd made the transaction at the Blue Flame. Even if Murphy had messed up, why was Miss Huntington sitting primly in the chair next to him?

Alastair opened a folder before him and produced two identical documents. He held them out for Tom to see. "As you can read, the warehouse at 47 Old Oak Road is deeded to both you and Miss Huntington. The clerk had recorded Miss Huntington's title on a Monday afternoon, and yours on a Tuesday morning. For legality's sake, it doesn't really matter whose was recorded first or last. Both are binding. If Mr. Magee was here with us, he could explain how he happened to sell both of you his warehouse. By his taking money twice, he's committed fraud"—the lawyer gave a slight shrug—"but who can prosecute a dead man?" After a chuckle, he answered himself. "My late wife would say *I* would if I could recover something."

Tom saw no humor in that. Accentuating the annoyance he felt with Stykem, Murphy, and Miss Huntington, who had begun to rummage through her purse, Tom brought his foot down hard on the floor and leaned forward. "What are you trying to tell me, Stykem?"

"You and Miss Huntington are both the legal owners of the parcel known as lot four, block two."

A cold knot formed in Tom's gut. Muscles on his forearms bunched as he took hold of the chair's arms and gripped the padded leather. If Murphy Magee weren't dead already, he'd go for the man's throat. He should have known better than to do business with a man basted with whiskey. But Tom hadn't wanted to leave for the week without having secured the warehouse, so the transaction had taken place in the saloon.

He heard a dainty cough and sniff, then glared at Miss Huntington. "What do you have to say about this?"

Miss Huntington had brought out a hunk of lacy stuff and lifted the edge to her nostrils. "Mr. Stykem, I find I'm feeling a little lightheaded. Could you please open the window for ventilation?"

"Open the window?" Tom echoed. "You've known about this for a week. If anyone is sick, it's me."

She kept her eyes forward. Curved lashes caught his attention; they were softly fringed and the exact shade of her hair. His gaze lowered. A kind of feathery blue fabric gently outlined her figure, cutting in at her narrow, sashed waist. He knew enough about ladies' fashions to appreciate that she wore pleats, bows, and trims in all the right places. As his eyes lingered on the controlled rise and fall of her breasts as she breathed into her handkerchief, he became aware of what he was doing. With a silent curse, he instantly stopped his appraisal of her.

Tom laid his palms on his thighs. "What now?"

The curtains fell back into place after Alastair unlatched the window lock and lifted the sash. He took his seat and pointedly gazed at the both of them. "Mr. Magee died on the installment plan. Meaning he owed people money." A shuffle of papers, and Stykem came up with a long list that he began to read from. "Eight dollars and forty-two cents to one Madame Beauchaine of Tut Tut, Louisiana, for astrological readings, ten cents to Dutch's Poolroom for dill pickles, three hundred and twenty-two dollars and four cents to the Blue Flame for a bar bill." Alastair waved his hand over the paper and set it down. "Et cetera, et cetera. Frankly, I don't know why he held onto the warehouse as long as he did. He could have used the revenue."

"What are you getting at?" Tom questioned.

"Murphy Magee's estate can't give a refund to either of you. After debtors get hold of what he has left of the money you gave him, there'll barely be enough to cover my fees." Stykem bent his fingers and cracked the knuckles in succession from pinkie to thumb. "I didn't want to suggest this without your being together, but one of you could buy the other out. Of course, that will mean you're paying twice for the property. You'll have to ask yourself how badly do you want it." Wiry brows arched as he waited for their reaction. Neither of them moved, so the lawyer continued. "Miss Huntington, you pay Mr. Wolcott five hundred dollars and the warehouse is yours. Or, Mr. Wolcott, you pay Miss Huntington four hundred and fifty dollars, and the warehouse goes to you."

"Four hundred and fifty?" came an indignant female squeak. "Mr. Stykem, I paid Mr. Magee five hundred dollars for the property."

"Yes, my dear, that is true. But the deal Mr. Wolcott worked out with Mr. Magee allowed him to buy the property for fifty dollars less than you paid."

Miss Huntington's rose-colored mouth thinned, and a blush crept up the ivory column of her neck. She was either highly embarrassed or angered to the boiling point. Tom couldn't tell for sure. He didn't really care. All he knew was he didn't have an extra four hundred and fifty dollars with which to buy her out. Nor could he afford for her to pay him five hundred for the right of ownership. No other site could enhance his store the way Magee's place could.

The warehouse on Old Oak Road was tailor-made for

his needs. It was tucked away from the town's populace, and the area surrounding it was semiwooded. A vacant lot sat on either side and to the rear of the building. He'd planned on setting up a target practice area out back, along with extension traps. Since stray clay pigeons and bullets would be no threat to another business or other persons, he didn't need a permit for open firearms other than the formality of an intent notice filed with the police department. He couldn't have that luxury in another building within Harmony's town limits.

"Well, hell," Tom said at length, exhaling. "That buyout idea doesn't work for me."

"Miss Huntington?" Alastair queried.

"My business adviser would caution me against it. My funds are tied up and cannot be released to buy the building a second time." The piece of lace had been lowered onto her lap. She wound a corner of the handkerchief around her slender forefinger, then unwound it. Wind, unwind. Wind, unwind.

"There ought to be some kind of law that says the warehouse is mine," Tom argued.

Miss Huntington cleared her throat. "Excuse me, but I paid for it first. After all, it was recorded to me on a Monday, and you on a Tuesday." Then, ignoring him, she spoke directly to the lawyer. "Mr. Stykem, don't take this the wrong way, but can't we approach a judge who has a higher definition of the law than you? Surely he could settle this as legally as possible."

"I've already consulted with Judge Redvers in Butte. When it comes to hard cases, he's got a reputation for using common sense as much as law." A toothpick rolled from the edges of Stykem's mountain of documents, and he absently fiddled with it. "Judge Redvers said he'd rule on any action like King Solomon. He'd cut the baby in half."

"We aren't fighting over a baby," Tom grumbled.

"I know that," Stykem cut in. "The baby is a hypothetical. The judge would rule to divide the warehouse, so there's no point in wasting time bringing the case to him when we already know what he'd say."

Miss Huntington's next query held a note of crispness. "So now what?"

"Now we'll have to proceed the only other way." Stykem went to yet another folder and produced a bid form. "I've taken the liberty of having Mr. Trussel look at the property. For a moderate fee, he can construct a wall that will evenly divide the building. And he can frame in another entry door on the east side. You both would have your own entrances; however, he advised me that the storage room in the rear that runs the length of the building cannot be altered. Several of its posts are main supports to the roof and tampering with them could be detrimental to the building's soundness. You would each have your own access to the area, only it wouldn't be sectioned in two like the main interior."

Tom mulled over the possibilities. He'd have to make everything fit in half the space. Perhaps he could still stock the same amount, but the aisles would be cramped. If he had to overload the walkways, where would he put his grizz? The bear had weighed six hundred pounds before he'd stuffed it. There had to be room for his mammoth eight-point bull elk and the lynx he'd gotten last winter. He had an endless amount of taxidermic fowl and small rodents that required counter space. Hunters liked to see trophies on display. And Tom had a shitload of them.

Massaging his temple, he fought against the idea of sharing the building with a woman who had a flower on her hat bigger than a moose's butt. He didn't like the thought of having to compromise with her. But it seemed to be the only choice he had.

"Forgive me saying so, Mr. Stykem, but I shouldn't have to pay half."

Tom gave the lawyer no opportunity to respond. "Sure you'll pay half."

Her gaze landed on his. "I shouldn't have to yield another cent." The tuft of lace resumed residency at her nostrils, and she spoke through the weblike pattern. "Already you've gotten your part of the building for fifty dollars less than me."

Alastair cut in. "I'm sorry, Miss Huntington, but the fact of the matter is, it doesn't matter if he paid one penny and you paid one thousand for the place. You both negotiated separate deals that have nothing to do with one another—except that they're for the same property."

She straightened. "Then my side should be at least a foot wider than his."

"There again, Miss Huntington, you can't measure against the original cost of the building. Both halves will have to be equivalent." A gold signet ring reflected light as Alastair twirled it on his finger. "So, are we all in agreement?"

"I'm afraid you leave us no other choice." Miss Huntington took the words right out of Tom's mouth.

"Mr. Wolcott?"

"It's like the lady said."

"Good, then everything is settled." Stykem tidied the documents on his desk. "It will be up to both of you to inform the postmaster that you'll each be getting your own mail. Miss Huntington, your address will be 47-A Old Oak Road, and Mr. Wolcott, your address will be 47-B Old Oak Road. I'll speak with Mr. Trussel and have him get started with the renovations right away."

Miss Huntington stood, then walked stiffly around the back of her chair to the umbrella stand and retrieved a folded parasol. "Good day, Mr. Stykem."

She'd gone out the door when Tom went to his feet and shoved his left hand in his pocket. "Stykem. I can't say it's been a pleasure."

The lawyer laughed. "I hear that a lot."

Tom stepped into the receiving office, where Miss Huntington and Crescencia were exchanging words. As soon as he came into the room, they shut up. He went past them, Crescencia saying, "G-good day, M-Mr. W-Wolcott."

"Yeah, same to you." He let himself out, thinking he heard Miss Huntington say something like, "Don't you fret about it, dear. You shall overcome, I assure you." Whatever that meant.

Once down on the street level, Tom went for his cigarettes and lit one while he stood on the boardwalk. As he waved out a match, Miss Huntington exited the building. She gave him a quick gaze, then proceeded. He had to go in her direction, so he trailed her. At the corner, they were forced to wait before crossing while the Harmony Fire Department backed its No. 1 engine into the firehouse.

He stood behind her. In height, he had at least ten inches on her, so he had an aerial view of the top of her hat. The air was as fresh as it could get out here, yet she started up with the handkerchief routine again. Then the reason hit him, dragging his pride down a notch. She thought he stunk. Hell, he knew he did. No wonder she'd had Stykem open the window.

On the toes of her proper shoes, Miss Huntington inched her way toward the curb. What did she think he was? A pig? He didn't like to be this in need of a bath, but when had there been time to put on his coattails before delivering himself to her presence?

Now that he realized she was bothered by him, he cut the distance between them. His chest nearly pressed against her shoulder blades. He would have gone in even further if his jaw hadn't been in jeopardy of being run through by the lethal pin sticking out of her hat.

When she moved again, she went a bit too far and teetered. He grabbed her by the elbow before she could fall into the street.

"What's the matter, Miss Huntington?"

"Nothing." She'd swung her body halfway around so that she could gaze at his face. Exotic green eyes held onto him as physically as his hand held onto her arm. It was a damn shame such pretty eyes belonged to a guardian of morality.

The silkiness of her dress felt good beneath his finger-

tips, so he didn't readily release her. Because he'd been
so bogged down in his business, it had been a while since
he'd held a woman and explored the delights of perfumed skin. He wouldn't have guessed that by touching
her elbow he could become aroused. But damn if he
wasn't.

What had started out as teasing her was teasing him.
He let her go, then took a deep pull on his cigarette.
"What are you going to do with your side?"

Her voice intruded in his head. Regaining a sense of
indifference, he replied, "Sell sporting goods."

Speculation filled her gaze. "Oh . . ."

He felt obligated—not that he wasn't curious—to ask,
"What are you going to do with your side?"

"Open a finishing school for ladies."

"What for?"

"To educate them in the rules, usages, and ceremonies
of good society."

"You mean to make them like you."

Her chin lifted, and for a minute he thought she might
jab him with the point of her unopened parasol. "I
should hope."

The boardwalk traffic began to move, but Miss Huntington stayed. "By the way, I hope you aren't *allergic*."
She said the word as if she wished he was. "I'll be bringing my cat."

After giving her an uneven smile, he crossed the street
and called over his shoulder, "No problem. I have a dog
who *loves* cats."

Edwina stood on the corner watching Mr. Wolcott dis-
appear from her view. She made a mental list of all his
offenses in the presence of her company.

Number one: Not removing his hat.

Number two: Reaching for cigarettes.

Number three: Not practicing personal hygiene.

*Number four: Openly staring at her without her
invitation.*

Number five: Using a swear word.

And number six: Verbally insulting her good character.

A half-dozen demerits. She would have counted touching her if his gesture hadn't been somewhat of a valiant attempt to keep her from falling into the street. But then he'd forced her into moving too far off the boardwalk.

Number seven: Unacceptable bodily contact.

In spite of herself, faint tingles rushed to the spot he'd touched. His fingers had been firm yet gentle when he'd held her elbow. Crystal blue eyes had scowled at her beneath down-turned brows. A mane of tawny hair laid in a disarray across unscrupulously wide shoulders. At first his gaze had been bright with humor, but then it had changed to a dark, unfathomable hue. She didn't want to think about what he'd been thinking about.

The man was a toad. She had to give today's women the opportunity to choose the right husband for themselves and not settle for whoever lived in Harmony's tight-knit circle. Ironically, Mr. Wolcott had unwittingly been her helper.

She had been aware that he entertained Eastern gentlemen by taking them on hunting jaunts. The steady visits of well-bred clientele had given her an idea this past summer.

Harmony's eligible young ladies should be introduced to men of respectable professions—not that the selection in town was dire. But those who stayed after graduating the normal school rarely set their sights beyond a trade or working at Kennison's Hardware Emporium. And the handful who had aspirations of bright futures left for college and didn't often return once they saw what the outside world had to offer them.

While in Chicago attending business college, Edwina had fallen in love with a man about town. Their relationship had been chocked with spontaneity, but it hadn't resulted in marriage. Smarter now, she realized she'd lost herself to a beau who heeded his mother's opinions rather than his heart. By enlightening girls about the facets of courtship—especially the do's and don'ts—she hoped to empower them to know the difference between real love and passing affections. There were good men who came from large cities, and just because Edwina had chosen the wrong one didn't mean that she thought all Easterners were mollycoddled. On the contrary, those who sought the West for recreation were of a different breed. She saw them as adventure-seekers.

Where Mr. Wolcott had thought of a way to bring gentlemen to their small Montana town, Edwina had thought of a way to show those very gentlemen that charming women didn't necessarily reside only on city streets. Perhaps her students would impress the men into staying, and those marriages could add a diversity to the community.

Edwina crossed the street, then proceeded on Main toward her residence on Sycamore Drive. Sugar maples shaded the walkway, their leaves showing vague signs of the autumn change. The season hadn't taken hold yet. Though nights brought a shivering chill, days could be warm beneath the buttery sunshine.

She had a seven-o'clock meeting that evening at her home. A cake needed to be baked and the silver tea service brought out. Tonight was an important night. Everything had to be perfect. The afternoon had upset her, but at least she'd been apprised of the situation before Mr. Wolcott had come to the law office.

When she'd first learned about Mr. Magee's selling the warehouse twice, she'd wanted to give him a stern piece of her mind. But immediately thereafter, she'd been informed that he had died in an accident, and she'd felt horrible for having wished he would have one. Only in her mind, he hadn't died . . . merely suffered some minor blood loss with a fracture. Or two.

She could hardly bear to think that she'd spent what precious little money she had left in the bank—just over five hundred dollars—much less being asked to come up with another five hundred with which to buy out Mr. Wolcott. To add insult to injury, when she found out that she'd paid fifty dollars more than him—for the *exact same property*—she'd felt as if Mr. Magee had made a mockery of womankind. He must have thought females pretty stupid when it came to business deals.

Edwina's lips curved down. Well, she'd been stupid enough, but right now that was a moot point.

Of course she didn't have a business adviser. But after finding out that she'd been made a fool of once, she wasn't about to be one twice. Especially not in front of Mr. Wolcott. He needn't know that she couldn't afford to buy him out.

She wouldn't have had this trouble if she'd taken that quaint suite in the Ellis building. But the deposit and monthly rent would have sent her to the poorhouse even quicker than she was already headed.

Turning down a sycamore-lined street with Queen Anne homes, expansive lawns, and multitudes of color in both trims and landscape, Edwina clicked the tip of her parasol on the hard-packed ground.

Sporting goods. Why did he need to sell that nonsense? The Sears and Roebuck catalogue sold the basics a man needed, and even then, the few items she'd seen while flipping to the ladies' section had looked rather silly.

A mere wall dividing them would surely not be enough. Among other things, his remark insinuating that his dog would eat her cat had cinched that. She'd take a waffle iron to that mongrel if it harmed so much as one hair of her precious Honey Tiger's fur.

But for the good of all the marriageable young ladies, Edwina would endure any inconvenience she had to. She longed to see happy homes with loving husbands, celebrating christenings, birthdays, and anniversaries. Of course, that wasn't to be for her. . . . No gentleman would ever marry her if he knew the truth.

So Edwina Huntington had to pretend to be an unapproachable old maid, uninterested in affections. Because she had a deep, dark secret. One that she'd rather take to a presumed spinster's grave than ever—*ever*—reveal.

Chapter

❦ 2 ❦

Edwina had left the downstairs windows partially open. The lace curtains whispered the soft autumn evening through the house, filling the parlor with the late scent of roses and second-blooming phlox. Warm ginger and cinnamon came from the kitchen, where Marvel-Anne was icing the batch of gingerbread Edwina had baked when she'd come home.

From her bedroom upstairs, an indignant Honey Tiger meowed behind the closed door. Her tabby had a fixation for Mrs. Treber's petticoats—she wore them fourfold. Honey Tiger would bat at the frilly hems and cause annoyance; Edwina didn't want anything to disrupt the evening.

Pausing at the hall mirror, she pinched color into her cheeks, then ran her hands down the smooth lines of her sage green dress with chocolate stripes. She plucked off a few stray honey-colored cat hairs before she squared her shoulders and took in a deep breath. Confident her pulley-belt encircled her waist snugly and her plackets lay neat, she turned away and went into the parlor as Marvel-Anne came through the dining-room portieres carrying the tray of confections.

"Did you want me to put these out now, Miss Ed-

22

wina?" The stout hired girl moved to the tea cart as if she knew what Edwina's answer would be.

"Yes, please."

Marvel-Anne had worked for Edwina's family as long as Edwina could remember. Because of the woman's good organization and no-nonsense personality, the parlor was always rigidly neat. Marvel-Anne dusted behind the pictures and never left the shades up in summer sunshine more than ten inches so as not to fade the Axminster ingrain carpet. The ceiling lamp's crystal pendants always glittered, as did the brass chain links that pulled down the globe so the red-colored kerosene could be lit. On Mondays, she did the washing; on Tuesdays, the ironing; on Wednesdays, the mending. Thursdays and Fridays, she gave the house an extra cleaning. Saturday, she did baking, and on Sunday, there was the Sunday dinner to prepare and the best china to wash afterward.

When Edwina's father had died four years ago, Marvel-Anne had practically moved in to help. Then she'd aided Edwina with the nursing of her mother, who had taken ill the past summer. Mother had gone peacefully in her sleep, and now Edwina was alone in the big house. She should have let Marvel-Anne go because the residence didn't need nearly the attention it was given—that, and there was the matter of money. Or, rather, the lack of any extra. When she'd tried to broach the subject of dismissal in a roundabout way, Marvel-Anne quickly minced her carefully chosen words. She'd say, "Never you mind, Miss Edwina. Don't worry a lick about me. There's nothing else I'd rather do with my time. After all these years, I know the routine and I like to keep routine in my life."

Edwina hadn't the heart to tell Marvel-Anne that she hadn't been thinking of her well-earned retirement. Simply, Edwina couldn't afford to pay for her services anymore. But after tonight, if all went well, she'd be able to stay afloat for a while.

The bell cranked, and Marvel-Anne lumbered to the

door. Within the next few minutes, the parlor was filled with a gaggle of ladies balancing steaming teacups and dainty plates of gingerbread.

"Ladies," Edwina announced while standing up in a motion so fluid and graceful one would swear she'd never practiced the move. "I'm so glad you all could come." Amid the clatter of china against saucers and silver fork tines against dessert plates, Edwina proceeded. "It pleases me greatly to inform you that the Huntington Finishing School is now a reality. I have secured a building for the girls, and it will be ready for occupancy—I hope within the week."

There were approving nods all around the group, but there were two abstentions: Mrs. Elward and Mrs. Plunkett.

Prudence Plunkett sat in one of the chairs ornamented with a tassel valance around the bottom. The cushioned hassock her large feet rested on swallowed her shoes whole; only the tips of pointed black peeked from the damask. "I don't want my precious Hildegarde to marry an Eastern gentleman and move away to the nasty city." Big, ungainly, and solid, she suddenly became afflicted with a pain in her side, which she gripped with plump white fingers; the other hand held firmly onto her third serving of cake.

Edwina had witnessed Mrs. Plunkett's "attacks" before; she suspected they weren't some foreign ailment that she professed the doctor told her was incurable, but rather plain old ordinary indigestion. "Are you all right, Mrs. Plunkett?" Edwina asked. "Shall I have Marvel-Anne make you a bicarbonate of soda?"

Waving a dumpling arm, Mrs. Plunkett's fleshy pink mouth frowned. "No, no. It shall pass." She snuck in another bite of cake.

The druggist's wife, Mrs. Elward, sat like a pencil on the divan's silken edge. A thin, nervous little woman, all curls and ruffles and beads and dangling ribbons, she ventured to say, "You don't know what happens to girls in a metropolis . . . married or not."

Mrs. Kennison set her cup and saucer down. "Fanny, don't be a boob." Rarely did anyone contradict Grayce Kennison. She was too stunningly beautiful to spar with. Her complexion seemed transparent, and she could pile her golden hair in a wavy pompadour higher and fuller than any of them ever could. "I don't think a city is an evil place. I for one wouldn't mind if my Camille could live in New York or Philadelphia. I'd be tempted to go with her."

Shallow gasps circulated through the room. Grayce gave a heavy sigh laden with frustration. *"With* Mr. Kennison, of course."

Brows settled reassuringly back into place.

"Miss Huntington," Mrs. Calhoon said, lifting her chin a bit and causing the light to shine on her nose. Her cluster of summer freckles had begun to fade. "You were in Chicago. Was the city wicked, as far as cities go?"

A discomfiting heat stole into Edwina's cheeks. Talking about Chicago and the business college wasn't something she wanted to do. Memories were all she had left, and it was heartbreaking for her to relive them.

"Chicago offered valuable resources that one cannot glean from a town of our size. But that isn't the question here tonight, ladies." Edwina commandeered the conversation down a different avenue. "What is of the utmost importance is that your daughters are properly educated in the deportment of our society so that they may marry men worthy of their wonderful charms."

"We wouldn't want them to become old maids," Mrs. Treber commented, "like that dear Crescencia Stykem." There was no imminent danger of a lack of suitors for her own daughter. Mr. Treber owned the men's clothing store, and Mrs. Treber eyeballed every male customer as a potential son-in-law.

"Poor things," Mrs. Calhoon said, seconding the sentiment. "They can't help it."

Mrs. Plunkett washed down the last of her gingerbread

with sweetened tea. "People ought to be sorry for them."

"Why nobody ever took a shine to Crescencia Stykem before beats me." Mrs. Brooks's mud-colored eyes were set deep in her narrow face. She admitted to sleeping in her corset to keep her figure straight and inflexible—much like her way of thinking.

"Why, yes," Mrs. Elward added, "now that you point it out. She's thrifty and capable. And from what I understand, a commendable cook."

Mrs. Treber chimed in. "She'd make a real helpmate for some good man."

"I declare," Mrs. Kennison said. "When you see the girls that do get married, it seems to me men haven't got the sense that God gave little apples."

Mrs. Calhoon nodded. "With Miss Crescencia's not having a mother to guide her, we should talk to her about enrolling in Miss Huntington's school. Why, my Lucille is sixteen and on the shadowy approach to being an old maid herself."

"So is my Ruth," Mrs. Elward sighed. "Good land— I shudder to think she should find herself on the shelf at seventeen." She grimaced.

"That Wayland girl married at fourteen," Mrs. Kennison said.

Mrs. Plunkett refused Marvel-Anne's temptation of a fourth serving of cake. "That's a little too young for comfort."

Mrs. Treber begged to differ. "Unless the man is reliable."

Grayce agreed. "Which Harvey Wayland was."

Mrs. Brooks tsked. "I'm glad I haven't got one of those lazy, easygoing fat men to contend with."

"So true." Prudence brushed the spicy crumbs from the voluptuous yards of black cashmere comprising her lap. "Mr. Plunkett has his faults, but I must say he is a good provider. I cannot imagine going through life without a husband to take care of me the way Mr. Plunkett does."

Quite by accident, the curtains rippled like ghostly spirits on a gust of dusk-borne wind. The parlor grew painfully quiet, as if the occupants suddenly realized that what they were talking about could be hurtful to a woman who didn't have a man in her life, namely one Miss Edwina Huntington who would never see twenty-four again.

Edwina told herself that she didn't care, that their talk of husbands didn't discompose her. But hidden away, in that closed-off place that protected the rend in her heart, their remarks did wound—only she would never let them know how deeply.

Mrs. Kennison spoke first. "Well . . . we can't have our girls gadding about uptown by the blacksmith's and getting into trouble for it. I was all for the idea when Miss Huntington told us about her plans, so I have no qualms enrolling my Camille in the finishing school. I can't think of a better model for my daughter."

A sigh of relief fluttered against Edwina's rib cage. She went to the parlor organ and picked up the receipt pad and applications she'd set on one of the jutting little shelves.

As she put the carbon in order and positioned her writing pen, the other five ladies announced their desire to have their girls enrolled in the school also. Edwina informed them that the tuition was to be five dollars a month. All replied that their husbands would see to it that she was paid before the end of the week for the first month's expenses.

Half an hour later, Edwina saw the clutch of women to the door. As Mrs. Plunkett's expansive skirt faded from her sight, Edwina stayed on the porch and wrapped her arm around one of the dark red posts. She pressed her cheek to the cool wood and gazed at the rising moon. Sycamore boughs spread dark against the creamy night sky, and frogs croaked from a distant pond.

She should have been totally elated, brimming with sheer joy. She had succeeded with the first phase of financial recoupment. Unhappily, that fact barely softened the edge of disappointment that she wouldn't be using her business diploma the way she'd envisioned.

The shock of finding out that her father's life insurance had nearly run out because of medical expenses incurred by both her parents still gave her cause for disbelief. Life insurance was supposed to ensure that the beneficiary bore no hardships. Her mother had weathered humiliation by mortgaging the house, then ignoring the mail in their postal box.

Delinquent bills from various cure-all doctors and druggists who advertised in newspapers had been adding up for nearly a year. Only in the past four months, since her mother's death, had Edwina found out about the debts. A week ago, a letter had come from the Equity Mortgage Company in San Francisco, California, stating the house would be repossessed in ten days if she didn't make an immediate payment. She'd written a check from the bank account that had been bequeathed to her and sent it off the very afternoon she'd received the intent-to-foreclose notice; then she'd gambled nearly all the remaining funds on the warehouse.

All her plans to leave Harmony and seek employment in Denver had come to a grinding halt. What Edwina Huntington wanted for herself no longer mattered. The family's respectability was at stake. She couldn't just pack up and ignore the responsibility.

Accepting her lot, she'd assured the debtors that she would take care of the bills as soon as possible. Her desire to educate the local girls was only one of the reasons for the school. The other was because she desperately needed the income.

So she would now help girls develop high standards of morals and manners. Silly, really, when coming from her.

Edwina sighed softly. When she was nineteen, she had thought she knew exactly what her life was going to be because she controlled its course. She had no intention of meekly accepting or making the best of anything— and that had meant not staying in Harmony. Armed with the discovery of her independence, she planned her bright future and left to attend Gillette's Business College for Ladies in Chicago, Illinois.

The first year had been wonderful, the second even better. During her third, she'd met Ludlow. Her fourth had been heaven . . . but with hell in the lurch. A mere week before graduation, the bliss crashed around her, and the frantic letter had come from home. She'd returned right away and stayed by her mother's bedside to the end.

She'd remained in Harmony after the graveside service, and she'd never gone back to that bohemian world in Chicago, that place of laughter and music and free thinking. She'd gotten her certificate through the mail, missing out on the pomp and ceremony with the other girls . . . with Abbie.

Always aspiring, and failing, to conform to social propriety, Edwina had come to know she was different. There was an energy in her, an almost disturbing capriciousness, that wouldn't go away—no matter how hard she tried.

With the handful of katydids shrilling in the trees, Edwina tapped her toe to the wavering beat, wishing she could dance for fun once more.

Tom opened the heater's swing cover with a rag and snagged the handle of a lumpy metal coffeepot. The hiss of burner wicks and the odor of fuel oil filled the warehouse, but the heat hadn't spread enough for him to take off his thick flannel overshirt.

Nudging the cover closed with his elbow, Tom set the pot of coffee on the end of a sawhorse where he had an empty cup. Shay had gone to the livery to pack up a few things while Tom stayed to lay out the modified store before Ab Trussel came by on Thursday to put up the wall.

After pouring himself a naked cup of the brew, Tom walked around the area holding his coffee. Barkly's bloodshot gaze followed his movement, but the hound's head stayed positioned on his forepaws; he didn't budge from the warm floorboards in front of the heater. Tom paused at the seven-foot spread eagle that he'd dragged to the morning light streaming from the window. Earlier while rummaging through the storeroom, he'd found tin plates, an assortment of tools, and unfinished projects. The tin bald eagle had been tucked in one of the corners with a dusty drapery covering it. The broad wings were amazingly lifelike in their depiction of feathers, and the tilt of the bird's head could only be described as proud. Tom felt like he'd stumbled onto Christmas. He wanted that eagle to mount over his entrance door. If Miss Edwina Huntington took a shine to the bird, she would have to fight him for it.

As if saying her name in his head could conjure her, there she stood, peeking into the window. He stepped out of the sunlight and into the shadows, watching as she cupped gloved hands to her temples to view the interior better. Her balance wavered, then her shoulders took a slight dip. She must have been standing on her tiptoes. The four-on-four glass didn't offer him clarity while perusing her; there were too many cobwebs and a film of dirt. What he *could* see was her expression: the brief white of her straight teeth as she bit her lower lip, then the singular arch of one perfect brow as she lowered her hands. She was thinking.

He didn't like that in a woman.

Taking a slow gulp of coffee, Tom went to the door but stopped before turning the knob.

"It looks locked," he heard Edwina say from the other side.

Another female voice replied, "Yes, Miss Edwina."

"I should have gotten the key from Mr. Stykem before Mr. Wolcott got it." A dull clattering sounded—like a hoop bucket with a cake of soap inside. "That man is an animal. You should have seen him at the lawyer's office. He looked like he'd been taking a dust bath with the chickens in front of Storman's feed mill. And he just about smelled as ripe as a pigpen."

"Barkly," Tom whispered. The folds of skin above the

dog's shoulder-length ears prickled to attention. "Come here."

"It's too bad he's got interesting eyes," Edwina continued. "A man like that ought not to have interesting eyes. I'm sure he's used them against innumerable women, trying to get what he wants, then he . . ."

Tom tuned her rattling voice out as the click of Barkly's toenails headed his way. As soon as the hound reached the door, Tom said, "Sit." The dog did so. Even sitting, Barkly made an intimidating foe. The top of his rusty-colored head came up to the start of Tom's hip.

". . . a lingering gaze like his could give women all the wrong impressions. Why, if I wasn't—well, never mind. I suppose we should find out if the lock's engaged."

Barkly licked the dangle of drool off his rubbery muzzle, but got only half of it as the door swung outward. Then a high-pitched scream of terror started a hellacious ringing in Tom's ears.

"Dammit all!"

Only after a scant moment, Tom comprehended that both he and Miss Huntington had uttered exactly the same thing at the same time. His gaze lifted to hers with a hard glare of surprise. A bloom of pink streaked across her cheeks, and she looked away before he could read anything from her eyes. Curiously regarding her, he pondered the possibility that indelicate thoughts might be hidden in that outwardly decorous head of hers.

"Next time you're wondering if a door is locked," he drawled, "why don't you see if it'll open first before you talk it to death. You never know who's on the other side."

"Or whose ferocious dog," she countered, warily keeping her distance on the stoop. "Can you please tell it to move so I can come in?"

Tom took another leisurely drink of his coffee. He rather liked having her at his mercy, especially after the colorful things she'd said about him. He'd never once used his gaze to get a woman to do what he wanted. His hands had always done all the convincing.

"Mr. Wolcott, will you?" came her impatient request.

Lowering the cup, Tom said, "Barkly. Out."

The bloodhound rose from his haunches but didn't walk directly outside; his wet nose began to twitch with the excitement of trying to corral a good scent. Soon, the loud sound of snuffling could be heard, and Barkly started giving Miss Huntington's skirts the once-over.

She took a hop backward, bumping into the woman at her side. Tom gave the other woman a fleeting glance. Built like an ox, her body looked more solid than a block of wood; an iron twist in her gray hair didn't do a thing to lessen her hard appearance.

"Do something!" Edwina squealed, the bucket in her hand swinging.

"Once he's on a scent, he goes deaf to my voice." Dragging his nose across the black-and-white–checked fabric, the dog inhaled sharply four short times, then snorted out the scent on the fifth beat, as if to clear his nasal passages. "Must be that cat of yours that has him all worked up."

Tom had witnessed Barkly go through this process countless times and knew there was no point in telling the dog to back off. To Barkly, getting in as much as he could of a good sniffing was worth any reprimand.

Edwina made an attempt to clutch her skirts away, lifting them higher. The dog's nose just elevated with her movement, rather than being deterred. Her gaze fell onto Barkly's face. "My goodness, this dog has no eyes."

"He's got two. Both brown." Using a gentle grip, Tom grabbed a handful of Barkly's scalp and pulled upward, giving the dog's face a lift. Undistracted, Barkly kept sniffing, navigating a path higher toward what would have been Edwina's lap had she been sitting. Of course, she misconstrued his investigation of the area as being of something else more vulgar.

"Stop that, you nasty thing!" she said, choking, swishing the side of her skirts to her middle for protection. The satiny swish of her petticoats sounded provocative.

Tom let the dog's skin go slack. Then with a sideways

glance, he took in an appreciative eyeful of black-stockinged ankles, a frothy swath of underwear lace, and even a little bit of some attractive shins.

Sneezing, Barkly left a spray of slobber on Edwina's skirt before he decided he'd had enough and trotted on.

"Oh!" she cried with outrage.

Downing a quick sip of his cooling coffee, Tom shrugged. "Must be a potent cat. He couldn't keep all the scent in."

Edwina entered the building with a shake of her skirts, the strapping woman close on her heels. She must have been hired help, because she carried the bulk of the cleaning supplies. The pair went to the center of the school's side and deposited a mop, bucket, rags, broom, window brushes, and bottles of ammonia.

Briskly running her hands across her arms, Edwina couldn't disguise her chill from him. She wore a tailored hip-length jacket, but the fabric didn't appear to be very heavy. Kid gloves encased her slender fingers.

Tom wasn't much for chitchat. He was here to work, but he figured he ought to offer what he had.

"If you ladies want to stand by the heater for a while, you're welcome to." He set his empty coffee cup on the sawhorse. "I've got coffee, too."

"No, thank you." Edwina's feminine voice filled the cavernous warehouse.

"I make a mean pot. Black as sin and hot as hell. You'll have to use my cup, though, if you want some." He sent her a suggestive smile.

"*Definitely* no, thank you," she responded tartly.

"Suit yourself." His mouth curved into a half grin, then he picked up a disk of red chalk and began to walk the perimeter of his area.

Tom more or less forgot about them as he marked off the floor measurements of his counters, shelves, and aisles and made the circles that denoted stuffed animals. He saved the grizz for by the heater, where the bear could be a topic of conversation. Standing with his back against the storeroom wall, arms folded over his chest, he surveyed his handiwork. A movement caught his peripheral vision, and his survey strayed to the sway of Edwina's hips as she scrubbed the top panes of the window while standing on an overturned crate.

A hairpin worked loose from her high twist, and she paused to nudge it into place with the back of her wrist. Stepping off the crate, she dunked her drab cloth into the water bucket, rung it out, then climbed back on the makeshift stool. An air of capability surrounded her, bringing a vigor to her concise movements.

Tom went to the heater, pitched the chalk nub into a box, and took a load off on the sawhorse. He ran his red-stained hands down the sides of his denims, then reached into his breast pocket for his Richmonds.

Lighting one, he dropped his elbows to his knees and settled onto the plank to enjoy his smoke while watching Miss Edwina Huntington's backside shimmy.

Edwina could feel Mr. Wolcott's hot gaze on her back and grew perturbed. Didn't he have anything better to do than to stare at her? She and Marvel-Anne had been working themselves to the bone all morning, and he'd done nothing to improve the appearance of his side of the building. All he'd accomplished was scratching red chalk on the floor, drinking coffee, and smoking cigarettes. He certainly wasn't as ambitious as she was.

At least that oversized dog of his hadn't returned to sniff her silly. She could only pray that Marvel-Anne hadn't heard her slip of the tongue. Mortified, she hadn't been able to meet Tom Wolcott's gaze. She should have stopped herself from blurting such crass words without thought. But she'd been surprised senseless, and not by accident. Surely that bloodhound had been positioned there as a deliberate scare tactic. She took it as an omen of things to come.

If only she hadn't said those things about his eyes to Marvel-Anne. Extreme humiliation washed over her anew. She'd never wanted him to know that in spite of his ill-kempt appearance the other day, she hadn't been immune to the appealing features of his face. They'd been made all the more appealing this morning by the time she'd entered the warehouse.

She hadn't been prepared to confront him after he'd given himself a stern grooming. Though he'd left his hair untrimmed, without his hat, the heavy waves fell half behind his ears—the right side deliberately put there. The not altogether unpleasing length ended softly over the collar of a royal blue overshirt. His beard and mustache had been shaved away to smoothness, leaving his square jaw visible.

Seeing him this way made her hard pressed to remember he was someone she didn't like. He'd finagled purchasing the warehouse for fifty dollars less than her. That meant he was a man not to be trusted. He took advantage of those—namely her—who hadn't had the foresight to negotiate the price down, too.

Getting off the crate, Edwina flashed a furtive look in Tom's direction. He still remained perched on the sawhorse, a cigarette dangling between his fingers. Gall rose inside her that he would openly gape. His slow gaze burned over her body, making her feel annoyingly warm and flushed—even with the warehouse's chill. He sat in a casual way, legs spread apart and boot heels hooked on the wood brace, as if he didn't have a care in the world. She only wished she could act so free and unrepressed.

Edwina freshened her cloth, then worked on the lower panes of the window. Any gentleman would have had the decency to offer his assistance once he saw that she and Marvel-Anne were tackling a big job. Though she didn't really want to be indebted to Mr. Wolcott, so better to chap her own hands than accept his helping one.

A brittle cold remained in this section of the spacious room, despite the heater on full service at Tom's side. This brought to mind a problem Edwina hadn't foreseen: sufficiently heating her school. She had the means, but it meant she would do without at home.

Marvel-Anne came toward her with the mop to swish the dingy ropes in the ammonia bucket.

"We'll have to use the heater from my room," Edwina said as water sloshed in between Marvel-Anne's fingers while she squeezed the mop head. "It's a good thing we didn't lug it in there from the attic already."

"But you'll get too cold without a heater."

"My bedroom is above the parlor. I'll keep the embers banked high in the fireplace so they stay hot most of the night. And there's extra blankets."

Marvel-Anne nodded. "I'll step out and do the other sides of the windows, then we'd best go home for lunch and a cup of hot tea."

If Mr. Wolcott continued with his unrelenting stare, Edwina wouldn't need anything hot. Putting her hands on her hips, she assessed what to do next, trying to keep from looking in that man's direction. She took a few steps in a small circle, envisioning where her entry door would be and how the windows would appear once she hung some handsome curtains. If she'd had the money, she would have had the walls plastered so she could paint them an eye-pleasing color. As it was, she'd been giving serious thought to putting a coat on the faded exterior. Buttercup yellow with white window sashes. Ideally, hiring a painter would have been best, but she couldn't spare the expense.

Turning, she stole a glimpse of Tom. He just sat there, staring with those clear blue eyes of his, as if he were trying to strip her raw. Fresh annoyance flared inside her. She bent to pick up the broom, intent on brushing the cobwebs from the walls. If she hadn't been so put out of sorts by his unwavering eyes, she would have grabbed the handle instead of sticking her hand in the scrub bucket. Snapping her wrist to fling the water from her fingers, she muttered her exasperation beneath her breath. The blunder wouldn't have bothered her nearly as much if the low chuckle coming from his corner of the room hadn't reached her ears.

"What?" she shot at him.

Broad shoulders shrugged, and a mild smile didn't mask his false innocence. "What what?"

She held her position for as long as she could, staring right back at him to see how he liked it. But rather than feeling any satisfaction, she felt increased discomfort. Her heart began to foolishly hammer, and her senses became disordered.

He could make her squirm inside her skin just by doing nothing, by sitting there with an attitude that exuded more masculinity than the whole baseball team, sponsored by Kennison's Hardware Emporium, had in its entirety.

Sharply inhaling to suppress her ire, she did her best to ignore him, but it was difficult, given that there was no place to be free from his prying eyes. That was unless . . .

With a satisfied walk, she went into the storeroom. The haven offered little space for contemplation; tools and curls of tin cluttered narrow shelves. Sheets of shiny metal, as well as unfinished projects, lay strewn here and there. One piece was a ceiling pendant from which to hang a gaslight.

Now that she was hidden, she wrinkled her nose and mulled over her next move. She couldn't seek sanctuary in the small storeroom forever. Leaning her hip against the wall, she crossed her arms beneath her breasts.

"Find anything you want?"

Edwina started, her pulse tripping. She absently laid the palm of her hand over her heartbeat. "I wanted a moment to myself."

"Coward." His face loomed over hers, and he'd positioned himself far too close for her comfort. "You're hiding."

Her gaze shot upward, and before she thought better, she blurted, "Yes! I don't like the way you keep looking at me."

"How's that?"

The rebuttal that formed in her head wasn't going to reach his ears. She wasn't about to tell him that he was making her feel undressed. He already knew that. "Never you mind."

She made a move to leave, but from where he stood, he blocked the only exit.

"Pardon me," she said, inching left.

"Okay." He inched left.

Frowning, she repeated, "Pardon me," and inched right.

"Okay." He inched right.

Her indignation bristled. "You're trifling with me, Mr. Wolcott."

The resonant sound of his laugh rippled through the air. "Yeah."

"Whatever for?"

"I wanted to see if you'd say dammit again."

Embarrassment gripped her. "I can assure you it won't happen again. In my defense, my father would occasionally use that word when discussing politics at the dinner table. I unconsciously picked it up, but I never use it." Then she went on in a rush, "Habitually, that is."

One corner of his mouth crooked, revealing a faint dimple that she found—to her chagrin—utterly seductive. "Whatever you say."

"I say I'm not saying anything more on the subject."

Relief overtook her discomfort when a familiar woman's voice called out from the warehouse, "Miss Huntington? Marvel-Anne said you were inside."

"Excuse me, Mr. Wolcott," she said firmly. This time her request wasn't met with any "trifling." He allowed her to pass, and Edwina made her escape to visit with Crescencia Stykem.

The statuesque young lady hovered over the tin replica of a large bird. Seeing Edwina, Crescencia squinted through her glasses at her. "I've never seen anything like this. Is it yours, Miss Huntington?"

"Good heavens, no."

"Lucky for me," Tom commented behind Edwina as

he strode to his side. "I was prepared to fight you for it. A real knuckle-bruiser knockout."

Crescencia's eyes widened, and she whispered, "He's not serious?"

"Don't pay any attention to him," Edwina said, brushing off his droll remark. "What can I do for you, dear?" The endearment seemed too matronly to be spoken to a woman only two years younger than Edwina, but she felt motherly toward Crescencia. She was pretty and should have been married—except for one slight problem: she couldn't hold a conversation with a prospective groom without stammering her way into a state of blushes and acute hyperventilation. By showing her how to converse and carry herself in a mixed crowd, Edwina hoped to help the poor thing overcome her shyness.

"I've brought my application by. Papa agreed to let me have the mornings off to attend class. He said . . . well, never mind what he said." She straightened her wire spectacles.

Edwina pressed her hand over Crescencia's. "It'll be all right."

"He said I'm as graceful as an elephant when I'm using the typewriter, and I have as much chance as a grasshopper in an anthill of ever getting a husband. Do you think so?"

Giving Crescencia's thin fingers a squeeze, Edwina decreed, "Stuff and fiddlesticks. I think you're a lovely and likeable young lady. You'll come into your own. Sometimes it just takes longer for some than others."

"Thank you, Miss Huntington." Crescencia smiled at the encouragement, then handed Edwina the quarter-folded paper and a bank check she took from her purse.

"I'll keep you informed as to the starting date of the school." Edwina walked her to the door.

"I hope it's soon."

Crescencia stepped through the doorway just as a man rounded the blind corner. They bumped into one another, brushing arms. He immediately laid his hand on her shoulder and made an apology. "Sorry about that, sweetheart. I hope I didn't hurt you."

Her glasses slightly askew from the encounter, she fumbled to adjust them on the bridge of her nose. Lashes flickered; a quiver hitched her breathing. "I—I—I—" Crescencia's face paled to ashes; even her gaping mouth went gray.

Then she dropped into a dead faint.

Chapter

3

Walking with his thumbs hooked in his denim pockets, Tom threaded his way between the aisles of Kennison's Hardware Emporium, taking in the inventory. With his lips together, he worked on a stick of spearmint chewing gum. The paint section loomed, gallons stacked on gallons. A dollar eighty a can: Light Blue, Quaker Drab, Old Gold, Myrtle Green . . . but Vermillion—thirty cents.

"Hey, Kennison, how come the vermillion is only thirty cents?"

Mr. Kennison came around from behind the counter. The suit padding bulged on his shoulders, and his neck was rigid in a starched collar. "Mrs. Kirby ordered that for the trim on her house, but then she changed her mind. She bought English Venetian instead. I'm overstocked on the vermillion, so I'm offering a discount."

The proprietor tapped his finger on a can of paint. "This reminds me. Miss Huntington said she'd come by this morning to pick up three gallons of the Canary and one of Old Revival White. I'd better write her order up."

Tom's brows thoughtfully lifted, and he exchanged glances with Shay, who'd been examining mailboxes.

"You aren't going to paint your side red knowing she's set on painting hers yellow?" Shay lifted the flap of a rectangular box. "You ought to get one of these. Then you won't have to go to the post office."

"I can get one if I save money on the paint. Ninety cents compared to five forty. I'd be an idiot not to."

"You're an idiot if you do." Peering into the mailbox's interior, Shay said to the depths, "What do you think she'll do when she sees you slapping up red next to her yellow? I think you should get yellow, too." The lid flapped into place, and he examined the price tag. "Sixty-five cents."

"I think you've gone soft in the head. Ever since you made that redhead faint two days ago."

"I felt bad about that." He set the nickel mailbox on the purchasing counter with Tom's small order. "Never thought my face could cause a woman to swoon."

"One whiff of ammonia, and she came around. Saw you standing over her," Tom chuckled, "and she about went under again."

"Yeah, figure that. I said I was sorry." Shay fingered his stubble. "She was a good-looking woman when she wasn't fidgeting. That hair color of hers reminded me of desert sunrise after a night of rain."

"You're turning poetic, Shay." Tom picked up two gallons of red paint and carried them to the cash register. "Her father's the lawyer I saw."

"Stykem?"

"Yep." After retrieving one more gallon, Tom reached into his back pocket for his billfold. "She's his secretary."

Shay's mouth lifted in appreciation. "Damn, a woman with a mind."

"I wouldn't go that far. When I saw her, she was battling a typewriter—and losing."

"Nobody's perfect." Shay met him at the counter, and shot him a hard gaze. "You're really going to buy the red?"

"I really am," Tom replied with a satisfied smile.

"You mud-snot," Shay said, good-naturedly badgering him. "You're enjoying this."

"As much as I can. Maybe I'll irritate her so much, she'll close up shop and go home, where a woman belongs."

Although he hated to admit that if she did, he'd be sorry the game between them would end so soon—because he could pull a fast one just as easily as she. She'd made the first move today, an underhanded, sneaky double-cross—one that he'd thought of himself but discounted because it was extreme foul play.

The tip-off had been catching her and Ab Trussel in a suspicious huddle this morning on the boardwalk in front of his house. Tom held back behind the cover of a lilac bush across the street to see what was what. When they broke up, Trussel had a secret grin on his face, and Miss Huntington beamed with pleasure from beneath the netting of her hat. Waiting until she entered the hardware store, Tom then approached Trussel, who had begun to walk down Dogwood Place.

"Hey, Ab," Tom said in greeting, falling into step with the carpenter.

Trussel's stride faltered a beat as soon as he gazed at Tom. The tools in his case rattled, and he gripped the strap tighter against his chest. "Mr. Wolcott, I'm on my way to the warehouse right now to do a rough-in on the wall with my chalk line."

"I figured you were headed there. I saw you talking with Miss Huntington." Tom casually slipped his hands into his pants pockets. "From the looks of it, she gave you some special instructions."

"No," the carpenter shot back quickly. "She didn't say a thing."

Tom was going to have to use the back-door approach. "I was up near Baskin Falls last weekend. The lake is made for hunters. It has wide ditches around the perimeter, and they're grown in with willow and cattails. You should have seen the water. Damn thick with ducks. A man could do a lot of pass shooting if he had the right decoys and calls. Get himself five hundred ducks in one day."

"Five hundred ducks!"

"Mallards, canvasbacks, and some redheads. I saw all three."

"Five hundred, you say?"

"With the right decoys and calls." Tom absently fingered a matchstick in the lining of his pocket. "As I recall, you said you were a duck-hunting man."

"Indeed I am. Haven't been out yet this year because of my workload—"

"Hell of a lot of ducks at Baskin Falls," Tom said with enticing zeal. "You'd be up to your ass in them."

"Meat packers back East pay seven dollars a pair for canvasbacks and even pick up the cold freight charge." Trussel eyed him with an expression of gleeful calculation. "I could make over fifteen hundred dollars if I got lucky."

"At least."

Tom's hand came down on Ab's shoulder and stopped him dead in his tracks. "I tell you what. When I get the store opened, you come see me and I'll give you a few of the newest duck calls to take up to the lake. You tell me if they can perform like the manufacturer says."

Ab's eyes widened with his musing. "Have you got that new super raspy model in? Or better yet, the double cluck? A man could lure himself a lot of canvasbacks with the double cluck. You know, I read they still blow when they're wet."

"You're absolutely right. A hunter can't miss with either the Sure Shot or the Duck Master. And Ab, I've got them both." Tom gave the man's back a few hearty pats. "So what's Miss Huntington up to?"

The light in Trussel's gaze dulled. Hesitation marked his facial features a moment, then he blurted out, "She promised me a case of Marvel-Anne's spiced plum preserves if I gave her side of the warehouse an extra foot. Being a bachelor, I don't have anyone to can fruit for me. And I like plums, so the temptation . . . um . . . it was . . . there."

Curses formed in Tom's mouth, but he didn't utter them. Instead, he feigned sympathy through gritted teeth. "I'm sorry she asked you to do that, Ab. You know that she paid Murphy fifty dollars more than I did, so she thinks she's entitled. But the fact of the matter is, the lawyer handling this case says it's unlawful to modify the property in favor of one or the other party. So you have to keep that line right down the middle—fifty-fifty."

"That's what I told her, but she said you'd never notice—"

"I'd notice."

"What do you think I should do?"

"Let her think you did what she asked."

"But what if she measures the distance and finds out I didn't?"

"Women don't possess the common sense to measure the distance of anything. She'll take your word for it." Reaching out to seal the deal with a handshake, Tom pumped Ab's arm.

Doubt furrowed the man's brows, so Tom had to go the extra mile. "As soon as you finish the job, I'll give you a dozen Reliable Bob decoys. Take the spiced plums if you want them, but keep your mind on those five hundred ducks. Seven dollars a pair? You're going to be a rich man."

Trussel got a face-splitting grin on his lips. "I might just be at that."

Tom had watched the carpenter continue on with a light step in his walk, his head obviously filled with canvasbacks and greenbacks.

Now standing in the hardware store and knowing what Edwina planned for the color of her exterior, Tom could play dirty, too. She'd started the war, but he'd win the first skirmish.

*   *   *

Great cumuli floated on a deeply blue sky. Yellowing leaves drifted from the oaks, falling on the expanse of property behind the warehouse and in the weedy ditches beyond where goldenrod was turning gray.

Inside the building, Edwina's side remained toasty from the heater she and Marvel-Anne had Mr. Trussel bring over. A pot of rich hot chocolate rested on the burner to stay warm. Extra mugs had been packed in a snack hamper with Mr. Trussel . . . and another . . . in mind. The carpenter had just finished framing the entryway for Edwina's school and needed only to hang the door. Already he'd marked off the dividing boundary. The white line, boldly imprinted on the floorboards, gave Edwina's stomach a pang of conscience rather than a sense of victory.

She hadn't liked resorting to trickery, but she'd had no choice. Since she'd paid more for the property, she should be entitled to more square feet. Her direct speech to Mr. Wolcott about how she felt had fallen on deaf ears, so now she had to handle the matter herself, guilty as she might feel. In any case, what was done was done. Mr. Trussel said he would begin constructing the wall tomorrow.

As the leaves sifted quietly to the ground, Edwina painted the exterior wall around the window. Careful not to drip the yellow, she made sure the brush dipped sparingly into the bucket on the ladder shelf. Standing several rungs up, she could see Tom Wolcott coming down the road from the livery. He carried the front half of a black bear mounted on a wall plaque. The two forelegs had been stuffed to give the appearance that the bear had been shot midattack; both limbs were raised high and had claws spread. Teeth were bared in the muzzle, the mouth open and tongue curled.

He saw her, and rather than go around his corner of the building, he strode across the back through the oak grove. To her displeasure, vanity bested her. The old duster she wore to keep the paint from damaging her shirtwaist and skirt was worn thin and transparent at the elbows. An unadorned straw hat covered her hair, which she had plaited in two heavy braids down her back. She hadn't wanted to be bothered by the multitude of pins required to keep her pompadour in place—not to mention that the mass of hair piled high on her crown more often than not gave her a headache.

Stilling the brush in her hand, she bit back saying something cheeky about the dead bear in Mr. Wolcott's arms. After she and Marvel-Anne had brought Mr. Trussel the spiced plums in the cover of darkness following last night's supper, she vowed from that moment on to be an amiable business neighbor because she had fairness—by the measure of one foot—on her side.

"Good afternoon, Mr. Wolcott."

"Miss Huntington." His gaze lifted to hers, the bear shifting in his arms so that the bulk of it rested on his shoulder.

"I see you're moving in."

"The trophy wall is."

"How nice," she replied, though she really thought a trophy wall nonsensical and bigheaded.

"You nail up the stretch of string down the back of the building?"

"No, Mr. Trussel did that for me. I didn't want to accidentally paint over the line on your side. He's strung a length down the front of the building as well." She dabbed a little of the yellow beneath the eaves, incorporating a spider's threads in the paint. "You wouldn't be thinking about painting your side, too, would you, Mr. Wolcott?"

"Haven't given it any thought."

"In case you do, this yellow is a lovely shade. It brightens up the entire area, don't you think?" He made no comment, so she proceeded in what she hoped was an inviting tone. "Mr. Kennison sells this color at the hardware store. Number two-oh-six." Viewing the look of disinterest on his face, she hastily added, "It's reasonably priced."

"I'll think about it."

She wished he would think hard about the paint. Although the clapboards in their weathered state weren't altogether unappealing, with the ray of sunshine on her side and his still drab as a wet newspaper, the building took on a nonuniform appearance.

"Looks like you're doing a pretty good job. Painting sheets and everything."

"You'll find, Mr. Wolcott, that I'm meticulously neat and organized."

"I expect I may have to be subjected to that."

She didn't like the dry tone in his reply, as if her tidiness were an offense rather than an admirable quality.

Since he wouldn't commit himself to purchasing the paint, she saw no reason to dally in conversation with him. Sinking the brush halfway into the bucket, then gingerly ridding the excess paint against the rim with a half-dozen neat passes, she proceeded with her task. He took the hint and went on his way.

Crouching slightly, she snagged a glimpse of him through the window as he entered the warehouse. Considering the expanse of the floorboards, the naked eye shouldn't have been able to tell anything was amiss. If he looked long and hard enough at the white chalk, he might detect the line was one foot in her favor. She, of course, had noticed the discrepancy immediately. But she had been pointedly looking for the difference.

Edwina straightened, then with tiny, even strokes, used up the paint on her brush. Dipping it into the nearly full can once again, she readied to smooth the bristles against the rim, when that odious bloodhound trotted up to her. Heedless of her painting sheets nicely draped over the ground, he trudged across them, leaving a track of mud prints and ruffling them away from the wall.

"Get away from here!" she shouted, forgetting that she held a wet brush in her hand. As she waved her arm at the dog, yellow splattered across the window. Horrified, she gazed at the globs of paint marring the fresh

white sashes and clean panes. In a slow drip, they began
to run down the glass squares. "Look at what you made
me do!"

A face other than her own reflected in the window.
Tom Wolcott looked out from the inside with arms
folded across his chest and a grin on his mouth that she
wanted to slather with number two-oh-six.

"Mr. Wolcott," she said loudly. "Your dog is out
here."

The grin turned into a comfortable curve. "He usually
is." Then the man had the audacity to walk away.

Twenty minutes later, she still fumed at him and at
Barkly, who kept running through the surrounding
leaves at a breakneck speed, chasing after squirrels and
making a hideous baying sound. She hadn't thought a
dog of his size could move so fast. At one point, he tried
to climb a tree. She'd smiled to herself, thinking her
precious Honey Tiger superior to him. Her beloved kitty
could scale the branches with no problem. All Barkly
managed to do was stir up the leaves. Then he rolled in
their crispiness until that got tiring, too. Finally, he
sprawled out, tongue lopped to the side, and began to
gnaw on acorns.

Up until the slack-skinned dog had come along, she'd
prided herself on not making a single drip on the cloths
or getting one fleck of paint on herself. Now her fingers
were jaundiced from all the turpentine and rags she'd
used to clean the windowpanes.

Ready for a cup of hot chocolate before she picked
up the paintbrush again, Edwina went to the front of
the building. Mr. Wolcott had left a short time ago, but
Mr. Trussel was just finishing hammering the door's
hinge pins into place. He then laid the key into her palm.

"I'll lock it from the inside, Miss Huntington. You try
the key."

Her fingers curled over the cool brass. A strong sense
of independence was her guide as she inserted the key,
then turned. The door opened to her touch on the knob.

"You're safe and sound now," Mr. Trussel decreed.

"But still exposed, so to speak, until the wall is completed." She gave him a knowing gaze. One he didn't return; instead, his eyes purposefully—and more than a little nervously—averted themselves from hers. Too late, she realized her imprudence at making even a cryptic mention of the wall. "Forgive me, Mr. Trussel. I shan't mention 'it' again. You have my utmost discretion," she whispered.

"I've got to head home to the shop and get some other tools."

"By all means," she said, pouring a cup of hot chocolate. With his departure, she sat on a hammock chair. She and Marvel-Anne had brought two such folding picnic chairs over that morning. The housekeeper had stayed a time and painted the front of the warehouse while Edwina worked on the side, but then Marvel-Anne had to return to the house to finish some mending she said needed her attention.

Edwina counted her blessings. Marvel-Anne was lending a hand above and beyond her duties, and without being asked. She volunteered. No matter how Edwina's money woes might affect her in the future, she could never cast the woman adrift. At least not without a tidy severance check as compensation.

While Edwina nibbled on a nut wafer cookie, a horse-drawn wagon driven by Mr. Wolcott's associate pulled up front. She could view the assemblage through the sporting goods store's open door. Boxes and crates, not to mention an abundant pile of stuffed animals, filled the bed. The brake went into place, then the man climbed down from the seat.

As he entered the premises, she was reminded that he wasn't an unpleasant-looking man—albeit his facial features were somewhat linear. Lines wore grooves at the corners of his eyes and mouth. Yesterday, after Crescencia had fainted and had been revived, he'd made his introduction. Shay Dufresne. His name had sounded French, especially the last: *Dew-fraine*. She'd thought him a gentleman when his concern for dear Crescencia had bordered on indulgent. His hand had taken hers, and he'd given her fingers a few quick pats before lifting her head so that Edwina could pass the ammonia bottle beneath Crescencia's nose.

Once her eyes fluttered open, Crescencia nearly fell into oblivion again upon seeing the man she'd collided with standing over her. Edwina would have to impress upon the other woman that contact with a person of the opposite sex wasn't cause for a fit of the vapors. That, in fact, a man's touch could be . . .

Edwina abruptly shook her musings from her head.

"Miss Huntington." Mr. Dufresne tipped his hat.

A nod blended with her reply of "Mr. Dufresne."

"You remembered."

"Of course."

Momentarily, he went outside to return with one of the boxes. "How's your friend Miss Stykem?"

"I'm certain she's very well today. How kind of you to ask."

Mr. Wolcott appeared around the door's corner, an animal's black-and-white-striped rear end hoisted in his arms. As it was for the bear, the wall plaque was only half of the body of the poor thing, definitely a victim of rigor mortis. But in this case, the unappealing half—muscled hindquarters with legs and hooves, and a tail with a tuft of black hair on the tip.

Though Edwina had promised herself she'd be congenial, she couldn't refrain from asking, "Was it necessary to remove its head?"

"Never had a head that I saw," Mr. Wolcott replied, setting the vulgarity on a sawhorse. "This was bagged on a safari in Africa."

She became duly impressed. "You've been to Africa, Mr. Wolcott?"

"Never claimed I was there. Said that's where the zebra bought it. I picked this up from a marketeer in the Galveston harbor."

A frown marred her lips. She should have known he'd say one thing to make her think another. Leaning into the chair's canvas, she tucked her legs beneath the seat. "If you cross the zebra with your bear, you'd have something whole."

Laughter erupted from him, a deep and rich earthy sound that unexpectedly gave her a shiver of delight. Against her will, she smiled with him. His lips were firm and sensual, the white of his teeth an engaging contrast next to sun-bronzed skin.

Too soon, he broke the spell and looked away.

"Wouldn't do me any good to put them together." The lid to his coffeepot was lifted, and apparently, the pot was empty, because he scowled. "One of these days, I'm going to make a clock out of the zebra. The tail's going to be the pendulum."

Edwina's brow arched. *A clock?* Out of a zebra's behind . . . ? How positively and utterly . . . stupid. Managing to speak in a serious tone, the best she could muster was "I'm certain it will be a conversation piece." And something she'd never care to see.

"No more coffee?" Mr. Dufresne asked.

Mr. Wolcott clattered the lid into place. "Just the dregs."

Opportunity had knocked, and Edwina graciously rose. "Gentlemen, I have hot chocolate. And cookies."

Mr. Dufresne accepted first, striding toward the hamper and extending his hand for several of the cookies. Then she poured him a cup of the hot chocolate.

"Thanks."

"You're quite welcome."

While turning, she said, "Mr. Wolcott, would you care for a—" The words were swallowed in a gulp of panic.

Mr. Wolcott stood on the chalk line, gazing from one side of the room to the other. Edwina's heartbeat slammed against her ribs. Pushing herself into motion, she took quick steps, with the cookie platter outstretched in her hand. She all but shouted, "Nut wafer cookie?" in hopes of distracting him.

His gaze remained planted on the floor, so she lifted the bowl higher to block his view. Eyes the color of blue ice lifted and plugged into hers. She couldn't face the indescribable expression in them, but neither could she take her gaze elsewhere.

"Was this your doing?"

Dismay clutched her. How had he figured out the line was off without even taking the room dimensions on each side? He must have measuring eyes, because he'd certainly sized up her intentions.

His premature discovery hadn't given her time to come up with a reasonable explanation other than the truth—which she intended to tell him. Just not at the moment—rather, after the wall had been framed and plastered and would be too much of an inconvenience to tear down and redo.

"So, can you paint and bake cookies?" His resonant voice intruded on her rioting thoughts.

"W-what?"

"The cookies. I asked if you made them."

"You did?" *Was this your doing?* Of course, he'd meant the cookies! "Oh, you did ask. Yes . . . I baked these."

Taking several, he popped one whole into his mouth and chewed. "They're good."

"Thank you," she mumbled, her nerves still wrapped in knots. "Can I offer you some hot chocolate?"

"Sure."

She went through the motions of pouring, but she didn't know what she was doing. The episode too close for comfort, she couldn't seem to calm down enough to catch her breath. Handing him the mug, he accepted and stayed right smack on that line, his gaze skimming its length once more. She couldn't stand it, so she all but took him by the coat sleeve and offered him her chair.

"Have a seat, Mr. Wolcott. You must be tired from all your moving."

He wouldn't budge. "I'm all right."

"But I insist."

Quite by accident, she gouged his instep with her heel

as she moved to stand closer to him in an effort to prod him away from the chalk line.

His eyes captured hers and all she could manage was an encouraging smile in favor of the chair. Finally conceding, he fit his lean body awkwardly into the soft canvas. The chair's wooden frame groaned, as if unable to take his full masculine weight. He balanced the steaming mug on one of the arms.

Seeing that he'd finished his cookies, she quickly offered more. He scooped a pile of them into his wide palm, then settled into the picnic chair with his right boot on his left knee, without taking another glance at the line.

She exhaled, unaware that she'd been holding her breath. She'd just averted a major disaster with nut wafer cookies. Thank goodness they were Marvel-Anne's speciality.

A sickle moon ascended above the silhouettes of the oak trees. Tom had told Shay to meet him at the warehouse at eleven. Standing in the shadows, he waited for his partner in crime to arrive.

The flame of a match momentarily took the chill off his fingers as he cupped his hands together to light a smoke. He would have rather been lounging on his bed with the funny papers, catching up on the wisecracking "Katzenjammer Kids." Instead, he had to do his ambushing under the cover of night because the element of surprise was just too tempting to pass up.

He'd almost changed his mind that afternoon when Edwina had stuffed him with fancy cookies and hot chocolate. But then he'd caught her furtive gaze on the chalk line, and he'd been reminded exactly why he was the recipient of her doting hospitality. His performance had rattled her, just as he'd intended, and she wanted to throw him off the scent. Too bad. He already knew what she was up to. Even so, he couldn't quite correlate the low-down tactic with a woman of her character.

Her green eyes were veiled by a reserve he didn't

entirely believe. She was smartly quick-tongued—a trait
that didn't go with a woman who held her spine without
compromise. Too many mannerisms about her seemed
to be contradictions. One minute in Stykem's office,
she'd been submissive with hands folded in her lap; then
the next, she'd been trying to bargain her way out of
paying for her share of the renovations because of the
fifty dollars. Not something someone's maiden aunt
would do. He knew. His Aunt Evelyn would have rather
choked on her own indignation than blurt her real
feelings.

Tom took a slow walk around the building's perimeter
to keep the circulation flowing through his limbs; his
thoughts occupied his mind while he waited for Shay.

Early adult experiences with women resulted in Tom's
tendency to be drawn to the types who flaunted themselves and had glittering eyes that meant anything goes.
But in his boyhood, he'd wanted the cream of the crop—
only he hadn't been good enough for her. All in all, he'd
had a lot of fond memories growing up south of the
tracks in Texas. Throughout his school years, he'd been
the class prankster. His mischief had gotten him into the
parlors of the well-to-do, where he wouldn't normally
have been invited, because he provided entertainment.

Elizabeth Robinson, a spoiled little minx but the prettiest girl in Texarkana, planned a Christmas party the
year he'd been expelled for a week for unbolting the
outhouse hinges. His family had been poorer than Job's
turkeys, his father being a dirt farmer and his mother
taking in wash. One day after school, he found the fancy
invitation waiting for him on the table. He couldn't believe Elizabeth had asked him to come.

Of course he wanted to go—to see how the rich lived.

The Robinsons' house could have been used for pho-
tographs on postcards. Pictures in heavy gilt frames almost covered all the white-and-gold wallpaper in the
parlor. Hand-painted roses glowed on the lampshades,
and bigger roses spread through the carpet pattern.
Crowded on the sofa and in chairs set close together,

the well-off kids from his school looked like real young ladies and gentlemen.

Elizabeth met him, looking more beautiful that night than any girl sitting in the room. She showed him to a seat, then proceeded to enlist everyone in a game of Spin the Platter. He'd never heard of it. Elizabeth's eyes were a sparkle of daring, so he said he was in. She spun the plate, then called out a name. His. Coaxed into standing up, he did so. A sticky crackling on his rear end made him whirl around to try to see what had affixed itself to him.

Flypaper.

When he glanced at Elizabeth, she was laughing so hard, tears had formed in her eyes. Cursing, he tore at the paper, but only small bits came off, and then they stuck on his fingers.

He'd gotten out of there, slamming the front door behind him, swearing all the way home. That Monday, he found out she'd invited him on a dare, and he'd been sap enough to fall for it. From then on, he never went back to that school. At the age of fifteen, he stuck to his side of the tracks and took up the plow like his old man.

Although he couldn't say that Christmas had been exactly when he'd decided, he could see that the incident had been the cornerstone. The Wolcott name wasn't going to be laughed at. It was that part of him that drove him to success. Even if there wasn't anyone in his family to see *Wolcott* on a business placard.

Thoughts of his older brother surfaced, as did the images of the turbulent life he led. After John was tall enough to stand over their father, he never broke a sweat in the fields again, choosing instead to spend his days in the saloons and gamble the money he made finding water for farmers. There was one thing about John—he had a talent with a divining rod that a rare few had. Too bad he wasted a talent that could have been used in a respectable, worthwhile profession.

Rarely did Tom hear from John. Old letters every once in a while caught up to Tom. Since he expected to stay in Harmony, Tom could write back now and tell John to come for a visit—if he was of a mind to.

And the last Tom had seen his father had been about three years back. What correspondence he and his dad had exchanged had been infrequent. When mail finally reached Tom, he'd been mining gold in the New Mexico territory. The words Henry Wolcott had penned had surprised him. After his mother's death, his father had deserted the land in Texas, moved to Mexico, and remarried. Rather than toiling over his own fickle soil and having to worry about the elements, he now worked on an *ejidos*—some kind of common farm.

For a couple of weeks, Tom had mulled over the letter; then he'd packed up his gear and gone down into Mexico to some town whose name he couldn't pronounce. He'd seen his dad and his new wife; she'd been younger than him by half. They'd already had two kids, and one more was on the way. He hadn't felt any kind of attachment to the weather-beaten man sitting before him. It was as if he hadn't been born the man's son.

At the age of thirty-two, Tom had lived half his life with his family and the other half making his own way. Any bond that had been forged between him and his dad had vanished. It was fair to say they'd gone their separate ways. When Tom rode out of Zacatecas, he knew he'd never see his father again. And he also knew Henry Wolcott would never see his youngest son by his first wife prosper in ways no one in the family ever had. Nor would his mother. John might, perhaps, if he dried out long enough to earn money for a horse.

Tom had hooked up with Shay in the New Mexico territory again, and they had roamed the countryside doing odd jobs, ending up lumbering in Washington. But nothing had satisfied Tom. He was tired of being another man's money maker. He had to do something on his own. So when Shay had said he was headed east to Idaho, Tom had said he was going farther to see what the lure was in Montana.

With a small amount of capital he'd tucked away in his wallet, he'd been able to advertise and bring men out west. Once he'd felt confident he could make a living as a businessman, he'd relaxed and settled into what he thought was the best-looking place he'd ever seen.

Harmony, Montana.

Giving the store and outfitting his best shot wasn't enough. He had to prove his worth to himself, to achieve everything on all accounts—business and family. He'd eluded marriage for a long time, and now he could finally think about taking the step in the next year—if all went well and he had enough money. He'd go to the altar only if he was financially settled. He'd be damned if any wife of his would have to work herself into an early grave like his mother had.

As for the woman he'd marry, he wanted someone who was fun, who liked to laugh and let her hair down. Someone as easygoing as himself.

Damn certain not that Edwina Huntington—which teed him off because he found her attractive. Even in that shabby getup she'd had on today. The length of her hair hadn't escaped his attention. The ends of thick braids fell well past her waist. He'd wondered what her hair would look like unbound . . . flowing over her bare shoulders. The image he conjured was provocative to say the least.

But she was a north-end girl through and through. Her deal with Trussel had proved she'd put flypaper on his ass without a thought. And that rankled him enough for him to get even and put a snap in her garter.

Footfalls crushed the dry leaves, and Shay emerged from the shadows huddled in a hunter's camouflage coat—just like Tom's.

"Did you bring the brushes?" Tom asked, meeting him.

Shay produced two fat ones from the deep-slashed pockets.

"I've got the paint around the front."

"Don't you think we ought to burn some lanterns on low so we can see what we're doing?" Shay asked, his breath misting.

"Hell no. Pickering doesn't lock up the Blue Flame until after midnight. We can't chance being seen." Tom ground his cigarette beneath his boot heel. "Besides, we're not here to see what we're doing. Contrary to what our primary teacher told us about our pen strokes, in this case, neatness *doesn't* count."

Chapter

❦ 4 ❧

Vandals! Hoodlums! Miscreants!

A thunderbolt could have slammed down right in front of Edwina and given her less of a shock.

The warehouse had been sabotaged! With red paint. Everywhere. Not only on the clapboards, but fat ugly drops on the ground, blobs speckling the shrubbery, and beads running down the windowpanes.

For some unknown reason, the culprits had only struck Mr. Wolcott's side. A ripple of relief assailed her, along with a faint pulse of shame for having thought of herself in a time of crisis. Still, that didn't dim the edge of despair that gripped her in its clutches. The building looked like the inside of a slaughterhouse with all that red splattered on everything. The steady yellow dividing line she'd painted cleanly down the middle had been sloppily cut into. Her sweet canary had been killed with vermillion.

A silent shriek surged up her spine and pinched the nerves in her neck. She had to report the crime to the police immediately.

Blazing with hot indignation, she marched up Birch Avenue with her skirts swishing immodestly. She should have checked her pace and not let her upset show. After all, she hadn't left the house without buttoning her gloves in the vestibule. To do so on the porch was gauche—not to mention that a lady never appeared in public until she was fully dressed. But all that ladylike folderol was inconsequential to Edwina right now. She didn't want to have to think about her actions when her reactions had her in the mood to kick something.

The police department came into view, and she stalked to the gate. She fumbled with the latch as she let herself in. The pickets on the fence had always seemed too wobbly, and as the gate slammed home behind her, they vibrated like a telegraph line. Two iron deer were planted in the lawn, looking somewhat startled and more than a little rusty.

Once at the door, Edwina stopped, her gaze angling in on the note pinned to the door:

> Gone quail hunting.
> You can like it or lump it.

"Dammit all," she swore beneath her breath.

Violations in Harmony didn't run the gamut the way they did in big cities, but a deputy officer should have stayed in residence at all times in case of an emergency. While the guardians of law were off in the bushes playing bird stalkers, the criminals were getting away.

"Of all the . . ." she muttered as she dug through her pocketbook. Finding her card case, she opened the clasp, withdrew a calling card with her name and address printed on the front, and stuck it in the door's crack.

Thoughtfully chewing the inside of her lip, Edwina turned and pondered her next move. Under any other circumstances, she would *never* seek Tom Wolcott out at his home. A variety of deportment infractions could be forgiven in a small town, but a lady's visiting a gentleman at his residence was not a small breech of etiquette—it was taboo. She herself didn't give a whit about the rule, but Edwina Huntington the finishing school teacher had to keep proper appearances. On the other hand, the call wouldn't be one of a social nature. This was official—and urgent—business.

"Oh . . . bother it."

Her mind made up, Edwina stormed down the walkway, pausing midstride to confront the deer. Looking quickly left and right to see if the coast was clear, she kicked one's leg, and the dilapidated thing fell flat on the brown lawn. Then she proceeded, feeling somewhat vindicated for having found no officer to take her complaint.

The street sloped toward the planked bridge over Evergreen Creek, and then climbed past the pasture behind the livery stable and the blacksmith shop. Able to take the back way, she didn't meet anyone on the main street. Above the livery, a loft had been converted into a small office, then in recent years into a rented residence after Mr. Hess had added onto the first floor. She knew this was where Mr. Wolcott lived, but she had never in her wildest dreams thought she'd be climbing the outside steps to his door.

Once at the top, she calmed herself into a forced display of refinement. She quickly looked at the blue-black foulard of her skirt with its all-over pattern in shaded grays to make sure no grass blades sullied the fabric. A check of her hat found it securely pinned, a cursory inspection of her glove buttons found that they remained in a perfect row, and a slight fluff of the white ruching that edged her boned collar made it stand up in stiff attention. Confident everything was in apple pie order, she sucked in her breath and rapped on the door.

Tom sat at the table next to his heater, wearing a pair of silk-fleeced drawers and a hole-ridden flannel shirt halfway buttoned. He might not have cared about flashy suits, but he did like his underwear to feel good cupped against him. As for the shirt, he'd thrown on his old favorite. The fabric had worn so thin in places, a few spots had frayed. A rag rug might have gotten better use out of the flannel, but Tom figured it needed a little more breaking in before somebody else stepped on it.

With bare feet tucked on the chair spindle beneath him, he drank coffee while reading the current issue of *American Hunter's Journal.*

GOOD SENSE-DEER SCENTS

Hunters, try the latest in lures—deer in heat estrus. This concentrated scent is highly respected, but be forewarned: you may be attacked if it's not properly used.

We also specialize in cow-pie cover scents. Cover your human scent with cow-pie extract. What better way to hunt in areas where deer live near cattle?

For orders, write to: Good Sense, Minnetonka, Minnesota.

Mulling over the possibilities, Tom scratched his fingertips across the stubble roughing his jaw. What kind of greenhorn would rub himself with cow shit? Besides, any fool could go to a pasture and pick up patties for free.

Now, chasing deer while they were doing the dicky-diddle was a whole different story. Could be this deer pee would sell for him. The concept was imaginative enough to attract a customer's attention.

As he made a mental note to order a dozen bottles, a knock sounded on the door. Shay usually came by about now to share a cup of coffee.

"Door's open," Tom called, thumbing through the journal, his gaze skimming an article heading on carbine kicks.

The knock repeated. *One, two, three.* Delicate-like, yet pressing. Barkly let go with a choppy snore from his sleeping spot by the bureau. The hound lay sprawled out on a bearskin rug.

Tom caught the bottom of the curtain and pulled the

faded cotton away from the window. From his place at the table, he couldn't see who stood on the landing.

Rising, he went to the door and opened it.

Give him a thousand guesses, and he would never have gotten one right. "Jesus . . ."

Edwina Huntington—put together in uncompromising fashion, from the top of her nutty hat—this one had a wide wreath of abundant foliage—to the toes of her shoes—these with big black bows on them.

He'd known she would find him and tell him about the paint, but he'd never figured she'd come to his apartment. Once again, her actions didn't add up to the external image.

"Miss Huntington," he remarked in a mock surprised tone.

She said nothing. Her mouth had gone agape. Her pupils were dilated and her eyes were wide. She gazed at him for quite a long time—something he didn't mind once he realized what she was looking at.

His half-open shirt revealed a chest covered with crisp brown hair. Though he didn't go around sizing himself up, he thought he was pretty muscular and broad through the shoulders. She obviously found something interesting about the body she was gawking at.

Lowering her eyes a fraction, her gaze fell on his drawers. Their cut fit him fairly snugly. Though the crotch area was half obscured by the hem of his shirt, what part of him did show was obviously defined.

A stain of red in her cheeks heightened her color. The depths of her bright eyes sent strong sexual suggestions to his brain, ones that probably would have keeled her over if she could have read his mind. It amazed him that someone as socially rigid as she could have such an affect on him. He knew better than to fall in lust with her type. But somewhere in those almond-shaped eyes, he could almost see a different woman. And she didn't have a shy demeanor.

It didn't help matters that he frankly appreciated her perfectly shaped breasts and trim waistline, outlined by the tightly fitted bodice. With his examining gaze, he reversed the tables. She balked.

"Mr. Wolcott," she murmured, her eyes darting to his face. "Mr. Wolcott. I . . . that is . . . you . . ."

With her trying to avoid staring at the more intimate parts of his body, he felt the heat pour out of the room in a rush. Irritated with himself for letting the situation play out of hand, he complained, "The cold air is coming in. Step inside so I can close the door."

She peered at him as if instead he'd just said, *Take off those clothes so I can ravish you.* "No, I couldn't."

"Then I'll come outside."

"No! You can't. Somebody might see us talking up here."

"Then come in."

"But—"

With a swift motion, he caught her by the elbow and reeled her in like a catfish before she could protest. The door slammed on her gasp, leaving it outside on the landing. Barkly opened one eye, barked once, then ignored them.

"Mr. Wolcott, this is highly improper," Edwina squeaked, keeping her back as close to the door as humanly possibly without going through the wood.

"I'd say your coming here is more so." He padded to the table to retrieve his coffee cup for a sip. Feigning censure, he declared, "Miss Huntington, I'm shocked. A woman of your untarnished reputation coming to a man's apartment. I thought you had better sense."

A spark of pique lit her eyes; her chin tilted in a way that could only be called saucy. Difficult as it might have been, he had gotten the other Edwina Huntington to show her face. This woman had spunk and verve. He found her a lot more amusing than the closed-up version. "Well, I wouldn't have had to come if the confounded police had been in their office."

His brow arched with the appropriate concern. "What about the police?"

"Well, my goodness, gracious me—never in all my

born days . . ." A perfumed hankie was brought out from the cuff of her sleeve and lifted to her nose. After a few dabs, she stuck the handkerchief back; then she checked the row of buttons on her gloves.

The refinement had slipped neatly back into place. He grew disappointed.

"What about the police?" he repeated.

"I went to report a vandalized property—our building. It's been seized upon by ruffians."

"What did they do?"

"Why, they've defaced your side with red paint."

"No."

"Yes!"

"Bastards."

"Mr. Wolcott, please guard yourself against uttering such vulgarisms in my company." Her obvious outrage let him know that his profanity had affronted her feminine ears.

"Unlike you, Miss Huntington, I habitually use *vulgarisms* when the moment is appropriate. And I'd say this is a pretty appropriate moment." He set his coffee cup back on the table. "Some low-down bastards just left their red signature on my half of the building."

"I understand your upset, Mr. Wolcott. Truly. Why, if it had been my side—which fortunately it wasn't—I'd be very distressed. That's why I went to the police to report the incident—in the hope the culprits were still close at hand and could be apprehended. Posthaste." Edwina took a step from the door. "But the arms of the law have seen fit to take up other arms."

"What are you getting at?"

"They've had the gall to close up and go quail hunting."

Tom found it increasingly difficult to keep a straight face. "Quail hunting, you say?"

"Yes!"

"Bastards."

"Yes!" Her soft lips twitched, then she bit the bottom one. "I mean . . ."

"You are forgiven, Miss Huntington. This is a desperate situation." He put his hand out to her, laying it on the small of her back and steering her toward the door. "I'm going to have to ask you to wait outside while I get dressed. Then we'll go over to the building together and see what can be done."

The door opened, and Edwina tripped over the threshold to stand on the landing. Facing her, he couldn't resist saying, "Red? They used red?"

"Vermillion," she replied, seriousness etched into the furrows of her forehead.

He shook his head, as if thoroughly disgusted. "I'll be ready in a minute."

Once the door had been clicked into place, Tom stifled the laughter roaring up his throat.

In the light of day, the building looked worse than Tom had imagined. She'd attempted to take one foot more for herself, so he had had to retaliate. But this war was messier than he would have liked. He might have gotten one over on her, however, that didn't fade the fact that he had to live with what he'd done. His store looked like it had been caught in an ambush between desperadoes, all brandishing Peacemakers.

"You're right," Tom said to Edwina, still staring at the destruction. "The place looks like hell." And he meant it.

"I'm so sorry."

The concern in her voice came across as genuine. He wished she would have felt that badly about stealing the extra foot. Then he would have felt sorry about things, too. But she didn't. So he didn't. It appeared they would both continue to be frauds.

"You could buy some new paint," she suggested. "A brown, perhaps, would cover the damage. I'll . . ." The starch in her shoulders lost a little of their rigid definition. "I'll even help you repaint."

With a dubious lift to the corner of his mouth, he countered, "You'd help me repaint?"

"Yes." The reply came laced with a little regret. "We may not have gotten off to the most pleasant of starts, but we are business neighbors."

Lying business neighbors. Tom didn't fall for this latest tactic. She wanted to help him repaint like she wanted to walk down Main Street naked. What was she up to now?

"I don't have any extra cash to buy more paint." Not on him, anyway. The Harmony Security Bank had four hundred ninety-three-dollars and eighteen cents of his locked up in a modern vault. He could have made a withdrawal if he wanted to. But he didn't want to. "After paying Trussel for the wall, I'm tapped out on funds to go into the store."

Crestfallen, Edwina's shoulders drooped a notch more. "Oh . . . well, perhaps if the hoodlums are caught, they'll be made to compensate for the damages by buying the paint themselves."

"Could be."

"If only we could speak to the police."

"If only."

"Of all the times to go quail hunting."

"Of all."

She looked at him with a hint of perturbation, but the narrowing of her eyes disappeared when Shay approached from Dogwood Place—just as Crescencia Stykem came down Birch Avenue. The two reached the front of the warehouse at the same time.

The redhead couldn't meet Tom or Shay in the eyes; rather, she kept her gaze on the building. "Whatever happened?"

"Thugs." The simple word fell hard from Edwina's tongue.

Tom glanced at Shay and repeated, "Thugs."

Shay, who hadn't really wanted any part of the painting, tucked his hands in his armpits and stood back on his heels. "I'd say this looks more like the work of snakes in the grass." Then he gave Tom a disapproving glare.

When Tom refused to challenge his accusation, Shay turned to Miss Stykem and doffed his hat. "It's good to see you, Miss Stykem."

"M-m-m . . . Mr. Du-Du-Dufresne."

"I trust your health has returned."

Freckled cheeks blossomed with smudges of pink. "I . . ." She averted her eyes from his. "I'm b-better."

"You look fetching in that shade hat. What color do you call that?"

Trembling hands lifted to adjust her glasses, leaving the left side cocked a fraction higher than the right. "Th-the catalogue c-called it v-violent raspberry p-pink."

"I can see why." Shay gave her a wink. "One look at a woman in that color, and it has a man thinking about making violent passion—"

Tom elbowed Shay in the ribs. "What are you doing?"

Shay shot him a dark frown. "Talking to the lady."

Lowering his voice, Tom said, "You don't say words like *passionate love* to a woman like her. She's liable to have a heart seizure."

In a whisper back, Shay remarked, "I think you're mistaken. I'll bet she's heard it before. She's a beautiful woman. Why can't I let her know I find her attractive? Your trouble is you don't know how to woo a woman with words."

"I never had any need to talk while I was wooing."

"I really have to go, Miss Huntington." Crescencia handed Edwina two large envelopes. "I'm here because Papa asked me to bring you these. One is for you, and the other is for Mr. Wolcott. They're your titles to the property."

"Thank you, dear."

"Yeah, thanks," Tom added, taking his copy from Edwina. With a single fold, he tucked the envelope into his breast pocket.

Crescencia fumbled with her spectacles again, then began walking backward. "Good day, Miss Huntington. I hope to be seeing you soon."

"Then I reckon you'll be seeing me again, too," Shay called to her retreating form. "Because I'll be here."

Practically tripping, Crescencia made an about-face and all but scurried away.

Edwina gave the building another once-over. "Since the police are unavailable, I'm going to see if I can get to the bottom of this. I'm paying a call on Mr. Kennison and asking him who's bought red paint lately."

"Bright idea, Miss Huntington," Tom agreed. "I'll stay here in case anything new develops."

She started down the street, Tom going for the pack of Richmonds in his shirt pocket.

"Is that really a bright idea?" Shay asked. "Kennison knows who bought red paint."

Tom scratched the tip of a match with his thumbnail to ignite a flame, then lit his cigarette. "I'll bet he's forgotten by now."

The inside of Kennison's hardware store smelled strongly of new leather and the iron of tools and faintly of sawdust, which had been scattered across the floor. Edwina went straight to the counter. Mr. Kennison's back remained toward her for a moment as he stocked his shelves with new merchandise.

"Miss Huntington," he said. "May I help you?"

"I certainly hope so." She rested her pocketbook on the counter. "I'd like to know who's bought red paint from you recently. Vermillion, to be exact."

Mr. Kennison's hand stilled on a box of drawer handles. "Well, now . . . let me think . . ." Eyes gazed upward; a thin mouth murmured silent words. He brought a palm down the white of his apron, as if to wipe off perspiration. Then he met her steady gaze. "No. I can't say I recall any vermillion being sold. Mrs. Kirby did order some for trim, but she had a change of color scheme, so I sent the cans back to Glidden."

Edwina visibly sagged. "I suppose anyone could have made an order through the Sears and Roebuck catalogue. Then we'd never know."

"No, we wouldn't."

"Thank you, Mr. Kennison."

He escaped back to his work, and she wandered around the store for a while to think about what to do next. She could question Mr. Calhoon, the postmaster, and find out if any packages from Chicago had come in from Sears. But even if some had, he wouldn't have known what was inside them.

What to do . . . ?

Unbidden, the image of Tom Wolcott standing at his door wearing bedroom clothes surfaced in her mind. She'd been taken aback by the slovenly appearance of his moth-eaten flannel, yet drawn to the highly masculine fit of what he wore as the bottom of his pajamas—if one could call an old shirt and men's ribbed drawers pajamas. Her interest had only lingered a few seconds—just enough for her to conclude Mr. Wolcott was physically . . . proportioned . . . with the rest of his large body.

For all her days at the business college, socializing at clubs and parties, she'd never crossed paths with a man like Tom Wolcott. He had an innately captivating presence that was lacking in the urbanized boys who wore the latest wool suits and spouted current stock market figures. In Chicago, she'd been drawn to fellows like Ludlow Ogden Rutledge and his cigar-smoking peers.

But that seemed like eons ago. Now Edwina had pressing obligations. A new path ahead of her. She had to make the best of the situation in Harmony and try to prove to herself that she hadn't changed all that much. That deep down inside, she was still Edwina—the same girl who used to sit in church and, with her eyes on the ceiling's rain spot, faithfully send her prayers through it to Heaven.

A weariness settled in her heart. Sometimes she wished she could turn back the clock and revisit those days of innocence. But of course she couldn't. Time marched ahead, and so must she.

Edwina summoned up the expression that had overtaken Mr. Wolcott's face this morning while viewing the warehouse. Disgust and disbelief. She hated to admit it, but she felt sorry for him. Vandals had done him wrong, and he didn't have the money to rectify the injustice. She herself was tight on cash, but since she'd been paid up on tuition fees, she did have funds she could spare for several cans of brown paint. Were it not for the fact she'd finagled that extra foot of floor space, she never would have considered spending the money on his side. But she had, so she would.

"Mr. Kennison."

"Yes, Miss Huntington?"

"I'd like to purchase three gallons of a brown paint—whichever hue you think would best cover vermillion."

"Miss Huntington?"

That he would question her purchase somewhat puzzled her. "It's for Mr. Wolcott's side of the building."

"I see . . . then I'll put it on his bill."

"You misunderstand, Mr. Kennison." The pocketbook latch clicked open, and she searched for her coin purse. She didn't usually keep much on hand, but today Marvel-Anne had asked her to stop by the butcher's and buy a roast for supper, so she'd left the house with extra money. A prime cut of beef would have to be forsaken; they'd have to settle for chops tonight. "I'm buying the paint for him. I feel bad that his shop's been vandalized. A good neighbor should lend support, so I'd like to do this." She thought, but didn't add, *It will make me feel better, since I shorted him out of an even half of the warehouse.*

"Miss Huntington," Mr. Kennison said as if he were plagued by indigestion, "I ask you to reconsider. Let the police handle the matter."

"I highly doubt they will find the culprits." Large coins left her fingers to sit on the counter before him. "I'd rather Mr. Wolcott paint his side now to smooth out the building's appearance. I've got my students to think about. The warehouse in its present state is an abomination. I'd rather not subject the girls to such an unsightly mess."

Mr. Kennison's hand covered the coins. His lips pursed as if he'd sucked a persimmon. The money slid toward her and he lifted his palm. "Oh, fiddlesticks, there goes my rubber froggy. But I can't let you do it, Miss Huntington."

Rubber froggy? "I don't understand."

"Mr. Wolcott bought that red paint himself."

Astonishment dropped her jaw open. "Pardon?"

"Just like I said." Mr. Kennison mussed his neat coif as he ran nervous fingers through his pomaded hair. "Mr. Wolcott bought that vermillion. Though I didn't see him do it, I'd bet he's the one who painted the warehouse. He said he'd give me a bass lure—a soft rubber froggy with a string-gut loop and treble hook—if I forgot about the transaction. I thought I could, but not when you're going to spend your money on him."

Anger whisked through her, quick and strong. *He tricked me! Why, that wolf in moth-holed clothing! And I actually felt sorry for him!* When she thought of how ridiculous she must have sounded to go on in such an animated way about the defacing of the property and the vandals, when all the while, she'd been talking to the rotten criminal himself!

Well, she wouldn't give him the satisfaction of knowing that *she knew* he'd crossed her bows. Fury choked her, making speaking difficult. "Mr. Kennison, your honesty is most appreciated. I don't want you to lose your . . . froggy, so we can keep this between us for now. Please let Mr. Wolcott think you told me nothing. I'll tell him when I'm ready."

"But, Miss Huntington—"

She raised her hand to stop him. "Your daughter will be attending my school, and I thank you for your faith in me. I'd rather not resort to the tactics Mr. Wolcott has seen fit to use. It's not what you'd want me to teach your Camille. So I think it best to let the matter drop and let all parties involved go on the way they were this morning before I found out about the paint. I'll inform him when the time is right." In turn, she slipped the coins from the counter's edge into her purse. The roast beef was back in the oven, so to speak. Then she clutched her pocketbook to her waist. "I thank you very kindly for your integrity, Mr. Kennison. Good day."

As she turned to leave, Chief Officer Algie Conlin and Deputy Pike Faragher entered the hardware store. Their noses together in a hat–to–hat brim conversation, they didn't see her.

"We never would have gotten back so early if it hadn't been for Tom Wolcott's insightful advice," Algie remarked. "He was right. For prairie chicken, use only an ounce of number-six shot."

"And for quail," Pike added, "load eights and nines."

"Save the tens for snipe."

Deputy Faragher nodded. "Good thing Tom had that nine weight, and damn nice of him to bring a couple of boxes of shot by the department last night when he dropped off that clay pigeon intent permit."

"An upstanding fellow, that Wolcott," Chief Officer Conlin declared. "A real asset to the community."

"Miss Huntington." Pike noticed her first. "We got your card on our door."

Algie straightened. "A coincidence we've run into you. This'll save us a trip to your house. What can we do for you, Miss Huntington?"

She stiffened her backbone and kept her gaze level. The realization that Tom Wolcott had not only bribed the hardware store owner, but he'd also conveniently gotten rid of the police this morning—however oh so subtle in his *nine load* ways—had her gnashing her teeth together. "Yes, it is a good thing you didn't have to come out to my house, because I no longer need your services. The matter has been taken care of. It was nothing after all."

"Whatever you say, Miss Huntington." Algie shrugged.

The pair of them drew up to the counter while she opened the door. As she exited the store, she heard:

"Kennison, we need an iron stabilizing rod. Some son of a bitch kicked down our deer."

Why did he do it? The question burned in Edwina's mind hours later as she sat on her parlor floor in her nightgown. What could Tom Wolcott possibly have to gain by painting his side of the warehouse that hideous red—and sloppily so—other than to drive her crazy?

Scissors in hand, she couldn't come up with a plausible answer, so she forced herself to put him out of her thoughts. The precise diagram she had drawn on the back side of a letter was of her school furnishings in miniature. The template would serve as a guide for arranging her furniture before she actually moved in. That extra foot was able to accommodate her desk and the sideboard on one wall, then two rows of desks—old extension tables she'd found in her attic—that would serve as stations for the girls.

With a single cut, she sliced off the salutation end of the letter. It landed faceup in her lap.

Madame Janetta DeVille

Edwina could hardly bear to look at the slanted signature. The salutation became her desk. The remaining piece of the letter was dissected into tables, the heater, a sideboard, and a few odds and ends.

As Edwina aligned them on a master board the exact scaled-down size of her schoolroom, she rearranged them in a pleasing manner. The *Dear Miss Huntington* turned into the sideboard. *I would be interested in* was now the storage area.

Hands stilling, Edwina closed her eyes and reread the letter in her head for the dozenth time.

My Dear Miss Huntington:

> *It has been too long since I last heard from you. Have you decided to remain in Harmony, or are you still considering a move to Denver? I would be inter-*

ested in meeting with you should you come to our
fair city. The job I spoke of, senior staff accountant
to our bridal salon, is still available. The clerk I hired
after your original refusal four months ago, didn't
work out for me. I would much rather hire a woman.
And a woman of your business talent is rare. Your
accomplishments at Gillette's are to be praised.
Please advise me as to what your plans for the future are.

> Yours,
> Madame Janette DeVille
> House of DeVille Bridal Salon

Edwina swallowed a heavy sigh. Out of courtesy, she
had given Madame DeVille a reply, but not the one the
woman wished to hear. Edwina had to stay in Harmony
until her family debts were paid off. She didn't know
how long that would take her, if she could ever be free
of them at all. When she'd sent her college credentials
to Colorado months ago, she'd been hopeful she'd be
given a position. But when the offer came, she'd had to
turn it down. By then, she'd found out about the second
mortgage and the pile of medical bills. Until she could
square all of them, she was stuck. Her dreams had to be
put on hold.

Honey Tiger padded to Edwina and brushed against
her arm, waiting for a scratch beneath the chin. As she
obliged the cat, its white whiskers twitched with pleasure. She took the loving for a moment, then fickle as
always, moved on. She stepped on the templates, her
pink nose bumping on the paper as she smelled them.
The map became ruffled. But Edwina didn't care. She
was too tired—not physically. It was more of a tenseness
from trying to hide things, from trying to be somebody
she wasn't. . . .

Moving a section of hair to her back, she leaned into
the settee and brought her knees up. Her hair flowed
freely about her shoulders. Her pale feet were bare and

she wore no wrapper. Within reach, an O'Linn beer bottle sat on the parlor table. Normally, she never would have indulged on a Friday evening, but Tom Wolcott's stunt had driven her to distraction.

She drank one beer a week each Saturday night; then on Sunday morning on her way to church, she cut across Birch Avenue and snuck the empty bottle in the rubbish bin behind the Blue Flame Saloon. Thus far, no one had been the wiser.

Great pains had been taken to keep her secret. She had the O'Linns sent to a post office box under an assumed name, and she'd told Mr. Calhoon she'd be picking up a parcel every so often for one H. T. Katz, an old family friend from Waverly too infirm to make the drive to Harmony to pick up his parcel. Not a brow had been raised, for it wasn't uncommon to take mail to others. She kept the bottles hidden in the cellar, where they stayed cool and out of Marvel-Anne's sight.

Edwina didn't think of herself as a drinker. She just happened to like beer, and unfortunately, a woman who indulged—no matter how harmlessly—was of a doubtful reputation. Which, she hated to admit, in her case was the absolute truth.

A wry smile caught her mouth as she recalled Tom Wolcott's earlier words of reproof: *A woman of your untarnished reputation coming to a man's apartment.*

If he only knew. . . .

As the taste of O'Linn washed through her mouth, she was reminded of the Peacherine Club in Chicago. She'd danced there many times with Ludlow. She and Abbie would sneak out of Abbie's bedroom after her parents had retired, and they'd meet up with Ludlow and his group to go to the music district, which had been *en vogue* for the college students. Edwina had never considered she might not be safe in the colorful dancing clubs; Abbie had said she'd gone there lots of times before.

Abbie . . . Edwina missed her. Abigail hadn't written in the past month, and Edwina wondered about her.

Their parting had been awkward. During the last week she was in Chicago, Abbie changed. She'd been strange . . . and a little secretive, especially when Ludie's name had come up. But Edwina had had to leave before she could figure out what was the matter. She'd asked Abbie in a letter. In Abbie's next correspondence, she made no mention of anything amiss.

Trying to come up with answers, Edwina reflected on their friendship. They'd become fast comrades as soon as they'd met. One of Edwina's mother's conditions for allowing Edwina to go to school in Chicago was that she had a respectable home in which to stay. The Cranes were related to the minister at the Harmony General Assembly church. Minister Stoll had sent a letter of introduction to the Cranes, and they in turn had opened their home to Edwina. Edwina's mother had thought she was sending her daughter to a fine Christian family—and that did describe Abigail's parents, but Abbie herself had turned out to be quite the opposite. Not that she'd been a shameless woman—Abbie just liked to frolic and dance. And Edwina had soon learned what a truly good time could be had when she let her hair down—not that she ever did in the literal sense.

The east side Peacherine Club could be described as nothing short of delicious. Edwina had been introduced to piano music she'd never in her life heard. And she'd learned to dance to the fast beats, too. Ragtime and the cakewalk. Ludie had taught her. They'd had the grandest of all times. And when the evening grew late, he and a friend would escort her and Abbie home as far as they dared; then the pair of them would strip right down to their corsets and climb up the porch roof to slip into Abbie's room.

Edwina took another sip of beer, her thoughts wistful. She could have been Mrs. Ludlow Ogden Rutledge if she'd been the kind of girl his parents had wanted him to marry. Or if he'd been the kind of man to stand up to his mother.

The hurt had lessened the more time passed. But she

couldn't forget the words he'd spoken to her that night, her last in Chicago. They still pained her too much to think about. So rather than dredge them up, she rose and went to the Victrola.

In the cabinet beneath it, she housed her respectable records in the front, but the popular ones in the back. She put on a recording of "Swipesy Rag," wound the turntable, then began to trot through the parlor as the upbeat piano notes played out the big trumpet. She hummed with the tune, gaily moving left and right. Honey Tiger perched on the settee and watched her as if she'd gone loony.

Inadvertently, she kicked the templates and the papers scattered. At least she didn't have to feel guilty anymore about getting that extra foot on her side. Tom Wolcott's painting party had stamped out all her wrongdoing.

Now if only she could stamp him from her head. The hour nearing midnight, she couldn't help thinking that at this very moment, he wore his atrocious . . . revealing . . . nightwear.

Not that she had gotten that good a look . . .

She wondered if he knew how to step around the floor doing the nice-and-light to the "Swipesy Rag."

Not that she'd ever dance it with him . . .

Although she was certain he knew the nice and light. . . . But in his repertoire, it was no dance.

Chapter

❧ 5 ❧

The dividing wall had been completed late the day before, providing Tom the privacy of his own store and entrance. First thing that morning, with Shay's help, he'd mounted the eagle on the roof line right above the door. Tom had also had a business placard made, with WOLCOTT'S SPORTING GOODS AND EXCURSIONS engraved on it; the sizeable piece of wood now hung from the eaves.

After skimming the length of white plaster with a quick gaze, Tom resumed stocking a glass case with knives and ammo while contemplating how he'd arrange some trophies on the new wall and where he'd nail up Buttkiss. One thing for certain, working in the newfound peace that came with not having to be subjected to Miss Huntington's usual cold stares was worth everything he'd paid Trussel—and then some, namely those decoys the handyman had walked off with last night.

Of late, Miss Finishing School had really gotten her Dutch up. He couldn't be sure what over because she hadn't spoken a word to him since last Friday. If she'd found out about the relocation of the dividing line, he figured she would have given him hell by now. Seeing as she hadn't reported the findings from her hardware-store investigation, Kennison must not have told her anything.

Tom wished he'd never bought the vermillion. The joke had been more on him than her. The outside of the building, even with the majestic eagle there to spruce it up, truly did look like it had been defaced by vandals.

Crouched on his knees, Tom could feel the floorboards vibrate from the other side of the wall, as if a lot of furniture was being shuffled from one spot to another. Although it was already well past lunch, the scraping sounds had been going on for a good few hours, as if whatever scheme she'd had for arranging her schoolroom wasn't working out.

He wondered how long it would take her to figure out his double double cross to her double cross—if she even had the nerve to come over and point out that she'd tried to cheat him first. Rather than second-guessing her, he continued unloading boxes.

A faded red Knickerbocker baseball cap, which he wore backward on his head, kept the hair from falling in his eyes while he leaned into the cabinet and arranged shell crimpers, extractors, bags, and belts.

Rising, he was about to get a box of Thunder Head fast flight archery blades, when the store's door opened and Edwina filled the vacancy. Before he realized her intent, a rolled linen measuring tape encased in hard leather left her hand, sailed across the room, and bounced off his head. Luckily, the projectile struck him on his ball cap. The felt band buffered part of the impact; the rest resulted in what he hoped was only temporary blindness in the right eye.

"You measured," he remarked in a dull tone.

"Not soon enough!"

While squinting and trying to sort out his vision, she charged at him with her fists clenched at her sides. In spite of the smart pulsing on his forehead, he couldn't help thinking her shot had been pretty good.

"How many froggies did you give Abner Trussel?" she shouted, her stride long and voice vexed. Reaching him, she put the flat of her hands on his chest and shoved him back. Fairly hard for a woman.

Tom hadn't been prepared for a physical assault, so he took a step backward.

Hands still on him, she tilted her face upward. "Well? How many froggies?"

When he didn't immediately answer, she gave him another shove. Although he outweighed her and could have overpowered her easily, he figured that in her warped reasoning, he was due some pushing around—not much. So he barely moved, just enough to make her feel satisfied she'd accomplished something.

"None," came his laconic reply.

"Don't lie to me, Mr. Wolcott." If she'd been taller, her nose would have been bumping his, the way she stood on tiptoes trying to get in his face. "You had to have given him something."

"Duck calls. Super raspies and double clucks. Some decoys, too."

"Oh, buster, I knew it!"

The heel of her shoe came down on his boot, then she rammed his chest with another strong push. He faltered a little, his foot momentarily shot through with a nagging pain. This was the second time she'd gouged him with her heel. The first time, he'd given her the benefit of the doubt and had called it an accident. Now, he wasn't going to be so generous. He picked her up beneath the arms and held her at arm's length.

While she dangled, he barked, "Don't step on me again."

"Put me down, you toad! You brute!" A shriek of horror left her lips.

He did so, but he didn't readily release her. "Are you going to calm down?"

"No!"

His grip remained unyielding. "Then I can't let you go."

"Of all the mean-spirited, dastardly, underhanded,

low-down things you could have ever done to me! I was entitled to that extra foot!"

"I think you've got the tables turned around wrong. The low-down thing was your bribing Ab Trussel first with spiced plums. All I did was up the ante."

"All you did was take liberties with half the people in this town. I found out about Mr. Kennison and the police. You should be arrested for tampering with law officials."

"I did nothing of the kind."

"I'd say number-nine shot is tampering when the police have to close up their office to try it out!" Wiggling, she tried to free herself, but his grip remained steady. She ineffectively cuffed him on the shoulders. Her hair loosened from its high pile, the curls at the top dancing with her as she struggled. "Unhand me, you vermillion oaf!"

In an attempt to kick him, her right leg swung out, but he sidestepped her in the nick of time, taking her with him. They bumped into the grizzly who stood guard at the heater.

She screamed.

He laughed.

"It's dead," he commented with a half smile, testing to see what she would do should he let her go. Since she made no other attempts to go for his shin, he slowly uncurled his fingers from her underarms.

Standing away from him, she put herself together, becoming the stuffy version of herself. Primly and properly, she swiped the invisible wrinkles from her puffy sleeves and skirt. Then she jammed a few hairpins in place before the coiffure tumbled down. After all was put to rights, she crossed her arms beneath her breasts.

"Mr. Wolcott, I do believe you owe me an apology."

"For what?"

Her eyes blazed. Their brilliant hue, lit by sizzle and fire, gave him wicked ideas.

"For taking what should rightfully be mine—one extra foot. I wasn't asking for the moon and stars, just a simple twelve inches to compensate for having paid more for my share than you did. I don't think that's an unfair request."

"Trouble is, you never asked me."

"I stated my feelings quite clearly in Mr. Stykem's office."

"But you never asked. You demanded."

She huffed, "Had I asked, would you have given me the extra foot?"

"No," he replied simply.

The hard-fought ladylike composure faltered once more. She reached out to slug him on the arm, but he caught her hand midswing.

With amusement, he asked, "What color is your petticoat, Miss Huntington? I'd swear with the way you're acting, it's got to be red." He went as far as reaching for the folds of her skirt, pinching some delicate fabric, and lifting until snowy white was revealed. "Damn, I'm disappointed. When you slammed into me, I thought for sure you'd left modesty at home and scarlet was your color today."

"H-how dare you!" she stammered, stumbling away from him and slapping down the rumpled print.

"I'm onto you, Miss Huntington."

"I'm certain I don't know what you mean."

"I mean," he took a step forward, pinning her between himself and the table of camp cooking outfits, "you aren't who you're pretending to be, Ed."

"Don't you call me Ed, you fresh thing, you!"

A chuckle escaped him, and he drew in closer, fully trapping her with hands pressed on either side of her onto the tabletop. "What I can't figure out is why you go to such extremes to hide your other personality. I like you a lot better when you're as spicy as cayenne pepper."

"I don't care if you like me or not." She turned her face away from him and gazed down at a stack of tin plates. He drank in her profile: wispy bangs that fell across her forehead, a nose that was charmingly sculpted, and lips full and rounded over perfect teeth.

"Maybe. Maybe not." She refused to meet his gaze. The scent of dried rose petals, the kind ladies scattered in their bureau drawers, filled his nose, sweet as any bottled perfume—perhaps even more erotic than a dose on the skin. The smell clung to her clothing, and when she moved, the fragrance moved on the air. Such a thing could drive a man to distraction. He'd never been this intimately close to her before. She smelled good. Too good. He had to put some distance between them, but he had a hard time moving.

Shifting, he said, "I tell you what—why don't we start over as of today? A clean slate. From now on, I'll be honest with you. Nothing to hide. Likewise, eh, Ed?"

With a toss of her chin, she said, "I don't have to tell you anything."

"Good. Then that means you don't have anything else to hide."

"I never did."

"I'd say different."

"Unhand me now, Mr. Wolcott," she said in a co-quettish tone, though her hot gaze was anything but.

Because she'd offered him a challenge with her eyes, he rose to the occasion and gave her a sideways smile. "Yeah, from now on I'll be totally honest. And I'll enjoy it, too." His fingertip lifted to her full lips, lingering a fraction from their quivering seam. "I like your mouth. I especially like this part here." He took the liberty of touching the bow on the upper lip, caressing just softly enough to bring forth a shiver from her.

"What do you think you're doing?" she asked, her voice low, yet soft and clear.

Although it hadn't been his original intention, he made a decision and said, "Kissing you."

Touching his lips to hers, he savored the softness of her mouth and the flutter of her breath against him as they joined. He claimed his kiss as if they were out for a Sunday-afternoon ride—slow, drowsy, and full of plea-sure. The shiver of a sigh she gave him tormented him to a certain degree. A desire for her to relax made him proceed in an unhurried manner, lightly grazing her lips, then slanting his mouth over hers.

She stood rigid in his arms, yet her lips didn't have the marble coldness of a spinster. He detected a sweet pliancy, a vague hint of experience—a few seconds of her kissing him back. Someone had kissed her before. And perhaps that someone had taken advantage, because her muscles tightened and she held herself very still. He didn't want her to feel threatened.

He tucked her curves neatly next to him, holding her close. Stroking a light path down her spine with his fingertips, he tried to coax her to ease into him and mold her body to his. When at last she did, he breathed in. Blood pounded in his brain.

Gradually, he deepened the kiss as she nestled against his chest, making no protest about wanting to be set free. He slid his hands up her waist, feeling the glide of fabric as soft as down against his palms. If she'd truly been an old maid, she wouldn't have felt so much like velvet . . . smelled so much like flowers.

Cupping her oval face in his hands, he stroked his thumbs across her smooth cheeks. The texture of her skin against his calloused fingertips taunted him as he traced a path down the satiny column of her neck. He wanted to pull the pins from her hair and sift his fingers through the thick curls.

Edwina let him hold her, but she didn't kiss him back again. She fought him without physical force, apparently waging some kind of battle within to not reduce herself to feeling something. Whether or not she meant to push him away, her hands came up to his shoulders, exerting pressure.

The gesture was enough to sober him. He pulled back, finding rational thinking difficult as he gazed into her heavy-lidded eyes. Her moist lips parted and a rose flush stained her cheeks.

"You're ruining my life," she whispered.

Because he didn't feel remorse for having kissed a

woman who'd rather have him in jail than in her bed, his reply could only mirror hers. "Likewise."

In a monotone, she requested, "Release me."

He did so, slipping his hands into his pockets and stepping out of her way.

She tugged on the cuffs of her sleeves, putting them in order and brushing off unseen lint. She did a quick check of her hair with a few pats and, finding nothing out of order, she angled her face at him. "Petty incivilities aren't in my nature, Mr. Wolcott. Although you deserved it, I shouldn't have thrown a tape measure at you. Should you incur any bills from Dr. Porter, forward them to me and I'll reimburse you." With a quiet but desperate firmness, she added, "I'd very much appreciate it if you didn't mention my name when you call on his office."

"You don't have to worry. I won't be seeing him."

"Suit yourself."

Walking around him, she went toward the door. Unlike when she'd entered the store, her stride was at a scrupulous and reserved pace.

"I'd say I was sorry for the wall if I was wrong in telling Trussel not to give you that foot. But I'm not," he said to her retreating form. "And just so there's no hard feelings, I'll share my mailbox with you."

She stilled, then slowly turned to glare at him. "Stuff your mailbox."

"What was that you said?"

"You heard me." She continued on, her dismissive attitude jabbing at him.

As he moved from the table, he stepped on something. "You forgot your tape measure."

"You can stuff that, too."

"So much for petty incivilities," he said beneath his breath.

"You're deplorable," she shot back at him.

"And when you're fired up, I find you adorable."

On that, she had no comment except to slam the door.

*　　*　　*

Edwina sat at her desk and put a hand to the back of her neck. She pressed her head hard against her palm, trying to rid herself of the headache that was giving her brain a pounding. The pain had erupted full force the instant she'd walked out of Wolcott's sporting goods store.

Through her uncurtained window, she could see outside; twilight cast the sky in plum. The day felt longer than a five-mile walk in new shoes. She resumed staring at the classroom's interior; a frown caught her mouth. Lit by the flame of a single lamp, the horror that was the room couldn't be disguised. The furnishings appeared lumped together. A hat rack nudged the sideboard, the extension tables made jagged rows, and her own desk sat so close to the heater, she'd had to smother the coals or risk being barbecued.

Moaning, she lowered her face to the open book on deportment in which she'd been marking pages for tomorrow's opening-day lessons. Her mind, plagued with a migraine, could no longer function. What little she'd managed to think out had been frequently pushed aside by visions of Tom Wolcott's hedonistic mouth on her own.

How could she have allowed him to kiss her? Hadn't she sworn never to kiss another man? But when he'd looked into her eyes, his own possessing such allure in their winter blue depths, she'd been reduced to a namby-pamby.

His lips had touched hers with a tantalizing persuasion. For a moment, she'd forgotten herself and kissed him back, stealing an instant's pleasure. In that time, she'd succumbed to the delight he'd offered. She'd enjoyed his sculpted mouth over hers and had reveled in the tingling sensations that had radiated through her body.

Oh, she loathed herself for her weakness. Now more than ever, she'd have to carefully watch her every move and gesture in his company. Actually, avoiding his company was the best plan. And there was no reason for her to ever have to be in it again unless they chanced to meet on the streets. It would be safer for her. She wouldn't be tempted to do something she'd regret.

Any outward signs of attraction to Tom Wolcott would jeopardize all that she had fought so hard to regain. Namely, her dignity. She could never be used in such a way again and recover from the humiliation.

Lifting her head, Edwina sniffed back unshed tears. She'd been on the border of crying for the past couple of hours. Nothing was working out the way she'd planned. Feeling sorry for herself had never been one of her failings, but now she found that wallowing in self-pity made her outlook on tomorrow a notch brighter.

Things couldn't go worse than they'd gone today.

A deranged barking began behind the building. That no-account bloodhound sounded hotly in pursuit of something. The bays rumbled from its chest, echoing a thirst for blood. He'd probably treed a squirrel and thought himself quite the conqueror.

Edwina glanced down at the beribboned basket at her feet. At least her dear kitty was safely inside, away from that nasty mongrel.

"Precious angel." She lifted the lid, wanting the comfort of her cat's silky fur to nuzzle against. Her anxious smile fell.

The basket was empty.

Rolling the chair back, Edwina poked her head beneath her desk. "Honey Tiger?"

In the dark recess, no marmalade cat with whimsical white whiskers could be seen.

She straightened, her eyes darting frantically around the room. "Kitty?"

A sweet little meow didn't answer.

Panic flew through Edwina as she went to her feet and began searching all the nooks and crannies of the room Honey Tiger had explored earlier. No Mama's-precious-lambie-baby-snookums kitty cat.

Honey Tiger had been in the basket many times. She'd always stayed inside once Edwina put her in there.

The cat had ridden in the coach compartment of the train to Chicago and back to Montana without a hitch. The only time she'd escaped had been at Abbie's after a neighbor's cat had moseyed along the porch and stuck its face next to the window glass. Honey Tiger had had a hissing and spitting fit and had gotten out of the house when a door had been opened. After chasing the other cat away, she'd climbed up the ancient elm in the backyard. Nobody but Edwina had been able to coax her down.

"Honey Tiger?" she called one last time, waiting a moment before accepting the idea that the cat had gotten out of the building. The cat must have snuck past her when she'd gone to see Mr. Wolcott. In her state of agitation, she hadn't noticed the tabby slipping through the door.

Where could her lambkins have gone? Honey Tiger didn't know the area over here; all she'd ever ventured onto was the sun porch of Edwina's house. . . . She could get lost or hurt or . . .

Edwina couldn't think with that blasted dog carrying on. "Oh, shut up, you good for nothing acorn eater."

Barkly!

Edwina bolted out the door and ran toward the back of the warehouse. Dry leaves crackled beneath her feet as she approached the bloodhound, who sat at the base of a tree. Seeing her, he ceased his barking just long enough to sniff her fingers—as if she'd bring *him* anything to eat!

A faint haze from an unseen moon lighted the grove sufficiently for her to make out shapes but not much else. Tipping her head back and straining her eyes, she could see through the network of oak branches. There, on a high limb, was the silhouette of her baby girl, her back arched in fright.

"Honey Tiger!"

The faint and distressed mews tore through Edwina's heart.

Barkly had shifted from a snapping bark back to that

pitiful howl. For lack of a weapon, she picked up two handfuls of leaves and hurled them at him. "Get out of here! Go home. Shoo!"

The leaves had no affect on him. In fact, he thought she wanted to play. His forelegs stretched out in front of him, his rump lifted, and the whiplike tail wagged.

"You're so stupid!" she yelled, then turned her back to him and made a split-second decision.

She began unbuttoning the side placket of her skirt.

When she'd had to get Honey Tiger before, she'd had a ladder at her disposal for propriety's sake. Where on earth would she get one now? Besides, she dared not leave her kitty alone.

Stepping out of the navy Panama cloth, she kicked the wad behind the tree trunk. Then she untied the waist of her petticoat and let the cambric slip down her stockinged legs. Standing in her knee-length drawers, she did several toe touches to limber up; then she began to scale the tree.

"Hush, my sweet baby!" she called. "Mama's coming."

Fortunately for her, she'd practiced climbing on Abbie's porch trellis. Neither the height nor the effort bothered her. She chose first one safe hold, then another, pushing twigs from her face as she went. Her hair got hung up on a branch, and a wince soured her expression as several strands snagged and tugged at her scalp. Hairpins came loose, and the pile of her pompadour sagged down her back.

Meow! Meow!

"Lambie precious! Hold on!"

Honey Tiger hadn't scrambled too far up the massive tree, but she had gone farther out on a limb than Edwina would have liked. Although the point where the appendage attached to the tree was thick, the end thinned dramatically.

Late acorns still attached to the tree rained to the ground as she bumped them. On a quick glance, she was surprised to see the dog not going after the nuts. Actually, she was surprised to find the dog was absent. He'd apparently run off.

Good riddance.

Fearful of crawling out too far and risking stressing the branch, Edwina slid on the rough bark, her hands propelling her forward. She went along fine until an ominous rip rang through her ears. Her drawers caught on a broken twig, and the sensitive flesh of her buttock cheek stung from the scrape.

Tears watered her eyes, but she couldn't stop. A short distance separated her and her cat. Honey Tiger's claws were dug in deep into the tree's craggy skin, but at least her meows had subsided.

"Kitty. Come to me."

Honey Tiger didn't move.

"Mama's pretty girl. Honey Tiger." She held her arms out.

The tabby's arched back realigned to normal and her tail quit its tight waving. But she still didn't come to Edwina.

Anchoring herself to the limb by wrapping her legs around it and pressing flat against it, Edwina stretched her arms as far as they could reach in an attempt to pluck the errant kitty free. In spite of extending herself to the point of an unsteady hold, she was shy of touching her cat by about a foot.

A foot. It would have to be that.

Leaves that hadn't fallen from the tree yet rustled with her motion as she inched forward. "Come to me," she said sweetly, trying to disguise the frustration in her tone. "Honey Tiger."

Meow. But the cat wasn't coming to Edwina. She had to try another tactic.

"Salmon. Salmon, salmon, salmon nummies."

Meow.

A crease furrowed her brows. The word *salmon* always worked to get the cat to listen to her. Against her better judgment, she crept out farther than was wise. Tamping down her impatience, she called in a no-

nonsense voice, "Honey Tiger, you come to Mama. Right now. Salmon. Mackerel. Sardines."

No comment.

As a desperate effort, she hastened to add, "Dittman's caviar."

Footsteps stirred the leaves below, and Edwina froze. She had a clear view of the ground beneath her, the particular branch she occupied being an offshoot of one of the lowest arms. No limbs grew below it.

Cigarette smoke came to her nose before she could see the person. The red nub swayed her gaze in its direction. Though she couldn't make out a face in the haziness, from body definition alone, it had to be Tom Wolcott. He filled out a shirt better than any man in town. And no one else wore a baseball cap at leisure—especially not backward.

Not daring to move lest she call attention to herself, she prayed he wouldn't linger. Honey Tiger was no threat in giving her away. The cat had decided to give herself a face bath. Edwina rolled her eyes.

Crunching sounds rose to her ears as Tom took a few steps. "Barkly," he called, then whistled once. "Let's go home."

The dog, who she'd been grateful had disappeared earlier, didn't show itself and give his master a reason to leave. Drat that mongrel anyway. Tom took a draw on his cigarette, then strolled through the grove while whistling every so often. It was her misfortune that he paused directly underneath her.

Both her hands had grown numb from the night air. In fact, she realized it was quite cold. Gooseflesh prickled her skin as a slight breeze made the boughs tremble. She couldn't be sure, but she thought she might have heard something else from the tree. A crack? A creak? Just the wind playing tricks?

Apprehension flickered through her. She shouted silently, *Please go home, Mr. Wolcott, so I can get down!* No such luck. He stayed, the tails of his overshirt fluttering against his thighs.

The noise came again, definite this time—a sharp snap, the kind of sound a limb made when it gave way abruptly under pressure and strain.

"Oh, no . . ." she moaned as the brittle crack caused her to drop several inches with the branch. Grappling to hold on, she attempted to back off the limb. At this angle, it was impossible to slide up. She was dizzy with fright and her heart thumped madly.

Crack!

"Look out!" she screamed just as the branch gave way, and she hurtled to the ground.

Tom Wolcott's upturned head cleared her vision just as her hands slammed down on his shoulders. Somehow, she flattened him on his backside, landing in the middle of his belly. Their foreheads bumped, shooting fresh pain through her head.

Dazed and disoriented, she let herself drape over him with her full weight before attempting to move. Nothing felt broken, but then she'd never had a broken bone before, so she didn't know for sure.

With arms spread on either side of him, she struggled to lift her chin. Using her elbows to prop herself up, she had to peer through a web of her disheveled hair. Before she could utter a word, he had the bad taste to say, "Miss Huntington, if you wanted me on my back, all you had to do was ask."

Aside from the knot throbbing on his forehead, Tom figured he'd gotten off pretty easy for just having had a body slam down on him from nowhere. Well, not exactly from nowhere—from the tree. What in the hell had Edwina Huntington been doing up there?

Darkness pervaded the grove, but there was enough illumination from a hidden moon to see by. Tom's hand automatically lifted to smooth the hair from Edwina's face. He tucked tangled locks behind both her ears. That done, he could read her expression clearly: shock, anger, agitation. A combination of all three lit her mouth, eyes, and brows, which were clamped shut, narrowed, and arched, respectively.

"How do you feel?" he asked, overriding any retort she might make about his prior comment. Genuine concern caused him to lay stock-still in case she'd broken anything.

"Not particularly well," came the weak mumble.

Consolingly, his thumb stroked her earlobe. "Where are you hurt?"

A trembling breath whispered, "Everywhere."

"As much as I find our present position has . . . possibilities, I think you'd better let me help you stand so I can check your bones."

Eyes flashed at him. "You're not a doctor."

"No," he said with a grin, running his fingertip over her shell-like ear, "but I used to play it in my youth."

"You're positively indecent."

"That's not what the girls said."

She gave an all-over shiver and batted at his hand. "Quit doing that to my ear. I find it . . . bothersome."

He didn't stop, enjoying the feel of her curvaceous body crushed against his. "Is that why your legs are hugging mine?"

"They most certainly are not." With that, she rolled off him into the leaves. Several stuck to her hair and littered her shirtwaist and . . . underwear. He just now noticed she didn't have a skirt on. Dainty drawers with lace-bound hems bunched up on her thighs, exposing the shape of her legs. *Very nice.*

Edwina laid a hand dramatically across her forehead and heaved a great big sigh. "I think I'm going to faint."

"I doubt it. Not unless you're suffering from a concussion. Are you?"

"How should I know?"

"You need to see a doctor. I'll carry you to Porter's office."

"Absolutely not!" She bolted upright, then moaned and clutched her head. "How would I explain falling on you?"

"The same way you'll explain it to me." He rose to his feet and offered her a hand—which she ignored. "What were you doing in the tree?"

"Rescuing my cat," she murmured through fingers that covered her eyes, nose, and mouth. Then she peeked upward over her fingertips. In a wavering voice tinged with distress, she cried, "Honey Tiger? Kitty, kitty, kitty."

A frazzled tabby skulked from a dark corner of the warehouse. Tan fur stood high on its back, and each slow step was low to the ground. The pitiful, plaintive yowl that issued from it filled the clearing.

The cat went to Edwina. She picked it up and held it close. Tom's tight gaze was riveted on the scene—most notably on the swell of her bosom above the cat she comforted against the row of buttons that traveled between her breasts. Her slender figure was seductive; the half-clad image she presented was an unwitting invitation to the bedroom. The wealth of russet hair tumbled down her back, falling past a narrow waist.

Lifting the cat, she put her nose up to its tiny pink one. "Honey Tiger, next time you come when your mama calls."

Meow.

Edwina grew oblivious to Tom, her focus on a worthless feline as she cuddled and cooed at it. He had as much affection for cats as Barkly did. They were stupid pets; completely worthless. Cats couldn't flush out game, and they couldn't retrieve anything bigger than a field mouse. They never chased after sticks or balls. Okay, so they could catch birds. Big deal. Just the powder-puff varieties. Your sparrows, hummingbirds, and songsters. Other than that, all cats did was sleep the day away, then eat liver and take care of business in a box of sawdust and sand. A pretty sad commentary for a life.

Irritated by the sugary endearments Edwina showered on her cat, Tom made a slight gesture with his right hand. "You lose your petticoat and skirt in the fall?"

"Hmm?" she replied, as if she'd forgotten he was there.

"You're not wearing a skirt and petticoat."

Quickly looking at her stockinged legs, she apparently remembered she was missing something. The palm she immediately placed over her bent knees did nothing to hide the obvious. "I had to take them off to climb the tree. They're behind that oak where I kicked them."

Tom strolled in the direction, perusing the area but not finding a skirt and petticoat. "Are you sure you left them over here?"

"Of course I'm sure." She pointed emphatically. "Right there. Right where you're standing."

Tom gazed down. There was nothing. Meeting her eyes, he remarked, "If they were here, they're gone now."

"They can't be gone!" Gaining her footing, she stumbled toward him with the cat clutched tightly in her arms. Leaves scuffled beneath her shoes as she walked around the tree in a circle. A slight rip in the seat of her drawers offered him the vaguest hint of the ivory skin beneath.

As she made another pass around the trunk, he moved in closer and took full advantage of the situation; he walked directly behind her, his gaze pinned to the rip as he gave not a second thought to the skirt he was supposed to be looking for.

She stopped and twirled around to face him. For a moment, he thought he'd been found out. Instead, she stared at him and insisted, "They were here."

"Maybe if you tell me exactly what happened," he suggested, opting not to tell her she had a tear in her drawers.

Exasperation colored her usually lilting voice. "I was in the building when *your dog* began barking. Then I looked for my cat in her basket. She wasn't there."

Unbidden, his line of vision kept inching lower. "Then what?"

She eased away from him while she continued. "So I

came outside and found out *your dog* had chased my cat up the tree. Not having a ladder, I climbed the tree myself. At some point, I realized *your dog* had run off."

He indulged himself in gazing at the flat of her stomach and the flare of her hips. "What happened after that?"

With all her sidling, she ended up standing behind the trunk for cover, with only her face peeking out. "Then you came outside. The branch broke and I fell. I landed on you."

"I know that part."

"Just to refresh your memory." She shot him an accusing glare. "I didn't think you were paying attention to what I just told you."

"I heard every word."

She exhaled heavily. "None of this would have happened if it haven't been for that menacing dog of yours."

Tom hated to have to tell Edwina, but Barkly had been known to bound off with things he knew he wasn't supposed to—clothing included. To Barkly's way of thinking—if Tom could think like a dog for a moment— it was a game of "catch me if you can." Most of the time, Tom never caught him, and whatever he stole ended up wherever he got tired of it. He usually made nightly rounds that included the billiard parlor, where he mooched peanuts off Dutch, and then the Blue Flame or the butcher shop, where he ransacked the rubbish bins.

Rather than sparing her, Tom said flatly, "Barkly made off with your clothes."

Denial flared in the set of her mouth. "Don't joke with me, Mr. Wolcott."

"I'm not."

Acceptance didn't readily come. But after a moment spent searching his eyes—as if to say *You're still joking—right?*—she buried her face in the cat's fur and moaned, "I'm ruined . . ."

Tom went to Edwina's side and awkwardly patted her shoulder. Condolences of lost propriety weren't his forte, but he gave it his best shot. "You're not ruined. Nobody has to find out."

Her pert chin jutted out. "How am I going to get home like this? I can't just walk down Main Street like the emperor in his new clothes. People are bound to notice."

Shrugging his agreement, he conceded, "I don't know about some emperor in new duds, but I'd definitely notice you." Then, as if he'd done this gentleman thing before, he unbuttoned his overshirt and slipped the flannel off his arms. Handing the coat to Edwina, he said, "Tie this around your waist. We'll cut across Birch and take the alley off of Elm to your place. The businesses have been closed for an hour. Everybody should be gone."

"You're walking me home? I don't know . . ."

Irritation marked his words. "If you've got a better plan, Ed, spill it."

She didn't.

In the time it took for him to lock up the store, she'd gathered her things and met him out front.

She looked a sight. The bump on her forehead couldn't be hidden by the brim of her hat. She had attempted to tame her hair, but to no avail. The tresses spilled across her shoulders. Gloves had been buttoned—a ridiculous offset to the matching holes at the knees of her black stockings. The shirt around her waist covered only her backside, not the front, except where the sleeves hung down. In the crook of each arm, she carried a pocketbook and a basket. He could guess what was in the latter. If it hadn't been a cat, he would have offered to carry it for her.

As they set out, he took hold of her by the elbow and guided her in the dark past the rear of the building and up the road. Main and Birch Streets posed the biggest problem. On both northern corners, the Brooks House Hotel and the Blue Flame Saloon stood out.

Making sure all was clear, Tom draped his arm around Edwina and swiftly ushered her across into the uneven shadows behind the saloon. The back door had been propped open for air; tobacco smoke rolled into the night along with the scent of liquor.

They cut through the rear entrances to the barbershop and garden behind the drugstore, bypassing the police department and dashing over Birch and Sycamore. Coming down the sidewalk and staying close to the shrubs, they reached Edwina's without trouble.

As he escorted her up the walkway, the moon came out from behind a cloud to cast silver on her house: three stories with bay windows and a tall, eight-sided cupola, a lot of gingerbread trim, a wraparound porch, flowers in beds, potted plants, and big trees in the yard.

His pace slowed as he took the setting in. Edwina Huntington was a well-off north-end woman. The place reminded him of Elizabeth Robinson's home, but the woman who resided here did not.

"Nice house," he remarked as he led her up the steps.

She turned and faced him, appearing out of sorts and uncertain. "I can let myself in."

He waited for her to do so; she didn't move. He also wondered how he was going to get his overshirt back.

Licking her lips and scooting her backside against the doorjamb, she said, "Mr. Wolcott, you've actually been very . . . diplomatic . . . this evening. Although the entire debacle was your fault, you've been gracious enough to rectify the error of your ways and—"

He interrupted, not wanting to hear her out. "With all these windows, I'll bet you use a lot of flypaper sheets in the summer."

Puzzlement shaping her brows, she replied, "Why . . . yes, as a matter of fact, we do."

"It figures."

He held out his hand.

She merely stared at it.

"My coat," he said in clarification.

"Oh . . . yes."

Before he could voice his protest, she shoved the cat basket in his hand. He stiffly held it while she undid the knot and gave him the overshirt. Then she took the basket back.

"Well . . ." she said, crossing her legs at the knees as if to keep herself covered.

"Do yourself a favor," he suggested, not wanting to linger any more that she wanted him to. "First thing in the morning, go to the police and file a theft report for your skirt and petticoat. Say they got stolen off your clothesline."

"But—"

"Trust me on this. G'night." Without a backward glance, he took the steps to the street.

Chapter

❧ 6 ❧

Edwina's fan-plaited skirt had turned up decorating the
disposal bin of Nannie's Home-Style Restaurant. Her
petticoat's reappearance hadn't been in such a forgiving
location. Found in the alley out back of Dutch's poolroom, the cambric had been streaked with mud and
smears of tomato sauce from pot roast bones. Had she
not informed the police of the so-called theft early that
morning, explaining how her clothing had gotten to two
different places would have been embarrassing, to say
the least.

But at the moment, Edwina couldn't think about Deputy Faragher's visit to the school a half-hour ago when
he'd informed her the clothing had been discovered and
that she'd have to sign a release at the office to reacquire
them. Presently, six students between the ages of sixteen
and nineteen were assembled in the Huntington Finishing School, along with Crescencia Stykem, who was the
oldest at twenty-two. They sat expectantly at their seats
with good posture, all eyes on their teacher.

Edwina's hands lay atop the book of deportment, but
gazing out into the fresh faces of these young ladies, she
wasn't quite sure how to begin. They were innocent and
unchanged by the vast temptations outside of Harmony's

quiet circle. Should she enlighten them? Put the idea into their heads that if they didn't marry, they should know how to financially take care of themselves? Better to prepare them to handle a variety of situations. After all, that was her objective.

"Good morning, ladies," she said, speaking clearly and distinctly. She hadn't had any practice acting matronly to girls precious few years younger than herself. To Edwina's way of thinking, she was still in her youth, too.

"Good morning, Miss Huntington," they returned in unison.

Although her purpose was to appear matronly, Edwina felt frightfully dusty on the old maid's shelf with that form of address. Changing times were at hand. In Chicago, young women had begun to address their husbands informally by their first names, rather than in the old-fashioned way of Mr. Whoever.

"You may call me Miss Edwina," she said, neatening the application stack, which hadn't been untidy to start with. "Allow me to tell you about this school and what you'll be learning here. A well-developed moral sense will prevent idleness and build in you a regulated character, which will in turn preserve you from the excesses of those tenderer emotions and deeper passions of women that are potent and can work for evil or for good."

The girls gave her blank stares, but she continued in a voice that held depth and authority she didn't necessarily feel. "You will be taught discipline and how . . . um . . ."—her sternness faltered—". . . not to run wild. You'll be trained to use a noble and harmonious self-restraint."

"Please?" A hand raised, and Edwina nodded. "What exactly do you mean, Miss Edwina?" queried Lucille Calhoon, lovely with her carrot-colored hair, pale blue eyes, and warm smile. She waited patiently for Edwina to elaborate.

Edwina wasn't given the opportunity—not that she had a ready and definite answer in her head—to reply.

Camille Kennison answered for her, her sunny personality matching the sunny blond of her hair.

"She means we're not supposed to go gadding around uptown and being idle or something. Don't look at or talk to men we don't know—even if we think they're delicious. And never do what you want to if it's uncultivated, because you have to show you're above trivialities." Her perfectly pouting mouth lifted in a smile. "Isn't that right, Miss Edwina?"

"Well . . ." she said, toying with the pencil beneath her fingertips. "That's not how I would have put it, but you have some fine observations. Idleness is a great cause of misery. You should be trained in the habits of household duties and the duties of married life."

Behind the back of her hand, Hildegarde Plunkett whispered, "Like submitting to the dark and secret degradation in the bedroom." In contrast to her lily-white fingers, her pretty round face grew pink. She was a little ungainly but concrete.

Edwina couldn't have been more shocked by the statement. She hadn't suspected these girls ever discussed such things. She knew she hadn't when she'd been their age.

"It must be terrible at first," Ruth Edward said in a timid voice. "I know I'll die of shame."

Johannah Treber, who had a thin nose and a dimpled chin, added, "I don't think that after a while you'll mind so much. Not if you really love your husband. I could do anything for love."

The conversation had taken a life of its own, completely befuddling Edwina. She herself had done things for love, and it had brought her trouble and a lifelong commitment to remaining unattached.

Camille joined in. "That's right." She was comely and pert, popular with boys, and always stylishly dressed. "If it's real love, you don't have any doubts at all."

"But real love comes after you're married," Ruth said. "You won't know if you can . . . do things . . . until after you're already a wife. And then, if you don't ever fall in love, you're stuck and have to . . . do things . . . anyway."

"I'm not going to be stuck in a loveless marriage, and that's flat." Hildegarde turned around in her chair to face Ruth. "My mother says that if you marry a good man and you respect him, you can make yourself fall in love with him. Just look at her and my father. Before she married him, she told me she used to think of him as a lummakin—part lummox and part bumpkin. Now she worships him every Friday night when he tells her how much money he's put in her household account."

Crescencia's hand rose and Edwina nodded, although she'd lost control of the situation. The other girls had been talking as frankly as if they'd forgotten where they were.

"Miss Edwina, tell us about Chicago."

Cressie's question stilled the room. Then Meg Brooks, who'd remained quiet until then, said, "Please tell."

Edwina hadn't counted on their wanting to know about her time in Chicago. But perhaps it was for the best. She'd make them aware of their options. "If any of you ladies ever has the chance to go to a big city, I suggest you do so."

"Did you see any automobiles?" Meg asked.

"Yes."

Johannah chimed in. "What were they like?"

"Loud."

"Did you ride in one?" Crescencia wanted to know.

Edwina thought about the time she'd gone touring with Ludie in his Pontiac motorcar. There'd been a dozen riders, all crammed in and having a joyous time. Abbie had sat in the front next to Edwina, who'd sat directly beside Ludie. They'd gone to the waterfront, where they'd frolicked on the beach. It had been later that night, as a bonfire burned high in the sky, when Ludie had proposed. And much later . . . when Edwina had. . . . She stopped the thought right there.

With an unyielding sigh, she knew not to encourage the girls in this kind of behavior. Her answer was "No,

I've never been in an automobile. But if you're ever invited to ride in one, make sure you're properly escorted. And that would go for all activities in public places."

"I know of public places that aren't so public during certain times of the day," Lucille said with a secretive smile.

"And just what are you getting at, Lucy Calhoon?" Meg demanded. "We all know you'll go with any boy in the hopes of getting a comb-and-brush set."

"What's wrong with that?" Hildegarde directed her gaze at Meg. "My mother says that a girl can accept a comb-and-brush set from a boy, but nothing else. *If* you know what I mean."

"Oh, I know what you mean," Ruth said, then mumbled, "kissing."

"What do any of you know about kissing?" Crescencia piped up, her spectacles firm on her nose. Gone was the insecurity and fluster when men were present. Her face shined with a thirst for knowledge, as if she'd never been privy to this sort of information before.

How did they get into this discussion anyway, Edwina wondered. She had had no idea the girls were this outspoken with one another about the opposite sex. With her father's illness at its worst during her last year in normal school, Edwina hadn't been able to partake in the social activities of girls her own age. She hadn't attended the coming-out parties and the ice-cream socials. She'd gone from schoolgirl to mother's helper, blindly unaware of what she'd been missing—until she'd gone to Chicago. She'd never had a bosom friend in school, a girl she could tell all to. Apparently, these young ladies had learned more by talking among themselves and exchanging tidbits than Edwina had ever gleaned from her mother in twenty-four years.

"Kissing men with mustaches is far preferable to kissing men without." This came from Camille Kennison.

"How would you know?" Lucy asked.

"I just do."

Meg, whose upswept hair shone like copper from a pool of sunlight coming in the window, said, "There was that notions and trimming salesman she thought devilishly handsome."

"I never did," came the hot denial. "And look who's talking. You get all those traveling men in your father's hotel. You've got the run of all of them."

"They're wickedly dangerous," Ruth whispered with a shy smile.

Hildegarde said, "My mother says they wear boiled shirts and stiff collars."

"And pinkie rings," Crecencia added with a giggle.

"So what?" Meg shrugged. "They pay a dollar a night."

"Have you ever dared to look in one of their sample cases when you make up their beds while they're out?" Johannah's close-together teeth bit into her lower lip.

With a sniff of displeasure, Meg replied, "I'm not allowed to go upstairs when the rooms are occupied. But I did see inside a man's case once while he opened it in the lobby."

"Tell!" the other girls shouted, leaning closer to Meg.

"Ladies' corsets! Not these wasp-waisted things our mothers make us wear. But real straight-front ones."

"Oh . . ." Crescencia sighed. "I could never let a man see me in a straight-front corset."

"Cressie, don't be such a goose," Camille hastened to say. "You're so fainthearted around men that if there's a knock on your door, you won't answer it, fearing tramps. What if the knocker was *the one* coming to pay a call on you?"

Blushing to the roots of her hair, Crescencia said, "A man's never knocked on my door . . . tramp or otherwise."

"Cressie, you never set your cap for any man so he *could* knock. That's your trouble. You're pretty enough. All you have to do is go after the right one and he'll be putty in your hands."

While Crescencia digested that news with thoughtfully

drawn brows, Lucy wistfully said, "I think Julius Addison is good-looking. Even though his nose is crooked."

"He broke it in a fight," Hildegarde informed her. "My mother told me to stay away from him. His hands are always dirty."

"It's from the oil on barbed wire," Lucy said in his defense. "He can't help it if he has to work at the feed and seed."

"He wears overalls," Johannah commented dryly.

"So?" Lucy was adamant in her affections for the Addison boy.

Camille toyed with a curl resting on her shoulder. "How can you be attracted to a man who doesn't even wear a padded suit and lace-up shoes?"

"I just can, is all!" Lucy shot back. "When he looks at me, my bones melt."

"What were you doing up by the feed and seed?" Hildegarde wanted to know. "My mother says . . ."

Edwina put both hands to her temples; she had to maintain a semblance of order—at least inside her head. Her intentions had been to teach the girls about men and life's responsibilities, not the other way around. But what she'd just heard was beyond belief. These girls were not nearly as innocent as she'd suspected.

She interrupted their chatter. "Ladies! Ladies, I think it's time we put this discussion to an end and focus more on the deportment of your person."

Having gained their attention, she put a hand on the top of the deportment book once more, as if for fortitude. "Just as you should prepare yourself for a city trip, you should prepare yourself for excursions in town. Before making a call or visit, a lady always takes her hair out of curlpapers, then changes her felt shoes and puts on either her best—or second-best—dress. Lastly, she puts on her gloves—which she has not buttoned on the stoop."

Just when she thought things would now progress in a more mannerly fashion, a commotion began outside. Shay Dufresne led a string of pack horses past the window, then tethered the lines on the rails he'd installed out front. A group of five men who looked well to do in new hunting suits congregated next to the animals while Tom Wolcott engaged them in a spirited conversation. Guffaws and loud laughs resounded, distracting the girls.

Bottoms lifted from desk seats as the girls strained to get a better look out the window. There were plenty of smiles of curiosity and whispers about the gentlemen, and Crescencia Stykem's eyes were fastened on Shay Dufresne.

From her position, Edwina couldn't view the whole scene. She did hear the deep drone of masculine conversation, and then horrid noises, like those of an animal in severe pain. Over and over, the hideous snorts echoed through the classroom. This wasn't to be tolerated.

Rising from her desk, Edwina calmly said, "Girls, stay seated. I'll attend to the matter."

But as soon as she'd passed through the open door, a swish of skirts could be heard as they all drew next to the window. One glance over her shoulder and she saw seven faces peering out of the glass.

Once outside, she noted the hunters all had a type of rippled hose device next to their mouths. When they blew into the tubes, a grunting call pierced her ears. It was deafening when they all sounded together.

"Mr. Wolcott!" she shouted.

He turned toward her, one of the offending contraptions in his hand. This being their first encounter since last night, she was unsettled by his presence, knowing that she'd pummeled him while in her underwear not twenty-four hours prior. And with a rip in the said unmentionables, to boot. She hoped he hadn't noticed the tear before she'd tied his shirt around her waist. But where Tom Wolcott was concerned, luck was never on her side.

She did have to admit she owed him a thank-you for the advice about the police. Had he not suggested making the report, she wouldn't have done so and thus saved face. On the other hand, had his dog not dragged her clothing off, she wouldn't have found herself in the situation at all.

She'd thought she'd seen the last of him, but it seemed there was no end to the grief he could cause her. Days ago, it had been vermillion paint. Today, it was obscene noises. Tomorrow . . . who knew. In spite of his innumerable faults, he had the audacity to look ruggedly handsome in a red plaid shirt with indecently tight denims hugging his lean legs. Tan leather boots with chunky heels added inches to the already towering height he had over the other men.

"What is it, Miss Huntington?"

His tone was businesslike, yet she detected an intimate warmth to it. Or had she imagined that?

"Mr. Wolcott, the grunting noises out here are disruptive to my classroom."

"Rutting," he said, correcting her, then ignored her to speak to the gentlemen. "Now, these elk calls are going to work nicely for you if you don't overuse them. But no bull is going to buy into a female making all the noise ya'll've been making at once. So in case you'd like to try something else, I do have the diaphragm type that is as effective but not as easy to use. They come in medium, small, old, and screamer."

One of the men, wearing a straw-colored outfit, asked, "What happened to large?"

"Sir," Tom replied with a grin, "I don't believe you're ready for the large. I knew an outfitter once who, while coughing, accidentally sucked the large into his windpipe. Every time since when he's belched, his throat makes a rutting sound."

A chorus of jovial laughter followed.

Edwina frowned. "Mr. Wolcott."

His smile softened as he faced her. "What is it, Miss Huntington?"

"I'm trying to give a lesson. The noise out here is intolerable."

"We'll keep it down," Shay politely assured her as he

ran his hand down the side of a half-asleep yellow dun. "Within the quarter-hour, we'll be out of here."

"I appreciate that, Mr. Dufresne."

Edwina gave Tom a final stare—one he met with those depthless blue eyes of his—before she returned to the building.

As soon as she headed for the classroom door, the girls scrambled for their seats—all except Crescencia, whose hands lay lightly on the windowsill as she stared outside. Closing the door behind her, Edwina went over and looked out for a moment with Crescencia. Mr. Dufresne walked around each animal, checking their saddles and touching them with a gentle stroke. His shoulders and his way of walking suggested reliability and common sense. Edwina liked him. And it appeared as if Crescencia had taken a shine to him. Edwina would encourage her, but only after she found out if he was available. Unfortunately, that meant asking Mr. Wolcott.

"Take your seat now, dear," Edwina said quietly.

Then she returned to her desk as well. But her thoughts weren't on the rest of the lesson. They kept drifting to the men outside . . . particularly one man— the wrong one for her.

Stuff and fiddlesticks . . . she had to quit fooling herself.

Any man would be wrong for her.

Tom sat behind his high counter on a stool. Given that the hour neared dinner, the store was empty. An assortment of scrap paper surrounded him, each with different figures on the pieces. One said *5 Big Buck horn mounting kits at $1.02 each.* Another read *2 Ugly Butt targets at 58¢ each.* He had a bunch of them, all meaning something important, yet he couldn't figure out how to put them on a single ledger sheet in an orderly fashion.

Mathematics had always been a perpetual pain in the neck. He'd never mastered any of it with a passing grade during the years he'd spent in school. Once he'd dropped out, he'd never had any use for it, so he'd gotten rusty with what he did know—which wasn't a whole hell of a lot.

He could add pretty well—subtract if he used his fingers. Multiplication was a lost cause, as was division. Fractions—no dice. But operating a store with a flow of inventory meant he'd damn better keep track of things. He had to know how much he had invested in stock, how much he paid out, how much he took in—just the basics of bookkeeping.

But he'd been sitting there for the past hour and he hadn't been able to come up with a single column that amounted to anything understandable. Everything looked foreign to him. Nothing added up to what it should. According to his figures, he was in the hole a couple hundred. That just couldn't be.

So he'd continued his struggle to put things to rights, but he was beginning to get frustrated. He rubbed his forehead lightly, which reminded him of the obnoxious lump. He'd put on his fishing hat this morning in an attempt to hide the injury from the prying eyes of customers who had been streaming in and out throughout the day for his grand opening.

Staring into space, then back at the mess in front of him, Tom procrastinated yet again making a tally sheet. The broken lead tips from two pencils smudged his wrinkled sheet of paper; he was down to one sharp pencil.

Taping the blunt end on the counter, he made himself a deal. When this last lead broke, he could go home.

Just as he was about to apply firm pressure, the door opened and Edwina came inside. She wore a short cape, hat, and gloves, as if she were on her way home.

"Mr. Wolcott," she said while approaching, "am I disturbing you?"

He leaned into the edge of the counter with his elbows. "Not at the moment. Do you plan to?"

She sent him an exasperated look. "Not intentionally."

Reaching the counter, she stood on the opposite side. "I wanted to inform you that my clothing turned up."

"Figured it would."

"Yes, well, your dog had quite a night of carousing. My skirt was discarded at the restaurant, and my petticoat, at the billiard parlor, of all places."

Hooking his boot heels on the stool's rungs, he rolled the pencil beneath his palm. "Could have guessed that one."

"I wanted to thank you for your tip about the police. Reporting the theft did save me from a scandalous predicament."

"Any time."

"There won't be a next time. I fully intend to keep a better watch on my cat."

Noticing her arm bare of a basket handle, he asked, "Where is the hair ball?"

A sharpness cut into her tone. "I believe you mean fur ball."

"Whatever."

She frowned, her lips forming an inviting pout that she was probably unaware of, or she would have set her lips more properly. "I left her at home today. She was too traumatized by yesterday's fall. But I'll be bringing her tomorrow, so I would appreciate it if you kept a leash on that dog of yours."

He didn't pay close attention to what she said, instead noticing that the bangs she normally kept wispy had more of a curl to them today. "You're wearing your hair differently."

A hand went up to the roll of curl at her forehead. She gave it a few nervous pats. "It just turned out this way."

He reached over and raised his hand. "More likely you're trying to hide this." With his fingertips, he brushed aside her bangs to reveal a purple bruise. He gently caressed her injury, thinking her skin softer than that of any woman he'd ever touched.

"I did think it best not to draw attention. It looks like you thought the same thing . . . that hat you're wearing . . ." Her voice sounded breathless as he continued to touch her. "How would we explain that we both have the same . . ."

He shouldn't be doing this. The only thing they had in common was that they were wrong for each other. She wasn't his type, not by a long shot. But there was something about her . . .

Reluctantly, he lowered his hand and relaxed on the stool. Picking up the pencil, he tried to look intelligent by scribbling a few numbers on his paper. From the corner of his eye, he could see her gaze taking in the place. Even though he'd had to cram his stuff in half the space he'd originally planned, the store had turned out all right.

Aisles were cramped, but he'd expected that. He'd assembled some cases and a run of narrow tables for his camping gear. The far wall was full of trophies of all varieties, as was half his countertop. Stuffed rodents in your small species and waterfowl, so lifelike they appeared ready to take flight, huddled around the powder scale. The back wall had shelves of hunter's hats and some clothing, basic shirts and trousers. With the south-facing windows occupying most of the space, the front wall was bare except for gun manufacturers' posters. The wall behind him was the focal point of the room. Aside from the Wild Turkey bourbon calendar, a beaver clock, and some fishing spears, Buttkiss had the solid stretch all to himself.

His eyes followed Edwina's as she stared at the clown head. He'd ordered the humpty-dumpty target out of a toy catalogue a year back, but he'd just now had the room for it. There were hinges on the base of the hat, ears, mouth, and tongue. The object was to throw a rubber ball at the mouth, knocking the teeth out and causing the tongue to appear. A thrower also got points for hitting the other parts. Twenty for the hat and ten for each ear.

"You want to take a shot at Buttkiss, Ed?" he asked, facing her. "With your aim, I'd lay odds you'll bust his teeth out first try. I've got a goose egg on my noggin to prove it."

She blushed but made no commit about the tape measure she'd pitched at him. "Why ever would I want to knock the teeth out?"

He shrugged. "For the hell of it."

"I never do things for that reason."

"I expect most of the time you don't, but I'll bet you have before." His prompting was met with the arch of a brow. "Come on. I dare you."

She took in a breath, then let it out quickly. Looking at him, then Buttkiss, she set her pocketbook on the stack of boxed rubber wading boots in front of the counter. She began to unbutton her gloves. "What time do you close?"

The wall-mounted clock—a stuffed beaver holding a luminous Beacon roman numeral face in its paws—read five minutes after five. "I did five minutes ago."

"Then lock the door and pull your shades."

False surprise punctuated his words: "Ed, you shock me."

She glowered at him. "That's all I need—somebody to come by and see me throwing rubber balls at a clown's head. And quit calling me Ed, Mr. Wolcott."

"Only if you call me Tom, Edwina."

He pulled the cords on the roller shades, flipped the OPEN sign to CLOSED, and locked the door.

Heading toward her, he said, "Have at it." Then he rested his backside on the hammock and tent table, put one ankle over the other, and folded his arms across his chest.

With dainty tugs, she removed both gloves. The balls were in a wide-mouth fishbowl on the counter, and she fingered a few before selecting one.

"Give yourself a disadvantage. Stand at least ten feet back."

His suggestion was met by an impaling stare tossed over her shoulder. "Ten feet won't be a disadvantage."

"Prove me wrong."

Counting off the feet with measured heel-to-toe steps, she turned in place, squinted at the target, and coiled her arm. He had to watch in wonder when she released the ball with as much energy as a professional in the baseball leagues. Buttkiss's painted white teeth shot through his tonsils and his tongue jumped forward.

"That's no country fair pitching," Tom commented as he left the table and went to reset the clown's teeth. He faced her. "How'd you learn to throw so hard?"

"Launching my shoes at misbehaved dogs." A smile cultivated a certain mischievous look in her eyes. He'd never thought Edwina capable of flirting, but damned if she wasn't.

He retrieved the ball from the floor and deposited it in her outstretched hand. If he had had an ounce of resolve, he wouldn't have brushed his fingers across hers to close them over the rubber.

Their eyes met and held. She was still smiling. Beautiful. Engaging. He liked her. He shouldn't. In an attempt to resist her captivating grin, he put some distance between them, taking up his watching spot again. "Harmony doesn't have that many dogs on the loose. Where'd you really shore up that aim?"

"The Midway Plaisance," she replied, her gaze steady on the target.

"Where's that?"

"Chicago." She bounced a little on the balls of her feet.

"This time, get him in the left ear," Tom suggested.

She drew back her arm and let go, knocking the hinge and pinning Buttkiss's ear to the side of his head.

As Tom strode to the clown, he mused aloud, "Never figured you for the type of woman to venture out of this mud-puddle town."

"I would leave this place in a heartbeat if I were able."

Turning toward her, he saw a hand cover her lips, as if she'd spoken secret thoughts. He detected melancholy . . . an almost quiet desperation in her eyes.

"Then what's keeping you here?"

She looked away and her words were directed at the floor. "Responsibilities I cannot ignore."

Before he could ask her what they were, her expression changed—a cool and unapproachable façade that warned him to back away. He'd let her get by with it for now, but they weren't through talking about this. Edwina Huntington lived in a cream-puff house. He figured the only reason she taught finishing school was out of boredom. What kind of responsibilities could she possibly have?

With a demure smile he sensed was forced, she changed the topic of their conversation as easily as the wind changes direction in a storm. What she said next hit him with gale force. "Your friend Mr. Dufresne is quite charming. Has he at present engaged a woman's affections?"

Annoyance bit into Tom's gut for no justifiable reason. It was just that he couldn't see her with Shay. He couldn't even picture her with anyone but . . . *him* . . . with her in her drawers and sprawled softly across his body.

Jesus, why had that thought come to him?

True, he'd lain awake for a long time the previous night thinking about how enticing those curves of hers had felt next to him, but he'd reasoned it was because he'd been too long without a woman. He had to get over to Waverly and visit one of the sporting houses, buy himself a lady of leisure for the whole damn night. One who had reddish brown hair let down to her hips and eyes a bewitching green. And one who wore sassy underwear. White frilly stuff. With a figure to do it all justice. A pretty face, breasts just the right size for his palms, a slender waist, and legs that didn't quit.

Scowling, Tom realized he'd been imagining Edwina.

"Well?" Edwina's velvety voice cut into his ribald musings. "Is he?"

Hell's aces, she was talking about Shay Dufresne, his friend and partner. If she wanted to go after him, who was Tom to tell her otherwise? He had no claim on the woman, so he wouldn't stop her from sinking her claws into Shay. Not that the match would be a very good one. Shay, he had some fine qualities, but what did he know about north-end girls? He'd never been invited to Elizabeth Robinson's house.

Ah, damn. He wasn't any advice columnist. Let Shay take his own falls and learn from them. But just the same, Edwina Huntington wasn't the right girl for him.

Dropping the ball into Edwina's hand, Tom replied woodenly, "He just got into town. He doesn't work *that* fast."

The smile of relief she tried to contain accentuated the twist in his stomach. He grew instantly irritable, his eyes hardening.

As she wound her arm back for another throw with that pliant curve still on her lips, he ground out seconds before the ball left her hand, "You aren't exactly the kind of woman he normally goes for, but I can tell him you're interested."

The ball missed Buttkiss by a mile and whacked the beaver in the snout. A crack of grass rent the silence as the clock's dial splintered while two buck teeth flew off the rodent's mouth and dropped to the floor.

"Dammit all!" Tom swore, and charged over to assess the damage. The beaver's nose was cockeyed, and the hands on the clock had both drooped down to read six-thirty. Crouching, he swiped his fingers beneath the counter to feel for the missing teeth.

Edwina came up to his side, her skirt grazing his arm. "I didn't mean to," she hastily apologized. "It's just that when you said what you said about me and Mr. Dufresne . . . well, you distracted me. You've got it all wrong—"

"Move back," he said, fuming.

She did so with a slight hop. He expanded his search and came up with both teeth. Rising, he examined them in the palm of his hand.

Edwina inched forward and ventured to say, "I truly

am sorry. They're repairable, right? Can't you rubber-cement them back on?"

"Rubber-cement?" The dubious lift of one side of his mouth shut her up. It had taken him a full winter to assemble the clock. It had taken Edwina less than a minute to bust it up. "What the hell happened to your concentration?"

Her breasts thrust out, and her chin shot up. "I was concentrating until you had Mr. Dufresne and me coupled off. I'm not solicitous for him. I was inquiring on behalf of someone else."

The heightened color on her cheeks did little to convince him. Depositing the beaver teeth in an empty beer bottle beneath the counter, he turned the tables on her with the first woman that came to his mind. "That Crescencia Stykem isn't a bad-looking woman when she's not fidgeting." Short of what he'd just declared, he didn't know what else to say about the ink-happy secretary. He hadn't really paid any attention to her looks other than that first cursory glance in the lawyer's office, so he stole Shay's words and used them to his advantage. "That red hair of hers reminds a man of a desert sunrise after a night of rain."

She stood there with a hot stare on her face. "Are you inquiring after her?"

"Nope. Just asking for someone else," he retorted, giving her some of her own medicine. "Not that I wouldn't be thinking of her for myself . . ."

When she didn't bite and run with the bait, he gave the line a little more reel and switched lures. "That Kennison girl . . . what's her name?" A smile of sinful delight lit his face. "Camille." Absently, he went for the dish of walnuts he kept for the customers' enjoyment and grabbed a nut. "She's enrolled in your school. Don't know what for. She doesn't need any finishing, from the looks of her." Using the butt of a hollowed-out pistol, he crushed the nut and sifted through the shells. "She's a beautiful girl."

Edwina cringed and pursed her lips. "I agree. She is a beautiful *girl*. She's only nineteen."

Trickling some of the nuts into his mouth, he shrugged. "So?"

"So? You're too old for her. You've got to be at least thirty."

"Thirty-two." His brows fell in a line. "How old are you?"

She started up that damn business of dusting herself off—the invisible lint routine. He hated that. "Not that it's any of your affair," she said, plucking at a spot on her sleeve. "Twenty-four."

"Twenty-four and never been married."

"Have you?" she shot back, clearly out of sorts.

"Nope."

Her voice grew gentler. "Do you aspire to?"

"Absolutely." He crushed another walnut. "Don't you?"

"Absolutely not."

Tom thought this strange. All women wanted to get married—even the ones who worked in the saloons. "Why don't you want to?"

For an instant, wistfulness stole into her expression. "The aspirations I have wouldn't conform to marriage."

"Why not?"

She tilted her head and gazed at him as if he were dense. "What man would want his wife to be employed?"

Tom had never given that any consideration. His wife would stay in the house and raise their kids. Bake cookies and sew junk for the tabletops. Hell, that's what wives were supposed to do. This working thing . . . it was too modern for him.

"I don't know what kind of man would want that. Because I'm not the kind of man who would allow it."

"I see. How do you feel about unmarried women being employed?"

She was baiting him for some reason; he could see it in her eyes. He had to ask himself if he was going to be a smart bass or a stupid trash fish. The bass wouldn't bite; the trash fish would feed on anything. Wary of the unidentifiable lure she used, Tom replied, "It's all right, I guess." Satisfaction marked her expression; he didn't want her to think he wholeheartedly approved, so he added, "If the woman's got nothing better to do."

They stood there for a few seconds, a standoff of sorts. It seemed that all that needed to be said had been said— for a lifetime—between them.

Edwina left his side of the counter and went to the other, where she collected her gloves. Tom had been littering shells across his accounting papers, causing her to give them a furtive glance. In her expression, he could see her brain working—a no-nonsense clicking inside her head.

While shoving her fingers into the prim white of her gloves, she commented, "You should hire yourself a bookkeeper. Your debit and credit columns are reversed, and you don't have a clue as to what your assets and liabilities are. The numbers are all wrong for what you've stated they represent."

Thoughtfully chewing his walnuts, he asked, "What do you know about it?"

"I have a certificate from Gillette's Business College for Ladies in the classification and analysis of financial statements. Do yourself a favor—get someone who knows what he's doing or you'll be out of business within the week."

It rankled him that she seemed smart about something about which he wasn't. Men had the God-given right to know everything; women only learned the leftovers from what men wanted to show them.

As she tucked and fluffed herself to order, she said briskly, "I'll be hosting a tea party on the lawn in back next Tuesday. I wanted to inform you so that you could show some consideration and not use the area."

"Yeah, yeah," he mumbled, pulverizing another nut.

"And I would greatly appreciate it if you kept your dog locked up somewhere. I don't need him traipsing between the tables, begging for cake." She picked up her handbag, then said sincerely, "Please bill me for the damages done to the clock. I hope you can have it repaired."

"Forget it."

After she left, he gazed dejectedly at the beaver. Then his eyes lowered to the calendar and what he'd penned on Tuesday's square.

Mayor Heston King and constituencies . . . from Big Horn . . . coming in to try out the new Flightmaster.

He'd forgotten about the mayor. If King liked the clay pigeon thrower, Tom could sell enough of them to put a nice sum away in the bank toward purchasing a house. He'd been thinking about real estate lately. A man couldn't expect a wife to live in a room on top of a livery. If he ever got serious enough to propose, he had to have roots. Be stable. Give a woman a place to nest.

So he couldn't cancel the mayor's visit. No way, nohow.

"Ah, hell," he grumbled.

How long could a tea party last?

Chapter

7

Edwina stood at her dining-room table alongside Crescencia. The pair of them arranged flowers for that afternoon's tea. Actually, Edwina could have done the centerpieces herself, but she wanted to converse privately with Crescencia.

Selecting a long-stemmed white zinnia, Edwina asked, "Dear, have you been reading the book I loaned you?"

"Yes, Miss Edwina. I read the whole thing." Seriousness was reflected in the lenses of her spectacles. "Twice."

"And what did you glean from the chapter titled 'Introductions'? Specifically relating to gentlemen?"

Crescencia poked a sprig of baby's breath into her arrangement. "I thought it was well intended."

"You didn't gain a sense of direction? A little insight into the correct forms of greeting between ladies and gentlemen? How to be yourself with confidence?"

"Not exactly that last part . . ."

Edwina reached for a daisy. "I think you can if you put forth your best effort."

"Oh, but I do try. It's just that when a gentleman talks to me, I can't seem to keep my words straight. I get all bothered."

"Why is that?"

"I don't know. . . . I wish I did." Crescencia finished her centerpiece and began work on another one. "I'm just not keen on how I look, I suppose. Nobody wants a girl with hair my color . . . or one who wears glasses." A hand went up to adjust the offending eyewear. "Papa says I'm no parlor ornament. That's why nobody ever asks me to have an ice cream with them."

Crescencia's discouraged tone aroused anger in Edwina. Mr. Stykem wasn't being fair to his daughter by uttering such things. "Cressie, don't you believe what your father says. He doesn't know everything."

Her eyes widened. "But he's my papa. I always listen to him."

"I think it's time you stopped listening to him and made up your own mind how you feel about yourself. I like your red hair, and I happen to think your glasses make you appear very intelligent." Edwina placed a stem of greenery in her arrangement, then stood back. "Parents don't always know everything. Mine were no exception."

"But you listened to your mother when she asked you to come home from Chicago."

She sighed. "Of course I did. She was ill and needed me to take care of her. But had I taken to heart what she told me about going to the school, I never would have left here at all."

Edwina's thoughts momentarily drifted back to the day she and her mother had argued about her applying to Gillette's. Her mother had said her character would be ruined should she go to the city alone. In that instant, Edwina had known that if her courage failed her, she would have meekly bowed to her mother's wishes. It had been with supreme effort that she'd shouted she didn't care what people said about her. She had a right to live her own life, to improve herself, to learn more than what could be taught her in Harmony.

Although she'd argued she didn't care about talk, she had. She still did. It was important for her to present herself with flawless deportment . . . an untarnished character—unlike her true one. But when she'd told her mother she didn't care, it had been liberating. She only wished she could feel that way now. Instead, she was trapped. . . .

After sobbing into her lifted apron and lamenting how hurtful Edwina was for wanting to leave her, her mother had relented. Edwina had won. She would go to business college. Her life was her own.

And it would never be the same again.

"Dear," Edwina said, letting go of a past she couldn't change, "perhaps if you told me what you want to do with yourself, I could help you."

Crescencia's eyes misted. "What I want will never happen."

Edwina set down her scissors and put a hand to the other woman's. "What is that?"

Cressie couldn't meet her eyes. "Get married and have a family."

"You can have that," Edwina assured her sympathetically. Then with gentle care, she asked, "Is there a particular gentleman you have in mind?"

"Oh, no." Crescencia's denial was too quick. "There's nobody."

Resuming her arranging, Edwina snipped the stems of sun king marigolds and pink roses. "Why don't we practice your introductions? Let's say we do the section on words of salutation."

"Well . . . all right." Crescencia set the flower in her hand on the table. "How will we?"

Edwina discarded her own posy and faced off with Crescencia. "Let's choose the gentleman we'd like to use as our role-play model." Putting her fingertip to her bottom lip, she suggested a single man of good qualities—if one could count having blood on an apron full time an engaging trait. "Mr. Gale, the butcher."

"I'm not that flustered by him. I go to the shop every Friday and I can say, 'Two pounds of ground sirloin' without a single stutter. He doesn't affect me. Not too much, anyway." In a lowered tone, as if she didn't want to be overheard by the walls, Crescencia added, "Have you ever noticed he parts his hair down too low? Don't you think he knows we know his hair's thinning on the top?"

Edwina bit back a smile. "Apparently he doesn't think we know." Then she said, "How about I pretend to be Mr. Sterling?" Burton Sterling operated the local branch of Manhattan Life Insurance. Somewhat mouselike in appearance, he was available for the taking, but there were no takers.

"Mr. Sterling comes by the office from time to time to ask Papa about legal matters. I can speak to him all right. I do get nervous around him . . . but do you have to pretend you're him?"

"Not if you don't want me to." Edwina affected an air of deep thought, then said, "I know. I'll be Shay Dufresne."

Crescencia swallowed, her neck taut. "I—I don't know."

"Don't you care for Mr. Dufresne?"

"Oh, it's not that at all," Cressie replied in a rush. "I think he's . . ."—she gulped—". . . he's very manly."

Just as Edwina suspected. "Then let's practice with him in mind."

Maneuvering Crescencia by the shoulders, Edwina positioned her away from the table and facing the grilled doorway leading into the parlor. "This will be fun. Now, you stay here. I'll approach you as if we were walking on the street and we chanced running into one another."

Edwina went to the opposite end of the dining room, then nodded to Cressie for them to begin walking. The other woman had a playful smile on her face. As they met, Edwina doffed an invisible hat and said in a deepened voice, "Good afternoon, Miss Stykem."

Crescencia's sportive mood immediately closed off. She mumbled, "Hullo . . ."

Frowning, Edwina put her hands on her hips. "You

don't address him in that fashion. You must reply, 'How do you do, Mr. Dufresne?' "

"I couldn't . . ."

"Certainly you could. Try it."

Crescencia wrung her hands, gazed at her toes, then muttered, "How do you do, Mr. Dufresne?"

"Well," Edwina said, exhaling, "at least you said it. Perhaps next time you can look me—*him*—in the eyes when you say it."

Her chin rose. "I'll try."

"Now, I'll reply, 'I'm quite well, thank you, Miss Stykem. And yourself?' "

"Um . . . I—I'm all right, I suppose."

Brows turned down, Edwina shook her head. "You must hold yourself with confidence, dear. Keep your backbone straight and tell me right to my face that you are wonderful."

Cressie's eyes widened. "But I'm not wonderful. Papa told me—"

"Oh, shoot your father, Cressie!" Edwina chided her, venting her displeasure over a man who would make his own daughter feel less than adequate. "He doesn't know anything about you and that's flat!"

"But—"

"No buts." Edwina wouldn't be put off. "Next time you see Mr. Dufresne, you tell him what we just practiced. And once you've built your self-assurance up, you extend your hand and invite him to shake it."

"Oh!" Crescencia moaned. "I couldn't let him touch me. Don't you remember? The last time he accidentally did, I fainted."

"Yes, I remember." Edwina went to the table and sifted through the basket of ribbons for a small item she'd tucked away to give the girl. Handing over a tiny corked bottle that could be fit easily into the palm of a hand, she explained, "Smelling salts. Keep them handy. If you feel lightheaded, give yourself a dose and you'll be fine. Hide them in a handkerchief and no one will suspect you're not sniffing your perfume."

Crescencia looked dubiously at the bottle, then nodded. "I guess I could."

"Certainly you can."

"I just hope I can get a word out before I feel dizzy."

"Well, why don't you keep this in mind next time you talk to Mr. Dufresne? Imagine he's wearing lip rouge."

"Oh, but that's not in the deportment book, Miss Edwina!"

"Yes, I know. I made it up. If anything, it should keep a smile on your face." Straightening her apron, Edwina said, "We'd better hurry with the rest of these. I told the girls to be at the school by eleven, and it's almost that now." She plucked a few daisies and added with a smile, "I couldn't have picked a better fall day. The sky is clear and the sun is shining. Everything's going to be perfect just as long as Mr. Wolcott doesn't forget to tie up that mongrel of his."

But within the hour, lead-colored clouds rolled over Harmony and a darkened horizon foreshadowed rain. Edwina and Marvel-Anne had spent painstaking hours earlier in the morning raking and bagging leaves in burlap to keep the grass area in the grove tidy and ready for a party. Afterward, they'd moved the classroom tables outside along with the chairs. Bringing from home a half-dozen tablecloths, Edwina had smoothed them out, then arranged for her best dishes and primrose flatware on top, and then Crescencia had placed the flowers in the centers of the tables. Marvel-Anne lined up the tomato sandwiches, sweet pickles, and burnt-sugar cake on a tea cart.

As the girls began arriving, Edwina hoped the rain would stall long enough to get through the luncheon. Soon everyone, wearing their Sunday finery, had taken a seat, and Edwina stood before them.

"Good afternoon, ladies."

"Good afternoon, Miss Edwina."

"I thought this would be a nice way to review general

rules on table etiquette, but I hadn't counted on poor cooperation from the weather."

The plumes, ribbons, and ornaments on hats fluttered in the tease of a breeze. Fresh faces watched her and gloved hands were folded neatly in every lap.

"While Miss Stykem serves you, I'll go over the basics. I'm sure your mothers have taught you much of this already, but it's worth repeating."

As Crescencia took plates of sandwiches to the girls, Edwina began the lesson. "It is rude to elevate your elbows and move your arms at the table. Tea or coffee should never be poured into a saucer to cool, but sipped from the cup."

Hildegarde raised her hand and Edwina nodded.

"My mother says that tramps and vagabonds drink coffee from soup cans."

Edwina's hands locked together behind her back. "Well, I wouldn't know for sure, but your mother may be right."

"I'm certain she is." Hildegarde accepted her plate and snuck a peek beneath the petite slice of bread to see what the sandwich contained. "My mother knows a lot of things."

"Yes, she thinks she does," Edwina replied, then bit her tongue, hoping none of the girls deciphered the disparagement in her remark. "Let's continue." Her tone leveled to a professional one. "If by chance anything unpleasant is found in the food, such as a hair in the bread or a fly in the coffee, remove it without remark. Even though your own appetite may be spoiled, it is good not to prejudice others."

Johannah Treber raised her hand, and Edwina gave her permission to speak. "Once on a trip to Sheridan, my parents went to a restaurant—more than one's pocket could stand, my father said—and when his order of veal cutlets with cream gravy came, there was a dead fly lying on top. He kicked up an awful fuss, calling over the headwaiter and demanding a new dinner free of charge." She put a finger to the dimple in her chin, as if pondering. "Miss Edwina, do you think the rules of etiquette can be bent a little when you're paying good money for a meal that has a fly in it?"

Edwina cocked her head to one side and said in concession, "I believe there are always exceptions."

The plates had been passed out and the mint raspberry punch served. "You ladies may begin while I talk. Remember to remove your gloves." Quiet movements followed as they neatly did so.

"The next rule is one I think very important. Neither eat too slow nor too fast. The former shows a consumption of time and the latter, greediness."

That said, Hildegarde Plunkett had popped a quarter-shaped sandwich in her mouth with one bite. Her lips locked, and she guiltily looked away, chewing slowly.

Walking around the tables, Edwina said, "Strive to keep the tablecloth as clean as possible and leave your napkin unfolded beside your plate when you are done."

While the girls ate, she debated whether to discuss the particulars of breakfast, luncheon, and dinner. Before she could come to a conclusion, a group of dandies sporting derbies rounded the corner of the warehouse, evidently exiting Tom Wolcott's store. He was with them; in fact, he led them to the grove. In his hand was a length of rope and attached to the end, Barkly.

Tom tied the rope to a tree branch, then motioned for the men to gather in a half circle. They stood around a gadget Edwina hadn't noticed before. It sat on a three-legged pedestal of a sort and had an arm attached to the top by a long spring. On the palm of the arm, Tom loaded a flat blue disk.

Curiosity crowded out thoughts that should have been at the forefront of her mind. She didn't realize immediately—until she noticed each gentleman held a rifle in his grasp—that they intended to commence shooting.

During her tea party.

"Excuse me, girls." Edwina walked grandly toward Tom and his entourage, trying hard to keep her expression affable. His voice drifted to her as he talked to the men, explaining something about pigeons and pulls. As soon as her presence was detected by the dandies, hats were immediately doffed.

Tom turned in her direction, blue plates clutched against his middle, his words of instruction trailing off. "Hey, Miss Huntington. We'll be out of here in an hour."

"Mr. Wolcott," she said through gritted teeth, "might I speak to you for a moment?" The smile plastered on her face caused her cheeks to ache. "Gentlemen, I won't keep him long."

Without giving him the opportunity to decline, she walked away and headed toward the front of the building. Once there, she disguised the tap of her toe under the hem of her skirt. The scatter of leaves told her he was coming up behind her. She whirled around, eyes lifting to his.

"Mr. Wolcott, I distinctly remember telling you my plans for this afternoon. I want to know what you're doing."

He'd gotten rid of the disks, his hands buried in the pockets of an unbuttoned duster. An easy smile played at the corners of his mouth, infuriating her. "Firing off a few pigeons."

"I don't know what that means, but you'll have to fire them off another time. Right now, it's my turn for the grove."

"Sorry about that, Ed, but I can't. The man with the handlebar mustache is the mayor of Big Horn. He's brought some prominent people with him to try out the Flightmaster."

"I don't care!" she shot back.

"Keep your voice down, Edwina. People might hear you."

"I don't care if they hear me from here to breakfast, buster." She stood in a battle pose with hands on hips. "What about my girls' tea party?"

He gave her a shrug and a grin. "They can watch?"

His reply was anything but amusing to her. Bitterness

put a bite into her voice. "You'll disrupt my class. Again."

"It shouldn't take more than an hour, then we'll be out of your way." He went for the breast pocket inside his coat and brought out his cigarettes. "And you've got to give me some credit."

A frown soured her mouth. "What for?"

"I tied up my dog."

On that note, he walked away.

Very childishly, she stuck her tongue out at him.

He must have had eyes in the back of his head, because he turned and warned, "Don't show me that unless you intend to use it on me."

Then he retreated from her view.

The debate was over. She felt drained and defeated. He could make her so mad, she didn't recognize herself.

Edwina had no choice but to return to the girls and make the best of the day. Once there, she saw that they stared at the men who had gathered around Tom, who had a rifle anchored against his shoulder as he talked a while—Edwina couldn't make out the words. Then he pointed toward a space void of tree branches. All fell silent when he took his position again. He motioned with his head to a gentleman crouched by the gadget. The man did something to a spring lever, then a blue disk went sailing in the air. A gunshot echoed as the blast of plaster exploded. Tom hit the tiny round plate midflight.

Barkly started baying and straining against his rope collar. Intermittently, he pawed at the ground and stuck his hind end up, his tail wagging.

"Girls, we're going to ignore them," Edwina announced. "We'll talk about the things to be avoided in a social gathering." These would be more of a reminder to Edwina than a lesson for the girls. "Do not permit yourself to lose your temper in society or show that you've taken offense at a supposed—"

"Pull!"

Bang!

"—slight," she concluded through the gunshot's echo.

"Every subject liable to provoke a discussion of disagreement should be—"

"Pull!"

Bang!

"—avoided."

Keeping her posture rigid and her eyes averted from the scene of destruction, Edwina silently vowed that when this was over, she was going to tell Tom Wolcott what she really thought of him—that he was a big-headed, trophy-happy, self-centered man.

Barkly started in with that frenzied bark of his, deep and strained from the back of his throat. She thought he might throw up, he was so excited. She wished he would. Maybe he'd gag.

"Should anyone assume a disagreeable tone of voice or offensive manner toward you, never return it in company." *Unless the disagreeable person is Tom Wolcott.* "Appear not to have noticed you've been slighted and make it seem the person has failed in his—"

"Pull!"

Bang!

"—objective."

A breeze came through the grove with enough force to disturb the flower arrangements, toppling the one at Ruth Edward's table. She quickly righted it as her napkin blew to the ground.

"It's all right, dear," Edwina assured as the girl chased down her serviette and replaced it on her lap. "To continue. Avoid stale and trite remarks, as well as coarse gestures." *Unless the offense is directed at Tom Wolcott in the form of a stuck-out tongue.* "To speak to a person in ambiguous terms is—"

"Pull!"

Bang!

"—rude."

Edwina was at her wit's end. She couldn't go on as if nothing were wrong. The entire afternoon was turning into a catastrophe. That dog wouldn't shut up, the sounds of gunfire made a completely inappropriate back-

ground for a luncheon, and to top it all off, big splats
of rain had begun to fall.

"Girls, I believe we should collect ourselves and return—" Before Edwina could finish her sentence, Barkly
made a strangling sound that caused her to look in his
direction. The hound had pulled his rope taut and
backed out of the collar to freedom. In a flash, he took
off after the pieces of broken plates, collecting one in
his chops and running wildly through the grove. He
rounded the trees, his galloping feet spraying leaves,
then ran back again, coming to a skidding halt. His nose
was to the wind, black nostrils twitching; Edwina could
swear he was homing in on a scent so strong, nothing
would keep him from seeking it.

The scent turned out to be burnt-sugar cake, for the
dog took off in a mad run for the tea cart. She was
unable to stop him in time; he gobbled two extra slices
in two extrawide gulps. Screams perforated the air as
Barkly made tracks to the tables, standing up on his hind
legs to devour what he could.

"Mr. Wolcott!" Edwina shouted.

Barkly, muzzle slathered with icing, had the nerve to
bound on top of Camille's table and steal the remnants
from her plate. Then, tail wagging like a whipcord, he
proceeded to leap to Meg's table and polish off the leftovers of her sandwich.

Rain increasingly spilled on the mayhem, Barkly doing
as much damage as he could before taking off in a
clumsy gait toward the large potted chrysanthemum, just
into a fall bloom, that Edwina had put out for color.
He lifted his leg and watered it—the final insult—then
scampered off through the trees.

"Girls!" Edwina called through their giggles, screams,
and chatter. "Everyone run home before you're soaked
through! Class is dismissed!"

There was a flurry of skirts as girls linked arms and
ran. The ill-fated tea party had been abandoned.

Edwina noticed that Tom Wolcott's group had dis-
banded as well, the dandies striding swiftly up Dogwood

Place, no doubt to the comforts of the Brooks House Hotel. Tom was nowhere in sight, nor was the thing he'd called the Flightmaster. He certainly cared more about taking that to cover than confronting her about the mess his dog had made.

Droplets fell from the brim of her hat as she surveyed the shambles. Plates and flatware littered the ground, napkins blew like little ghosts, punch stained the pretty tablecloths, and the leaves that she had taken such care to get rid of were now thick on her side of the grove—compliments of Tom Wolcott's side.

With a heavy sigh, Edwina whispered, "Dammit all."

"That about sums it up," came a masculine voice.

Edwina turned with a start. Tom had snuck up behind her.

The brim of a Stetson kept the rain out of his eyes. His mouth was set in a grim line around a cigarette; smoke swirled on a current of wind. Water marks dappled the front of his buttoned linen duster. Her own striped taffeta bodice was peppered through with rain spots, but she didn't care enough to get a cape from the classroom. Why bother when she was nearly soaked already?

She didn't say a word to Tom when she set out to gather things on the tea cart to bring inside the building. That he pitched in was his own idea.

Together, they cleaned the mess without one utterance between them. Then she locked the school and headed toward home.

Through the general delivery grating, Edwina could see Mr. Calhoon's wide back with suspenders crossed upon it, his visored head bent over a stack of letters.

She cleared her throat to make her presence known.

Mr. Calhoun lifted his head and made a hasty apology for his neglect. "Miss Huntington. Good morning."

"Good morning."

She noted his black mustache, stylishly trimmed and

waxed. When he spoke, the ends wiggled. "You just missed your mail."

She stood there, surprised, her face blank. "What do you mean?"

"Mr. Wolcott picked it up along with his. He said you'd be sharing the same mailbox."

"He did, did he?" The question was more like an attack.

"I normally don't make door deliveries, but sometimes special circumstances arise and permit me to make exceptions. From now on, no need to come in and get your mail. It'll all come directly to 47-B Old Oak Road." His merry eyes slid onto a handled net of some sort, and Edwina couldn't help following the line of his gaze to see what was the object of his broad smile. "It's a beauty, isn't it?" Mr. Calhoon picked up the gear and appeared to weigh it in his hand. "Peerless fyke net with wings. Always wanted one of these. You know, back when . . ."

But Edwina didn't hear the rest. She'd gone storming out the door and was headed straight for 47-B Old Oak Road.

Tom had made a mistake in not checking with Edwina about events; Edwina needed to know that the mayor's visit couldn't be helped. But everything else had been out of his control. To his credit, he had tried to keep Barkly on a rope. Things might not have been so bad if the dog hadn't escaped.

Barkly had really bungled things, putting away food like a glutton and dancing on the tabletops. The hound had just hit his stride when he'd posted a letter on the chrysanthemum pot. Tom had watched Edwina's face change to red fury with that one.

Because the episode had turned into a hell of a runaway train, Tom felt compelled to make things up to Edwina. Even though he'd already made the offer about sharing his mailbox, she hadn't taken him up on it. He figured it was a matter of pride and her not wanting to be obligated and all. So he did the manly thing: he took charge.

He told Calhoon to deliver her mail to his box, too—even though it had cost him a damn good landing net to convince the postmaster. What the hell was sixty-five cents when the outcome could soothe a woman's ruffled feathers?

She'd better be talking to him today. Yesterday afternoon, he'd have rather she shout blue murder at him than give him the silent treatment. He hated when women clammed up.

Dipping a brush into a bucket of brown paint, he proceeded to make his entry door a little more presentable. With Shay still gone, it would take Tom a while to get his half of the building looking decent, but he'd do a stretch at a time.

The brush tip connected lightly on the frame, and with a steady hand, he smoothed the bristles down in a long and even stroke.

"Mr. Wolcott!"

A trail of brown shot across the window glass as Tom flinched, then clenched his teeth while surveying the damage. When Edwina Huntington said his name in that shrill nasal tone that had maiden aunt all through it, he wanted to stuff the paintbrush down her throat.

Turning, he forced an air of congeniality. "What is it, Miss Huntington?"

"I just left Mr. Calhoon. He informed me you've stolen my mail."

"He said that?"

Pink lips turned down. "Not in those exact words, but that's precisely what you've done. He didn't have the authority to give you my personal property without my consent."

"I thought mail was government property."

"All the worse. Theft of government property is a federal offense."

"Only before Calhoon gets it," Tom countered, smearing an old rag across the window glass to get the paint off. "After that, mail is a free-for-all. If it's stolen, it's up to a town what they want to do to the perpetrator."

Her hands fell to her hips, purse strings looped over a wrist, and she took a militant stance. "Apparently you've stolen mail before."

"Nope. I just have my facts straight." With a clean cloth, he wiped his hands clean the best he could. Brown stained his fingers and dirtied his nails. "Ed, let's not argue about this. The reason I had Calhoon give me the mail is to save you the bother of having to pick it up— my way of apologizing for yesterday, for Barkly and all. If I could have, I would have changed the mayor's arrival, but he'd come in from Big Horn and there wasn't another train he could have taken."

Even to Tom, his explanation sounded satisfactory— although he hadn't looked up the train schedules. For all he knew, King could have hopped a ride on a different connection. He hoped Edwina wouldn't see the need to double-check his story. Just in case, he added in a gentleman's earnest tone, "I really, really am sorry, Edwina. My fault entirely."

For that, she didn't censure him. Instead, her hands relaxed, and she exhaled audibly. "I appreciate your integrity."

He wasn't quite sure what *integrity* meant, but he didn't think he had any if it had to do with stuff like honor and chivalry.

"I'd like my mail now," she said, body aligned in perfect form, toes aimed forward, right in line beneath the angle of her chin. It was as if the Edwina who'd slammed down on him from a tree had never existed. This double personality she had was wearing on him. He wished she'd make up her mind and just be one of them, rather than teasing him with her fun side, then reverting back to the starched-up version.

"I'll get it. It's on my counter." He went inside and grabbed the assortment of letters, accidentally blotching them with brown. Once outside, he handed them to her. "Sorry about the paint."

"Don't be. I'm glad to see you're cleaning up your side." She didn't give the letters a glance, not a single furtive look. Hell, he got personal mail so rarely, he could barely make it out the post-office door without tearing into it. Just last week, his brother John sent him a letter from California asking for money. Tom sent him some. John wrote he was doing part-time oil drilling, and part-time water finding—and Tom deduced he was probably doing part-time drinking if he was short on cash.

"From now on, I'd prefer it if you left my mail in the box." She motioned to the black mailbox hanging to the side of his door. "I can get my correspondence out of it myself." Then she entered her side of the building, firmly closed the door, and didn't bother to lift the shade.

Could be she wanted to read through all that mail in privacy. He hadn't been able to help scanning the return addresses on the half-dozen letters she'd received.

The Glenwood Sanitarium. Scott's Emulsion. Cuticura. Procter's Vegetable Glycerine. Crab Orchard Water Co. Noyes Bros. Blanket Wraps.

For a woman who appeared to be quite intellectual, didn't Edwina know that snake oils and all that crap didn't work?

Sunday morning, high clouds gathered in the sky, but the temperature was mild enough to be outdoors without wearing multiple layers of clothing. After returning home from church, Edwina gathered a rake from the toolshed and left for the warehouse. She'd felt restless and idle indoors and had looked for an escape to bring her outside, where she could exercise. She'd never objected to raking, as it stimulated her mind as well as kept her busy. Though there was no point in raking the grove, she wanted to anyway.

Anything to keep from facing the tower of bills that were accumulating in the pigeonhole of her desk.

Three more had come since Wednesday. And although she now got her own mail out of the box, she was certain Tom Wolcott was still going through hers. How could he not? Her telling him that she would get her own mail wasn't preventing him from sorting through the letters, which led to reading her envelopes as well. But as of two days ago, she'd outfoxed him. She'd gotten to the mailbox first. Even if that had meant abruptly halting her class mid-lesson to hurry out the door and take the items from Mr. Calhoon before he could slip them in the black box.

Embarrassment washed over Edwina anew. It was bad enough Mr. Calhoun thought her foolish enough to send away to those backwater companies. Now Tom knew as well. What he must think of her? Not that she cared . . .

I do care. But she hated to admit she did.

Oh, when this all ends, I can do what I want. She kept telling herself that she was doing all right, that she was paying whom she could and staving off those whom she could not. But the stress was wearing her down. She resented having to be accountable. She hadn't been the one to make such a mess of things, yet she was the one who'd gotten stuck bearing the burden.

As Edwina rounded the back of the building, she stared at the vast expanse of golden leaves littering the ground before her. There truly was no need . . . but if she didn't, she'd have to go home and face the likes of Crab Orchard Water Co. and Noyes Bros. Blanket Wraps.

With a nod of conviction about the therapeutic effects of physical activity, Edwina began to rake.

Tom had cracked more walnuts than he had cracked ledger columns. In over an hour, he hadn't gotten a single row to add up and match its corresponding posting on the opposite side of the chart. According to his calculations, he didn't have jack. All his money was gone. Which couldn't be true. Because he'd gone to the bank on Friday and had taken out eight dollars and sixty-four cents to pay cash on a collect shipment of life-sized rubber deer—your does and bucks. If he'd been broke, the teller wouldn't have given him the money—along with a receipt that showed he had six hundred thirty-two dollars and sixteen cents remaining in his account.

So he was obviously doing something wrong when it came to tallying debits and credits. And he'd even tried working things Edwina's way.

She'd pointed out that his columns were mixed up and he'd tried to remember how she'd told him to put them. He'd thought he'd done it right, but neither side was in accordance with the other. One saw red, the other black; once, one totaled zero.

He slammed another nut with the revolver, the hulls scattering. With a flick of his fingertip, Tom played a game of points to see how many he could get off the accounting paper without spilling any onto the floor.

In a sloppy shot, a hull flew over the counter and beaned Barkly, who'd been sleeping on the floor by the stool, on the right ear. Snorting, he lifted his boxy head and glared, with one bloodshot eye, at Tom.

"Ho, there, Barkly. Penalty on Wolcott," Tom commentated.

The dog reclined once more, gave a heaving sigh, then shut his eyes.

Drumming his fingertips, Tom slouched on the stool's seat and gazed across the store, not seeing anything in particular, just losing himself and trying to figure out what he could do to avoid bookkeeping.

He wasn't in the mood to throw balls at Buttkiss. And since the store was closed on Sundays, he couldn't count on the customers to keep him from the worksheets. He'd gone as far as dusting his small rodent trophies with a signature paintbrush. The eyes and ears of those weasels and foxes had never been so damn clean. He'd even polished their teeth.

After that, he'd gotten out his beaver clock and examined it for repairability. In five seconds flat, he'd concluded the thing was history. There was always the zebra clock. That motorized pendulum he'd ordered to install in the tail had come in. But he wasn't in the mood to work on that, either.

He'd finished painting the exterior, so he couldn't use that as a distracting excuse anymore. Shay wasn't due back until late afternoon of the following day. No camaraderie to be had today.

He ought to go fishing, pick a fight with a cutthroat trout. Once they took the hook, they ran against the stream bottom and then did a little broad jumping. It'd been too long since he'd dropped a line. But Tom couldn't rationalize putting that much distance between himself and the store. The way he saw things, if he stayed in the warehouse's general vicinity—within, say, twenty yards—he was within mindshot of the accounting pages. Anything beyond that and he couldn't say he was actually working on them.

"Ah . . . hell," he mumbled.

Flat. His life was flat, at the moment. Deader than the stuffed field mouse he'd mounted on a block and used as a doorstop. Tom stared at the rodent with its two beady glass eyes, his fingers tattooing out "Three Blind Mice" on the countertop. When he was through, he muttered his disgust and stood.

"I've got to get out of here or I'm going to go crazy," he said to Barkly as he reached for his overshirt, which was hung on a peg by the door. A walk outside and a smoke ought to clear his head, make him see things in a different light.

Tom stepped through the door and Barkly shot past him, banging into his leg as he dashed out to chase after a squirrel that had been nibbling an acorn. Had he the capability, the hound would have run right up the tree. Instead, he stared the squirrel into quivers with his hollow eyes while it clung to high bark.

Lighting a cigarette, Tom started walking around the corner of the building but stopped shy of the warehouse's grove. He hung back to spy on Edwina as she raked leaves toward a fairly big pile. She must have been out there a while.

Smoke curled through Tom's lips on an exhalation. As with most of the things she did, Edwina used a stringently frugal method. Three even strokes. Left, right, and center. Then swish, swish, swish toward the main mound.

That she could be so meticulous annoyed him. That she would even bother to rake the leaves when the trees were still sifting them down made him wonder about her soundness.

A slight smile curved her mouth. She was sound, all

right—in all the places men were drawn to, himself included.

An image of her wearing drawers and a shirtwaist— all long legs and disheveled hair—flashed in his mind. She'd forgotten herself that evening of the tree fall, and he'd enjoyed her company all the more for it, even with that cat as her foremost concern. She'd been able to make him smile. He liked to provoke her into losing hold of that rigid mold she poured herself into each day.

So to break his morning of monotony, a little frolicking was in order.

He was getting his rope.

Edwina choked on a gasp when she saw Tom Wolcott bearing down on her with a coil of fat rope in his grasp.

"Hey, Ed," he called, a cigarette dangling between his lips. "Nice day."

Her eyes narrowed automatically. "Nice day for what?"

The lift of his shoulders had more innocence in it than had a newborn babe. "Leaf raking." He said nothing further and proceeded to unwind the rope to lay straight on the grass. A few seconds later, Barkly rounded the corner and came charging at her pile of leaves.

Taking a position of defense, she held the rake out in front of her to ward him off. He merely circled and caused her to spin, then took his opening when her back was to him; he dove headfirst into the crackling leaves. Delight lit his face—she could swear he smiled; he snapped up several oak leaves in his teeth and took off at a run. He zoomed between the trees, then skidded to a stop, tail wagging as he spit out the stolen leaves. The excess skin under his chin and his long ears made a flapping noise when he shook off.

Edwina stared at the damage. Her neat and tidy pile had been ransacked. It wasn't a big mound anymore. Stragglers and ragged pieces of leaves littered the area surrounding her.

Her focus switched to Tom, who examined the high limbs of the oaks and then studied her scattered leaves.

"Stand back a little, Ed," he said at length, looking not at her but at the high, gnarled branch of a stately oak off center above her head.

Skirting him, she gripped the rake's handle and watched as he took the rope in his hand. Like a cowboy, he somewhat circled a long length, then began to swing it. Momentum gathered and his arm came back just before he released the rope, its end sailing high into the tree and right over the limb. With a few twists and jerks, he made crimps that slammed against the branch's underside to hold the rope secure. That done, he created a series of knots in the length that dangled about a foot from the ground.

"Give it a try, Ed?" Tom asked while pitching his cigarette and snuffing the nub with his boot toe.

Gazing at the rope swing, she was reminded of the one hanging in her own backyard, long unused, though she'd performed many acrobatics on it as a child. Her father had hung it up when she'd been around six years old. The thought of the trouble he'd gone to made her sad—made her feel guilty for not appreciating all the things he'd done for her when he'd been living. Both her parents had taken care of her. Her father had worked to feed and clothe her; her mother had cooked and cleaned alongside Marvel-Anne to make sure their house was always inviting and presentable to Edwina's friends.

Shame burned hotly inside of Edwina. Not an hour ago, she'd been full of bitterness over her current set of circumstances. But her parents had taken care of her; now she had to take care of them. She'd done so physically; however, family didn't die when a loved one was laid to rest. She would make sure the Huntington name wouldn't suffer slander. Financial obligations would be met, and without another grudging thought from her.

Why had it taken Tom's silly tree swing to make her see this?

Tom's voice intruded. "So what do you say?"

With her hand shading her eyes against a shaft of bright sunlight that took advantage of a part in the clouds, she replied, "No. I don't think so," even though the temptation pulled strongly at her.

His easy shrug said that he didn't believe her. A tug on the rope proved it to be secure. Then he walked away, turned, and gave her an easy smile. A wisp of a breeze caused his hair to fall across his nose; he swiped the unruly strands off his forehead. Then, striking a run, he aimed for the rope, grabbed on, and lunged forward. With the motion of his body, he got himself into a good swing.

Back and forth, higher and higher. He made apish sounds, like he was a jungle primate. If he hadn't sounded so ridiculous, she wouldn't have laughed—or egged him on in turn.

Clamped between his legs, the rope gave him firm support, and with the sides of his boots against one of the knots, he could pretty much free up his hands without falling. He let go with his right, then left. Her heartbeat hitched in her throat. She knew he was athletic and could very well do tricks on the rope, but she worried anyway. She didn't want him to fall.

"Okay," she shouted at him, "you can stop that now! You'll get hurt."

"Wooooooooo!" he hollered into the sky, thoroughly ignoring her sage advice.

Why was it men thought they needed to prove themselves to women? Edwina grew perturbed. She ought to just turn away and go home so he'd stop acting like a ham bone and behave.

But she couldn't pull her gaze off him.

She'd never known a man quite like Tom Wolcott. Ruggedly handsome, totally masculine, yet boyish and still full of pranks at his age. His inordinate height was emphasized by being up higher on the rope. With each pass, his hair flowed around his face. Long hair had never intrigued her before; Ludie had worn his clipped short and quite distinguished, styled with pomade. But

Edwina found she rather liked the look of Tom's wild and careless mane. She also liked his smile—broad and genuine, easygoing, nice teeth.

Both her gloved hands rested on the top of the rake's handle, and she set her chin on her fist. A smile claimed her lips as she watched, listening to him hoot and holler. She wished she could soar free like that, be six years old again and not care a whit what people thought of her— or in Tom's case, be thirty-two and not care.

On an extraordinarily vulgar monkey sound, Tom let go of the rope and flew into her pile of leaves. He landed on his chest, arms sprawled out from both sides, his face turned, eyes closed.

Lying deathly still.

"Tom!" The rake fell out of her hands. She raced to him and dropped to her knees. Barkly came barreling in behind her. His slobbery tongue slicked her cheek, so she shoved him, hard—enough to make him move. Insulted, the dog sat back with his head hanging low.

"Tom, can you hear me?" Edwina asked, bringing her face close to his. Her fingers rested beneath his nose to feel for breath. It was there. Labored and moist. She bit her lip and worried the tender skin. "Tom . . . ? Tom, wake up."

He remained unmoving.

Bracing her hand on his shoulder, she jiggled him. Nothing happened.

She slipped his hair from his brow and tucked the length gently behind his ear. Moving closer again, she tried to view all of his face. No blood. A promising sign. Or was it? Head trauma . . . he needed to wake up. Should she leave him and get Dr. Porter? Or should she shout for help? Who would hear her down here? *Oh, help.*

She would have cried if she thought it would do any good.

"Please . . . Tom . . ."

A blue eye opened; one side of a firm mouth arched.

And in a manner that could only be described as sinful—certainly not painful. "Please, Tom . . . what?"

She gasped. Sputtering her shock, she said, "Why . . ." Then she straightened, appalled. "Why . . . you horrible toad. You baboon. What's the matter with you? Are you crazy? You scared me half to death."

In her upset, she went as far as slapping him on the arm—with as much force as she could muster. His wince gave her a slight satisfaction as she rose to her feet and shook the leaves off her skirt.

Tom rolled onto his back, then casually crossed his legs at the ankles while his hands linked behind his head. "You never called me Tom before."

"I'd call you something else," she said, flinging the words at him, "but my language isn't that base."

Deeply, he laughed, making her want to squash him under her shoe. On a huff, she trudged toward her rake, but she never made it. Tom must have shot to his feet, because he jogged past in a burst of speed. Then, pivoting, stood in front of her and blocked her way so she couldn't go anywhere without running past him.

"Don't be mad, Ed. I was just trying to get you in the mood."

"Mood for what?" She scowled. "To bash you in the head with my rake? You are the most infuriating, most insensitive, most—"

"—fun you've had since you got back to Harmony." A lopsided grin caught his mouth. "Admit it, Edwina. You want to have a turn on that rope."

She would confess no such thing.

"I tell you what," he said in that tone that foreshadowed her undoing. "I'll make you a deal. You swing on the rope and I'll be your target. See if you can hit me."

"It's a tempting offer, but the answer is no," she conceded. "So quit daring me to do things. I don't like it."

"Yeah, but you love the challenge."

At cross purposes, she could say nothing to the contrary.

"You're missing an opportunity to let your hair down.

You know you want to," he said, fanning the flames of desire to do just that.

"Absolutely not."

"One little swing."

Forcing an air of reservation, she said more to herself than him, "Somebody might see me."

"It's Sunday. Who'd come down here?"

"I don't know." And that was the truth. She couldn't think of a soul who would happen to be this far down on either Birch Avenue or Dogwood Place on a Sunday, unless they had to go by the mill to get to Evergreen Creek, which wasn't very likely on a Sunday. Unless they wanted to get to the eastern side of the creek because the brick footbridge on Maple Street was still under repairs. Which wasn't a very likely trip to be made on a Sunday.

Groaning with resignation, Edwina walked toward the rope.

Tom called to her, "I knew it."

She knew she wanted to, too. A wicked smile brightened her from within, but she'd never let Tom Wolcott see it. It had been a long time since she'd done this. Rope swings made her think of dragging the wicker lawn chair to the line of hemp in her yard so she could be high enough to get a good grip and swing wide.

Unfortunately, there wasn't any lawn furniture here, so how was she going to get a thrust going?

"I'll give you a boost." Tom's voice wrapped around her, much like the man himself. He'd drawn up so close to her back, she could feel him breathing in her ear. "On the count of three, jump up."

She nodded. He placed his hands on her waist as she stretched out her arms. Trying to displace the river of excitement rushing to the places his wide hands were splayed, she focused on Tom's hoist up.

"One. Two. Three."

Then came a shove and she was lifted into the air. Her gloved hands caught the rope, gaining a firm hold. She felt confident, excited, silly—but unprepared for the electrifying contact of palms on her behind as Tom began to push her.

"You don't have to do that," she chided over her shoulder.

"Just giving you a hand."

More like two hands.

Within five strong pushes, Tom got her going fairly high. Despite her vow not to show him she was delighted, she giggled. And once she started, she couldn't stop.

Leaning left or right could determine her course. Tom shot out in front of her, and she grinned while taking aim in his direction. Just when she could have winged him, he dodged out of the way.

"Hey!" she cried through a wide smile. "Don't move."

"The hell I'm not." He ran circles around her, laughing as he eluded her on every swing.

A drop of water fell on Edwina's nose. Another on her eyelid. Rain. Oh, not now! This was too enjoyable to abandon so quickly.

As she swished through the air, the force tugged the pins keeping her hair piled on top of her head. She could do nothing to remedy the situation, and slowly they slipped free until the Gibson style came tumbling free. She'd taken her hair down in the literal sense.

Rain began to fall more densely, splattering across her. She turned her face heavenward and let herself get soaked.

"How're your arms holding up?" Tom asked.

They hurt. So did her legs. She wasn't as agile as she used to be. But she didn't want to let go. If she did, she was afraid she wouldn't have the courage to get back on.

"I'm fine."

With that, Tom gave her another strong push that sent her almost level with the warehouse's roof when she added her own weight into the swing.

The image she made must have been disgraceful, disreputable: soaked all over, hair down, skirts and petticoats lumped halfway up her calves, swinging like a hoyden—and loving every minute of it.

Barkly began to anxiously bark, but she couldn't see him. He must have gone to the building's front and cornered a bug or something stupid.

If the hound hadn't ceased his howling to snarl, Edwina doubted Tom would have turned his head to shout, "Barkly! Come!" at the precise moment she soared right at him. In that split second, her legs collided with his chest and threw him off balance. Her arms, aching from the impact, released the rope. Tom fell backward. She toppled across him.

A jumble of leaden skirts and trouser legs, all wet through, prevented them from immediately disengaging. Edwina thought for sure he'd kill her. This was the second time she'd fallen on him. But in her defense, both times were unintentional.

Rather than getting yelled at, she felt the rumble of laughter in his chest as he started to chuckle.

"Oh, God, Ed . . . only you."

She lifted her chin enough to look into his face. Thank goodness, no lumps were rising on his forehead this time. Through his laughter, which now she had deemed overwrought delirium, she said on her behalf, "There wasn't any time to say 'Look out.' "

"Wouldn't have done any good if you had." The smile he gave her sent her pulse racing. Those white teeth flashing from such a face were . . . what was it Camille had said about men . . . ? Delicious. His face was delicious. She had no doubt he could have made even the most stodgy old maid fall into a fit of the vapors.

Why did he have to be so . . . so . . . *him?* Why couldn't she have fallen onto a man who was bald and had a wart on his nose? Temptation would not be running amok in her brain if she had.

But it was. And at an alarming rate. If Tom so much as moved his mouth a fraction toward hers, she would let him kiss her. Again. She wanted him to. Desperately.

Rain pelted them, but she barely noticed she was wet,

much less cold. On Tom's face, droplets rolled off his cheeks, his chiseled jaw. His smile died, and in its place came a fiery heat in his eyes. *He knew.* He knew what she wanted and he was going to do it.

Breath stilled in her throat. Her heartbeat thrummed. She lowered her head. Slowly. He lifted his. Slowly. Her eyelids flitted closed . . . and she waited . . .

. . . to be pounced upon by a soggy mongrel. Her lashes flew open with a start. Hot and cold clashed inside her. A dousing with ice water couldn't have sobered her more. The bloodhound conked her on the head with what felt like a stick. She turned to see he had a shredded umbrella clamped in his mouth. Water dripped off his ears, but he wouldn't shake off; it meant he'd have to drop his prize.

"Barkly, where in the hell did you get that?" Tom asked with a tight edge of annoyance in his tone.

"From me," came the curt response.

Edwina recognized the voice instantly. "Mrs. Elward," she whispered. She would have gotten up if she could. Mortification ran through her like a dull blade—painful and torturous. She was in big trouble.

Not a moment too soon, Tom came to her aid and managed to untangle her skirts enough so that she could sit up. He went to his feet and offered her a hand.

Once standing, Edwina saw that Mrs. Elward wasn't alone. Mrs. Plunkett, Mrs. Brooks, Mrs. Treber, and Mrs. Calhoon flanked Mrs. Elward as if she needed protection. Barkly growled. Edwina could see why. The ladies did look frightening with their wilted feather hats, dripping flounces, and muddy-hemmed skirts.

Whatever were they doing down here on a Sunday?

She visually searched them for clues. Their hands clutched tiny green cloth books and umbrellas—minus the one; binoculars hung over their sodden shoulders. Then it dawned on Edwina. They were the local chapter of Amateur Ladies Avifauna Ornithologists.

Bird watchers.

"Ladies," Tom gallantly began, "this isn't what you—"

"I collapsed," Edwina cut in with barely a breath in her lungs. "It . . . it was the sermon this morning. Heaven's tears. That's what Minister Stoll calls the rain. The rain made me think of my mother. I . . . I became overwhelmed with grief and fainted on Mr. Wolcott. Quite unexpected. I knocked him over."

"Your hair fell down in the faint?" Mrs. Plunkett said accusingly, a brow arched in a perfectly horrible gesture of disbelief.

"It was—" Tom started.

But Edwina talked over him again. "Yes," she lied coolly, her tone daring them to say otherwise. "I was so distraught, wanting to go to my mother's grave, that Mr. Wolcott had to subdue me. Forcefully."

"Really?" Mrs. Elward remarked, each syllable of the word emphasized to the utmost.

Edwina flushed, then got mad. "Yes, really. I want my mother." She lifted her face to the sky and shouted for good measure, "Mother! Mother!" Then quite unexpectedly, tears formed in her eyes and she truly did want her mother—wanted to be cradled in her mama's arms and comforted, brought back to childhood, where the worst thing to happen was a scraped knee. "Mama," she said through a sob.

Stepping forward, Mrs. Treber said consolingly, "There, there, dear!" And took her against her bosom and held her. "We know you miss your mother. It's a burden to bear, but a burden you must."

The other ladies gathered around her and patted her shoulders, which were now quivering in earnest. She couldn't seem to stop crying. Somewhat hysterically, too, Like mother hens, the ladies clucked and fussed, and through it all, she heard bits and pieces of the reprimand they gave Tom. Something about Barkly's attacking Mrs. Elward's umbrella. Vicious dog. And being rained out of their club meeting yesterday and trying it again today. Scouting the *Sitta carolinensis*, the white-breasted nuthatch. Rained out again. Going home. Vicious dog— that came twice. Tom offering to replace the damaged umbrella. Offer accepted. Conversation finished.

"We'll walk you home, dear," Mrs. Brooks said. "You shouldn't be left alone."

"Marvel-Anne is at the house," Edwina said with a sniff, not venturing a look at Tom.

Then Edwina was shuffled beneath Mrs. Calhoon's umbrella and guided, with an arm about her waist, to the street. At the last minute before the oak trees would obscure her view, she chanced a quick glimpse of Tom.

With legs apart and hands at his sides, oblivious to the rain slamming down on him, he stared at her. In his expression, she saw regret . . . and the subtlest hint of longing. For what? Her? The very idea was . . . compelling. Potent.

She had the strangest urge to break free of the ladies and tell them they were making a mistake: she was headed the wrong way.

The rain had lost its force and trickled to a drizzle that Tom ignored while he walked to Edwina's house under the cover of darkness. Tucked beneath his arm, he carried a bouquet of damp wildflowers he'd pilfered from the lot next to the livery. He'd waited until he felt sure Edwina would be alone and calmed down enough so she wouldn't slam the door in his face.

That . . . and he didn't want to be seen bringing her flowers.

Not that he didn't think it a noble cause. It was just that he'd never been sap enough to go this far. He was new to this sort of tactic—in a nutshell: romance.

The word sounded foreign in his head, and he wasn't quite sure what to make of it. In the past, sweet offerings had never been required to make things up to a woman. He gave them an irresistible smile, a kiss here and there. End of story. Life went on. No complexities. No . . . flowers.

Tom was probably taking the romance thing a little

too far. This was strictly an apology mission. He'd pushed her too far. She hadn't wanted to go on the rope swing, but he'd baited her into it. And she'd gotten caught. He could understand why she'd be upset. She was probably still crying. He needed to make things up to her. Flowers soothed frazzled women—or so he'd been told. He'd soon find out.

At the walkway to Edwina's house, he opened the latch on the gate and let himself inside. Lights on the lower story told him she was still up. It wasn't yet seven o'clock, so he'd assumed she would be.

He took the steps to the veranda, then stood on the stoop for a few moments to figure out a plan. All he'd thought through so far was shoving the flowers at her. After that, he was hoping something would come to him.

Gazing at the wilting bouquet in his hand, he felt like a jerk. This wasn't his style. Why he'd opted to do things this way, he couldn't quite determine—other than he'd been desperate for an idea, any idea that could mend fences.

The front door muffled music. It wasn't loud to begin with; it was a phonographic recording that sounded like it came from the side of the house. He couldn't quite make out the tune.

Now or never.

"Ah, hell . . ." he muttered.

He cranked the doorbell and stuck his fingers in the collar of his shirt that was neither particularly tight nor buttoned to the highest closure. He just felt like he was choking.

His gaze stayed on the leaded stained glass that decorated an oval cutout in the front door. No shadowy movements could be detected behind the pattern. The doorbell went unanswered.

Shifting on his feet, he rang again.

A minute must have passed before he decided to walk around the veranda to the side of the house. The bay windows were covered with sheer curtains. A door led to the porch; it was also swathed with a lacy fabric.

The beat of a two-step filtered through as Tom reached the door. He could finally make out the tune. *Joplin. "Maple Leaf Rag."*

Leaning close to the window, he peered inside what looked to be the parlor. A motion to his right caught his eye, and he tracked the figure to the center of the room.

"Jesus . . ." The word left him before he realized he'd even breathed.

So much for crying. . . .

Edwina was doing the high-stepping strut . . . in her woolies. A fitted white lace corset cover—minus the corset—hugged her breasts and showed fine cleavage in the V-shaped neck. Her drawers were some frilly type that matched the lace on the top piece. Black stockings covered her legs and feet, fancy embroidery in three colors at her slim ankles. Unbound hair fell in a curly cloud past her waist. Ivory skin, a lot of it bare, teased his senses as she pranced by a settee, then back down the length of the room to the end with a right sideward step.

The recording ended on her breathless smile. Cheeks rosy, breasts rising and falling from the exertion, she held her pose. Those tantalizing curls dusted her nose and she blew them off. With a soft giggle, she went to the player, lifted the arm, and turned the handle a few times to reset the phonograph.

When he thought she wasn't going to dance anymore, disappointment settled in his chest like lead. He couldn't explain why, but watching her move to ragtime's nice-and-light aroused him more than would a floozy in a full strip.

Lively notes drifted through the parlor again. She flitted about, taking a hop over her cat, who lay in the center of the rug with its tail softly moving.

Clearly, if he announced his presence, he would be interrupting a very private moment, when she was involved in something she obviously didn't want getting around. Edwina Huntington the finishing school teacher prancing in her whites, dancing the two-step—and being pretty damn good at it, too.

Thinking the situation through, he had two options.

A gentleman would walk away and forget what he'd seen.

That one got quickly scratched off the list.

He went for the second choice.

He knocked loudly on the parlor door glass.

Chapter

9

By dancing, Edwina hoped to forget about that afternoon. But the scene with the ladies dropping her off on her doorstep kept replaying in her head.

"Have Marvel-Anne steep you some wormwood tea, dear," Mrs. Treber had suggested, fussily tucking dripping hair back into her ebony coiffure.

Fanny Elward seconded her. "Yes, do. It always works to calm my Roger. And he would know what's best. He is the druggist."

Iris Brooks chimed in. "Wormwood is the best. A soother when my George is in a tantrum over politics."

"Don't I know," Mrs. Plunkett added, her skirts leaving a wide puddle on the porch.

In a mousy voice, Mrs. Calhoon pointed out, "It's a good thing an election is more than a year off."

Edwina had nodded to be sociable, but she'd wanted nothing more than to go inside and hide. Especially when the topic had abruptly turned to Tom Wolcott.

"He's not a bad-looking man," Lulu Calhoon said.

Olive Treber threw in, "No, not at all. I wonder why he hasn't married."

"Self-absorption," Prudence Plunkett said in speculation.

Unyielding in posture, Mrs. Brooks said, "His business."

"It's taken all this time. Perhaps we should consider him available . . . ?" Wet ribbons flat on her hat, Mrs. Elward grew thoughtful.

Edwina didn't want to hear about their plans to fix up Tom Wolcott with one of their daughters. She'd been about to beg forgiveness and take her leave when Mrs. Plunkett's words stopped her short.

"We're forgetting Miss Huntington. She may already have designs on him."

"A handsome man," Mrs. Treber pronounced.

"Quite," Lulu Calhoon agreed. "We wouldn't blame you if you wanted to encourage him, dear."

Mrs. Elward quietly asked, "Do you want to encourage him?"

"No," Edwina said vehemently. Then tried to imagine Tom with one of their daughters. "I don't know. . . . Maybe." She thought about her resolve not to get involved with a man. Not ever again. "No, definitely not," she said, recanting. But if Tom Wolcott was an option, he could be . . . perhaps. "I might." Confusion slammed around inside her head. Tom had said he thought Camille Kennison was very pretty. But Grayce Kennison wasn't here to put her daughter into the courting market.

Conviction, Edwina told herself. "No, I shan't encourage him." Her head hurt. She squeezed her eyes closed. She couldn't think.

"Poor dear."

"She's not herself."

"The grief."

"She needs to lie down."

"Shall we come in?"

"No!" Edwina shot back, her eyes flashing open. "I appreciate everything. I just want to be alone."

Then she'd slipped into the house and took refuge. That had been hours ago. Now she just wanted to dance and lose herself in the music.

At first, Edwina wasn't sure the knock had come from the parlor door. But it persisted through the notes of the music, causing her to stop midtwirl and stare at the sheers. The form of a person, barely discernable, stood outside.

Had the bird watchers come back? And at the side of the house?

Caught off guard, she bit her lower lip. Warning alarms clattered. No, it couldn't be the mothers. There was only one shadow. One mother?

Frozen in limbo, Edwina mentally ran through a list of possible callers. Marvel-Anne had a key to the front door, so she should have come directly inside if there had been a need for her to return. But she'd left at six-fifteen after serving supper and helping Edwina out of her wet clothes. Not wanting to take a bath before she ate, Edwina had slipped her China silk kimono on and sat at the dining-room table with her hair down to dry. Crescencia Stykem might drop by unannounced, although her doing so was doubtful. They'd covered the protocol of calls in class this week. One of the mothers might have returned alone. If that was the case, she'd be in an awful jam, worse than the umbrella incident. How could she explain dancing to Joplin?

The knock repeated.

Without further rumination, Edwina put a stop to the music and grabbed her colorful blue-and-red wrapper. If she hadn't gotten heated doing the sugar cane and taken the robe off, the circumstances wouldn't have been as bad as they were.

Dancing to popular music was one thing; dancing to popular music in one's underwear was another.

Edwina slipped her arms into the geisha sleeves, then strode to the door. A grab at the curtains to view the person outside before unlocking the knob brought both a jubilant yet sinking feeling in the pit of her stomach. At the sight of Tom Wolcott, she frowned.

"Open the door, Edwina." Tom's resonant voice came clearly through the beveled glass.

She shook her head. "I don't want to talk to you."

"Edwina." Dark brows knit together. "Let me in."

"That's all I need—to have to explain myself again."

"Nobody saw me coming over. I took the alley."

Edwina stared a moment, perhaps—but not quite consciously—debating whether to let him in. A bouquet of drooping flowers filled his hand. They had to be for her. But the goodwill gesture baffled her. This type of sentiment was uncharacteristic of a man who liked to show off dead animals.

But whatever the reasoning behind his visit, her secret had been discovered. And that threw her into the awkward—and potentially dangerous—position of having to defend her actions. She'd always worried she'd get caught one day, but the appeal of dancing had been too much to resist, so she'd taken the risk. She hadn't counted on Tom being the one who could expose her.

He could use the information to his advantage—namely by letting the town know that she danced to so-called hedonistic music. With her name ruined, the school would be also.

Edwina didn't want to believe it, but she could see Tom making roast meat out of her . . . then stuffing what was left to tack onto his wall—yet another trophy. Silently, she groaned. She had to find out what he intended to do—if he intended to do anything at all.

She undid the lock and took several steps backward, her hand rising to the bands of satin down the robe's front to make sure the edges fit snugly together—as if that were an issue now. He'd already gotten an eyeful.

No matter, she couldn't let her deportment slip in his company. She had to stand on ceremony in spite of the way things looked.

"Whatever the reason, Mr. Wolcott, evening calls are paid only to those with whom one is well acquainted," she stated primly, her hand remaining on the robe's folds.

Without a word, he shoved the flowers at her.

She was helpless but to accept with her free hand. "Oh . . . well . . . thank you."

"Hell, I owed you." His fingers slipped halfway into his pockets and he rested his weight on one foot. "For this afternoon . . . and all."

The blue of his eyes bored into her own; they lowered a fraction, then slowly inched back up. Flustered by his blatant perusal, she forgot to remind him about his language. She clutched the silk more securely to her breasts. At least the robe came to the floor and covered her feet. Aside from the curves of her body that the kimono accentuated, nothing was revealed.

Why, then, did she feel stark naked?

Turning away so he couldn't hold her captive with his gaze, she went to the center table and set the bouquet next to the family photograph album. "What happened this afternoon wasn't entirely your fault, Mr. Wolcott," she said, running her fingertip across the picture book's mother-of-pearl cover. "I was a willing participant."

She heard the dull tread of his boots as he came toward her. Stiffening, she waited for him to reach her and . . . do what? What did she expect . . . or want?

When he paused, she felt his presence. Close. Very close. The fragrance of shaving cologne pulled her attention. She tried to decipher the scent . . . musk and a hint of bayberry. Nothing overdone. Pleasant. And there was the lingering trace of tobacco smoke. She found that scent on a man appealing.

A wave of euphoria washed over her and prickled her skin. Did she imagine him lightly caressing her hair?

Facing him without warning, her breath caught in her throat as she backed her behind against the table's edge. Indeed, he stood close, close enough for her to fall into his arms. She couldn't do that . . . not again. "So . . ." She sighed foolishly and damned herself for doing so. "Is there anything else you wanted?"

Without a hat on, his richly hued brown hair glistened beneath the light of the oil lamp hanging from the ceiling. He had a way of styling it that was careless, yet utterly flattering to his sportsman physique. It was brushed away from his strong forehead; the wavy lengths that fell over his ears came to rest on his collar. The overall effect was disarming.

"I didn't want anything else until I heard the music on and saw you."

She lowered her eyelids and tried to remain composed. She'd inadvertently shown him her true colors and now he was going to tell.

There were two things she could do. Plead her case—without going into any details of course—and hope he sympathized. Or outright fib. The latter seemed the surest way out.

"I can assure you," she said in an unwavering voice, "I don't make a habit of dancing—fully clothed or in my unmentionables. In my defense, I was trying out a recording that a friend sent me. But I found it trite and dull as an old penny."

"Didn't look that way to me."

Unable to meet his eyes, which could penetrate her and bring her to destruction, she stared at the outline of a cigarette pack in his breast pocket, visible from a part in his duster.

"Well, it's true," she reiterated. "I don't habitually dance. Not ever . . . rarely."

His voice seemed to vibrate through her when he said, "You don't make a habit of much, but I seem to catch you doing more rather than less of what you claim you don't do."

The heat of a blush spread across her cheeks. "You just think you're finding me up to no good. I can assure you—"

"Assure away. I'm not buying."

A sinking feeling pitted Edwina's stomach. She was his sitting duck and he had enough ammunition to blast the decoy feathers right off her. She had to try to save herself. "On my behalf—that is, I don't really—on the contrary—" She could go no farther. What else could she say? She was trapped. A different tactic was in order. "Ragtime does seem to be getting around, and to not give it a try would be quite close-minded. Don't you think?"

"You've got a pretty good flare for Joplin," Tom commented. "A nice take on the double shuffle."

Her gaze grew wide as the moon. She'd meant to distract him, but it was she who was distracted. She couldn't believe he was familiar with the popular artist. Tom Wolcott lived in a den. How could he know Joplin, much less a ragtime double shuffle?

"You know Scott Joplin's music?" she questioned, forgetting she was supposed to be throwing him off the scent. This was the first bit of compatibility they shared: music.

"I know Scott Joplin."

His reply took her for a loop. He didn't imply that he knew the music; the implication was he knew *the man*.

"Excuse me?" she blurted in disbelief.

"We grew up together in Texarkana," he replied matter of factly. "Hell, when we were five, we watched the inaugural run of the Texas & Pacific come into town, and we said we were going to be one of those grimy-faced, cloth-capped, thick-glove–wearing men working for the railroad."

"You're kidding me."

"Am not." The glimmer in his eyes was deadly serious. "We lived just two blocks apart. His folks had a house on Pine Street off of State Line Avenue on the Texas side."

Dismissing her plan to draw him away from the fact that she'd been dancing, she slipped past him and sank onto the settee. Scott Joplin was her idol and now took priority in her thoughts—although she did remember to clamp her legs together before resting both elbows on her knees. Long hair fell over her shoulders, and she absently curled the ends of a piece around her forefinger. "Scott Joplin . . ." she whispered in awe. "I can't believe you know him—grew up with him."

"Played in the sandy hills and spring mud holes. I

haven't seen him since we were thirteen. His father left them and his mother moved him and the other kids over to the Arkansas side."

"Did he ever play for you?"

"I went to a few of his lessons. I didn't know squat about classical music, but he had perfect pitch and could remember any tune his teacher played to him."

"My, my." She spoke in a broken whisper, lost in thoughts of the composer. She forgot Tom stood in front of her until she viewed the tips of his boots.

"You've been figured out, Ed."

Lifting her chin, Edwina unsteadily countered, "I don't know what you're talking about." But she did. Too well.

"You like Joplin. You like to dance rag. So what?" He began to slip out of his duster, and she grew expectant. *Oh, goodness. He'll blackmail me now.* A tussle on the sofa in exchange for his silence. "I don't know why you think you have to hide it, but what the hell. I won't tell anyone." The duster dropped to the back of the settee, and he held out his hand for her. "Come on."

"Come on?" she blurted. Heaven help her, he expected her to take him to the bedroom. "I . . . um . . . I . . ."

"What's the matter, Ed?"

Heat consumed her, and not of the passionate kind. More like the panicking kind. She hadn't expected things to go this awry. But even in the chaos, a spark of triumphant conquest flashed through her. He must find her alluring.

"Let's see what you've really got, honey baby." He grabbed her hand when she didn't put her palm in his. She shot to her feet and came precariously close to having her breasts crushed against his chest. In a low voice that sent a shiver across her arms, he murmured, "Put the recording back on and I'll show you how a real ragger dances with his girl."

Relief and astonishment clashed within her. *He wants*

to dance. If she refused him . . . he might change his mind about not telling. . . .

Gulping, Edwina walked on stiff legs to the Victrola and cranked the handle. Tom came up to her and took her hand, then positioned her in the middle of the room. As soon as the first notes came through the big trumpet, he began to move with the rhythm of the beat. At first in step, then clapping his hands.

"Right in line," he called.

She knew that phrase meant to follow his lead. He stepped forward on his left foot, took another with his right to close in, then lifted the weight on the right and stepped left. This was a classic two-step, and she was amazed that he knew it.

Very hesitantly, she moved parallel to him. This could be a trick . . . a plan to undo her completely. She had to be cautious.

"Walk into it," he said, then orchestrated a turn that left his back to hers. She was to do likewise until their backs met. In a move that surprised her, he hooked his elbows through hers and took her dipping first left, then right.

A jolt of unbridled sensuality shot through her at the touch of his muscled back to her shoulders. With each move, sinewy cords rippled, and she felt the power in his body as it skimmed hers. She held herself stiffly and unyielding.

"Relax," Tom urged. "Relax . . . relax. Have fun." His tone blended with the musical notes. She wanted to do as he suggested, but she feared ulterior motives.

"Why is it you want me to dance?" she asked with a hard-fought effort not to show her skepticism.

"Because it makes you happy."

Oh . . . how right he is. How could he tell?

Tom lunged right and took her with him, her forearms still hooked through his elbows. Tight biceps held her and controlled which way she moved. She couldn't have gotten away from him if she wanted to. The question was, did she want to? Not really. . . .

Ludie had been a flawless and patient dancing teacher. When they'd linked arms or stepped into a waltz position, his muscles had been as pliant as putty. He had been a man of books, not of the outdoors, so he'd had no hard body definition. His hands had felt like a diaper flannel—smooth and soft. Tom's were rough and calloused, the fingernails too short but clean. Dancing with him was like being partners with bendable steel that had all the right moves.

Staying with the fast tempo and the compromising position, their backsides bumped with each body drag.

Edwina should have put a stop to the music. Frolicking with Tom in her home, in her underwear, was dangerous. More than dangerous—catastrophic. She knew *she* would never breathe a word. But Tom . . . if he told . . . she shuddered to think. She could always deny everything. It would be his word against hers.

"Break it down." He let her elbows go and stepped right sideward for a count, then brought his leg in for a left close.

On the second count, she gasped with surprise as he executed a pivot and a forward shuffle. His foot landed smack between her own, his knee brushing against her inner thighs. The silk of her robe parted and the belt slipped free of its satiny single tie.

Before she could catch her breath, he put firm hands on her waist and swung her in the air in a circle. Just as quickly, he set her back down.

By now, the kimono's tie lay on the rug and Honey Tiger swatted at the end.

Slender fingers attempted to keep the wrapper together as Edwina asked, "W-what do you call that?" Wisps of hair fell across the sides of her face, but she couldn't brush them back without giving up her hold on modesty.

"The happy-go-lucky." He tipped a mock hat at her and swaggered in a circle while waving his right hand. "I figured a hot shot like you would know it."

Whenever he used that challenging tone on her, she

forgot reason. Now she also forgot she wore nothing more than cambric and a dressing robe. Suddenly, it didn't matter that Tom might tell all of Harmony she was a dancing fiend. She'd take the chance. Pride was at stake here. She certainly didn't think of herself as the cat's meow when it came to improvised steps and gestures, but she knew a trick or two.

Demureness was temporarily abandoned as her hands rested on her hips. With a shake, she rid the hair from her eyes and narrowed her stare on him. "Crazy bones," she shot back with defiance. "On the two count—clockwise."

She waited a few beats until the tempo was just right, then began to shuffle in the designated direction. From the slow steps Tom took to her lead, she didn't think he knew it. She was sure after she abruptly pivoted to counterclockwise and slammed into his chest.

"What are you doing?" she blurted, taking a hop backward.

"Following you."

"You followed the wrong way."

His fingers raked through unruly hair. "Then start over. I'm with you this time."

Black-stockinged toe tapping to the syncopation as she gave no thought to the gap in her robe, she began the dance again. This time when she turned, Tom did so also on the same measure. Six counts later, she was in the lead again.

She shifted into a pattern of low positions that were interrupted by cross-kicks with right and left legs alternating. Pretty limber herself, she could get her leg up fairly high—high enough to kick Tom in the chops if she wanted to.

"Jesus," he muttered behind her.

Smiling, she called over her shoulder, "Crazy bones." Her shoulders loosened and she let herself sway in time.

"You do the pigeon wing?"

Tossing back, "Do birds fly?" she went into a step

that was a half shuffle, half stamp. His hands encircled her waist as he matched her step for step.

Inhibitions gone, Edwina allowed herself to enjoy the harmony of moving as one to the upbeat piano notes filling the parlor. The secure grip of Tom's fingers around her middle sent a volatile current through her. Filled with a strange inner excitement, she couldn't stop smiling. She felt blood rushing from her fingertips to her toes. At this moment, she couldn't remember how Ludie danced. Tom Wolcott outshined any memory of Ludie she had.

"Hop it down front and doodle back."

She did as Tom directed.

Just as the music reached its fevered pitch, Tom snapped his fingers and she turned.

"Time for the end." He laid a hand on her shoulder and on her waist, taking a swing position. Copying him, she let her head fall back as he whirled her around in a fast circle.

"Put the nippers on," he called. His hand fell off her shoulder and slid down her arm to her wrist. She didn't know what the nippers were, so she didn't grasp onto his hand like she should have. Reeling backward, she stumbled and fell out of his reach—but not before his fingers snagged the cuff of her wrapper. As she spun away from him, she slipped right out of the geisha sleeves of her kimono. The backs of her legs hit the chair Mrs. Plunkett favored, and she landed on the cushions.

Her curls cascaded around her cheeks and on her shoulders; she blew them off her brows with a pant. Drawer-clad legs apart in a thoroughly unladylike pose, she pressed her shoulders into the chair's tassel-decorated back. "What's the nippers?"

Tom stood over her, his own hair untidy. He leaned in and put both hands on the chair arms to trap her. The steady pound of her pulse skipped a beat. She thought for sure she was doomed. He'd now tell her that he'd gotten her just where he wanted her, and her life would be over . . . ruined.

"Handcuffs." The simple word barely registered. "You lock on my wrist and we spin around with the nippers on—like we're handcuffed together. Haven't you ever been on the whip end of a skating line?"

"Not in years," she managed to reply through a tight throat. Perhaps he was just buying time . . . toying with her like Honey Tiger did with the occasional mouse she found.

With Tom's exertion and sweat came the heightened scent of bayberry. He leaned in closer, and she could almost taste his lips against hers. She didn't slink farther down in the chair and try to envelop herself in its plump cushions; she remained where she was . . . waiting expectantly for something that never came.

"Let's try it again." His suggestion melted through her and clarity rose to the surface.

Flopped in the chair without her robe, she was an easy target for unraveling. Her corset cover neckline plunged precariously low over the tops of her breasts. The lawn of her drawers was thin enough to reveal certain unmentionable parts of her anatomy.

And he wanted to dance with her again.

Bewilderment jammed up her mind. She couldn't discern his motives. She had to know exactly what he intended. Although he'd proclaimed he'd not reveal her dancing to anyone, she had to be reassured.

"Will you not tell anyone about my dancing? Truly?"

A droplet of sweat fell off his brow and landed on the delicate fabric covering her breast. Practically on the nipple, to be exact. She shivered, the rosy peak going hard in spite of her best efforts to remain unaffected.

A gaze as stormy as that afternoon's skies swept her away. His words were low and deep and brought gooseflesh out on her arms. "I won't tell."

She tempted fate. "Why not?"

"If I told you, you'd never dance this way with me again."

On that, he straightened, held out his hand, and waited for her to take it.

Shrugging back, she bit her bottom lip. "But I'm not dressed."

"Honey, if I was of a mind to try something with you right now, you wouldn't have to be half dressed." His lean fingers curled around hers, and he pulled her up flush against him. Aching breasts pressed against his shirtfront, and she was on the verge of burying her face in his collar. "In fact, when I feel like kissing you . . . and more, if you say so, I'd rather you were fully dressed to start with. Then I could enjoy untying the ribbons and unfastening all the buttons." His lips caught the tangle of hair at her temple as he gave her a breathy kiss. "Kind of like opening a present. It's not as much fun when somebody else undoes the wrappings."

Edwina couldn't move. Breathe. Think.

His raspy voice echoed inside her. *And more, if you say so.*

Tom Wolcott did things to her head. Crazy things. If this wasn't her house, she'd have to get out of here, go someplace alone and pull herself together. She didn't recognize this person standing in her place, this woman ready to throw her head back and bare her breasts for a man she hardly knew—much less liked half of the time.

"Put the record on, Ed." His breath, spent and hot, clung to her forehead and made her woozy. A good woozy. Like the feeling she got from lazing on the window seat with the sunshine pouring in while she indulged in a box of fancy chocolate creams.

The ninny she was, she probably would have stood leaning toward Tom until dawn if he hadn't propelled her toward the Victrola. Methodically, she reset the phonograph and walked to him. If she'd been thinking with her whole mind, she would have put on her wrapper; she merely gave the colorful swath on the carpet a cursory glance before following Tom and clapping to the introduction of the tune.

They went through the routine once more, this time with minor mistakes and missteps. As soon as the song was over, Tom told her to play the "Maple Leaf" again.

They were going to dance it until they got it right. After the fourth try, they ran through the happy-go-lucky, crazy bones, and nippers without a hitch.

Static filled the room while the record circled and circled under the needle; the music finished. Out of breath, Edwina raised a hand and placed her palm on her heart. A faint dew clung to her cleavage, and as her fingers landed slightly above the swell of her breasts, Tom's eyes followed.

It didn't occur to her until now that Tom had seen more of her than Ludlow ever had in the time they'd known each other.

Catching her breath, she grew embarrassed. She should say something, but words failed her.

Tom, who'd rolled up his cuffs for the second try at the rag, now let the fabric down; he didn't button the cuffs. She had the strangest urge to make the offer to do them for him. But the casual way he'd left the cuffs had her mind brimming with racy thoughts to the contrary. Of touching the small pearl buttons down the front of his shirt and slipping them free. Then sliding her hands inside, across his chest . . . that chest she'd seen bare once.

And more, if you say so . . .

Edwina's lungs fought for air.

Tom shook the hair from his eyes, then made his way to the settee and picked up his duster. He flipped its length over his shoulder. "Buy you dinner Saturday night, Ed?"

Without thinking, she replied, "All right."

"Six o'clock."

Then he showed himself out the parlor door, and she sank into the chair.

Honey Tiger was sprawled on the lower shelf of the center table and Edwina murmured to the cat, "What have I gotten myself into?"

"Hell, Shay, you'd have asked to buy her dinner, too, if she stood in front of you wearing a hankie."

Tom leaned toward the smoky mirror above his bureau. All he could see was his collar and the yoke of his new shirt. But it was enough to tell him he was overdressed. With a grunt of disgust, he began to unfasten the cuff buttons.

Shay lounged on the unmade bed. Lying on his side with his ankles crossed and his booted feet hanging halfway over the side, he rested his head on his palm. "If a woman stood in front of me wearing just her whites, I'd be more apt to be thinking about dessert."

The twilled wool shirt glided off his shoulders, and Tom threw it at the bed. It landed on Shay's face.

"What's wrong with this shirt?" Shay asked, peeling the wool off his nose and pitching the garment on the floor.

"It's too much. I'm not going over there all decked out. I don't want her getting the wrong idea." Turning, Tom gestured to the other crisply folded shirt on the sheets. "Hand me that."

Shay tossed it to Tom. "What's the right idea?"

"No ideas. Friendship straight across the board. Cut and dried."

"Is that so?"

"Damn right."

Tom finished buttoning the cashmere shirt and objectively stared at his reflection. *And more, if you say so.* What in the hell had he been thinking? That was his trouble. He hadn't been thinking.

And level-headed thinking hadn't yet returned. When he'd told Shay Edwina Huntington had answered her door in her robe and underwear, he shouldn't have felt the weight of guilt crush him afterward. He'd promised only that he wouldn't spill about her dancing to ragtime—not about what she'd *not* been wearing.

In the past, trading information like this with Shay had just been shooting the breeze. It was a man's thing to run off the mouth about—scantily clad women. But that was the problem. He wasn't feeling about Edwina as if she were the kind of woman men talked about. But

Tom did have to credit himself with not discussing her breasts. At least he'd drawn the line at that—*them*—although it hadn't stopped him from picturing the deep cleavage when he was flapping his chops about the underwear. Those breasts . . . full and round, jiggling when she danced. Jesus . . .

He was getting too caught up in her. He'd liked it better when he thought she was an old maid. But he knew different now. An attraction for her was a dead end all the way around. She'd claimed she'd never marry. He wasn't the man to change her mind. He preferred women who were spontaneous, real corkers, carefree types. Unfortunately, he was imagining Edwina. She could fit the bill, especially when she danced to Joplin in her woolies.

Ah, hell. Why had he gone and asked her out to dinner?

Tom frowned at his alternate shirt in the mirror. "It's still too much."

From the bed, Shay suggested, "Maybe you ought to just go in your union suit. She could relate to that."

Edwina sat at her dressing table, then stood, then sat back down. She was a bundle of nerves. Absently, she ran her brush through her hair. "Honestly, I don't know why I accepted. I have a hundred things to do before Tuesday."

Crescencia occupied the window seat with a demure pose. She'd dropped by to return Edwina's Mousquetaire sleeve pattern. Having bought it in Chicago, Edwina was the only one in Harmony who had the stylish pattern that required two extra yards of dimity.

"Don't worry, Miss Edwina. The girls and I finished the bats last night, and this morning, Lucille and Meg are working on the skeletons."

"I never should have let Mrs. Brooks talk me into hosting the party at my house. Eastern doctors—thirteen of them arriving tomorrow for a hunting excursion."

When the Halloween party had been proposed by

Mrs. Brooks, Edwina had thought it a grand idea—until none of the other ladies present made a proposal as to who would pay for it all. Thank goodness, Grayce Kennison came to Edwina's rescue and suggested that everyone's next tuition check should compensate for the expenses. There had been reluctant nods, then finally smiles of agreement—as what was a few extra dollars when their daughters could be meeting the men of their dreams at the party?

"What time is Mr. Wolcott coming?"

Crescencia's question had Edwina glancing at the boudoir clock. "Half an hour."

"I can help you get dressed if you'd like." Crescencia rose and went to the open armoire. She fingered the green nun's veiling trimmed with black lace appliqué. "This one's lovely."

Edwina had tried the dress on over an hour ago, and after staring hard at her image in the full-length mirror, she'd told herself she couldn't possibly wear such a thing in front of Tom Wolcott. She'd had it since she turned eighteen, and while it was as beautiful as the day she'd made it, she'd outgrown its style. The green was too light, even though the black toned it down. Colors like mint and spring leaves were meant for younger women, not those who knew better than to pin their hopes on a romance at this late stage.

Of course Edwina was too smart to let herself think of the dinner invitation as anything other than a cordial offering—one business owner to another. Only she wished she never said she'd go. It was pure nonsense to be feeling butterflies in her stomach, as if she truly were young enough to wear the green. . . . For a heartbeat, she dared herself, then quickly thought better of it.

"No, dear," Edwina said, setting the brush down. "I won't be wearing the green."

"This one is nice, too," Crescencia said, skimming her fingertips down the champagne-colored princess dress of batiste.

Edwina put fingertips to her left temple, willing a

headache away. "No, I don't think so. It's too . . . too much. I don't want him to think I'm trying to impress him. All he sees me in are day dresses. If I were to suddenly dress to the nines, he'd get suspicious."

"Suspicious of what?" Cressie tamed a flame-red curl by tucking it back in the twist on her crown.

"Oh . . . just suspicious is all."

Shrugging, Crescencia went through the dresses, and Edwina declared them all unfit to wear. The striped lawns, imported rep, linen trimmed in cadet blue—they were unsuitable for the occasion.

With a dismayed sigh, Edwina put her head in her hands. "I don't know why I accepted . . ." Then lifting her chin, she said with a sniff, "Dear, you have to do me a favor. Tell him I've become suddenly ill and won't be able to go."

"Still too much." Tom hurled another shirt.

He'd gone through the two new shirts he'd bought at Treber's, then made his way through his better oxfords and duck cloths. Now he was down to flannels, which suited him fine; he was a flannel man. They were worn out at the elbows, but no holes. He was no damn slob.

After buttoning the double-breasted blue- and black-plaid shirt, he tucked the hem into his Levi's. Then he ran a comb through his hair. Glaring at himself, he swore. Who was he trying to kid? He wanted to impress her. Get to know her and find out what made her tick . . .

. . . find out if her skin tasted as sweet as it had looked. . . .

Contrary to what he'd told her, he *had* had a mind to try something that night. And he wasn't altogether sure she'd have turned him down. Any future encounters like the one they'd had, he had to know what he was getting into, who he was messing around with.

Turning, he asked Shay, "How do I look?"

Trickling walnut pieces into his mouth, Shay replied

while chewing, "If I say sweet as saltwater taffy, will you buy me a dinner, too?"

A retort was on the tip of his tongue, then Tom thought better of it. In fact, he had another idea. One that would keep him from doing or saying anything not completely on the up-and-up. This idea he had would keep tonight on the friendly level that he'd sworn to Shay it was.

Snagging one of the shirts from the floor, he sailed it to his partner. "Put that on. You're coming with me."

Nutshells flew off the bed as Shay sat up. "The hell I am. I'm not gussying myself up for your girl."

"She's not my girl." Tom felt his shave-smoothed chin. "In fact, she's more likely yours."

Eyes narrowed. "What are you telling me here, Tom?"

"She told me she's interested in you." He neglected to inform Shay that she'd insisted she was inquiring for a friend.

"Interested in me?" Panic flickered in Shay's eyes. "She can't be. Why, my heart's set on Crescencia Stykem. The only reason I haven't called on her yet is I've been gone from town more than I've been in it. I don't need Edwina Huntington to get her mind set on—" Without completing the thought, he began to unbutton his shirt. "Damn. I'll go. Only to set her straight."

"I most certainly will not, Miss Edwina," Crescencia said with a firmness Edwina hadn't thought her capable of. "No arguments. You're going. Chances like this don't come around every day for ladies like us. You'll have a wonderful dinner with Mr. Wolcott. And I really think you should wear something stunning."

Edwina was taken aback. The younger woman charged headfirst into the closet and produced the green nun's veiling.

"All right," Edwina begged, "I'll go. But not in *that.*"

Gingerly fluffing the collar, Crescencia said in a wistful tone, "Why, if I had the opportunity to have dinner with a man as good-looking as Mr. Wolcott, I'd wear something so beautiful he couldn't take his eyes off me. You're missing an opportunity, Miss Edwina."

An opportunity . . . that's precisely what she had. Why, left alone with Mr. Wolcott, she might do or say something she'd regret. She didn't know him at all. The best way to do so would be by staying on neutral subjects, exchanging pleasantries. And with another present, that couldn't get muddled.

"Cressie, dear, you're coming with me."

The eyes behind the lenses widened like saucers as she hung the dress on the top of the open armoire door. "Me? I can't go with you."

"Of course you can." Edwina took Crescencia's hands into her own. "It's better for a couple, when making their first appearance in public, to be seen with a chaperone."

"I-I'm no ch-chaperone," she stammered. "And besides, Mr. W-Wolcott wouldn't want me to come along . . . I'm certain."

"Quite the opposite. He'd welcome your presence. He told me he thought you were a very attractive young woman."

"H-he did?" Her palms grew clammy in Edwina's. "Oh, this is terrible. I don't want him to find me . . . that way. I don't think of him l-like that."

"Well, then you'll just have to come along with me, and we'll make sure he understands that you don't think of him in a romantic capacity."

"Oh . . . but I just couldn't come. Papa wouldn't like it. . . . I'd have to tell him what I was doing. . . ."

"We can speak to him on the way. When he finds out you're with me, he'll make no fuss."

"Yes, but . . ." In a desperate plea, she blurted out, "I'm not attired appropriately at all!"

"Never you mind, dear. I've got just the thing. And it's perfect for you."

"Mr. Dufresne," Edwina said with a start upon seeing Shay Dufresne standing with Tom Wolcott on her doorstep.

"Miss Stykem," Mr. Dufresne blurted out in a surprised tone, ignoring Edwina and directing his undivided attention on Crescencia.

Not immediately acknowledging Shay, Crescencia gaped at Tom Wolcott with clear disapproval. "M-Mr. W-Wolcott."

"Miss Huntington," Tom said in greeting, his low voice a little awkward.

After their round of mismatched salutations, a strained silence blanketed the four of them.

At length, Edwina and Mr. Dufresne said together, "Well."

Edwina smiled.

Mr. Dufresne laughed.

"You ladies are looking especially becoming this evening." Mr. Dufresne spoke to both of them, but gazed only at Crescencia.

The nun's veiling dress on her was almost the color of summer twilight reflecting in a meadow; her pale face and orange-red hair were enhanced by the matching hat that Edwina had loaned her as well.

"Yeah, fetching," Tom mumbled, shifting uneasily on his feet.

Edwina noted that Shay Dufresne wore a crisp new shirt beneath his opened coat; the smell of cedar chips that Mr. Treber kept in his cabinets drifted across the air. Tom, on the other hand, hadn't gone to any trouble for this evening's dinner. From the part in his duster, she saw he'd chosen a faded blue plaid that had seen better days. The Stetson on his head was the beaten-up one he wore while on hunting jaunts; the band was marked with a rim of sweat, and the creases on the brim were well set. But she could make no criticism of his attire. She had dressed in a black worsted voile skirt with a plain tucked shirtwaist.

It would seem neither of them had expected anything more than a simple meal and general conversation.

"Miss Stykem, this is a pleasant surprise," Mr. Dufresne said. "I hope this means you'll be accompanying us to dinner."

Her arm trembling, she brought a handkerchief to her nose and delicately took a small sniff of the salts concealed within. "I-I s-suppose I-I am. I d-didn't expect t-to see y-you here."

Shay knocked Tom on the upper arm. Tom glared at him. "Tom insisted that I come. Glad I said yes." To Edwina, he went on, "I really am glad Miss Stykem is coming." His tone sounded accusing, as if he were trying to make her understand something.

Looking pointedly at Edwina, Tom remarked, "You must have been thinking what I was thinking by inviting a friend along."

"As the saying goes, the more the merrier."

"I'll vouch for that," Mr. Dufresne said with a chuckle. "Shall we be off?"

Crescencia turned her head to Edwina, her eyes beseeching. A blush worked its way up her neck as she mouthed, "Papa."

"Leave that to me, dear," Edwina replied as if nothing were wrong.

The ladies gathered cloaks and put them on; then the two couples left the porch and began walking down Sycamore Drive. The members of each sex kept their distance from one another, the women in the front, the men bringing up the rear, their voices droning in some private conversation—somewhat heated from the inflections Edwina could hear.

"Whatever am I going to say to my papa?" Crescencia murmured behind her hand. "You didn't tell me Mr. Dufresne was coming."

"I had no idea," Edwina whispered. "But we'll still follow the plan. We'll go to your house and tell your father that you're having dinner with me."

"And t-two gentlemen," she squeaked.

"That's a minor detail."

"Not to my papa. He doesn't think a man's attentions toward me will be honorable because I'm an old maid, so he'll want to know why Mr. Dufresne wants to take me out to dinner. He'll interrogate him like he was in the courtroom and Mr. Dufresne was on trial. It'll be the most embarrassing thing I'll ever have to live through."

"No, it won't. I'll be with you and I won't let your father do anything to make you uncomfortable."

Crescencia lived one house up from the corner at Sugar Maple, and as they approached, Edwina's steps slowed.

"If you'll excuse us a moment," Edwina said, "there's something we need to do."

Edwina linked her arm through Crescencia's and they hurriedly took the walkway and went inside. Mr. Stykem lounged in a smoking jacket, the parlor thick with cigar smoke. When Crescencia came bursting in, he looked over the newspaper's edge.

"What's that dress you've got on, Crescencia?" he asked, then gruffly accused her. "Are you wearing French perfume?"

"Oh, heaven's no!" she lied. "I wouldn't ever . . . I'm . . . allergic. And the dress—I borrowed it from Miss

Edwina," she blurted out. "We're going to dinner at the restaurant because I haven't eaten any dinner—"

"I'm aware of that. I don't smell anything in the oven—"

"There's corned beef in a tin and bread's in the pantry. The can opener's in the drawer by the sink and . . . and, well, that's all. I won't be home late. Good-bye, Papa."

She dragged Edwina from the room before she could get a word out, and the pair scurried down the porch steps. They'd barely reached the street when Alastair Stykem's lawyer voice boomed from the veranda.

"Crescencia, what's all this folderol? Who's out there? Is that you, Wolcott?"

Mr. Dufresne stepped forward, gently took Crescencia by the elbow, and guided her up the walkway. "I believe I should get your father's permission to buy you dinner."

That was the last Edwina could hear. She and Tom stayed on the sidewalk, neither making eye contact with the other. Both gazed at the porch, where Mr. Dufresne seemed to be doing all the talking while Crescencia intermittently buried her nose in her handkerchief and held onto the railing.

Tom reached into his breast pocket for a pack of cigarettes, one of which he tapped out. Edwina was obliged to give him a reproachful glare.

"Sorry," he muttered, and put the pack back. Then he hunched his shoulders while digging his hands into his pockets. "Going to get cold tonight."

"Do you think it will snow on Halloween?" she returned, her question just as unimaginative.

"The almanac said it's a possibility."

She rolled a pebble beneath the toe of her patent leather shoe. "We didn't have snow on Halloween last year."

"Do you like snow?"

"I don't mind it."

Edwina wanted to scream in agony. This was ridiculous. It wasn't as if they were meeting for the first time.

He'd seen her in her bare nothings—twice. They were beyond strangers. Or rather, they were—sort of, but more along the lines of intimate strangers. They should have been able to carry on a conversation that wasn't meaningless.

"Aside from the time I took you home, I've never been on this street." Tom's eyes fell on the tree-shadowed lot next to Crescencia's home. A sign with FOR SALE written on it had been stuck in the weeds.

Edwina followed his gaze. "It's a nice street."

"North-end," he replied simply.

A layer of quiet so heavy descended upon them, Edwina's shoulders ached. Fortunately, Crescencia and Mr. Dufresne soon returned. Crescencia actually had the hint of a smile on her mouth. "Papa said it was okay that I accompany you. He gave Mr. Dufresne permission to walk me home afterward."

Edwina detected a glow on the other woman's cheeks, but unlike that of her shy blushes, this was born of optimism. From where she got her courage, Edwina couldn't be sure. But it must have been something Mr. Dufresne had said, because no longer were her words clipped with stutters.

This time when they set out, there was a distinct pairing of the couples. Mr. Dufresne and Crescencia took the front—her hand tucked into his arm on his kind insistence, while Edwina and Tom strolled in back. A twinge of envy took hold of Edwina. But she ignored it.

As they passed residences, gentlemen returning from their outings and the few ladies who happened to be at the door to receive their husbands all hushed as if at a funeral. Nobody had ever seen Crescencia Stykem and Edwina Huntington in the company of callers.

Walking by the town square gazebo with its honeysuckle vines going bare for the winter, they ran into Mrs. Plunkett. She nearly dropped her parcel but didn't utter a word other than a muffled greeting as she proceeded on her way with light feet unbefitting of a woman her size.

As soon as Mrs. Plunkett had cleared them, Edwina glanced over her shoulder and saw that the woman had broken out in a cumbersome run—heading straight for Mrs. Elward's residence.

Edwina knew that soon the ladies would be like bees in a stirred beehive. Voices would be buzzing in the thickening dusk. Gossip would be swapped over side fences and humming through Harmony better than by any telegraph line.

Edwina held her skirt high enough to elude the mud on the sidewalk, but not so high as to reveal an instep. The nighttime scene around them was quite different from that when the four of them had gone to the restaurant. Lamps had been lit in houses, and people had tucked themselves into parlors for the night. No one came out to their stoop to get a good eyeful. What they'd already seen had been enough to last them through the week.

Nobody could find fault in the two couples' being together. That wasn't what had caused the commotion. Ladies and gentlemen of unmarried status often went out singularly or in couples. In this instance, the chatter had been ignited by the fact that Edwina and Crescencia had never before been asked to do so. To the town, they were old bachelor girls resigned to solitary lives.

Edwina had gone through the motions of dinner, not tasting her food or even relaxing enough to enjoy the conversation Mr. Dufresne monopolized with Cressie. The other woman had calmed enough that a time or two, she'd actually tittered behind a coy handkerchief. The transformation was incredible. What could Shay Dufresne possibly have said to Crescencia's father?

She and Tom had sat next to one another, but they might as well have been a mile apart. Barely a word exchanged was between them aside from yes and no, or "Is that so?" When the bill came to the table, it was a relief for Edwina that she could finally go home.

After leaving Mr. Dufresne and Crescencia at her

picket gate, Tom continued on with Edwina. Flower bed
borders made a ghostly fringe along the sidewalk, and
leaf piles that had been burned earlier in the day still
gave off a fall scent that clung to the air. A full moon
had risen to the height of rooftops; bare sycamore
boughs spread like dark veins against its creamy face.

From the distant mill pond, frogs croaked. The only
other night song was made by Edwina's voile hem and
muslin petticoat ruffles swishing at Tom's ankle as they
walked side by side.

Once at her fence, Edwina laid her hand on the latch
and turned to bid Tom good evening. But he rested his
fingers over hers and undid the lock himself, holding the
gate open and standing aside so that she could pass
through first. He followed.

She took the steps and stopped on the porch. "Thank
you again for dinner."

"You didn't eat much."

"I'm sorry."

"Don't be."

She fidgeted with an uncharacteristically loose thread
on her glove, then glanced at him. At first, she'd felt this
way with Ludie: expectant, unsure, spoiling for trouble.
But all the times after he'd proposed, their good-nights
had been filled with quick, breathless kisses and entwined fingers that didn't want to separate until the very
last when he tipped his hat and whispered he loved her.

With Tom, she felt inexperienced, confused. Her mind
told her to be wary, while her body gave her a distinctly
different message: longing and want, the desire to be
held and adored, kissed, touched. How she missed
intimacy . . . a stolen glance of affection that spoke vol-
umes, a brush of a hand on her cheek. A meeting of
bare feet, flirting . . . connecting.

Suddenly, Edwina wanted to cry. She'd given up so
much . . . and for what? To live alone. Be lonely.

For the rest of her life.

"I need to go in," her voice, fragile with heartbreak,
cracked as she spoke.

Tom stopped her before she could reach the doorknob. "It's not that cold yet." His hand slipped around her waist. "Sit with me."

Guiding her to the wicker porch swing, he made her sit, then lowered himself beside her. Black fabric met a denim-clad thigh—her soft skirt and his sinewy leg. He lowered his arm over the swing's back. If he chose to, his fingers could brush her collar . . . stroke her hair . . . trace her earlobe.

Tightly knitting her hands and resting them on her lap, she told herself not to imagine such things. Instead, she looked at the inky sky—what little could be seen with the porch awning as a canopy. Swathed in darkness, the swing provided total privacy. Even if she'd turned up the parlor lamp to somewhat illuminate the outside, tall camellia bushes created an arbor in which to hide.

With his long leg stretched out in front of him, Tom set the swing in motion, a slow and lazy pushing forward and back. The chains gave off a rhythmic yet soothing squeak. Having not been used in years, the metal hardware had rusted from inattention.

"You sit out here much?" Tom asked, his voice sluicing over her like a warm afternoon.

"I used to. I haven't had the time since I've been back."

"I remember when you came home."

"You do?"

"Saw you walking alongside the baggage car at the station. I was down there meeting some fellows."

Edwina snuck a glimpse at his profile. The brim of his hat kept half his face in obscurity; his mouth was barely discernable. She watched, mesmerized, as his lips moved while he continued. "I've been to a lot of places. Never Chicago, though. Think you'll ever go back?"

"No. Never." Her reply came too quickly and too emphatically.

"You didn't like it."

Disquiet caused her to shiver. "I liked it too much."

Tom's hand slid to her shoulder. His fingertips grazed

the side of her neck—whether intentionally or not, she didn't want to guess.

"You said you'd leave here if you could. Where would you go?"

Through the creak of the chains, she said in a quiet voice, "Denver. Or maybe California."

Calloused fingertips whispered across her nape. No accident. Tingles worked their way across her skin.

"Why don't you?"

Enthralled as she was with the leisure of Tom's touch, his question didn't immediately register. When it did, she bit back the truth. It was too humbling to admit; she couldn't tell him that she was tied to Harmony until she paid off her parents' debts, that she could not abandon this house because her mother had made her promise—actually swear on the Bible—that she wouldn't sell it. It was all Edwina would have as a legacy from her family. The home had belonged to her paternal grandmother before she'd passed it onto Father.

"I just can't, is all," she said, forcing her melancholy to remain at bay. "But I will. One day."

"So you'll leave. You won't get married because you're going to work for your keep. Aspirations, you said." His recollection wasn't patronizing, yet it didn't sound as if he approved.

"Yes, I am. As an accountant." Pride caused her to sit up and face him. "I'm efficient with numbers. I've already been offered a position, but . . ."—a lump caught in her throat, and she slumped back into the seat—". . . but I had to turn it down." On a swing of the seat, she extended her legs out in front of her, pointing her toes. "I'll get another offer when the time's right."

"I'm sure you will."

Smiling, she asked, "How do you know?"

"Don't. Not really. Just figuring."

A peaceful lull fell across them, as snug and cozy as an heirloom quilt.

Edwina broke the silence. "What about you? Where have you been?"

"Texas mostly. Washington. Idaho. Wyoming. The New Mexico territory."

"Doing what?"

"Whatever paid." The flash of his grin caught her attention.

" 'Whatever' sounds disreputable," she remarked in jest.

"Could be."

"Is that how you learned to rag?"

His leg raised even with hers; in a playful manner, his ankle nudged the top of her shoe, as if to engage her foot in a suspended dance. "I picked it up here and there. At the troubadour shows in Near-Town on the Arkansas side. And Jig Top tents that came through wherever I happened to be when they came through." With a dip of his toe, he caught her foot behind the ankle so that her calf rested on his. Such a seemingly innocent gesture, but it had her somewhat breathless.

"Where'd you pick up the moves?" he asked.

If she told him about the Peacherine Club, he'd think her immoral for going to the so-called arcades of sin. But he'd already seen that many things about her didn't add up. And as far as she knew, he'd kept everything to himself. He had the means to destroy her reputation and had not. Why?

Tom smoothed the seam of her cape down her shoulder as nonchalantly as if he'd done so countless times. His voice came to her, a little defensive, a little resigned, when he said, "Hell, after some of the low-down tricks that have gone on the past month—and I'm blaming both of us—I could see why you wouldn't want to tell me squat about yourself."

Her soft laughter couldn't be suppressed. "Does this mean you're calling a truce?"

"I can speak only for myself. Barkly's his own man."

Tom lowered his leg; Edwina's knee naturally rested on top of his. The black of her skirt draped intimately over them; petticoat ruffles peeked out in a seductive tumble of lace. She couldn't stop staring at the place where they touched.

"All right, I call a truce, too." If she had the morality she purported to have, she would have immediately rectified their sitting arrangement. But she didn't. She found herself growing more and more seduced and liking it—even wanting to flirt with the possibilities herself. Did she dare? "I learned how to dance in the Peacherine Club, a waterfront arcade in Chicago."

"Who taught you?"

The answer to that question was harder to admit. She hadn't spoken Ludie's name aloud since leaving. Not even to her mother. While Edwina had tended her, they'd spent long hours talking about Edwina's childhood, her father, and how times were changing. Chicago never came up. Or when it did, Edwina steered the conversation away. How could she reminisce about college without talking about Ludlow? Her mother never knew she'd had a beau to step out with, never knew she'd been engaged . . . however briefly.

Edwina's mother's fondest wish was that Edwina marry and raise a family. She'd told her so frequently those last days when she drifted in and out of delirium. But Edwina had never encouraged that hope. Instead, she'd reminded her mother of the business degree she had and how wonderful it would be to travel and know she was qualified to support herself.

"Ed?" Tom's resonant voice broke through her reverie.

"Boys from the Merchant's College went to the Peacherine," Edwina replied vaguely. "There were always a few willing to show us how to dance."

"Sounds like college might be more than books and stale teachers." His tone held a lightness and measure of joshing, as if he knew she was battling the ghosts of her past and wanted to keep her from growing too wistful.

"You could go to college," she said. "It doesn't matter how old you are."

"Hell," he mumbled, his fingers resting on her shoulder. "No college would take a man who never made it through school."

That he'd confess such a thing to her held her in suspended surprise. Surely a man like Tom Wolcott didn't go around letting people know his weaknesses. He was too confident of other abilities. Like the ones that allowed him to guide Eastern gentlemen on hunts and own and operate his own store—no small feat. That took ingenuity and drive. Many wouldn't attempt such a venture.

"I think you could get a school diploma through correspondence classes. It's not as if you'd have to sit in a classroom again."

"I'm too old for book learning," he scoffed. "What do I need to know about who was president in 1854?"

"Franklin Pierce." The reply came automatically. Too late she could see that she'd flaunted her superiority when it came to education. She took liberties by laying a consoling hand lightly on his wrist. "I didn't mean that. It just slipped out. And really, you are right. I've never had to use that information for anything."

His silence made her self-conscious, and she withdrew her hand. What had gotten into her to touch him so?

Everything was getting muddled up. She couldn't pretend with Tom. He'd seen too much. She really should try to be more careful about what she said . . . what she did. She couldn't let him know anything more. There were certain things nobody could find out, things that couldn't be blamed on youthful whim and curiosity. Tom, with his nonliberal views, would condemn her.

"Why won't you get married, Ed?"

The query startled her and caused her heartbeat to race. She could say nothing—at least not the truth.

"You seem like the type to me. A lot of variety to offer a man if you show him your true colors." The latter was said with a smile she didn't have to see. "You're smart, and you're something to look at."

At the base of her throat, her pulse drummed. The

emptiness in her heart was momentarily filled. She wanted him to find her desirable, but to what end? A dangerous one. *An affair . . . that's all it would be. Oh, help. Where did that thought come from?*

"Although I can't attest to all your cooking," he continued, "you bake a fine cookie."

On that, she had to laugh. "I didn't make those nut wafer cookies. Marvel-Anne did."

"Is that a fact?"

"Yes."

Through a lift at the corners of his mouth, he said accusingly, "Why, you liar."

Still smiling, she fought against further laughter. "I'm sorry. The situation was dire."

She could view the flash of white from his teeth. He had a smile she enjoyed. But too soon, the curves fell and his mouth grew serious. "So why is it?"

He didn't have to specify what *it* was. She knew.

With a sigh she hoped sounded airy, she replied, "Oh, I don't know. . . . It's just not for me. I don't want to be tied to one place. One person."

Her eyes lowered. She couldn't face him. Lying wasn't easy for her, yet she seemed to be doing a lot of it lately—mostly to herself.

"Okay, Ed," came his quiet response. "Whatever you say."

There was a lot she wanted to say.

There was nothing she could say.

Warm fingers meshed with hers. Tom's left arm reached over to pull her into his chest, comforting and secure. She allowed it. If only for a moment, she could fool herself into thinking there was no harm.

The creak of the swing and the sound of Tom's heart against her ear were the only things she heard. She ignored the voice in her head that cautioned, warned. She didn't want to worry about anything—nothing but the tenderness she felt with Tom's arms around her.

His mouth found her temple and grazed it with a light kiss. She pulled in her breath and tipped her face toward his. In the disguise of darkness, she succumbed to what felt natural: snuggling next to Tom and drawing in the warmth of his clothing, his smell until such a closeness became sweet agony.

Why was she allowing herself to be wooed on a porch swing? Nothing could come of a relationship between them. Innocent flirtations would only wound. She had resolved her fate to be an unshared life, an unshared bed. Unless . . .

She wasn't good enough to marry. Every man wanted an ideal woman to be his bride. That wasn't her. Not anymore. Even Tom Wolcott deserved better. It wasn't out of any kind of pity for herself that she thought this. Truth was a strong adversary. She couldn't fend it off and think it didn't matter.

So, why then, did she welcome Tom's kiss when his mouth crushed hers? All rationality fled. The well-rehearsed arguments against this sort of thing that she'd waged in her head were lost. In their stead, she moaned in blatant ecstasy as Tom traced the seam of her mouth. They softly mapped out each others' lips, slanting and giving, searching and seeking pleasure. Pure fire shot through Edwina. She'd never known such an intensity. Tongues gently stroked as she explored the velvet satin of his mouth.

She shamelessly slid her arms over Tom's shoulders to pull him closer. His hands hastened down her sides, seeking the swells of her breasts. Her nipples beaded. Their breaths mingled, fevered and raspy. Tom lowered his mouth to the side of her neck, the sensitive curve leading to her shoulder. Her rained kisses across her hot skin, up toward her ear, teasing the lobe with his teeth. She tingled everywhere. His mouth captured hers again, possessively.

Madness. She should tell him to stop. She cried out, but her words were lost in a whimper as his tongue swirled across hers. Her hand rose to his chest just enough to push a slit of distance between them. Her intentions had been to try to clear her head, but the small opening gave room for his palm to cup her breast, run his blunt fingertips over her puckered nipple. The exquisite sensations raging through her body were nerve-shattering.

But she knew better . . . she'd been down this road before.

"Tom . . ." she whispered against his mouth. "Please."

The word wasn't a plea for more. Her tone begged that he be the one to put a stop to it all—because she couldn't.

His hands fell still. Their lips broke apart. An instant of regret fluttered in her heart.

Tom mumbled, "I'm sorry. I shouldn't have—"

"No." Her trembling fingertips pressed against his lips. "It's not your fault. It's mine."

She quickly went to her feet, unable to bear being close to him without his arms around her. Out of the need to occupy her hands for fear she'd reach out to him, she fidgeted with the frogs of her cape, adjusting, straightening. "I have to go in. Thank you for tonight."

"Edwina. Don't." His warm fingers closed over her wrist; her pulse tripped against his hold. "Don't run away." Then quietly, "Are you afraid I'm thinking less of you?"

She couldn't speak. Her breathing was still hurried, her face still flushed.

"If you do, you're wrong."

Grateful the dark veranda hid her shame, she refused to meet his eyes. If he only knew what kind of woman she really was—the kind of woman she was in agony considering being again . . . with him.

"Edwina . . ."

"You were right when you said that I'm not who you think I am. You don't know me."

"Then let me."

The words that followed were barely audible. "You'll be disappointed."

He released her. His voice hardened as he said measuredly, "Don't decide for me, Edwina."

She could say nothing further.

He'd gone for the steps and was soon enveloped by the night.

Tom had asked Shay to mind the store for a couple of hours. He'd told him he wanted to try out a new lure and get in some angling before the weather turned too raw. In actuality, he was counting on the diversion to keep his mind off Edwina.

With a smoke clamped between his lips, Tom stood on the bank of Evergreen Creek where it spilled into a natural pool about a mile down from the sawmill. Using an over-the-shoulder technique, he cast his line into the murky green water. The lure—a luminous soft rubber grasshopper—plunked through the tranquil surface and sank. He began turning the reel handle immediately, trying to bait a cutthroat into striking. Thus far, there had been no takers. The faddish lure came up empty again. He recast.

He must have repeated this motion some fifty-odd times already. Frankly, he didn't give a damn if he caught a fish. Any other day out, and he would have enjoyed himself. Fishing was something he liked; the peacefulness relaxed him. But rather than forcing his head elsewhere, like on the picturesque stream and the golden scenery around it, the automatic motions of cast after cast freed his mind to think about the woman who'd been avoiding him for the past three days.

Many times since, he'd rehashed the night they'd shared on her porch swing. Edwina had more complexity to her than the assembly instructions for a Kankakee portable section boat. No matter how carefully he read her, he couldn't put her together. On the outside, she presented Harmony with a woman of strict decorum and modesty, reserved, flawless conduct. But on the inside, when she allowed herself freedom in his company, she was dynamic, witty, intelligent.

She was much smarter than he. He'd spoken about his lack of education only to see what she'd say. He'd waited for her to look down on him, to ridicule his stupidity. Instead, she'd encouraged him. That hadn't been what he'd expected—or maybe it had, but he'd wanted to think otherwise. He'd wanted her to be like Elizabeth—selfish and unkind. It was easier to think he was toying with her, that he felt nothing.

But he did.

Admiration for Edwina was blossoming. More than idle curiosity, it was an interest far too deep for him to interpret, much less comprehend. He'd never felt this way about a woman, and there had been a fair share of women in his life: different types—those he'd flirted with, worked with, slept with. But he'd never met any that he'd wanted to get to know. He couldn't exactly say why. Perhaps he'd been too restless, too unsure of where he wanted to go, on the move with nothing to offer. But now that he'd ended up in a town where he intended to set down roots, things had changed. He'd changed.

And he thought that Edwina might have, too. He hadn't known her before she went to Chicago, but he sensed that something had happened to her there. She'd tried her wings and liked flying. He couldn't fault her for that. Everyone was entitled to see a little slice of life before settling down. But along with gaiety and dancing at the Peacherine Club and pitching balls at the Midway Plaisance, she'd taken her awakening a step farther. How far, he wasn't sure. There was a reason she overcompensated with the proper lady stuff. She must have done something improper . . . and now she didn't want anyone to find out.

Tom considered himself a forgiving man. God knew he'd done his share of hell-raising. Whatever Edwina thought was so terrible, he probably would think nothing of.

Reeling in his line and sailing it out over the water once more, Tom reflected on his conversation earlier in the day with Otto Healy, the agent at Granite Home and Farm Realty. The office walls had been crammed with framed architectural sketches, representations of

Gothic, Italian, Norman, and Swiss styles, the typical eclectic homes with such features as mansard roofs, arched windows, Elizabethan stickwork, and pinnacles. His ignorance must have been obvious, because after he'd looked bewildered at the sketches, Healy had pointed out the various facets.

"What can I do for you, Mr. Wolcott?" The agent had taken a seat at a desk and gestured for Tom to do likewise.

He slipped into the chair and lifted his heel on his knee. "That property on Sycamore Drive next to the Stykem place. How much are you asking for it?"

After rifling through a mound of papers, Healy had slid a sheet out of a folder. "It's a full acre. Semiwooded. You'd have to get rid of some trees if you wanted to build on it." Gazing down through the document, he'd said, "Eight-forty."

Tom had nodded, the spark of hope he'd been holding onto fizzling.

"Are you interested in the parcel, Mr. Wolcott?"

He hated to lay down his cards, especially when he didn't have a hand to play. "I might be. How much would it cost to put a house on that lot?"

An assortment of home catalogues had littered the edge of the desk. "Depends on what you want to build on it. You can hire your own architect and have him draw up customized plans. Of course that'll mean you'll have to go up to Helena. I don't have those services at my disposal here. Or you can look through the catalogues and pick out something already drawn up."

He had shoved one toward Tom and, out of courtesy, Tom had thumbed through it. All the houses had seemed elaborate to him—big, more than enough room for one man. But if that man had plans on putting a wife and family inside, they were just the ticket. Only from what he saw, they were so far out of his budget, he couldn't imagine ever owning one. A three-story with a stone foundation and latticework had caught his eye. It had a long veranda and molded itself around the porch. The whole of the house had reminded him of Edwina's.

"This one." He'd handed Healy the catalogue. "How much for it?"

The agent had cross-referenced design number five-seventy-six to a specification chart. "Twenty-nine hundred."

Tom had folded. He was out. Not a chance. No way, nohow. Not in this lifetime.

"There would be other costs, of course. Excavation of the land is twenty-five cents a cubic yard. Any rough stonework below grade would run the same. And if you want to modify the plans, there would be an extra charge." Seeing Tom's lack of enthusiasm, he'd rushed to add, "Now, I do have properties available for occupation. No builder's fees. I'd be happy to show them to you, Mr. Wolcott."

"Do they run considerably lower than twenty-nine hundred?"

"Well, some . . . but most are over two thousand." Once again, detecting Tom's uneasiness, Healy had quickly added, "You could still build, Mr. Wolcott. Loans are available. Have you checked with the bank?"

"No."

"I suggest you do so. And if Sycamore is too expensive for you, I do have a small lot parallel to the tracks that's two hundred and eighty."

South of the tracks. Tom had already stood and extended his hand. "I thank you for your time, Mr. Healy."

The agent had grasped his hand. "Anytime, Mr. Wolcott. If you have any further questions, please don't hesitate to drop on by." Then with a jovial curling of thumbs under the suspenders over his shoulders, he'd commented, "As soon as I'm able, I'll have to get by your store and check out the camping equipment."

"You do that."

Tom had departed with the feeling of complete failure suffocating him. He'd been fooling himself when he thought he could buy a house that . . .

. . . that Edwina might like.

The thought had sobered him. He hadn't even realized he'd been thinking along those lines. The notion was premature. He was getting ahead of himself. They hadn't spent very much time together.

But sometimes a man just . . . suspected.

Staring at the water, Tom didn't bother to recast his line. He packed up what little he'd brought in a creel and headed back to the store, feeling no less discontent than when he left.

A bank loan.

Hell, that meant he'd have to put up his business as collateral. But the building and everything inside was worth around a thousand, maybe fifteen hundred. Would that be enough? And if his business did poorly or failed, he'd lose everything. Risky. But was buying a house worth taking the risk? Tom had no answer as he walked into the store and set his pole on the counter.

Shay handed him a witch-shaped card. "Cressie brought this by while you were out. It's for both of us."

Tom took it and said, " 'Cressie'?"

"I see no reason to call her Miss Stykem. We've seen each other every day since Saturday—making it a total of fourteen hours in each other's company. In my book, that's long enough to be calling her something more familiar. Besides, I don't think Crescencia suits her. It's too prissy."

Gazing at a white invitation written with drippy red ink, Tom read:

FELLOW SPOOK:

YOU ARE HEREBY NOTIFIED TO ATTEND A GHOST CONVENTION ON THE 31ST OF OCTOBER, OTHERWISE KNOWN AS HALLOWEEN. COME AT EIGHT O'CLOCK AND PARK YOUR TROUBLES AT THE DOOR. THE PASSWORD IS "FUN." FULL GHOSTLY REGALIA IS REQUIRED. BE SURE TO COME TO SEE WHAT HAPPENS AT THE STROKE OF TWELVE.

MISS EDWINA HUNTINGTON

HIGH GHOST

10 SYCAMORE DRIVE

Looking up, Tom frowned. "Why does she want us to come to some costume party?"

"It's for those doctors that're in town—you know, the ones I'm taking up to Elk Flat on Thursday. Cressie said the whole thing is some kind of matchmaking session." Shay chuckled. "This ought to be good, watching those women fall over themselves for attention."

Tom didn't necessarily like that idea. But what did intrigue him was seeing Edwina. She'd conveniently been gone from the school by the time he closed, and she hadn't come to class until the girls had arrived, so there'd been no time to talk to her beforehand.

Setting the invitation down, Tom asked, "So what're you going to wear?"

With a wide grin, Shay pointed toward the corner. "That."

Tom had to crack a smile. "You've got to be joking."

Chapter

❦ 11 ❦

On Edwina's porch, a cluster of jack-o'-lanterns glowed. They sat on the railing and the steps leading to the front door. She had even put them around the side of the house so that those taking some air through the parlor door could do so and still enjoy the atmosphere. Sun-golden cornstalks had been decoratively tied to the porch posts. On the front door, a big bunch of orange crepe hung in a bow.

Edwina, Crescencia, and Marvel-Anne worked in the kitchen, preparing last-minute items. While stacking the sand*witches,* Crescencia chattered ceaselessly. Periodically, Edwina would sneak a peek at her and smile. This evening, the young woman was actually stunning. Her complexion softly glowed, and she'd put up her hair with rhinestone combs and a barrette. The costume she'd chosen was a rose-printed mousseline de soie made up over all silk; and she'd brought a white parasol with chiffon ruffles half a yard wide. She said she was portraying Jane Austen.

"Did I happen to tell you what Mr. Dufresne said to Papa that night we went out to dinner?"

Only a hundred times. Giving Crescencia an inviting

smile, she said warmly, "I think you might have, but please refresh me."

"Well, he went right up to my papa and shook his hand. He said he'd been intending to call on me sooner but that he'd been away on business. Then he just came right out and said, 'Mr. Stykem, I'd surely like your permission to take your daughter out for dinner. And even if you don't give me it, I'm going to take her anyway.' Well, of course, Papa gave him his permission. Then Mr. Dufresne said that my mother must have been a very beautiful woman because I surely reflected the image of that beauty. And *then* he said he hoped my papa would approve of him, because he planned on calling for me as frequently as he could." Crescencia put the sandwich platter next to the deviled eggs and devil's food cake Marvel-Anne had just finished icing.

"I'm happy that you're happy, dear."

"Oh," she exclaimed, "I'm so very happy! Why, I've hardly stuttered a bit since Mr. Dufresne said what he did to my papa. I can't imagine why."

"I think it's because Mr. Dufresne gives you the confidence that you didn't believe enough to give to yourself."

"Maybe." Then she giggled, as if recalling some private moment—of course having to do with Shay Dufresne.

Ever since Saturday night, Crescencia hadn't been herself. Edwina had witnessed her breathlessly laughing in class over the most trite things. She'd never heard her laugh so. Her voice wasn't the same; neither were her eyes, now wide with joy behind the lenses of her glasses. Even her face seemed softer, more mature.

"Well, what else shall we do?" Crescencia asked.

Marvel-Anne set the last pumpkin pie on the table and said, "If it's all right with you, Miss Edwina, I'd just as soon serve in the parlor so no one has a reason to traipse through our dining room and get any ideas to come into my kitchen."

Edwina nodded. "Of course." Though the kitchen

area was flawless as usual. Even the sink had been scrubbed bone white.

Edwina and Crescencia brought the food to the parlor. Warmth pervaded the room from a softly burning fire in the hearth. The bay window, full of houseplants and a lace-clothed narrow table, was perfect for the array of food. Soon, all was set out. Edwina quickly studied the decorations to make sure she hadn't left anything half done.

Candlelight had been used rather than the oil ceiling lamps, save for the one that lit the stairwell leading upstairs. Sheets were draped across the furniture, as well as over Edwina's dress form and two brooms, for ghosts must have a ghostly atmosphere. Dangling by threads from the ceiling were bats constructed from brown cheesecloth and whalebone; ghosts and skeletons made of brown sticks and sheets had been strategically played in the vestibule. In a corner of the parlor, on a sheet of gutta-percha, a large tub filled with water—apples floating on the still surface—waited for partygoers to bob in.

"Well, now all we need are the guests." Edwina finished the slow circle she'd made and folded her arms beneath her breasts, which were corsetless. For her costume, she'd chosen a Greek chiton of royal purple silk and gold thread that she'd made the previous winter while in college. The party she'd gone to had been with the set of friends she and Abbie traveled with, quite in vogue and liberal. Perhaps Edwina had made a mistake in selecting such a costume to wear within Harmony's little circle. The short loose sleeves ended at her elbows, revealing her arms, and yards upon yards crossed over her shoulders and down her back to form a type of train. The body of the dress flowed narrowly over her legs as if she wore a film.

Just when she felt inclined to go upstairs and change, she recalled the Greek tragedy the ladies' drama club had put on several years ago. All had worn similar such outfits, though not of silk, and headdresses of grape leaves, but not with their hair unbound like hers. So who among them would cast a disapproving eye?

Perhaps she wanted to tempt fate, to prove to herself that what she'd told Tom Wolcott about herself was true. She wasn't what she seemed.

"I hope Mr. Dufresne will be on time," Crescencia said hopefully, making a few adjustments to the rows of flatware; she lined up the punch cups so that they made a perfect semicircle around the crystal bowl.

"I'm certain he'll be here at eight." Edwina glanced at the clock. Only ten minutes away.

"Oh, I'm certain, too." Crescencia said airily. "I wonder what he and Mr. Wolcott will be wearing."

The breath was knocked out of Edwina. "Mr. Wolcott?"

"Why, yes, of course. I invited him on Mr. Dufresne's invitation." Sheepishly gazing through her glasses, she said, "For you, Miss Edwina."

"For me?"

"I believe he's sweet on you." The seriousness in the other woman's gaze was uncompromising. "I saw how he looked at you during dinner. I wasn't so occupied with Mr. Dufresne that I didn't notice."

"Whatever you want to believe, Crescencia, is your business, but let me tell you: Mr. Wolcott and I are never going to be a couple."

"Don't say that. There seems to be hope for me, so there has to be hope for you. I know it."

Edwina put hands to her cheeks. How could she explain to Crescencia that she would never marry? That there was no point in trying to pair her with Tom, much less anyone else?

The opportunity to at least try to set the other woman straight never came. The doorbell cranked, and the first guest arrived. Soon thereafter, the house was filled with people for Edwina to oversee, and she didn't have another moment to speak with Crescencia.

The doctors came as a group—all thirteen of them. Most wore pepper-and-salt suits; some wore peg-top trousers and knobby-toed shoes that were up-to-date. Since they had no costumes, the hotel had supplied them with sheets, which they draped over their shoulders. But their everyday clothes were visible. As smart dressers, they immediately garnered the undivided attention of her students' mothers, who had been milling around with their offspring, awaiting the prominent men's arrival. One in particular caught Edwina's attention as she circulated a tray of oysters.

There was a sort of dash and glitter about him. A diamond horseshoe pin in his tie winked when the candlelight caught it. Black pomaded hair parted smack down the middle and was oiled over his ears. A handlebar mustache curved like two parentheses on either side of his mouth. Edwina noted Mrs. Treber taking a detailed survey of him with her gaze, then nodding to Johannah, who smiled.

Edwina went toward the man and introduced herself. "Welcome to my home. I'm Miss Huntington." She extended her hand. "And you are Dr.—?"

He grasped her hand and vigorously pumped it. "Dr. Fred Teeter. It's a pleasure, Miss Huntington." She slipped her hand from his, none too smoothly; he didn't seem to want to let go and was moving in closer. Nonplused by his behavior, she grew especially perplexed when he leaned forward and examined her half smile. "Beautiful arch. No malocclusion. Flawless gingivae."

"I . . . I beg your pardon?"

"It's nothing, Miss Huntington. Forgive me. Always a professional, I just can't seem to speak to anyone without a *visum scrutari.*" Not giving her the chance to comment, he continued on. "Now who is that fetching young lady over there?"

He motioned in Johannah's direction and Mrs. Treber fluttered her fingertips in a hello while nudging her daughter to stand straighter. "That's Mrs. Treber and her daughter, Johannah. Would you care for an introduction?"

"Indeed I would."

The proper salutations occurred and Edwina left the three of them to move toward the refreshment table. Mr. Brooks and Mr. Calhoon stood there in a discussion she chanced to overhear.

"My wife is trying to convince me to rid myself of an entire dollar on a new corset for my daughter," Mr. Brooks declared through the hum of partygoers.

Mr. Calhoon replied, "I've heard that very same notion in my home. Newfangled folderols. What difference does a corset make?"

"Precisely. Don't these women know the gold standard has been ruined by the trusts?"

"Damn right. The common man will never see good times again."

Edwina politely closed her ears to them, secretly glad she didn't have such a close-minded father in her life to dictate what kind of corset she wore.

Now choosing the petite sandwiches to offer to her guests, Edwina set off again through the room. At her request, Mrs. Kennison played the organ. The lovely notes filtered through the buzz of voices, making for a merry atmosphere. Edwina had seen little of Crescencia and wondered about the woman's absence—until she went into the vestibule and found her monopolized by a man wearing a bearskin. His back was toward her and the mammoth animal had been strapped onto his arms and legs by strips of leather; the massive head rested on his head.

From the way Crescencia blushed and chirped, Edwina quickly deduced the man in question was Mr. Dufresne. She was set on turning away when Crescencia called out to her.

"Miss Edwina, look at what Mr. Dufresne has worn!" She giggled. "Isn't it too much!"

"Oh, my, well . . . yes indeed." Edwina gave Mr. Dufresne a soft smile, yet she didn't keep it for long— Tom came from the darkened hallway that led to where Marvel-Anne was hanging up wraps and coats in the closet.

The stairwell cast half of him in light and the other in the dimness from the parlor. She took in his clothing; no costume. Or perhaps to some, it would be—hunting regalia. Wide shoulders filled out a chamois shirt the color of straw that looked to be as soft as Honey Tiger's fur. Pants made of waterproof duck encased his long legs. About his waist was a gun belt; anchored against his hip, a pistol that looked quite deadly. Boots that reached his knees were supple brown leather; affixed to the side of one was a sheathed knife. On his head, he wore a type of hat with two bills. If he didn't look so devilishly handsome in it, she'd say the headpiece was ridiculous.

"Miss Huntington," he greeted her, his gaze giving her as thorough an inspection as she had given him, sending a thrill up her spine.

"Mr. Wolcott." And that was that. Suddenly quite self-conscious, she felt the need to excuse herself. After all, there was nothing further to be said. "I've got to check on Marvel-Anne. Please enjoy yourselves."

She took her leave through the hallway that connected with the kitchen. Of course Marvel-Anne needed no checking on. The housemaid was as reliable as a church bell.

Once in the kitchen, Edwina found it empty, but no matter. She'd needed the distraction—a moment to gather herself after seeing Tom. She had hoped he wouldn't come, that he wouldn't want to be in her company after their night on the swing. She'd avoided him the past few days, thinking that distance could make her forget about him.

She'd been wrong.

How could she pretend that he didn't exist when at every turn, there was something to remind her of him? In the building they shared, she read his name next to hers on the mailbox. In the grove out back, she couldn't look at the trees without remembering the rope. . . .

Edwina, stop doing this to yourself. It's not to be.

Voices sounded and laughter grew closer to the swinging door that joined the dining room to the kitchen. Not realizing until nearly too late that tears had moistened her eyes, Edwina couldn't let anyone see her. Reaching for the door to the back porch, she let herself out. Only after she'd closed off the jovial voices did she realize she still held a plate of sandwiches. She smiled, then sniffed. She stared at them and let a tear fall down her cheek.

The cool evening drifted over her. She wasn't dressed to be outside, but she wasn't ready to return inside, either. She brushed away the tear. Sinking down onto the steps, she put the plate beside her and gazed at her sandal-covered feet. Cold feet.

A movement from the shrubbery caught her attention and her chin rose. No one she knew would be skulking about. Sitting taller, she called, "Who's that?"

More rustling. What little leaves were left on the shaking bushes sprinkled down into the flower beds. A head appeared, then a long body, slack skin, a tail that wagged. Edwina wrinkled her nose.

Barkly drew up to her, stopped at the base of the steps, and sat. The tail kept on with its to-and-fro motion. He licked his chops. There was a dogged looked about his eyes—what she could see of them, which was mostly the bloodshot whites.

"You've come to beg for food. I believe that's a profession of yours." Gazing undecidedly at the plate of sandwiches, she then looked back at the hound. "Do you know how to do any tricks? Like speak?"

Nothing.

"Shake hands?"

Again, no response.

"Roll over?"

A tongue lolled to the side.

"I should have known your trick capabilities were dead."

At that, Barkly lowered himself onto his haunches, half rolled, and raised his legs, the front paws folded. He went quite still. Even the tail.

Edwina couldn't contain herself from bursting out

laughing. "Of course! He taught you how to play a dead animal!" She picked up a tiny sandwich quarter. "Well done." She praised him in her teacher's tone. "I suppose you've earned it."

By now Barkly had gone back to sitting and glaring and salivating. A long trail of wet spittle drooled from his mouth. She held back a shiver of revulsion over his sloppy deportment, then tossed him the morsel of ham and cheese. He caught the piece in midflight by raising up on his back legs and diving into the air. The tidbit was swallowed whole. Not a single chew. Her precious baby kitty cat would never have been so vulgar—a few sniffs, perhaps walking away as if not interested, then circling back around, a finicky lick here and there, then finally, acceptance. And it would be a good several minutes before the sandwich would be disposed of—sans the bread.

After that singular swallow, Barkly shot back to his begging position.

Edwina shook her head at him. "You'd have to show me something else before you could be rewarded, and since all you know is hooves up, I'm afraid you're out of luck."

"You didn't ask him the right things."

With a start, Edwina turned her head. The door slipped closed behind Tom as he came onto the stoop to join her. He must have been watching through the half window for a while. She tensed, debating whether to rise and go back inside. But before she could think of an appropriate excuse to leave, Tom had slid the plate to the side and sat down next to her.

"He knows a few tricks, but none of the ones you asked him."

Tom made no inquiry as to why she was sitting outside in the dark when her home was filled with party guests she should have been seeing to. She was grateful that he didn't. Explaining herself wouldn't be easy. For she had no answer other than pure melancholy—and over what? *Him.*

To keep her mind off the proximity of his thigh to hers, she asked in a tone that she hoped was conservative, "What other things does he know?"

Reaching for the sandwich plate, Tom said, "He does better when there's a reward. Can you spare a few?"

"A few." She couldn't meet his eyes. It appeared as if he were reading every inch of her. She hated when he undressed her without even so much as touching a single button on her person.

Tom glanced away and held a wedge of bread to Barkly. "Squirrel."

Edwina's brows rose, but even more so when the dog's two front legs came up to his chest and he pressed them together, as if mimicking a squirrel gnawing on a nut. Then going a step farther, the hound made a chittering noise with his teeth. She had no idea how he did it.

"Good boy. Good squirrel." Tom tossed the sandwich, which was consumed in the same manner as before.

Edwina smiled. "I wouldn't have believed it if you told me."

Tom gave her a conspiring wink that sent an avalanche of shivers cascading through her body. "Watch this. Barkly: duck."

The dog got up and proceeded to waddle around in a figure eight, legs loping left and right.

"Good boy. Good duck." Another sandwich wedge flew through the air.

Edwina hugged her knees and good-naturedly said, "I don't suppose he knows how to imitate President McKinley."

"No, but he can salute to Walter Zurick."

A musing curve held Edwina's mouth. Walter Zurick, otherwise known as the Old Soldier, was a Civil War veteran who walked weekly with the aid of his cane to the mercantile for pipe tobacco. Never mind that the store was a square block from his residence; it always took him a solid half-hour to reach his destination.

"Truly?" Edwina queried. "Let me see."

Tom picked up another ham and cheese. "Barkly: salute."

The dog lifted his paw and put it to the length of his nose while lowering his head.

Delighted, Edwina clapped. "I take back half the mean things I said about your dog."

Giving her his most charming grin, Tom said, "What about the other half?"

"He hasn't won all my good grace. He eats like a pig and has no manners. But I do concede he can be . . . amusing."

Tom laughed. Edwina wanted to laugh, too. But not with him. She couldn't. It would be encouraging him. She didn't want to do that . . . but she didn't want to push him away, either. She was torn.

When Tom's laughter died, a spark of purpose lit his eyes. "Edwina," he said and laid his hand over hers. She didn't move. She didn't breathe. "I've missed you."

She hadn't expected him to say that, to admit such a thing. She was touched, immeasurably. As she looked away, the sounds of the revelers filtered through to her ears. "I should go inside" was all she could think to say. That was her problem. She couldn't think. Not when he stroked her fingers with his thumb.

"I know you should, but I want you to myself for a little longer." He didn't wait for her to reply; she didn't think he anticipated her to have one. She probably would have argued the point; he would have insisted she stay. She would have lost.

She was glad when he stayed on a neutral subject. "Shay and Miss Stykem seem to be getting along."

"Yes, they do." The tiny spot where Tom's thumb pad massaged was tingling.

"That's good. Don't you think?"

"Yes." Even her scalp radiated pleasure from just the very light circles he made on her knuckles.

"Romance is good."

"What?" she blurted out, half listening to him.

"I said romance is good. Isn't that why you invited all

these doctors here tonight? In the hopes of pairing some of them off?"

"Well, yes . . . that thought had crossed my mind."

"So why, then, aren't you looking at them for yourself?"

On that, she grew still. She looked askance at him. "You know why. I'm not in the market." The words came out tight.

"Could be you already found somebody."

Oh, she knew now where he was leading with this. Abruptly, she rose to her feet, Tom right on her heels. He put his hands on her shoulders and made her face him. "Admit it, Ed. You like being with me."

"I never said I didn't." Shrugging from his hands, she bent down and picked up the sandwich plate.

As she faced him once more, Tom reached out and smoothed a curl over her shoulder. "You should wear your hair down every day."

She kept her chin level, refusing to let him see how he affected her. He could make her melt inside. "I'm not in costume every day."

"I think you are." His fingertip came down along her jaw. "Because the real Edwina wears her hair down and dances in her underwear."

Edwina opened her mouth to contradict him but didn't get a word out. The door opened and Marvel-Anne filled the doorway. Edwina jumped back, trying to hide the guilty flush on her cheeks.

"So there it is!" Marvel-Anne laid a big-boned hand over her heart, relief set on her face. "They've eaten nearly everything in sight and I thought, 'My heavens, they've eaten Miss Edwina's best English china plate with the pretty bluebirds on it, too!' "

"I was circulating with the sandwiches," Edwina hastily said, "and I came here to see if anyone was in the back . . . which of course they weren't. Mr. Wolcott was just outside looking . . . for his dog. We happened to run into each other."

Marvel-Anne waved off Edwina's explanation. "Well

and good. I just worried myself sick over that plate. It was your grandmother's, God rest her soul. I thought to myself, 'There is a thief amongst us who would steal a treasured plate.' "

Edwina went for the door and nervously laughed. "Well, now we know that isn't true, don't we?"

"Yes indeed!" Marvel-Anne took the plate. "Miss Edwina, you're trembling. My heavens, you don't have a wrapper. Come in before you catch cold."

Without a backward glance, Edwina entered the house and left the door ajar for Tom to come inside whenever he wished. She made her way to the dining room, where she came upon Mrs. Calhoon, Mrs. Elward, and Mrs. Brooks chattering like sparrows. Spying her, they ceased their chirping and gazed speculatively at her. A sinking feeling claimed her stomach. Of course, she should confront them and get it over with. Whatever they were going on about wouldn't die away. On the contrary, it would grow bigger and bigger until it lost proportion and definition.

"Ladies," she said with wax smile on her lips as she approached. "Are you enjoying yourselves?"

"Yes, quite."

"Certainly, my dear."

"Splendid evening."

And then quiet. Quiet as a stone—and just as heavy. Dreading the answer, she asked the question anyway. "Is there something amiss?"

Mrs. Calhoon patted her ginger-colored hair. "Why, no, dear. Should there be?"

"I don't know. You were looking at me as if . . ." She couldn't continue. *As if you know something about me.*

"We were just being inquisitive," Mrs. Brooks said, then gave each of her two companions an exasperating stare. "I see no reason to lie about it."

"I agree." Mrs. Elward plucked at the stiff lace ruching high on her neck. "Mrs. Plunkett told us she saw you and Mr. Wolcott dining out with Crescencia Stykem and a Mr. Dufresne."

An uncertainty crept through Edwina. Slowly, she replied, "Yes, that is true."

"We don't mean to pry," Mrs. Calhoon stated and was quickly seconded by Mrs. Brooks.

"No, we don't mean to pry."

Mrs. Elward added her disclaimer. "Of course we don't mean to pry. Crescencia has bloomed into a rose these past few days, and we know why: the woman is in love."

"Never thought it possible." Mrs. Brooks sighed with a dreamy smile. "She's such a shy thing."

Mrs. Calhoon nodded. "Yes, very shy."

Mrs. Elward took up the slack. "We can see why that dear Crescencia is in the throes of true love, but we couldn't help be curious about your relationship with Mr. Wolcott."

"Curious." Mrs. Brooks's narrow nose looked even narrower as she looked down it. "After all, you told us you had no interest."

"No interest," Mrs. Calhoon repeated.

Then the trio stared at her, all agog to hear her side of things. Surely it did look strange that after claiming to have no regard for Mr. Wolcott, she'd entertained him not a few days later.

Edwina didn't want to say anything they could challenge, so she went about her reply in a sideways manner. "In relation to the teaching of your daughters, how would you feel if I did want to be courted by Mr. Wolcott?"

Mrs. Calhoon's orange brows rose. "For myself, I see no problem so long as your courtship wouldn't interfere with classes. Ladies?"

"He's an upstanding man," Mrs. Brooks remarked, then added, "as far as I can tell."

"He is quite the handsome one," Mrs. Elward concluded with a wide smile on her mouth, as if considering what it would be like were she years younger and not already attached.

"Well, then," Edwina said, smoothing down the waist

of her chiton, "should I decide to permit Mr. Wolcott to court me, I needn't inform you." Mouths fell open, as if they realized they'd somehow just been tricked. "I'm so glad we got this all out in the open. I, for one, feel much better. Please make yourselves at home, ladies. And if you need anything at all, don't hesitate to ask Marvel-Anne."

Edwina left them and tried to keep her small smile of victory inside. It was quite difficult.

The rest of the evening passed with a good time had by all. Edwina made sure she occupied herself with guests every moment so she wouldn't have to face speaking any further with Tom. She saw him from the corner of her eyes as she conversed with the doctors, then as she spoke with the girls and told each of them they were doing splendidly with their deportment.

Somewhere around nine o'clock, the parlor games began and the atmosphere grew chaotic. They played charades and Whistling Biscuits—which turned out to be Dr. William Froggins's forte. Edwina had been introduced to him in passing. He appeared dignified but as bland as a head of lettuce. So when he bested them all by quickly eating his allotment of biscuits, then furiously whistling "Where Did You Get That Hat?" she'd clapped joyously with the others. Since Dr. Froggins could not be beat, they abandoned that for Buzz—a mathematical game that centered around the number seven or multiplications thereof. This was received with enthusiasm; and soon all those playing were laughing and patting backs when one missed his or her turn. They never got past the number sixty-nine before all had dropped out.

Edwina stood off to the side, watching and smiling as Crescencia and Mr. Dufresne joked with one another after their turns. On the opposite side of the room, Tom rested an elbow on the mantel. She caught him watching her. She blushed, then turned away.

Much later, parlor games were given up for the apple bobbing tub. Edwina cleared a remaining dessert dish from a chair in the vestibule, intent on returning it to the kitchen. Afterward, as she passed through the dining room, she came upon Mrs. Calhoon and her daughter, Lucille, speaking in hushed whispers. They were cloistered to the side of the grillwork, out of sight of the parlor.

"Now, precious," Mrs. Calhoon said in a low voice, "you do this little thing for your mother."

"But, Mother, really! I've never fainted in my life."

Stroking the shining red curls of her sixteen-year-old daughter, Mrs. Calhoon insisted, "It's not like you're really fainting. Do you want Camille Kennison to get every man in this room?"

"No."

"Then you must do something." Her frown lost its vigor, and she pressed on with a purr, "Fall in front of Dr. Teeter, my dear. He's the one with the tie pin. The expensive-looking one."

Lucy pursed her lips. "I don't think he's very handsome."

Forgetting herself, she snapped, "What's handsome got to do with it? He's rich." Then she sighed and said, "If ever there was a little angel on earth, it's my Lucille. Now you do like your mama says and you'll be married by June, my precious."

Lucy eyed the doctor who stood conversing with Camille Kennison. "It's not fair she gets all the boys. She always has. All right. I'll do it."

Mrs. Calhoon pinched her cheek. "What a good little dear you are!"

Edwina stifled a gasp, but not in time to stop the young woman from walking directly to Dr. Teeter, gaining his attention with a heavy sigh, then dropping dead at his feet.

"Miss!" Dr. Teeter exclaimed and bent down.

A rush of guests closed in. Edwina had to fight her way through them. She wouldn't expose Lucy, but she wanted to make sure Dr. Teeter didn't get caught by the situation.

"The girl has fainted and hit her head. She needs a doctor!" Dr. Teeter declared, frantically searching the faces gazing down at him.

Mrs. Calhoon, who had rushed to kneel at her daughter's side, screwed up her face. "But you're a doctor."

Dr. Froggins offered to fetch a medical man. "Where's his office?"

"You're supposed to be doctors," Mrs. Plunkett burst in, elbowing her way through.

One of Lucy's eyes opened, and her mother put her hand over it. "Now, wait a moment, Prudence, let's not be hasty." Mrs. Calhoon glared at Mr. Teeter. "Are you or are you not a doctor?"

"Not in a medical capacity, madam."

"What?" Mrs. Calhoon lifted her hand. "Lucille, get up. You're spoiling your costume."

Lucy's eyes fluttered open and she went on with the act to save face. "Why . . . I must have fainted. . . . I feel much better now."

Mrs. Plunkett wanted an answer; her tapping toe was a severe indication. "If you're not medical doctors, what are you?"

"Dentists, madam."

"Dentists!" Mrs. Plunkett gasped, then grimaced.

"Yes, madam," Fred Teeter said in confirmation. "We're from the Mt. Plymouth Dental Conservatory in Massachusetts. We thought you knew."

"She said you were doctors!" Mrs. Plunkett pointed an accusing fat finger at Mrs. Brooks.

Mrs. Brooks blurted out, "But they signed the register as physicians!"

"We are," Dr. Teeter said, intervening. "General practitioners in all phases of dentistry—doctors, just as we call ourselves. The travel arrangements were made under our professional titles—physicians."

Mrs. Plunkett wasn't appeased. To Mrs. Brooks, on whom she blamed the entire fiasco, she growled curtly, "If you had snooped through their rooms as I suggested, we would have known in advance that they were . . .

dentists." Her voluptuous body, dressed as Queen Antoinette, shuddered, as if dentistry were akin to plumbing.

Before Mrs. Brooks had an opportunity to reply, a muffled scream came from across the room. There by the apple bobbing tub, Hildegarde Plunkett stood, wide-eyed, an apple stuck in her mouth.

"Good Lord!" thundered Mr. Kennison, who happened to be nearby. "She's bitten too hard on the apple! She can't get it out of her teeth!"

"Hildegarde! My baby!" Mrs. Plunkett screamed and vaulted toward her daughter, wide skirts and hoops knocking over anything in her way. A slice of cake was lost from the service cart, as was a candle from the center table. Luckily, one of the dentists snuffed the flame before damage could be done.

"Hildegarde!" Reaching her daughter, she shrieked, "Help me! Somebody!"

"Pat her on the back!" someone suggested through the poor girl's choking coughs.

"Pry it out!"

"Slap her!"

"Pull! Hard!"

"You'll do no such thing," Dr. Teeter said through the animated shouts. "You may damage her lateral incisors!"

"Get a knife, then!"

Hildegarde's round face had begun to turn red.

"Cut it out!"

A nasally plea snorted through Hildegarde's nose. "Nnnnnnnoooooo!"

Mrs. Plunkett moaned, "My baby! She needs a doctor!"

"No, madam!" Dr. Froggins shouted above the melee. "She needs a dentist!"

And quite handily, there were thirteen readily available.

Edwina had planned on playing the letter game, Ghosts, at midnight, the winner to be proclaimed the

Halloween spirit for the night, but with the drama Lucille and Hildegarde had stirred, things had broken up, guests exhausted, just before the strike of twelve.

With a hug for each of the girls, Edwina had seen people off at the door. The last was a weary Marvel-Anne, who'd kept up with the dishes as quickly as they'd been soiled. The rest of the clean-up, such as removing the decorations, could wait until the next day.

Leaning into the open doorway while she watched the gate fall closed, Edwina let out a tired sigh. She'd bid Crescencia and Mr. Dufresne good night, but not Tom. He must have left without her noticing. That he hadn't at least said farewell gave her an inexplicable feeling of emptiness. It shouldn't have . . . but it did.

She rested a hand on the jamb, her head down, and was about to shut the door when a deep voice came to her.

"You don't bring in these pumpkins tonight, I guarantee half of them will be in the street tomorrow morning."

"Tom?"

She went out to the porch, hugging her arms against the moist cold. The tiny red glow from a cigarette burned in a shadowy wedge by the camilla bushes. As she approached, she made out his figure. He leaned against the porch railing, one foot crossed in front of the other.

Her voice was barely a whisper. "I thought you'd gone home."

"I was waiting for you." Pitching his cigarette onto the lawn, he pushed away from the rail. "You're cold. Go inside. I'll bring the jack-o'-lanterns in. Where do you want them?"

"I can help," she protested, lowering her hands.

Tom went to her and stood close. The dark heightened her sense of smell; he wore the bayberry cologne. It was heady; she loved the fragrance. He rubbed his warm palms down her bare arms. "You are cold."

The shiver across her skin was caused by something

entirely different than the night air. As she peered through the fringes of her lashes, a tide of pleasure moved through her at his touch. In an unsteady voice, she responded, "You can put them on the dining-room table if it isn't too much trouble."

"No trouble."

"Thank you." Edwina returned to the house, walking through the parlor and finding two candles as she went into the dining room. Setting them on the table, she collected more of the candles while Tom brought in the pumpkins. When they were finished, the parlor had been cast in black and only the dining room glowed in bright light.

Facing each other, Edwina knit her fingers together. "Thank you again."

His eyes held her still. "You're going to bed now?"

The question threw her off guard. "Um . . . yes . . . I . . ."

"Then blow out the candles and I'll walk you through the parlor so you don't trip on anything."

It was her parlor. She'd walked through it countless times in the dark and had never bumped into a thing. She knew its layout by heart, but his offer was too gallant for her to turn down.

With a knowing smile she couldn't wholly contain, she began to blow out the candles, until one by one, they died in a curl of smoke and the room grew bathed in gray. The acrid scent of burnt wicks floated on the air. A hand found hers. She let him hold it. She reached out her other hand and rested it on his arm. The chamois sleeve was indeed as soft as her kitty's belly.

She would have allowed him to kiss her, but he didn't. Instead he said, his voice cloaked in the dark, "You must be tired, Ed. You put on one hell of a party."

A soft laugh passed her lips. "I think that since Dr. Teeter got the apple out of Hildegarde's mouth, there could be a romance budding. Did you happen to notice how she fawned over him?"

Tom's deep laugh mingled with hers. "I heard Mrs.

Plunkett inviting—no, make that *insisting*—he come to dinner as soon as he gets back from hunting."

They'd begun to walk through the house, quietly reminiscing about the party and what they'd seen and heard, just like a married couple. It made her heart ache.

"Who would've figured they'd turn out to be dentists?"

"I should have guessed. He said I had flawless gingivae."

"Whatever that means."

"Hmm." She smiled.

Once at the base of the stairs, Edwina paused with her hand on the newel post. Above her, the lamp's wicks drank oil with a cozy purring. She expected him to kiss her now. But once again, she waited in vain.

"Good night, Edwina." Tom opened the door. "I can see myself out." His glance cut the distance between them. "Sleep well."

Then he was gone. No overtures of affection. No attempts at trying to make her open up to him.

She stood on the step and stared at a pane of the colored glass that was on either side of the door. A revelation came to her: it was the little things a man did for a woman that could make her fall in love with him.

On a quiet sigh, she sensed Tom had been entirely aware of this.

Chapter

❧ 12 ❧

Snow sifted down in tranquil white when Tom got the idea. It had been over a week since the Halloween party and in that time, he'd been doing little things for Edwina, such as raking her side of the grove—or as much of it as he could rationalize was worth the effort. Now the trees were completely bare, so that chore wouldn't have to be done anymore. In the mornings, he arrived early and went in the storeroom and out the closet door on Edwina's side. He built a fire in her heater—moved away from her desk—so that when she came to school, the room was warm. The mail was delivered in the early afternoon, and he would have handed her share to her if she hadn't always beaten him to the mailbox.

He'd gone out of his way to show her that having a man take care of her could have some promise. That an accounting job in Denver or California wouldn't be a likeable trade-off for what she could have here, namely him.

They'd make an unlikely pair, but the possibilities of such a relationship gave him cause to pursue her. He had to find out if Edwina Huntington could be the one for him. No woman before her had made him want to hang around for no good reason other than to talk, smile, joke—dance.

But so far, she hadn't fallen into his arms. And why should she? Aside from what was inside him, what could he give her beyond emptying her rubbish can in the bin? A house didn't seem a likely prospect, but he hadn't given up on one. He had gone to see the bank manager, Fletcher, to see if he could get a loan for that lot on Sycamore and a house on it. For how much, Tom wouldn't know for a few days. He hated to get his hopes up.

Even if he was able to get the money, there was Edwina's world beyond the superficial—the house with the picket fence and all the trimmings women liked: there were her friends, those old bats she hung around with. She obviously liked them or she wouldn't associate with them. He didn't think he'd fit in with them, even if Edwina welcomed him.

He recalled the night of the Halloween party and him standing in the parlor with his mouth clamped shut while others shouted out numbers in that game called Buzz. Even Shay, who'd dropped out of school when Tom had, had gotten into the spirit. Shay had a memory beyond anything Tom could comprehend. When Shay had been taught a subject in school, he'd remembered it. But Tom, he'd felt so stupid. He couldn't even play an asinine parlor game because he didn't understand math.

So he'd been doing some thinking, mostly while staring at his botched ledger sheets. Edwina had studied accounting. She said she was a crack shot at it. She could show him how it was done. She could make him book smart like the others. And in the process, he could spend some time alone with her.

He'd asked her out for dinner this past week; she'd declined. He'd offered to hire a rig and take her for a ride; she'd declined. From the expression on her face, he sensed she wanted to go. Why she said no, he couldn't fathom—unless she was still convinced he wouldn't like her if he got to know her. That was a bunch of bull.

Sitting at the store's counter and tilting the stool on its back legs, Tom watched the snow float in the sky while he waited for Calhoon to deliver the mail. When he did, Edwina would run out to the box and find a surprise waiting for her.

The door opened and a customer came in, full of talk about the weather. For the next few hours, Tom busied himself waiting on the flow of men bustling in and out, standing at the heater drinking hot cider and smoking while talking the latest traps with them. By the day's end as he restocked the corner woodpile for the stove, he'd forgotten about his plan until Edwina came inside, bundled up for her walk home, the cat basket hooked through her arm and a note in her gloved hand.

He straightened, clapping the moss and splinters from his hands. Walking toward her, he said, "Hey, Ed."

She gave him a smile that shot through his heart; then she began to read the unfolded paper: "Required: the services of an accredited accountant. Pay flexible. If interested, apply in person." Looking up, her tapered brows arched. "I take it this is from you."

"Yeah, it was from me." Shoving aside the clutter, he leaned his elbows on the countertop. "So, what do you say? Think you can save my books from ruin?" He stared hopefully at her.

Snow that had fallen on her hat had begun to melt and droplets shimmered in the puffy cluster of flowers and ribbons. The short straw brim was a forest green and brought out the color of her eyes. Loose curls escaped from her upswept hair to tickle her ears, which were decorated with a pair of gold drop earrings that looked to him like acorns.

Her teeth caught her full lower lip. She took a pondering bite of the flesh, then nodded. "All right. Why don't you give me everything you have and I'll take a look at it tonight. I can promise you my rates will be reasonable."

"No, Ed." At his refusal, she tilted her head. "I want you as my bookkeeper, but I want you to show me how you do it. The math and all."

She gazed at him a long moment. The cat moved in the basket, and she gave the lid a tap and soothed the feline with her voice. "But I think you could do better if you had a schoolteacher and schoolbooks to show you math."

"We went through this before. I'm not going back to school. I never will. It's either you or I'll forget it."

Her sigh sounded soft and sweet to him. "It's commendable that you want to learn, and I'm flattered you want me to help you. It's just that . . ."

"What?"

"That," she began with a lick of her lips, "what you're asking would take a lot of time. We'd be alone together a great deal in the evenings. People might talk."

"Let them."

"You might not care about your reputation, but a woman has to—"

"To what? Watch her every move even if it's innocent?" In a jerky motion, he pitched the now-mechanical tail of his zebra clock beneath the counter. "For crying out loud, Edwina, you act as if my proposition is illicit."

He'd gotten her. Color had risen up her neck. "Where do you propose these lessons take place?"

"Wherever you're most comfortable," he replied without a breath. "At the store here or in your classroom."

"My classroom would be more convenient. A desk is better for you to sit at. Posture and correct breathing go with learning."

"Good. I'll get my pencils and ledgers." He'd slipped off the stool and was in midgrab for the books when her voice cut through the room.

"Right now?" she exclaimed. "I didn't think . . ."

"Now's as good a time as any. I'm in the mood."

She gazed at him, indecisiveness written in her eyes. "Marvel-Anne expects me home for dinner by six."

"It's five now. You've got an hour." Then on a whim, he added, "Teacher."

With a squaring of her shoulders and a shake of her head, she declared, "You are the most persistent man."

"Yeah. Because it always pays, Ed." Then in a lower tone, "Always."

Weeks later, Tom still didn't understand multiplication. He'd gotten through the addition and subtraction, the latter giving his patience a good run. For him, it wasn't a matter of reversing the addition like Edwina explained. He just couldn't see that adding backward was subtraction. But with a lot of effort, and counting beneath the desk on his fingers, he'd been able to add and subtract digits up to one hundred—that carrying-over part throwing him for a few days. Edwina told him thousands and ten thousands were the same, just a digit or two more.

"Have you finished?" Edwina's voice drifted to Tom.

He sat at the desk in front of hers where she'd been occupied with work of her own. The paper before him, aside from her neatly penned multiplication problems, remained blank.

Slouching down in his chair and stretching his long legs out, he grew angry with himself for not understanding. For saying he got it when she told him three times three equaled nine. Or four times eight equaled thirty-two. How was he supposed to resolve this when he couldn't grasp the concept? Couldn't make any headway out of it?

"No . . ." he mumbled with irritation. "I haven't finished." His idea of learning math to spend time with her had been a foolish one. He should have come up with another way to get her alone, because his plan had one big flaw: he couldn't learn it. He never would. Some of what she told him made absolutely no sense. And in the process, it made him look more inept at numbers than before.

Edwina rose from her desk and came toward him. She sat in the vacant seat next to his at the long desk. The fragrance of roses clung to her skin. He breathed in and took her inside him. Being math illiterate did have its benefits.

"You haven't done any of them." Her tone was patient, soft, and comforting.

As he looked down at the untouched sheet, humiliation gripped his belly. "I was thinking about them. In my head."

"Tom."

Reluctantly, he gazed at her. She had the prettiest eyes he'd ever seen. He could lose himself in the green . . . pretend he was in the middle of a forest where the civilized world didn't exist. Her hair was in a nimble bun today, the topknot sort of sagging after a long afternoon of class. Tendrils fingered the collar of a white shirtwaist with lace on it and pearly buttons, all in a neat, straight row. A silver filigree pin was anchored in the frothy bow at her throat. If he looked long enough at its base, he could watch her pulse.

"What? Are you giving up on me?" He couldn't keep the deflated tone from his words. He'd failed. They both knew it.

"Absolutely not," she replied. "I wouldn't quit—only if you asked me to." She laid her hands on the desktop and knit her fingers. "Are you asking me to?"

"Maybe I should. There doesn't seem to be much hope."

"Of course there's hope." She stood and went to her desk, gathered several sheets of paper, scissors, and a pen. "It's my fault you're struggling. I've been going about this the wrong way." Taking the seat next to his, she began to cut up the paper into palm-sized pieces, then she wrote simple multiplication problems on them. With the answers. "Some people just can't understand the concept of multiplication. You're one of them. There's nothing wrong with that. For you, it will just mean memorizing your facts. I know you can do that."

"But I won't understand what I'm memorizing."

Stacking the papers, she held one up for him to read. "That doesn't matter. Read these aloud as I show them to you. Like this: One times one is one." Her brows slanted in a frown. "And sit up straight. You can't think properly when you're sliding out of your chair."

It didn't matter how he positioned himself. Concentrating became a struggle when she sat close to him. The urge to caress her cheek, mesh his fingers with hers, was there. He shoved himself upward by the heels of his boots until he was in the chair the way she wanted him. Gazing at the paper, he repeated, "One times one is one."

"Very good." She put that paper behind the ones in her hand. "Next."

"One times two is two," he responded in a monotone. She should have given him a crayon instead of a pencil.

"Next."

"One times three is three."

This continued until he got up to one times ten. Then she cut up more paper and went to numbers timed by twos. Afterward, timed by threes. And so on. She didn't go past multiplications of fives, saying he'd had enough to remember for one afternoon. She gave him the papers and told him to study them. To repeat them aloud. To embed the numbers in his head so that when she showed him a problem without the solution, he could give her an answer in under five seconds.

At five minutes to six o'clock, she didn't begin putting on her outer wear as she had done in the past. A food hamper rested on her desk.

"Not going home for dinner?" he asked from his seat.

"I'm eating here. Marvel-Anne was under the weather, so I sent her home at noon. You can go, if you have to. I've got some things left to do." A little nervously, she shuffled the notebooks in front of her. Her lashes shadowed her cheeks as she looked down, then raised her eyes level to his. "I have more than enough food if you'd like to stay and practice."

The soft hiss of the heating stove surrounded them with a drowsy warmth. Outside, dusk had fallen. A few stars had come out, their light reflected from the snow that he'd shoveled in drifts at the school's walkway. If he left now, he'd be going home to a cold room above a livery, a dinner alone. Only a fool would turn down the opportunity to dine with a pretty woman. And Tom was no fool.

"Sure, Ed. I'd like that."

The shy smile on her mouth was reassuring. She'd wanted him to stay, but she didn't want to come out and ask. "Would you care to eat now?"

"If you want to."

"All right." She rummaged through the hamper and pulled out wax paper–wrapped sandwiches and small cloth-covered containers, then two plates. His brows rose. She'd planned this. He caught her eyes with his; she blushed lightly but said nothing. After she had the food laid out on the table, she invited him to join her. "Please help yourself. I have plenty."

They ate in companionable silence. Honey Tiger, who'd been nosing around on the bookshelf, jumped down on Edwina's desk to beg, using a technique quite the opposite of Barkly's. The cat kneaded the desktop, then rolled on its back and pawed Edwina's hand. The thrum of its purr vibrated in the room. She gave her pet a morsel of cheese and a few soft strokes on the head.

When Tom finished his apple, he asked, "You don't have to tell me if you don't want to, but what was in that big box that came for you today?"

Edwina pushed her own plate away and stood. "Oh, I don't mind telling you. Actually, I'll show you. The reason I'm staying late is to see if I can do it." She went to the storeroom and dragged a box out about a square yard in diameter with the flaps on top already opened.

"Let me help you move that."

"It's not heavy."

But his hands had already pushed hers out of the way. The brief contact of her slender fingers against his brought a tightening to his chest. Ignoring the heat that worked over his skin, he lifted the package to where she directed. Standing back, he watched as she removed one of a dozen tubular hoops that had a bell inside it. The thing reminded him of a large bicycle tire without the spokes.

"What's that?"

"The catalogue called it a bell hoop." She shook the circle, then smiled at the jingle. "It's for balance."

"Balancing what?" Tom leaned into the edge of her desk and folded his arms across his chest.

"Posture," she said simply as if any bonehead would know. Then she put the hoop over her head and fit the back of it against her waist and held snugly to the edges. "I've already read the instructions. You're supposed to keep your chin level." She did so. "Keep your back in uncompromising form. Straight." She stacked herself up neat and tidy. Without moving her head, she said, "Oh. And I forgot one more thing. Hand me a book. That one on my desk. Not the fat one. The red book."

Tom reached behind him and picked up a volume that read *Courtship, Love, and Matrimony.* Interesting. He stretched his hand out and gave it to her. She had to rest the hoop around her neck a moment to put the book—of all places—on her head. The tome promptly fell down. She frowned.

"My hair's in the way," she said as if he knew why. She made adjustments, pulling pins out and shoving them back in at different places. Now the puffy lump of hair, a soft mahogany color in the lamplight that flickered above his head, drooped at her nape. With a confident air, she proceeded once more, settling the book on her head and slowly fitting the hoop back around her waist.

"There," she exclaimed with satisfaction.

Tom didn't see the benefit to this. He'd rather slouch if the mood struck him. "That's good, Edwina." He didn't want to hurt her feelings. "So how long do you have to stand like that?"

"This isn't all, silly," she said, eyes forward and her nose cutely wrinkled with thoughtfulness. "Now I let go of the hoop and keep it around my waist by moving my hips—"

He didn't listen to the rest. That part about her hips had gone straight to the part between his hips. Because she started swaying hers notably. Forward. Sideways. Backward. Sideways. Faster. Bell jingling. Swaying. Seductively. Pivot. Pivot. A mathematical equation popped into his head: silky times whispers equals petticoats. The hoop began to slip down to her undulating hips. She rotated them faster. Forward. Sideways. Backward. Sideways. Bell jingling.

Tom hadn't realized he'd been pressing his fingers tightly on the desk's edge to keep him from lunging. He would have jumped into that damn hoop with her in the next second.

Thwack!

The book fell off her head and slammed onto the floorboards. Her attention challenged, she lost momentum. The hoop came down next, but she struggled with a valiant effort to keep it rotating with a shimmy, shimmy, and a shimmy, but to no avail. It continued to descend. Hips to thighs, knees to full skirts, finally resting at the tips of her shoes after whirling around her, then coming to a wobbly landing.

"Jesus," Tom swore, using his sleeve cuff to wipe the sweat that had beaded on his forehead. "That's no posture equipment. That's . . . that's . . . just not."

"Of course it is. This hoop came with excellent references from the company and quite a testimonial printed in the *Boston Monthly*."

Her lips in a frown, she bent and picked up the hoop. Then she stuffed her hem into it, not without a hang-up in the front that provided a provocative view of stockinged calves. Finally she managed to slip it up the full hem of her skirt.

"Bet you wish you were in your underwear," he commented, taking a bite out of another apple. He had to put something in his hand or he'd be putting it all over her soft curves. "Then you could really give the thing a run for its money."

With a sigh of aggravation, she replied, "When you say things like that, you exasperate me."

He was a little cloudy on what *exasperate* meant but he took it that he'd made a bull's-eye remark because her eyes sparkled with that prideful determination of hers and her lower lip grew faintly rosy from the light snag in which she'd caught it with her teeth.

"I'll exasperate you whenever I want to," he drawled, then took another bite from the apple and slowly chewed.

She shot him a sideways scowl, which was overtaken with an expression of determination. The book went back on her head. The hoop was fitted at her waist. She started over. That swaying of hips that nearly made him choke on the fruit sliding down his throat.

If she were in her underwear, he wouldn't be accountable for his actions. As it was, he could barely stand to watch her. Didn't she realize this was making him go crazy? Forward. Sideways. Backward. Sideways. Faster. Hips thrusting, arms held out, breasts pushed up.

Edwina times bell hoop equals suggestive thoughts from Tom.

He had half a mind to knock the book off her head so she'd stop. But the cat intervened for him. Honey Tiger bounded onto the desk in front of Edwina, then promptly batted at the hoop as it sped within reach of its paw. The book plopped to the floor. Distracted by the cat, she let the hoop come to a slow revolution at her feet.

As soon as she stepped to the desk's side, the cat brushed its long whiskers against her waist. Cradling the feline in her arms, she reprimanded it. "No, no, no, angel kitty. This isn't your toy. No touch. Only Mama." The cat rubbed its head thoroughly over her breasts where she held it close. The cat's paws gingerly kneaded into the soft mounds, pushing lightly as it nuzzled. "No loving, Honey Tiger. I have to practice something right now." This was spoken in a sugar tone. More kneading and whiskers rubbing on breasts.

Feeling like his skin was itching from the inside, Tom couldn't stop himself from saying, "The cat was weaned too soon. It has nipple anxiety."

Her chin flew up. "I beg your pardon?"

"Ah, hell." *Damn cat.* "Never mind."

He ate the rest of the apple and kept quiet while she reassured Honey Tiger, then set her "precious," after much cooing and scratching beneath its chin, on the bookshelf.

"Well," she said, hands efficiently on hips, "I've deduced that the book isn't necessary. The hoop can achieve its purpose by working alone." She reached for the circle on the floor.

"You're not going to do that again."

"Certainly I am." She fit it over her head this time, the hair in the back sort of dragging on her collar, a curl tumbling down her back. "It's kind of fun." Then her face brightened and she reached for another hoop from the box. "Here. Try it."

"The hell I will." He raised his hands.

She shoved the hoop into his palm. "You're always telling me to try things. I ask you to use a simple child's toy and you're . . . well, you're . . . afraid it will insult your male . . . whatever it is you have that's male."

Eyes narrowed. "All of me is male."

"Yes, I'm sure it is."

Brows lifted. "I could show you."

She laughed. Dammit all. *She laughed.*

"What the hell's so funny?"

"You are when you get that look on your face."

"What look?" he asked self-consciously.

"Just that look."

Her vagueness exasperated him. Yeah, that's what it did. It exasperated him. He liked the word.

"Come on. Now you do it like I did. Put it over your head."

That shiny curl kept easing down her back, lower

toward her waist, until the pin keeping it in with the rest of the mass shot out and fell to the floor. She was oblivious to the metal *plunk,* too intent on showing him how to make an ass out of himself.

"On the count of three," she said. "And remember, it's all in the hips."

How could I forget? "I know."

She gave the call and began wiggling. Giggling.

If it were anyone else asking him, Tom wouldn't have done it. But he let the hoop go and started to shimmy his hips like a dancing girl. If anyone ever found out about this . . .

Her window shades weren't closed.

But that slipped his mind when he looked at Edwina, watched her moving in such a seductive way that he ached all the way to the marrow of his bones. His hoop fell onto the floor. He wasn't concentrating. Other things ribaldly fogged his head: breasts, hips, hair falling down, blushing cheeks, parted lips, panting, giggles.

When Edwina's hoop spun down to her feet, she paused. The bow above her upper lip was a little dewy. Her eyes were unusually green and bright and her high cheeks the color of iced roses. The smile she gave him had his heart racing. "Don't you want to do it—"

He couldn't let her finish; his thoughts had been pinpointing in one direction, on one thing. "I'll tell you what I want to do." He cut the distance between them with one big step. "No. I'm not going to tell you. I'm going to show you." His arms slid around her and pulled her tightly against him. Then he kissed her solidly on the mouth. Practically sucked the startled breath right out of her.

She was pliant beneath his exploring hands. He smelled flowers, no rose sachet powder. The fabric cloaking her shoulders felt satiny instead of like simple warm cotton. His fingers wove through her hair and gave the other curls their freedom.

For the briefest of moments, she hesitated. Then she kissed him back. Her frantic breath touched his face; her arms went around his neck. He intensified the kiss, moving his lips over hers. Harder. Every muscle and bone inside him felt like hot iron. The pressure of her mouth on his had him cupping the back of her head to bring her closer. But it was impossible. She was already inside him—not physically, but in his mind, his heart.

His tongue edged her lips farther apart, met with hers, teased. This was no flirtatious porch swing kiss. This was fire and passion. This was unlike anything he'd ever experienced with a woman. It was total, a total engulfment of every part of him.

"You taste like apple," she said through his smothering lips. "Sweet. I like it."

"You're too sweet." His voice was a growl. "Smell too good."

They backed into her desk; something clattered to the floor—pencils. Kisses kept them together; neither cared. God, he could lean over her, open her legs, press himself next to her. A loose ribbon; a slide of linen. Then in her. It would be easy, so easy, but a bittersweet satisfaction. She deserved better than to be taken on a desk. He knew it. And that left him in turmoil: sexually aroused more than he had ever been in his life, but knowing there would be no gratification.

He should stop. He knew he should. In just a moment. But first, he had to steal what he could, imprint the feel of her body into his memory.

"I can't do this . . . not here."

Her rasping words slammed him in the gut. *Not here.* Did that mean she'd wanted more? Was willing to give him more? He would never ruin her and walk away. Not Edwina. Never her.

"You're right," he said against her damp lips. "I shouldn't have . . ."

". . . *We* shouldn't have."

Heartbeats still tattooed against one another. Chest to breast. Hard and flat, soft and rounded. Different. Exquisite.

Her head fell back slightly, her eyes closed and her

lips parted. "I . . . I can't believe this. Me. It's me. I know it is . . . I'm . . . I'm just . . . trouble."

"You're anything but trouble." He couldn't resist kissing the column of her neck. It was so bare. So inviting. Then exhaling, he made her straighten and look at him. "We're playing a game, Edwina. Give a little, take a little. Stop. Start."

Through quick pants and a slow shake of her head, she whispered, "I know."

"What do you want to do?"

She gazed down and pressed fingers to her temple. "I don't know. I just don't know. You make me feel . . . but then I can't . . . Dammit all . . . I can . . . I have been . . ." The thought was left incomplete. Another slow shake of her head. "I just don't know."

Tom let her talk until she ran out of words. Then he gave her a moment in case she wanted to add anything more, hoping that she would say she'd had a void in her life until he'd shown up. But she didn't. And after she fell quiet, he spoke.

"When you decide, Edwina, you tell me. I'll be waiting for you."

The moment would have been poignant, tender, endearing—all of those romantic things that had eluded him all his life with women. But the cat—that damned cat—pounced onto the desktop and purred against her back. The spell broke and she turned to take the creature into her arms. He sensed she'd reached out to a lifeline. Something familiar. Safe.

He might have been able to salvage the mood if it hadn't been for Barkly. He came into the school by way of the storeroom. Tom had left his closet door open in the store. It was how he got to Edwina's for his lessons so he wouldn't track in snow on her floor. Barkly had just discovered the route.

The dewlap on the hound's neck swayed as he lumbered forward, nose stuck to the floor to make sure he didn't miss any scents. When he picked up Tom's, that mournful expression he often wore lit into his red eyes.

The hound looked laughable. His lips were working on something and causing quite a lather on his muzzle. White suds were everywhere.

Edwina caught sight of him and snuggled the cat deeply into her arms as if to shield it from his dog. "Oh my God! He's foaming at the mouth! He's got rabies! Tie him up! He'll get vicious!"

"It's not rabies," Tom said reassuringly; then with irritation, he admonished the hound. "Barkly, damn you. Quit eating soap."

"Soap?"

"He's been finding pieces of it here and there ever since Halloween. After the kids were done soaping windows, they must have pitched the cakes in bushes and flower beds. Because he's been gorging himself on soap for weeks."

"Soap?" she squeaked for the second time.

Tom shrugged. "His favorite is Colgate. But he's not picky. He'll eat any kind."

"How did he get inside the store?"

"He knows how to open the door."

"A soap eater and a lock picker."

"I didn't lock it. He just knows how to turn open knobs."

The cat squirmed, its four feet pushing and fighting. The gold in its eyes diminished as the black irises grew big and round. The look was feisty, a don't-mess-with-me signal. Barkly's wet nostrils twitched. He'd gotten a whiff of what he couldn't see. A deep and resonant bark echoed inside the walls, soap foam splattering from the effort. Then came a growl, a dribble of soap onto the floor, a distracted lick of chops—and a burp.

In spite of Edwina's possessive hold, the cat took off out of her arms, spitting and hissing, then bounded up the bookshelf and perched on the highest possible ledge. Its hair stood on end and it bared needlelike teeth, then gave a prissy spit.

"Get control of your dog!" Edwina said, backing away from Barkly, who in spite of his ominous rumble, was wagging his tail.

Tom took hold of his scruff and dragged him toward the door, a difficult task. The dog weighed eighty-some pounds. "Outside." Before he released him, he opened the store's door and turned the lock, then shut it so Barkly couldn't get in again. Left on the snow, the hound sat. "Stay outside." From Barkly's hang-dog expression, it was clear he was insulted.

Tom went back into the school, and it felt like the cold air had come with him. Edwina had packed her cat in the basket, from which issued muffled meows, and was moving through the room as if he weren't there. The closet door was shut. The coals in the heater had been tamped. She retrieved the rod for the lamp; she pulled it down and turned the wicks. They sputtered into the hot oil. Then darkness fell. The only light came in from what young moonlight reflected off the snow through the windows. He could see her silhouette as she threaded her way between the desks. He kept quiet until she had everything put away, her coat and gloves on, the hat pinned over unbound hair that had been tucked down the back of her wrap.

Her voice came through the cloaking dark. "I think we should go home now. We've done quite . . . enough . . . for the evening."

He didn't feel that way about it. To him, they hadn't done nearly as much kissing as he would have liked.

From the outline of her shoulders, he could tell her stance was businesslike, yet she was upset—she was trembling. Her tone was that of a tutor when she said, "Practice the cards I made for you. Memorize them. Tomorrow we can do sixes if you feel ready."

Disquiet marked his voice. "Will there be a tomorrow?"

"Yes, of course." Then she added softly, "If you want to come back."

"Edwina." Her name sounded fragile to his ears. "I'll come back until you tell me not to."

* * *

Thanksgiving came and went. Edwina had been invited to the Stykems' since it was the first time she'd have to spend the holiday without her mother. Mr. Dufresne had been asked to the residence as well. Tom Wolcott had not. Edwina had been painfully aware of this, but she also understood that the growing relationship between Cressie and Shay Dufresne was a two-way one.

The day before Thanksgiving, Tom gave Edwina a turkey. They'd been going over his eights tables for the third day, the numbers eluding him despite his daily practice with the cards. When they were finished, he went into the store and came back with the paper-wrapped bird. She'd bit the inside of her lip, trying not to give in to the smile that threatened, but the gesture was so Tom—so unsentimental, so wonderfully original. She'd loved the gift all the more.

The next few days had been torture, but not of the hurtful kind. It was an ache inside her, a longing. They hadn't kissed since that night. And each moment that passed without an embrace, without any form of physical intimacy, put Edwina further into a well of tension. Every time she sat next to him, their fingers seemed to have a reason to brush, to touch. He sent an electric current through her, sharp and alive with need. She knew he felt it, too. But he made no move toward her beyond the innocent. He'd said it was up to her.

She knew it. She'd agonized over a decision. When they'd fallen into each other's arms in the school, her shades hadn't been drawn. Anyone could have seen. She'd lost her head; she'd not been thinking. But that was exactly the problem. When she was with Tom, she didn't think about repercussions, only the pleasure she could have.

This afternoon, she'd almost kissed him, been brazen enough to do it. His pencil had fallen and they'd both reached for it. Their hands met, their eyes held. Their foreheads were close, so close. She had but to give in, part her lips, invite him. But fear prevented her from telling him with her gaze, because she could not surrender—not without trying every means to resist him.

But she'd lost.

She knew that now. She'd known it for days. Weeks. Maybe longer. Since before Halloween, the notion had been there . . . the thought of having an illicit . . . She couldn't bring herself to think it, but there was no reason not to. She knew what she was getting into. She had experience.

She had tried to ignore the feelings. When she let them in, they came to her with the force of thunder and whirlwinds—in, of all places, the kitchen, as she'd stood with her hands in greasy dishwater, Marvel-Anne talking to her about keeping a pig in a pen out back as a means of disposing of scraps too old to use in cooking. Edwina had been listening with only vague attention. She'd been meditative, but then her breath had halted and she'd grown cold.

For the first time since returning to Harmony, it was real to her that she could die an old maid, never again to enjoy the feel of a man. Marvel-Anne had gone on in a drone. Edwina had merely nodded, thinking that this is what it came to, spending evenings talking about pigs—and after Marvel-Anne left, spending what remained alone, talking to a cat.

She'd decided right then the risk was worth it. An affair. No marriage, but sex. Oh, could she go through with it? What would he think of her? But hadn't he suggested such already? *More, if you say so.* Men were open to this sort of thing. Tom had said he'd wait for her decision. What other decision could he be waiting for? She trusted him. He'd proven himself by not telling about her dancing. He would keep their relationship to himself. . . .

Discretion must be foremost in this . . . this seduction. *Seduction.* The word played in her head. That's what she was going to do.

Tonight.

Saturday. It was Saturday night, and she'd told Tom

the previous evening that she'd have his books ready for him. He'd progressed enough to know basic math facts, but not debits and credits, assets and liabilities. She'd put his accounting to order in short time. She could have easily given it to him at the store, but she was going to use it as an excuse to get him to her house.

Seven o'clock.

Snow fell in wet plops. The kind everybody cursed. It clung and numbed in seconds. Nobody would be out. Even if somebody saw him walking, they'd have to follow him to her gate to know where he was going.

She'd rolled down all the shades. A single lamp was on in the dining room, where the books waited for his inspection.

Edwina had bathed and perfumed with an essence of roses. She'd dressed in a blue-and-white satin foulard with skirt pleats running all the way down to the hem. Its Gibson collar was white lace; three segments of piping over the shoulders emphasized the shape of her bust. No pins held up her hair. A single grosgrain ribbon kept it tied together. She stood in front of the vestibule mirror. There was barely enough light to see by. In her reflection she looked . . . bewitching—out to bewitch— to seduce.

The doorbell cranked. She gasped, swallowed.

Inhaling and trying to keep her heartbeat steady, she opened the door.

Tom had been about to say hello. His mouth was poised on the word, but he lost sight of it when he caught sight of her. The gaze that he boldly raked over her body, from every facet of her face and hair to her bodice and waist, just about made her crumble. His reaction was more than she could have hoped for.

The seduction had begun.

Chapter

❦ 13 ❧

They sat at the dining-room table. Edwina had positioned her chair directly beside Tom's. She went through the columns and explained how she'd arrived at the figures. Each time she ran her finger down a length of numbers, she leaned toward him. She'd gotten so close once, his hair tickled her cheek. She spoke, yet she did so automatically—just a series of words leaving her lips. Her thoughts were elsewhere. On the aftershave Tom wore. That hint of musk, bayberry. The way he nodded, seemingly intent on what she showed him but obviously distracted.

He asked questions. She watched his mouth, the way his lips moved—firm and sensual. She studied the squareness of his jaw. The way his hair fell over his collar, the ends a little damp from snow that snuck past the brim of his hat. His eyes—she would meet them every now and then, read the message inside them: desire. She saw it. She knew it.

His facial expression changed as he went from being intent on understanding her methods of bookkeeping to being preoccupied. At every opportunity, she touched him. Lightly. Flirtatiously. On the back of the hand. His wrist. His sleeve, where his muscle and broad shoulder filled it out. His neck tendons strained. Yet he remained polite, pretending to be unaffected.

When they had examined every sheet of paper, closed the last book, Edwina wasn't sure what to do next. She'd tempted him at every turn, practically flung herself at him. Did he want a verbal invitation? Did he want her to spell things out?

Nervously toying with the button at her throat, she asked, "Would you care for some tea?"

"No." Hair fell across his brow. The lamplight picked up the various colors of brown, even a hint of bronze.

Biting her lip, she quit fidgeting with the button. "Do you have to leave?"

His eyes bore into hers, silver-blue, icy in color. But the sensual message in them anything but cold. His voice was raspy and low when he replied, "No."

She sighed silently, relieved. She relaxed just a little. He'd stay. Now what? Do what? *The next order of business will be to take Edwina upstairs. No . . . don't say that. Show him what you want if you cannot speak it.*

The low-banked fire in the parlor popped and cracked on the other side of the wall. Its light was barely enough to see by in that room, but its warmth floated marginally through the first story of the house.

She wove her fingers around the handkerchief tucked halfway inside her cuff. She was fidgety; the soles of her shoes could barely stay flat on the carpet. "Would you care to listen to a recording?"

"If you want to."

A compromise.

She rose on unsteady legs. Wetting her lips and keeping her breathing even, she went into the parlor and selected the "Emperor's Waltz." Several cranks of the Victrola and the music played through the wide horn. Melodic violins resonated. The tempo was lyrical, light and pleasant, romantic—not like the jerky and foot-stamping ragtime.

Edwina turned to return to the dining room, but barely took a step. Tom had left the table and come into the parlor. The light behind him cast his face in near darkness. She couldn't read what was in his eyes or clearly see his smile, but there was a hint of white teeth, perhaps a curved mouth. He seemed taller. Broader.

"Dance, Ed?"

"Yes." Her voice was barely a whisper. "I'd love to."

He held out his arms and she fit herself into them. Her hand laid softly on his taut shoulder; the other fit into his strong fingers. They glided around the floor, smoothly and in sync.

"You didn't learn the waltz in a troubadour show." She could hardly keep the count straight in her head. *One, two, three.*

As they whirled together, thighs nearly meeting with their footwork, he disclosed, "I must have picked it up somewhere on the road. I can't remember."

"Did you like traveling?"

"Sometimes."

"Was Mr. Dufresne with you?"

"Mostly."

One, two, three. Edwina felt the ribbon slide from her hair. She smiled, not caring. Tom maneuvered them quite adeptly through the room, circling around the center table. On the final notes, he suggested, "Take a twirl."

She let go of his hand and turned beneath his arm in one revolution. Then he brought her back into his embrace. His arms went around her waist. Her hair clouded over her shoulders. Their breaths mingled; their eyes locked. It seemed as if time had stopped and this moment would be theirs forever.

"Want to dance again?" Tom asked in a husky whisper.

She quietly shook her head. "No."

The beauty of a kiss lies in its impulsiveness and its impressibility. The words came into her head. She'd read them in her courtship book. How true they sounded at this instant. When she tried to speak, her voice failed her. He peered down at her waiting . . . waiting for her.

The prolonged anticipation of what she'd intended for this evening was almost unbearable. She had to do something. . . .

Closing her eyes, she dared to kiss him within a fraction of his mouth, just the corner seam. So warm and pleasant. Then ever so softly, on his chin and cheek. Raising on tiptoes, she cherished his forehead. What she could not say, she showed. She spoke her tenderness by pressing kisses to his lowered eyelids. Then her reverence by a caress against his brow.

He took her chin in his right hand, knuckles touching her throat, forefingers and thumb holding her face up to his. His mouth covered hers, persuasively and quite divinely. She sighed against him, parting her lips, snuggling closer into his embrace. Her mouth tingled. The kiss was rapturous and consuming.

When he gently broke away, one brow lifted . . . or so it seemed by the tone of his voice. "You've been drinking, Ed. Beer."

"Heavens, no." The denial came out in a rush. "Absolutely not. Never." His silence goaded; she dissolved like mush with a defeated sigh and slump of her shoulders. "Only one."

His low chuckle wrapped around her. "You always manage to surprise me."

"I surprise myself, too." To her ears, she sounded hesitant. Unsure. But she was sure. Very. "I . . . I don't want to dance." Then before her courage faltered, she took his hand in hers and led him through the parlor into the vestibule. He walked with her, but stopped at the base of the stairs. She turned, her eyes downcast. It was difficult to look at him. It wasn't as if she felt immoral, it was just that she'd never done this sort of thing before—been the aggressor, that is. Embarrassment did have a slight hold on her. "I've been thinking—"

"Edwina . . . Edwina." His fingers tightened over hers. "You don't have to do something that you don't want to. I never meant for you to—"

"No." She silenced him with a finger to his lips.

"Where this is leading isn't something I'm afraid of. I'm twenty-four, Tom." Then to make herself perfectly clear, she repeated, "I know what we're doing."

Uncertainty could be seen in his stance, but nothing was definable on his face. It was too dark. "Do you really, Edwina?"

Her hand lowered. "Yes. I do." She felt no blush. No heat on her cheeks. Perhaps it was because the vestibule was nearly black. "Come with me."

She began to climb the stairs, one hand on the railing, the other clutching Tom's. Once on the second-floor landing, she proceeded down a narrow hall, very dim, illuminated by a single taper on a side table. The channel of cool air brought out gooseflesh on her arms. She went into the third doorway on her right, where yet another slender candle flickered, its thin wick just barely burning enough to see by. In here, the atmosphere was warmer. The space was built above the fireplace downstairs; the heat from the fire rose enough for comfort.

This was her bedroom, of course, large and simple. Actually, it was very feminine when she stood back and gazed at it through Tom's eyes. The bed was canopied in swags of floral-patterned fabric that fell in pools by the head of the bed on either side of the oak frame. She favored pillows; a collection of them added dimension. Most she had made herself. Some were lace, others were satin—heart-shaped, delicate ovals. A tall wardrobe stood against one wall; the bay window on the other wall had cushioned seats, the very ones on which Crescencia had sat, suggesting Edwina wear the green nun's veiling. What Edwina planned *not* to wear very shortly would be far more scandalous than the youngish green on a woman of her age.

Off the bedroom, there was a bathroom. And inside it, a claw-legged bathtub with hot and cold running water. Her mother had had it installed two years ago, an expense Edwina agreed was worth every cent. On the marble-top bureau, her toiletries lay neatly arranged: brush and comb, bottles of perfume, ribbons and fancy pins, a porcelain hair receiver—a gift from a distant great aunt—that she never used. Beside it was a silver-handled mirror. Had Tom ever been in a lady's bedroom before and seen such personal things? Probably.

She kept walking forward until she reached the foot of the bed. Once there, she faced him and took both his hands. She squeezed. He squeezed back.

"I've never brought anyone up here. Above all else, you have to know that." She was thinking about his reaction . . . when he found out—the secret. He would know. Men did. She had to make it clear that nothing had ever happened here, at the house. This was special. For them. Only them.

Tom nodded, reached out, and took a curl between his fingers. "I believe you."

"And also . . ."—she inhaled, shaky and needing to stay composed—". . . I don't expect anything . . . after-ward. I don't—"

"Edwina, I wouldn't hurt you." He brought her close and cradled her in his arms.

She allowed herself the affection and comfort, just enough to let her be able to continue, then lifted her head to look directly in his eyes. "You need to under-stand from the start that what this is is two adults being together because they want to. It has nothing to do with anything outside this room. No society pressures. No de-mands. I'm not asking you for anything."

A frown marred his lips. "You make this sound so . . . damn calculated."

"It's not . . . not really. I'll never speak of it again. I just don't want you to think that you have to say things to me that you don't mean. That you have to pretend. I don't want that. I couldn't bear it." *Not again.*

"Edwina . . . somebody—a man—hurt you." He laid his palm on her heart where its beat skipped beneath his tender touch. "Right here."

She couldn't deny the truth. But she would not ask for his pity, either. "I survived."

Quietly, compassionately, he said, "But you still have the scars. I won't add to them."

"You're not. Because there is nothing for me to give up. So there is nothing to hurt me." Lowering her head, then raising it slowly, she gazed longingly into his eyes. "I have made the decision never to marry. Does that mean I cannot fulfill my life? Cannot enjoy the company . . . affections . . . of a man?"

"You can do whatever you like, Edwina. I was only trying to be honorable."

"Don't be *honorable.*" She nearly spat the word. "Be anything else but. I don't want honor. I want passion. Give me that. Only that." Quietly spoken into the darkness, her plea was murmured against his lips. "Kiss me. Make love to me. That's all I ask. Nothing more."

She laced her arms around his neck and waited. This time he would have to kiss her first, show her that they understood one another. The kiss came, gentle, testing, as if he was exploring. She sighed, able to kiss him back. The pressure of his lips remained feather light. The stroke of his tongue against her was as against a fragile thing.

"I will not break," she assured him, her fingers slipping into the ends of his cool, silky hair. "I know. Tom . . . I know."

That was all that she had to say—two words. In them, she'd admitted to not being a virgin. No surprise discoveries. Better to be honest. At least she hadn't had to come out and say it, explain it to a husband on her wedding night, cheat him out of what he expected his bride to be—untouched, perfect.

So. The dread secret was revealed. What next?

She held her breath until her lungs ached, waiting for his reaction, for him to turn away, be disappointed, even though they were not married. His opinion of her could change—drastically.

He held her face within his large hands. "I don't care." Then he kissed her softly on the tip of her nose.

Unexpectedly, tears filled her eyes. She blinked them

back. *Of course he cared.* He would care if she was his wife. But she wasn't. And he was so sweet, so kind, so wonderful for putting her at ease, for not judging or condemning. But of course he cared.

The pull at her heartstrings toward loving him was strong, overmastering chaotic emotions, but too irrational for her to give way to. She couldn't love him. Everything would change if she did. Stolen moments wouldn't be enough. She needed to grab hold of reality. And the only reality she knew at this minute was how impassioned she felt when Tom kissed her, touched her.

"Edwina . . ." He tipped her chin so that he could look into her eyes. To her, it seemed he searched for an answer. To a question she didn't know. His large irises reflected a seriousness that stilled her. "I have to ask . . . what about the possibility of you becoming—"

"I've taken care of it." She loathed having to speak about pregnancy just now.

"What have you done?"

She wouldn't tell him in exact words about the sponge. It was too much, even for her. "In Chicago . . . I learned about what to do."

"All right, Edwina. I didn't mean to upset you. I just had to know if I had to do something."

She shook her head. "No. So we don't have to talk about it anymore."

Her trembling hands lifted to his shirt collar. She unbuttoned the first one. Then the second. In between her arms, Tom's rose. He sought the tiny jet buttons of her bodice and slipped one free. Neither of them spoke. She finished before him. It was quite apparent that her dress was maddening to him. He groaned. She almost smiled. His big hands battled the minuscule buttons.

"Shall I?" Her voice was unreproachful.

An impatient edge mottled his reply. "I can do it."

She stood still, breath held in, her lower lip caught in her teeth.

He finished, and she gave a startled gasp that had her eyes flying to his when he slipped his hands inside her open bodice. Lean fingers grazed the fullness of her breasts where they pushed up from the boning in her corset.

"I can do it," he reiterated, then slid the sleeves off her shoulders.

In her own way, she touched him—not by teasing lightly, just palms flat, fingers splayed, against the hard planes of his chest. She dragged them through the light sprinkle of hair that curled softly there. His nipples tightened. She rubbed one with her thumb pad. He made an animal-like cry that he contained in his throat.

With a lack of haste, he continued with her buttons until the dress fell in a satin puddle at her feet. The pristine white of her underwear reflected the low light, brightening her image and giving him an unshaded view. She stood there proudly, not shyly.

She peeled the shirt away from his broad shoulders; the flannel fell like a blue river behind him onto the floor. She saw all of him, the contours and definitions— purely male, entirely masculine. She'd teased him before—with the hoops. She'd known he was all man. It was so plain to see.

She drank in his body, touching and mapping. His skin was so smooth, so warm. His heartbeat pulsed at his neck, strong, steady, in a thrum to equal her own. He explored her as well with caresses—gently with fingertips, all down her arms. She shivered, delighted.

They kissed—once, quickly.

Then Edwina sat on the bed and unlaced her shoes. Afterward, she removed them and would have rolled down her garters if Tom hadn't stood over her and held onto her wrist to prevent her. He grasped and flung the ruffled hem of her petticoat upward; white fluff landed in her lap. She leaned back on her elbows, hair fanned around her. With agonizing slowness, he rolled the elastic band down first one leg, then the other. Stockings came next. Using that same lazy glide, he stripped the sheer black away from her skin. Next, she was divested of her petticoat and corset in amazing dexterity. He had a knack for hooks, not buttons. They sprang free with simple turns of his wrist. Then it came down to a simple chemise and midthigh drawers—not fair.

She sat up and her eyes came level with the placket on his Levi's. Boldly, she unbuckled his belt and slid the length of leather free from its loops. She let it drop on top of her discarded petticoat, then undid first one steel button and another. She wasn't so experienced that she could tug his pants down his legs without a profuse blush. She stopped, gazed at him for help, and was glad when he stepped back and slid the heavy blue from his legs and kicked it aside. He was in only cotton drawers, the thin material revealing molded ridges and valleys, the indent of his navel and the whorl of hair that disappeared into the waistband. Her gaze traveled across his lean physique. She thought of the time she'd gone to his room, had seen him half like this—had wanted to touch him . . . but hadn't dared.

Without any outward appearance of self-consciousness, Tom hooked thumbs into the cottony band of his drawers and shed them in a single motion. She stared at him, poised nude before her, a little in wonder. She'd thought she'd been prepared, that she knew about this. But apparently not all men were created equal.

The pressure of his knee dipped the edge of the mattress as he came to her. "Lift up your arms."

She followed his instructions, not questioning. He took hold of the bottom of her chemise and pulled the cambric upward and over her head. It disappeared. He paused. Her eyes watched his as he looked at her—the expanse of her throat, the thrust of her breasts, the nipples that pouted beneath his bold gaze.

"Lie back."

She did so.

"You're beautiful, Edwina."

"So are you."

"Men aren't beautiful."

"To me, you are. A beauty like an old Roman statue.

Chiseled and marblelike. But with no fig leaf," she added with a smile.

"You'd never catch me wearing a leaf. I'm a cotton man."

As he spoke, her drawers came free of her legs. Now naked herself, she felt an instant's vulnerability. But it quickly vanished as Tom placed unbent arms on either side of her legs and moved upward on his knees. Nowhere did he touch her with any part of him. The urge to lift her pelvis, to feel him against her was there, but she couldn't act out her desires because he'd gone to his side next to her. She'd assumed this would be the end—no preliminaries. They would come together and in a few seconds, it would be over—with them sated, satisfied—but it would be brief.

Not so.

His fingers traced the curve of her shoulder. Then blunt fingernails dragged across the length of her arm and ended at her wrist, then trailed back up again to her collarbone. Then over the top of her breast, but not around the full sphere. Then in between them. Down lower past her ribs and across her belly. Everywhere he touched, sensations erupted. Sometimes they were gentle like a breeze, and other times, raging like a storm.

The pads of his fingertips were rough, yet not hurtful. They were deliciously arousing. A muffled whimper slipped past her throat when he finally stroked the crest of her nipple—in slow, circular motions that had her biting her bottom lip. In an alternating dance, his fingertip slowly drew a path between her breasts, giving each equal attention.

She leaned forward and kissed him. He gave back only sparingly, enough to satisfy, yet leave her wanting more as soon as his lips broke from hers. He dipped his head and his mouth found her. She shuddered as his tongue swirled around the tight peak. Her back arched. For long moments, he did scandalous things to her breast with his mouth and tongue, things she'd never known about.

She rolled onto her back, taking him with her. Her

hands rose to sink into his thick hair and hold his head close. The pleasurable assault went on, his lips closed around one breast while his hand molded the other. His lips tugged gently; his teeth nipped. Both sent spirals of ecstasy through her. Their legs intertwined. Rough hair on his thighs skimmed against her.

Dizzying thoughts ran rampant in Edwina's mind. *When I'm old and gray and by myself, I will remember this. If there is but one memory I can have, this will be it. I refuse to lose the magic of this night to senility.*

When she could stand no more of this sweet torment, he rained kisses up her throat, then caught her mouth. The kiss was frenzied and urgent. In a move she was hardly aware of, his body imprisoned hers. She caressed the length of his back, her legs parting. The need for release had built inside her with a fevered pitch; she squirmed beneath him. He pushed forward slowly; she took the hot, thick heat of him as he slipped inside.

And then there was only a raw need that ignited between them. Between the thrusts and burning tempo, kisses were exchanged, no longer soft or gentle. They were greedy, untamed, unlike anything Edwina had sought or given. But they were what she had to have as Tom's rhythm increased. She raced ahead, grasping for the telltale signs of release. Needing it now. Wanting it more than anything.

Completion came for her, too fast. A cry rose from her throat; her fingers dug into his muscular shoulders. She hadn't been able to help herself. He'd done things to her mind, made her feel wanton. She'd let all inhibitions go.

His kiss captured her breath, the panting that held her in its clutches. He kept moving his hips against her, over and over, until he shuddered with his release, breath coming from him in choppy gasps. Tom's impassioned groan filled her ears as his head lowered.

And then there was only the fragmented silence, broken by spent breathing, heartbeats that still pumped in unison. He nuzzled the curve between her neck and shoulder, kissing lightly. He didn't leave her. His weight felt right, like a layer of completeness. She didn't want him to move yet.

What she'd known before had been quick—gratifying, but quick. Tom did things in a way that unraveled her. Even now, in the aftermath, a multitude of effusive sensations skittered across the dips and peaks of her body. Every pore was alive. This was all so new, unknown.

Kissing his temple, she wrapped her arms tightly about him. Oh . . . Heaven help her. She could fall in love with him. It would be so effortless.

The light from various candles flickered and bounced off the royal blue tiled walls. Edwina had put them on the flipped-down commode seat, the floor, around the bathtub, and on the marble-slab sink counter.

The steaming, sudsy water felt indescribably good to Tom as it seeped into his body. The livery had a foot-bath with hot and cold running water that he used downstairs; but he couldn't sit in it, much less sprawl out. And in spite of the flower-scented salts and bubbles Edwina had dumped in the bath, he loved this, loved lying with his back against the slanted rim with her in front of him, his arms sheltering her in a soft hold. His legs could nearly make it to the end, but not quite. He either had to bend them or stick them out. He'd opted for the latter, only because Edwina could rest hers on top of his.

Soapy water slid down her calves, dribbling into the hair on his. Against the top of her head, he murmured, "You have cute toes."

Her gentle laughter vibrated next to his chest. "Such a thing to say. Feet are not cute."

"Yours are. Mine aren't." He stretched his leg up for her to view. "I have hair on my toes. You don't."

"I would hope not." She giggled.

He breathed in the scent of her wet hair; the fragrance of her shampoo had been heightened by that of the scented water.

Each fell silent, maybe because they both were content. He knew he was. He couldn't remember when he'd been so at peace, so filled. Absently stroking the sides of his thumbs up and down her ribs, he eased his head back on the tub rim and closed his eyes.

With her wit and charm, her candor and amusing mannerisms, he could fall in love with her if she let him. But she'd been perfectly clear. This would have to be enough. He would respect her wishes—for now. Maybe down the road, after they'd spent some time together, she might change her mind.

His thoughts drifted back to what she'd said. *I know.* At first, it hadn't been evident to him what she meant. Then she'd repeated herself. The second time, the message came across.

She'd been with someone before.

He wasn't altogether reconciled to her not being a virgin. But maybe he'd had a moment's relief: he wouldn't be the one to take her virginity from her. On the other hand, he'd instantly hated the other man who'd been in her life.

When Tom had made love to her, he'd wanted to tell her that he would wipe the other's touch from her memory. But that would have been selfish of him. Whatever memories she had, they were hers. He had no right to defuse them. It did anger Tom, though, that whoever he was, he had hurt her.

Edwina began to make some sense to him—the reasons she overcompensated with her primness and properness. In her world, it was better to be labeled a prude than to suffer hints at anything remotely akin to being a loose woman. But in his world . . . it didn't matter— not a lot. Perhaps just a little. He wasn't entirely used to the idea. He could forgive her, though—no question. Not that she required his forgiveness. He'd never apply the double standard to her, which said that men were able to seek their pleasures, but women were not—that those who did were women of easy virtue, tolerated by society only if they knew that their place was in brothels and the like.

But where did Edwina fit in? In neither place. So she would make her own—alone. It unsettled him.

Edwina dreamily sighed.

"What are you thinking?" he asked, crossing his arms over her breasts and loosely hugging her.

"This is nice." Her hands came up to rest on his forearms.

"Better than nice." Tom lifted his head and lowered one foot into the water to warm it. "Too bad you don't have any more of that beer."

"A delivery should be coming this week."

"You won't tell me how you get it."

"Hmm" blended with a smile he couldn't see but knew was there. "I have my ways."

His chin rested on the top of her head. "I know you. But I don't know anything about you. What was your life like when you were little?"

She didn't immediately answer. Then she began to explain. "Well . . . my parents had me when they were older. My mother lost two babies before I was born." She swirled the water with her fingertip. "I had a happy childhood, if that's what you mean. I did all the normal things a girl does."

"I don't know what the normal girl things are. I didn't have a sister."

"Dolls and dress-up. Parties on the lawn with friends. Skating. Drawing. I don't know . . . lots of things."

"What were your parents like?"

"Controlling." The word held a degree of bitterness. "My father worked as a teller at the bank. He kept long hours. And even on the weekends, he wasn't the most pleasant to be around. I think he disliked his position intensely but could do nothing to change his set of circumstances, since he had my mother and me to take care of. We left him alone, mostly. But when he was in a 'mood,' he could go on and on and tell me what's wrong with the country and why I should do this and that. And that I should marry only if I have money of my own so I don't have to rely on my husband for everything."

Tom smoothed a curl back from Edwina's wet forehead.

"My mother had strong opinions of what and who I should be. I fought with her about going to business college. We had a horrible argument. But finally, she relented." Edwina turned her head to gaze at Tom. "And the funny thing was—after all her fuss and tears—when we next saw Mrs. Plunkett, my mother told her right away what my plans were and how happy she was that I was going to the city to further my education. Mrs. Calhoon happened to be in the mercantile at the time and she declared, 'Edna'—that was my mother's name—'Edna, what's this world coming to that young girls can roam into the city alone?' The women didn't know I'd be staying with Minister Stoll's relations in Chicago. And even when my mother informed them, they still were prissy about it. So she said, 'At least my Edwina has gumption.'"

Facing forward again, Edwina fished out a porous sponge from the suds. "My mother went on to say that I'd be the same girl in Chicago that I was in Harmony and told them that she trusted my good judgment. That put their disjointed minds at ease."

Tom wouldn't like having his private affairs dissected and judged. How could Edwina stand it? No wonder she wanted to get the hell out of Harmony.

"You've lived here all your life?"

"All my life." She ran the tubular sponge down her arms, then up his thigh. His muscles tightened. "Except for when I was in Chicago."

"How long were you there?"

"Almost four years."

He wanted to ask if that's where she'd met *him*. But he didn't feel it was any of his business. She'd tell him if she wanted to.

"And what was the school like?"

"Big." Water trickled down his leg where she squeezed the sponge. "Bigger than I'd imagined."

"Co-educational?"

"Of course not. Only young women." She grazed his inner thigh with her knuckles.

He just about jumped out of his skin. "What is that you've got?"

"A Japanese loofah."

Smiling, he observed, "It must be a woman thing. I never had one."

Her easy laughter shook her body, rippling the water.

Settling her closer, he went on, "Tell me more. What about the girls? They all wanted to be accountants?"

"Oh, we didn't call ourselves that. Women can't be, you know."

"Then what were you—are you?"

"A certified bookkeeper."

"Sounds like the same thing."

She shrugged. "It is."

"When you go to Denver or California or wherever, will any of the others be there with you?" He hated the thought of her by herself. He didn't want to think of her there at all.

"I don't know. The only woman I was close with was Abbie—Abigail Crane. I lived with her and her family while I was at school." The loofah dipped into the water. More trickling, all down his arm.

"The minister's relatives."

"Yes, but they weren't . . . well, the parents were staunch reformists, but Abbie . . . she was her own person."

"How so?"

"Well . . . you could say she was . . . adventurous."

He understood. "Ahh . . . she liked to have fun."

"Yes. She corrupted me."

"For the better?" He bent his leg once more, and she doused his knee. His hands slipped lower down her waist. He sought her navel and traced it.

"It all depends. You didn't know me before. Maybe

257

you'd have liked me more the way I was than the way I am now."

"I like you just fine as you are." He pressed an ardent kiss to the shell of her damp ear. "Did Abbie show you the clubs?"

"Yes."

"And that's where the other college boys were."

"Yes." Vagueness came into her tone.

He knew he was getting closer to finding out about the one who'd defiled her, left her.

"Was there anyone special you danced with?"

"No . . . I . . . There was nobody in particular." She twisted and looked at him. An unspoken pain lived in her eyes. Tom wanted to rip in two the bastard who'd done this to her, put the hurt inside her heart.

In a calm voice that contradicted the turmoil in her gaze, Edwina asked, "What about your life before you came here? Tell me everything."

"There isn't much to tell." He put his disappointment aside; he'd back away if that was what she wanted.

"Of course there is. You've been places." She reached up and brushed a stray lock of hair from his forehead. "Why did you leave Texas in the first place?"

"To get the hell away from my father."

She gasped. "He beat you?"

"No. He just fell into the bottle a little too much and turned into an . . ."—Tom caught his language—". . . turned unpleasant."

She slipped back around and pressed her shoulders into his chest. "What did your father do?"

"He farmed. I did it for a while."

"You didn't like it?"

"Not at all."

"Then I should think you'd have wanted to stay in school so you could get a good education and make something of yourself." She turned quickly and took his chin in her fingers. "Not that you aren't something now. . . . I just meant . . ."

"I know what you meant." He gave her a soft kiss.

She sighed, then smiled into his face before resuming her cuddle position once more.

"I told you why I dropped out of school. It wasn't for me. I wasn't going to sit behind a damn plow, either. That was for my father—and my brother, before he left."

"You have a brother?"

"Somewhere."

"You don't know where?"

"Only when he writes."

"But don't you care?"

"I care, but what can I do? John's living his life on the edge, one town to the next. I never know if my letters catch up to him."

She pondered that a moment, then asked, "What about your mother?"

"She died. Worked herself to death."

"And your father? He's gone, too?"

"He's gone, all right." Tom couldn't help the sarcastic rumble of laughter in his chest. "He's gone down south. To Meh-he-co."

"Where?"

"Mexico." Tom turned his foot at an angle to play with Edwina's toes. "He's got a new family. A new wife. Some kids. I saw them once, years back. No reason to go again."

"But he's your father."

"So? He's got his place, I've got mine. Not everyone has to be one big family. I have Shay. He's more a brother to me than my own is."

"Did you and Mr. Dufresne grow up together?"

"Yep."

"And when you left, he went with you."

"That's how it went."

"Where did you go?"

Tom laughed. "First stop: the Lamar County Jail."

Edwina turned with such force that soapy water sloshed over the tub's rim. "To jail? What for?"

The way she stared at him, he expected she thought

he'd been arrested for a heinous crime of some sort. The truth of the matter was somewhat embarrassing—though at the time, it'd been more than somewhat. He saw no way to sugar-coat his reply.

"Being in an establishment of ill repute without sufficient funds to cover the tab."

Her delicate brows lifted. "Oh."

"Yep—oh."

After a moment, she said, "Oh." And with a frown this time. She settled in once more. "Then what?"

"We went north for a spell. I got a job working in a stockyard. I hated it."

"Smelly, I imagine."

"That's only the half of it." In thought, he rubbed a thumb over the stubble on his jaw. "From there we headed into the New Mexico territory. I did some mine work. Good pay. Hot as hell down in the hole. I spent most everything I earned as soon as I got it. Shay, he's better at saving than I am. He always had money in his pocket."

"What made you decide to go into business?"

"That idea," he said, "came to me while I was in Seattle. A lot of men came back and forth from Alaska. They were looking for ways to spend their money, and I guess to them, going off into the woods to let off steam was the best way to do it. I made some fair money, but I didn't like weather. It rains nearly every damn day."

"I like rain."

"I like it, too, when it's not living on my clothes everywhere I go."

"And what about Mr. Dufresne?" She rested her cheek against his chest. "Why didn't he come with you when you left?"

There was no reason not to tell the truth. It was in the past now anyway. "He had a girl that he was seeing steady. It didn't work out."

"I should hope so, for Crescencia's sake. She's quite taken with him."

"Likewise for him."

A few moments passed, Tom thinking about the serious steps his friend was taking, talking with him about. The word *marriage* had come up more than once. Shay had found a woman he loved deeply. Tom envied him.

"The water's getting cold," Edwina whispered. "Do you want to get out?"

"I suppose the bed's warmer."

"If it's not . . . we could make it warmer. . . ." She lifted her face to his, just as a chime sounded from a clock in the bedroom: 10:30. "Marvel-Anne comes at seven. You'll have to be gone by then."

"I know." He kissed her eyelids, then nose. "But we've got eight hours left."

"Then let's not waste them," she said against his mouth, kissing him and pressing the side of her breast into his chest.

261

Chapter

❧ 14 ❧

The next morning, life resumed as usual for Edwina. A Sunday sun rose to salute their small world nestled in the clutches of Montana's white winter splendor. As was the case every Sunday, those flocking to Harmony General Assembly church walked differently. Their carriage held a greater propriety and stateliness. Greetings were more formal, more subdued; voices were more meticulously polite. Perhaps it was because they were going off to hear Minister Stoll tell them how impious they'd been during the week—even if not a one of them had strayed down the garden path. That was just the way of things.

But one amongst them had departed from convention . . . quite delectably last night. However, to look at Edwina Huntington in her black silk grenadine dress, one could swear she was no different today than she was last Sunday, or the dozens of Sundays before that.

Edwina had sat staidly in her pew, gazing at the backs of bald heads and the old-fashioned bonnets of the old, devout, and deaf who had assembled in the front. It struck her then that she felt no guilt, no remorse. What she did in her house was her business. But the luscious thoughts that came to her in church were quite another matter, so she had to push Tom Wolcott from her head for an entire hour. After that, she'd been free to think of him as much as she liked—until next Sunday, when she had to give him up for an hour again.

Their paths did cross, very briefly, that midmorning. The congregation had been milling around the church-yard after services, rambunctious children throwing snowballs, when Edwina had been pulled into a conversation about the Ladies Aid Snowflake Ball that was held each New Year's Eve. Tom and Shay had exited the restaurant just as she'd been asked her opinion on Chinese bucket-shaped lanterns versus Japanese ball-shaped lanterns. Mr. Plunkett could get a better price on the Chinese, but Mrs. Treber argued the Japanese came with better paper and were figured.

If Edwina had had an opinion, it had failed her as soon as she saw Tom. She'd wanted to walk over to him and slip her arms around his neck. But obviously, that was out of the question. As a second choice, she'd wanted merely to speak with him and hear his voice. But that wasn't to be. As soon as the men had caught sight of Tom, they had invited him and Mr. Dufresne into their group. Loud guffaws had sounded; there were pats on the backs. She and Tom had exchanged glances across the segregated circles. Then excited male talk about something called a coyote howler had gotten them stirred up, and they had begged off to their wives, saying that they were going to Wolcott's to give it a try.

Edwina had watched them leave, mumbling something about paper lanterns of any kind being acceptable to her. Mr. Dufresne had remained with Crescencia, and the pair had strolled arm in arm down Hackberry Way toward the town square gazebo that had been decorated with pine garlands and big red bows. It was acceptable for them to show affection publicly, for their relationship was leading to respectability—marriage.

Monday, Edwina had thought for sure she'd be able to steal a moment alone with Tom. But he'd been occupied by a flow of customers; she'd been engaged with the girls and their lessons. She'd stayed in her classroom long after her students had gone home, in the hope she could see Tom before she had to leave. Five o'clock hadn't come soon enough. At last, he closed the store and came into her side of the building through the storeroom closet. She was waiting for him. The window shades were closed; the front door was locked. As soon as they met, she fell into his open arms and they kissed.

After long, breathless minutes when their mouths were together and their hands were exploring, she could hardly think. When he lifted his head, she saw only his eyes and the longing in them. She felt it, too, and wanted more than anything to be with him.

"We can't go to my house again. I just can't risk it. Last Saturday . . . it was chance enough. . . . Tempting fate isn't something I'm good at."

He nodded. His fingers cupped her face. "I understand. But we can't go to my room. If someone saw you going there . . . you just can't. I won't let you."

"I know." She sighed.

"We can be together here. For a while, anyway, without causing suspicion."

Her heart ached beneath her breast. "I want to. But I can't stay. I promised Mrs. Elward I'd come over and help her set sleeves on a dress she's making for Ruth. I'm late as it is."

She would have regretfully slipped out of Tom's arms then if he hadn't held her tight and kissed her. The strong hardness of his hungry lips over hers made her blood flow through her like a raging river. His mouth upset her balance and she leaned into him, crushing breasts against his chest. Clinging to him, she left common sense behind. So easily, the situation could get out of control. Then, fearful that it would, she backed away from the kiss, her fingers covering her mouth as if to keep the feel of him there.

"I have to go," she said in a rush. "Tomorrow. I'll bring another picnic dinner and we can share it." She added with a soft smile. "And practice your nines tables—I haven't forgotten. I'll leave the window shades up. Everything will look perfectly legitimate. And it will be. At least we can be together."

"Sure, Ed." He put his hand on her cheek. "I can come for dinner."

But the next evening, he couldn't keep his promise. Something had happened to a shipment of costly hunting skiffs; they'd been damaged in transit, so he'd had to send Mr. Dufresne to Butte to assess the property and file a claim report with the railroad. A meeting at the Brooks House Hotel Mr. Dufresne was to have had with a party of newly arrived hunters from New York had fallen to Tom—at five o'clock. The picnic had to be canceled.

She didn't see him on Wednesday the entire day. He'd had to close the shop and take the men out himself. Thursday, she came to the school early hoping to find him at the store. He wasn't there. Around noon, she heard movements on the other side of the wall. He must have returned. She went through the school day and dismissed her girls by two o'clock. She quickly went out the door and entered Wolcott's Sporting Goods and Excursions. Two customers were present, so she couldn't say what she wanted to say. She had to act very dignified.

"Mr. Wolcott." She greeted him with an air of unfamiliarity, checking to see if they were being watched. They were. "It's nice to have you back."

He looked more handsome than ever, his complexion having turned a shade darker from his adventures in the mountains. Tall and exceedingly muscular, he filled out a striped wool shirt well enough to make a woman heady.

"Miss Huntington." His gaze fell on the two men for a moment, too. Then to her, he said, "It's good to be back."

She strolled to the counter that he stood behind and looked for a piece of paper on which to write. "Everything was fine while you were gone." She tried to be inconspicuous when she nudged a stuffed bird aside to get what appeared to be a scrap piece. "The note on your door yesterday was quite sufficient. Only one person knocked on mine to inquire about your return."

"I hope I didn't put you out." Their fingers touched briefly, electrically, as he rolled a pencil in her direction.

"Not at all." She began to write.

"Glad to hear it."

Finished, she slipped the note to him.

Meet me in the storeroom at five o'clock.

"Well, I'll leave you to your customers, Mr. Wolcott. Good-bye."

" 'Bye, Miss Huntington." He gave her the briefest of nods. Had she not been looking for a sign, she wouldn't have detected it. Then she left, her heart beating in anticipation.

Tom wrote up the two men's purchases and they departed. Now alone, he put a foot on the bottom rung of his stool and gazed out the windows, pensive. The mood was unlike him. He should have been champing at the bit for five o'clock to come. It wasn't as if he didn't want to see Edwina. He did. In the worst way. But the fact that he had to meet her in a closet bothered him. With other women, the bits of fluff he'd dallied with in the past, he would have taken the meeting in stride, laughed about stripping off clothes amidst inventory. But not with Edwina. She wasn't a floozy. She deserved better than a storeroom.

The question was, where did he see their relationship going? It was too soon to decide the future. But he could see she was what he was looking for. He enjoyed her sense of humor most when she was trying to be serious. Thought she danced great. She was intellectual, especially with numbers. Had the best set of legs he'd ever seen on a woman and a mouth that said *kiss me* every time he gazed at it.

If he listened to what she said, he knew she'd never marry—him or anyone else. If that's what she wanted, he supposed she was entitled. But he didn't like it. What was he supposed to do if he fell in love with her? Not only was a cut-up heart at stake, so was his manhood.

Tom had gotten his reply on the loan. It was a no-go, at least not for the amount he'd asked for. The bank offered him two thousand if he used it on a housing loan. And if he put up the store and all its assets as the collateral. Everything he had was tied up in Wolcott's. Risking its worth on a signature for a house . . . Tom just didn't know. He could make the monthly payments just fine, but the property wouldn't be what he wanted—it was a stinking weed patch by the lumberyard.

Lighting a smoke, Tom clamped it between his lips and took out the battered tackle box beneath the counter that contained clock pieces. As he sorted through the tiny coils and springs, minute metal cutouts and gears, Edwina stayed on his mind.

She mystified him. He'd thought himself broad-minded—to a degree. But this notion of a woman not marrying so she could have a career, and her asking not for a wedding ring from a man, but rather sex instead—it all went against the grain of his thinking.

On the other hand, times were changing. Hell, the twentieth century was just around the corner. *Modern* was the word of the day. Automobiles, electricity, and flushing commodes were gaining in popularity. So why not change attitudes as well?

Tom mulled this over while he worked on the clock and spent the next hours talking with customers who came and went. At five, he locked up and dropped the shades. By 5:01, he'd combed his hair and gotten rid of the stick of spearmint gum he'd been chewing. Ten seconds later, he went through the storeroom door and left it open behind him so that light could spill inside.

The long, narrow space, semidark, was jammed with overstock. Life-size rubber deer that came apart in four easy-to-screw-in sections stood along the wall beneath the shelves. Next to the deer was a crate of number 13 bore leather cleaner. And some pistol kits with oil and polish, and Buzzacott's patented complete camp cooking outfits. On the shelves themselves were tins of hunter's camouflage makeup—your pine green and bark brown—along with bowstrings, floats, reels, black fly paste, collapsing telescope cups, and slingshots.

Halfway down the storeroom, the scene changed. White aprons with ruffles hung on pegs in neat rows. A fancy china service took up a shelf, below which were books about etiquette and stuff. Plain white gloves were lined up next to a basket of hair ribbons. Ink pens and bottles. Sample party invitations and calling cards in cream paper. A dried bowl of rose petals. Two bottles of perfume.

Tom took it all in—the broad picture.

One side drab, one side colorful.

One side harsh, one side soft.

One side, Tom's life; one side, Edwina's life.

If ever two people were mismatched, it was obvious in the contents of their closet.

Edwina's door opened and she slipped inside the cramped room. She looked so pretty in her green dress, his heart ached in a way it never had before. Her eyes, even in the vague light, matched the color of the dress—a kind of mint, just the hue he'd first noticed in her eyes in Stykem's office. Her mahogany hair was swept up, neat and tidy, held in place by gold combs on both sides. Seeing him, she broke into a beautiful smile.

"You're here."

"I told you I would come."

"Yes, I know. But after the last time we arranged to meet . . ." Her downcast lashes shadowed her cheeks. "I prepared myself to be disappointed just in case."

That she would be so honest about her desire to be with him brought special meaning to the moment. He'd known he wanted to be with her as well, but not until now had he realized how much he'd come to look forward to her company, to actually crave it. In the beginning, she had been a challenge, an amusing pursuit, when he'd tried to get her to break down and show her true self. But now that she had, he realized the complexities that made Edwina were the reasons he'd become utterly intrigued by her.

"Come here." He opened his arms and she tucked herself into them. Keeping her close, he breathed in the scent of roses, closing his eyes and imagining they were someplace else, someplace they didn't have to hide in order to touch.

She buried her face in his neck, and he pressed a kiss to her brow. Then their lips met like a whisper, soft, tentative. Their kisses grew more persuasive and drugging. He held the back of her head in his palms, keeping her close. Her hands rose to his neck and wrapped around him. The crush of full breasts against him made him draw in his breath.

He kissed her with a reckless, devouring abandon that she matched. That was how he felt—like the heat of her body had entered and consumed him until he lost all judgment. His fingers splayed over her back, then farther to the nip of her waist and then to the curve of her buttocks. He cupped the softness and pulled her to his groin. Delving into her mouth with his tongue, he tasted her, sought the pleasure she gave. The blood that pounded in his brain made him forget reason or where he was.

Inasmuch as he hated to, he broke their kiss.

"Edwina . . ." His voice, laden with unsated desire, sounded husky and thick to him. "What are we doing?"

She stared into his eyes, lips moist. Her reply came softly. "Kissing."

"In a damn closet."

"Not a damn closet. Our closet."

The beginning of a smile caught his mouth and overtook it before he could stop it. "A closet just the same."

She met the smile with one of her own. "Well, it's private. You have to give it that much."

"Not quite."

An arch lifted her brows. "Hmm?"

"There's a deer watching us."

Her laugh was sweet. "It's rubber. It doesn't count."

A spell of thoughtful quiet hovered in the room for a short moment.

"We could go to Alder," Edwina suggested. "It's far enough away that nobody knows who we are."

"What do you have in mind once we're there?"

Pink spread across her cheeks; then shyly, the words drifted from her mouth. "There's a hotel . . ."

"I don't like the idea of sneaking around, Edwina."

"I'm not fond of it myself. But what else do you propose? Walking directly to my front door? Staying long enough for tongues to wag?"

His hold on her eased with his indrawn breath. "I know what you're saying. And I know it's the way of things. But I don't have to like it."

"Nor I." She placed a hand on his shoulder. "It is our business. It shouldn't matter. But it does. If sneaking to Alder means we can be together, then so be it. I'm not ashamed of this—of us. I simply can't flaunt an affair and expect everyone to take it in stride. It won't work that way. You know it."

He nodded his agreement, his eyes narrowing. "I know it. But you need to know I'm not with you just for sex. Hell, I could pay for it if that's all I wanted."

Her gaze clouded with what he could have sworn were tears. But she blinked them back so quickly, he couldn't be sure. "That's very sweet of you to say. I never thought otherwise, Tom."

They stood motionless in the storeroom. Maybe each of them was thinking over going out of town; maybe each was wondering how wise such a plan was. Tom knew that was how he was looking at things. Even though what Edwina had said was true. If they chose to see each other intimately, it shouldn't be anyone's affair but their own. Going to Alder so they could be together was the only idea he could come up with, too. So he'd be damn careful to cover his tracks.

Edwina began talking first. "I'll take the train on Saturday. I'll tell Marvel-Anne that I'm going to look at flatware. There's a silversmith in town there. You can

ride over on the Mill Creek Road. It should be clear—
it's the mail route—and it wouldn't take you longer than
two hours. Can Mr. Dufresne watch the store on
Saturday?"

"Shay gets back tonight. I don't have anything booked
until next week. He'll be around. He can do it."

"All right. Then I'll take the nine o'clock. There's only
one hotel there. It's called the Knotty Pine."

A dubious curve hooked one side of his mouth.

"That's knotty—k-n-o-t-t-y. Not n-a-u-g-h-t-y."

"I didn't say anything."

"You didn't have to." She put a fingernail to her
teeth, thought marring the smoothness of her forehead.
"I'll get a room in my name. And you can get one in
yours. We'll meet in one of them and . . ."

She closed her eyes, shakily pulling in air, then opening the thick-lashed lids once again. He could see she
was struggling with this.

Tom brought her close once more, the blunt stubble
on his jaw catching in her hair and pulling several glossy
strands loose from their confinement. "Edwina, we don't
have to go. We could . . ." He paused before he said it.
The words exploded in his head, powerful, potent. No
thoughts went beyond the day that could change
things—they stopped at the day itself. Maybe the want
of it had been there all along. "We could get m—"

"No." She pulled back quickly, not letting him finish.
"Things are fine the way they are. I told you I don't
want anything else." An edginess marked her body
movements as she stepped away and hugged herself.
"I'm not deluding myself into thinking about things that
just aren't for me." A forced calm, a forced smile eased
the tension in her shoulders. Then she leaned forward
and briefly kissed him on the lips. As she stood back,
her features were soft and sincere—too damned sincere.
She really meant it. "I don't need chivalry, Tom. I'm
not a maiden you have to rescue. I'm fine just the way
I am."

"So you've said." He smoothed wisps of hair from her

ear and intently searched her face. "We can get rooms, but we're going to do this my way. There's a restaurant there—Creek-something."

"The Clear Creek Café."

"Meet me there at noon. It'll look like we're acquaintances and ran into each other. There's nothing wrong with sharing a table."

"No . . . there's not." With a thoughtful little huff, she continued in a tone that was strictly a teacher's. "Well, now that we seem to have settled Saturday, have you memorized your nines tables?"

The abrupt change in topic needled him. He was still trying to resolve her independence and accept it. "Dammit all, no. What good will it do me anyway?"

"You never know when you may need a mathematical equation to help you decipher something." Her lips pursed in thought. "For example, if you caught nine rabbits and then nine more. Two times nine is what?"

"I haven't the foggiest. Are the rabbits dead or alive?"

Her nose crinkled. "Well, my goodness, it makes no difference."

"Sure it does. If they're alive, what do I want them for? I'd let them go, so the answer would be zero. But if they're dead, I'd have enough pelts to make a couple of pairs of snow boots, a few hats, and meat for a helluva big pot of stew."

She folded her arms beneath her breasts. "You're impossible."

"No, I'm not. I'm a logical thinker."

A gleam lit her eyes. "All right, then. You have eighteen dead rabbits. How many lucky feet will you get from them? Eighteen times four equals—?"

The variables went over his head. "We haven't gotten past nines."

"Uh huh." Her nod was all-knowing. "See how wise it is for you to know the tables from one to ten? If you don't, you'd never know that you could have seventy-two good luck charms."

"One is all it takes."

"But with seventy-two, your chances are seventy-one more times likely to go in your favor."

Tom decided to quit and cut his losses. Arguing reasoning with Edwina was a losing battle.

Friday morning, Edwina sat in the classroom absently staring out the frost-covered window while the girls hung up their scarfs and coats on the wall pegs and set their hats on the shelf above. Her elbow resting uncharacteristically on the desktop, chin on her palm, she let her thoughts drift, with the scuffle of shoes, the purr of voices, and giggles in the background.

She and Tom had been alone together before and she hadn't put any tag of promiscuity on it, solely because what they had been doing had been harmless. A wistful arch touched her mouth. Nearly harmless. Impassioned thoughts didn't count. Nor did the couple of kisses between them. That was chaste compared to what they'd done in her bedroom. But a planned trip to another town so they could get a hotel room seemed calculated, cold. Edwina didn't like having to suggest it, but that was the only option.

Thinking back to what he'd said . . . *We could get m—* . . . her throat went dry. She hadn't wanted to hear him say anything about changing the arrangement to one of a more permanent nature, about a legal commitment that bound them forever. She couldn't think about it, for very good reasons—ones that went beyond her belief that a wife should be pure going into a marriage. She still felt that way. But she also had other opinions about wedlock. She had pushed them aside when she thought she'd marry Ludlow. Romance had overridden common sense. But never again. She shouldn't have ignored her better judgment, or her father's advice. A woman needed her own security when . . . if . . . she married.

Edwina's mother had relied entirely on her father to take care of her, never once inquiring about banking matters or insurance policies. When her father died, Edwina's mother didn't know the first thing about financial independence. Edna had gotten into a fix, and it had fallen on Edwina to take care of it, which she was doing fairly well. A couple of weeks ago, she'd sold the ceiling pendant for the light—among other odds and ends that she'd found in the storeroom before moving in. From the profits, she'd been able to pay off two accounts. The tuition she charged for her school was keeping her afloat, with enough to pay Marvel-Anne and the mortgages and a scant amount to continue to make good with the creditors.

If Edwina ever decided to marry—which was so doubtful the thought really wasn't worth the effort . . . but *if* she did—she wouldn't go into the union penniless. She could never fall victim to helplessness like poor Mrs. Lancaster. That had been awful. Several years had passed since Mrs. Lancaster had moved—*without* Mr. Lancaster, who had stayed only a month after his wife's abandonment before boarding the train himself, never to be heard from or seen again. The shock of the scandal had died down over the years. But Edwina decided the girls should be reminded of its repercussions. The lesson needed to be reinforced.

It had been in the back of her mind when she'd opened the school: instilling financial self-reliance in her students as well as grooming them for husbands. She hadn't been sure they were ready or would be receptive to her views. But now that she'd gotten to know the girls better, she could see they needed this information. That was why she'd ordered the pamphlets several weeks ago. They'd just come in today.

The girls were taking their seats, so Edwina cleared the distant cobwebs from her mind and moved her gaze to her students. She was immediately drawn to Crescencia, who had not removed her hat like the others. Chin up, oval spectacles shining, and fingers folded in front of her, she waited expectantly. As if nothing were out of the ordinary at all.

But her hat wasn't ordinary . . . surely not one to be bypassed without comment.

It was a turban of purple pansies, with a purple bow and a bunch of wheat standing up at one side and a chenille-dotted veil that came just over the tip of her nose. It was very . . . showy. Quite unlike Crescencia's tastes.

Ruth Elward had no problem in saying so, either. "What kind of hat is that you've got on?"

Crescencia straightened with a smile. "Do you like it?" She gave the girl no room to reply, which was a good thing, because Edwina could tell the others weren't taken with the turban. "Mr. Dufresne bought it for me on his trip to Butte. He got it ready-made from a millinery shop. Isn't it too grand?" Her head tilted left and right to give them a good view.

"It looks like—" Johannah began, but Edwina cut her off because she saw a deep wrinkle of distaste on the girl's nose.

"I think Crescencia's hat is lovely because it pleases her," Edwina said, more to Johannah than the rest. "I'm reminded of one of the maxims we learned the other day; perhaps now would be a good time to refresh ourselves. 'In private, watch your thoughts; in your family, watch your temper; in society, watch your tongue.'"

Guiltily, several looked away. Then Camille said, "I think your hat is just peachy, Crescencia."

Lucy chimed in, her freckles seeming more prominent against her pale winter's complexion. "So do I. And twenty-three skidoo to them who don't."

Hildegarde nodded her agreement. "It's purple. My mother says purple and blue are fashionable. And that plum is a color that means 'keep promise.'"

"I surely like the veiling. It's as sheer as a whisper," Meg added.

Crescencia tittered behind her hand, and at first her words were so soft, they couldn't be heard. Then she cleared her throat and admitted in a sinful tone, "I've bought a straight-front corset."

Gasps sounded. Then:

"When?"

"Why aren't you wearing it?"

"Does your father know?"

"Did he give you the money?"

"You were at the mercantile? My mother didn't tell me."

"What color ribbons?"

Edwina was surprised, too. The corset was quite fashionable. The stays were the straight-front part, giving support but leaving the figure graceful and supple while elegantly narrowing the back. Edwina had been thinking about getting one herself.

Blushing, the pink a flagrant contrast to her hair, Crescencia filled them all in. "Well, Mr. Dufresne took me for a coach ride last Saturday and we went over to Waverly. That's where I bought it." She hastily went on. "He never knew that was why I went into the store. I'd die if he did. I would have had it a day sooner—I got the courage last Friday—but when I went to your parents' store, Hildegarde, your father was behind the counter. I just couldn't tell him what I wanted. There's a nice lady in Waverly, and she helped me." Straightening her glasses, she continued. "As I said, I got it Saturday—wrapped in paper so Mr. Dufresne wouldn't know. I told him it was two yards of batting for a quilt I'm making. I'm not wearing it yet because I'm still a little nervous about it. And my father doesn't know. I paid for it with the savings hidden in my Bohemian glass vase bank. And the sateen ribbons are the prettiest pink you'd ever see."

"Oh, buster, do I want a straight-front corset, too!" Hildegarde wailed. "My mother won't let me. And we have one in the case that's grand. Only it's a number twenty-two and I wear a . . . never mind. But she could order one in my size!"

"I wear a number twenty-two," Lucy said, musing. "And I've got some birthday money tucked in my underwear drawer. How much is it?"

"Three dollars," Hildegarde replied.

"Three whole dollars!" Lucy screeched.

Hildegarde defended the corset's value. "It's mercerized brocaded coutil. It's splendid material with a long directoire hip and back."

"Oh, Hildegarde, quit spouting the catalogue features." Meg turned in her seat. "We'd buy it if it was made out of burlap, so long as it was straight-fronted."

Inspiration lit Lucy's pale face. "Why, I'll go to Waverly just like Cressie and buy one there with my own money."

Ruth interjected, "You'll do no such thing, and you know it. None of us can go against our mothers. Cressie's lucky because she doesn't have one. Huuuhhh!" She clamped her slender hand over her mouth and her eyes bulged. "Oh, Cressie, I didn't mean it. You must miss your mother terribly. . . . I'm sorry. Please forgive me."

"It's all right, Ruth." Crescencia gazed downward at her desk, the lenses of her glasses reflecting her folded hands. "She died when I was seven. I'm used to not having a mother."

The furor over the corset vanished as soon as Johannah asked, "Well, that's enough talk about something we're not likely to get. What I want to know is has Mr. Dufresne kissed you yet?"

Edwina stepped in. "Johannah, it isn't polite to ask a lady such a thing."

Meg raised her hand. "But if Crescencia wants to tell, can she?"

Sighing, Edwina leaned back in her chair. "It's up to her."

A barrage of questions hit Crescencia all at once.

"Well?"

"Has he?"

"What was it like?"

"Did you kiss him back?"

"Well . . ." Crescencia blushed. "Yes . . . he has."

"Tell!"

Crescencia put the back of her hand to her forehead—on the dotted veiling, to be precise—and gazed dreamily at them. "I . . . dissolved."

Hildegarde sat straight and proper, took in a gulp of air, and said in a rush, "My mother says it isn't proper to be kissed unless you're married."

From the corner, Camille frowned, her lovely blond brows furrowed. "Stuff your mother, Hildegarde. Make up your own mind for a change."

Lucy seconded her sentiments. "Yes, do. It's always 'My mother said this and my mother said that.' Poop on your mother."

"Lucille," Edwina warned. "That's not acceptable language."

Her muttered "sorry" was appeasing.

Face red, Hildegarde lashed back. "At least I don't flaunt myself in front of men. I went to Mrs. Kirby's house to borrow a cup of blueing for my mother and when I walked by the feed and seed, I saw you standing with Julius Addison and he was making goo-goo eyes at you. And you were making them back!"

Defiant, Lucy shot back, "So what!"

Edwina stood and tapped the end of a ruler on the top of the desk. "Girls, this is quite enough," she said sternly. "The conversation has gotten out of hand. While I don't mind our discussing the opposite sex and our feelings toward them, I think you need to remind yourselves that you are young women who have the potential to enrich your lives until you get married. If you get married." She went around the desk to stand before them. "I think marriage is a wonderful thing for you and that's part of the reason I started the school—so you could learn how to make a home pleasant and be educated in sociable skills.

"While I'm not opposed to your wanting to be courted and to marry, I think you should also think about how you can sufficiently take care of yourselves and learn ways to be independent. I fear with all the other material we've been covering, I've fallen short of my duty to teach you this. You'll notice the pamphlet on your desk called 'Women's Vocations: Voices of the New Century.' We'll be studying that today."

Hildegarde's hand rose, the sleeve cuff of lace softly falling down her wrist. "My mother said independence breeds willfulness."

"Independence and willfulness are not the same." Edwina set the ruler down behind her and rested her backside on the desktop's edge. "The latter refers to a lack of compromise. The former refers to not being dependent on others. I don't think they are interwoven, unless the person chooses them to be." She gazed at the faces intently fixed upon her. "Has any one of you ever thought about ways you could earn your own money?"

Horrified brows rose and most shook their heads. It was a given that until they left their parents' houses and the responsibility of supporting them fell onto their husbands, they would be taken care of completely, without having to lift a finger.

Only two of the students raised their hands.

"Meg?" Edwina called.

The girl's coppery hair had been done up high with gold barrettes on the sides, and when she talked, her head moved and the gold flashed in the pulled-back strands. "I've always thought I could run my parents' hotel. I think I have a knack for people. I can talk to most anyone about most anything. I've even, on occasion, checked salesmen into the register."

"You told me your father let you hand them the pen," Hildegarde pointed out.

Meg glared at her. "Well, it should still count. I did give them the means by which to sign in." Her full lips pouted. "It's all so unfair, Miss Edwina. He's let my brother take over the entire operation before. And now that Wayne is in college, I don't see why I can't. Why, if given the chance"—she pointed a tapered fingernail thoughtfully in the air—"I could run that hotel with my eyes closed, and I'll bet I'd increase the room reservations by serving tea and scones in the lobby at four o'clock and offering free cigars to the gentlemen to smoke while they read the newspaper."

"That's an outstanding idea, Meg," Edwina said with enthusiasm. "I think you should propose it to your father."

"Little good it would do. My parents are going on a twenty-fifth anniversary trip this spring, and they don't trust *me* enough to keep the hotel running. They're having my grandmother come in to take over. It's as if my parents think I'm an infant and need watching. I'll be twenty next week and I'm still being treated like a child."

Not wanting Meg to see her reaction, Edwina kept a grim smile to herself. She'd had this very same argument with her own mother at Meg's age. All she could offer was knowing advice. "Keep trying, Meg. Your father may come around to your side eventually. If not, I've found mothers have softer spots in their hearts. After all, they were once girls your age, too." Edwina pushed away from the desk and walked in front of the crooked rows where the girls sat watching her with attention. "Camille, you raised your hand. What is it you'd like to do?"

With her blond good looks, Camille Kennison could very well be married to any man for which she set her cap. Edwina thought it admirable the girl had set her sights beyond that. "It may sound silly, really, but I want to be a part of something and know I changed its outcome. I can't define what it is I want . . . perhaps a project. A charity. A way to add fulfillment to my life. A larger-than-life something . . . I don't know." She shook her head in frustration. "I'm not making any sense."

"I think you are, dear." Edwina paused and pressed her palms together in front of her. "There's something out there for you that's calling to your ingenuity and spirit. You'll know it when it comes along. Keep looking. In the meantime, is there anything else you can do?"

"I've been thinking about enrolling in a music school

to take voice lessons. I can sing passably well, and I thought the experience would be good for me."

"I quite agree. If you need character references, I'd be happy to supply them for you." With a clasp of her hands at her waist, she continued. "Before we return to our deportment books, I'd like to tell you the story of Mrs. Lancaster. I know you all have heard it before—actually, we all lived it with Mrs. Lancaster. But it bears repeating. If you recall, she'd wanted a parlor addition to her house. Mr. Lancaster was opposed and voiced his displeasure by telling her a parlor would cost too much money. So Mrs. Lancaster began taking orders for hats and making them morning, noon, and night so that she could get the money to pay for the parlor herself. If you recall, she rented space from Mr. Knightly. She worked her fingers to the bone, never seeing any of the money—it went toward her rent. You might not have been aware of it, but Mr. Knightly set up an account for her so that she could charge her supplies through his store. Everything she bought and sold was tallied on Mr. Knightly's books. When her calculations told her she finally had enough to engage a carpenter for the parlor, she went to collect her due from Mr. Knightly. She found out she didn't have a cent. The money had gone to pay off Mr. Lancaster's debts to Mr. Knightly. Mrs. Lancaster had toiled entirely for her husband and not a cent went to her."

Impassioned with ire over Mr. Lancaster's duplicity that left her more than a little shaky, Edwina gazed seriously at her students. "This is why you must think of entering into marriage with your own funds so that you will never be subjected to working for nothing."

Chapter

❧ 15 ❧

Smoking a cigarette, Tom stood beside the open window-dowsill and gazed at the scene below the second story of the Knotty Pine hotel. The air rolling in through the opening was brisk and there was a feeling of Christmas in it. Outside, snow and ice gleamed in the paths and wheel ruts of Alder's streets. The sun had begun to set over the western pines, splashing the background behind them in muted hues of salmon.

He'd just come in and gone to his room after he and Edwina had spent the afternoon having lunch, then walking through the small town. They'd looked in shop windows and taken in the modest sights. Then he'd rented a bell-rigged sleigh and they'd ridden through the back hills with a fur blanket across their laps. It had been a good, relaxing time full of laughter. He'd enjoyed himself.

After they'd returned the sleigh, she'd gone back to the hotel without him. He'd gone inside the general store and picked up a few things for their dinner. The bags were on a table near the foot of the bed.

Pitching his smoke, he closed the window and walked through the room. His travel bag rested alongside the wall and his wet boots dried by the fireplace. A softly crackling fire burned within, warming the room and chasing the cold he'd let in from the window. In front of the fireplace, he'd laid out his bearskin rug, and on top of the dense fur sat a postal parcel in brown paper that he'd brought from Harmony.

Withdrawing his pocket watch, he glanced at the time before setting it on the table along with his change and billfold. He scraped a chair back and sat in it with a slouch, propping his feet on the tabletop. Knitting his fingers behind his head, he stared at the fire.

He'd been doing some thinking. He wondered if Edwina had had an affair with the man she'd been with before. If that was why she felt fine about all this—because she thought she knew what she was getting into. But Edwina didn't know what she was getting into with him. For him, he didn't think a purely sexual relationship was going to be enough.

Though he hadn't fallen in love with her, he'd felt the stirrings of it when he had her in the sleigh and got her laughing about a story he'd told her that involved him and Shay in Texas. When she'd smiled and gazed at him, her eyes warm with humor and tenderness, he'd been hit by a fast fist in the gut—an unseen one, but one no less powerful than if it had been Shay slugging him.

A light knock on the door had Tom jumping to his feet and twisting the knob to let Edwina in. Her room was down the hall and around the corner toward the front of the hotel and by the stairway to the lobby. He'd requested a room at the end of the corridor so she could come with little opportunity to be seen.

"Hey, Ed," he said and closed the door behind her. She walked to the center of the room and turned to face him, arms at her sides, a bit of bashfulness on her face.

"Hello." She raised her eyes to catch him watching her.

She'd changed dresses since they'd parted. This one was a two-piece thing in what looked like silk fabric with a shimmering effect to it. The outfit was a garnet color that appealed to him. It had a collar he knew was called a Gibson—he'd seen a case of them in Plunkett's mercantile with a sign selling the attributes. A type of sailor's tie at the base of the collar knotted at the top and fell over the fullness of her breasts. Her narrow waist was cinched with a belt the same color as the bodice. The skirt buttoned in the front all the way down to the floor.

He went toward her. "You're beautiful, Edwina."

Giving him a demure smile, she gazed at her dress, then at him. "This old thing?"

"It doesn't look old." He took her into his arms and lightly kissed her lips.

"Well, it is." She kissed him back.

The kiss was more of a greeting than anything else, an affirmation that they were together as a couple. As soon as he loosened his hold on her waist, she slipped free. Sweeping her gaze through the room, she commented on the bearskin. "Isn't that Mr. Dufresne's Halloween costume?"

Looking at the spread-out hide with its mammoth head and long body, Tom conceded, "Yep. I brought it from home."

"Whatever for?"

"To sit on. Haven't you ever sat on a skin before?"

Thought lit her eyes. "No . . . I can't say that I have."

"You'll like it."

Edwina further assessed his room. "You've got a fireplace. I have only a heater. How did you manage that?"

"I asked for one."

"Well . . . my goodness. I should have, too."

"There's only two in the hotel. This one and one in the room directly below mine."

"Then I'm glad I didn't ask. Walking past the registration counter and coming upstairs would have surely had the clerk wondering."

She seemed to be at ease, but telltale signs—like fidgeting with the folds of her skirt with her right hand, and trying to do it discreetly—tipped him off to the fact that she was more nervous than she was letting on.

"I got us some dinner." Tom moved to the table. "Do you want to eat?"

"If you do."

He didn't like when women wouldn't come out and state their preference. It wasn't like Edwina to be undecided. She normally said exactly what she meant or wanted. With a turn, he faced her. "You're being mealy-mouthed, Edwina."

She reacted exactly how he'd hoped—irritated. With fire in her eyes, a lift of her chin, and her hands placed belligerently on her hips, she begged to differ. "I most certainly am not being mealy-mouthed. I thought I was being polite."

"Don't be polite with me. I like you best when you're on your worst behavior."

"Well, what a thing to say. I pride myself on good manners."

Reaching inside one of the bags, he spoke in a mild tone. "Unpride yourself when you're with me." Before she could comment further, he held a tin of crackers in front of her. "Boston butters."

"Yes, so they are," she replied tightly, miffed at him.

He laughed at her pique. "I got sardines, too."

Nose crinkling, she sniffed. "I won't eat a single one. I dislike them."

He laughed harder, glad she was noncompliant. "I didn't really get any. I knew you didn't like sardines. I just wanted to see what you'd say."

Following the crackers, he produced a picnic carton of assorted cheeses, a jar of pickles and olives, and a box of lemon snap cookies. Rather than leave the food on the table, he piled it into his arms and carried it to the bear rug. "It's warmer over here. Take your shoes off and sit down."

Edwina sat on the chair and lifted her skirt hem enough to untie her shoes and loosen the laces. He watched as she set them neatly aside, both toes lined up with one another. The strangest vision came to him: her shoes on the end of a bed—their bed—and them lying in it . . . eating crackers, making love, not having to leave in the morning, staying together.

He shook the thoughts from his head as she came to him and lowered herself onto the rug, fanning the garnet silk around her bent knees.

"What's that?" She motioned to the package.

"Calhoon gave it to me this morning when I was on my way out of the livery. He caught me by the post office and said it was for you. Asked me if I'd bring it to the store to give to you on Monday." He stretched his legs out and leaned back on his elbow. "I took it. Couldn't help reading the label. Then I asked him why it wasn't addressed to you. He told me once a month you get a delivery for this said person and bring it over to this said person in Waverly. An old family friend."

Edwina pressed her lips together to stifle a grin.

Tom went on. "I got to thinking . . . H. T. Katz. It sounded familiar. Then I figured out who it was." Pointing at her, he said, "Your cat." As he opened the cracker tin with one hand, curiosity filtered through his voice. "Why would you have something sent to your cat and tell Calhoon it was for someone in Waverly?"

"You know why."

"Yeah, I think I do. There's beer in that package. O'Linn's."

She peeled the wax from a cube of cheese. "True."

"I knew it."

"Of course. You're smart."

"No, you're smart." Placing a large handful of crackers in the center of the rug, he regretted not thinking about plates and napkins. "How long have you been getting beer shipped to you like this?"

"Nearly six months."

"You're ingenious, Ed."

"Such flattery," she said flirtatiously.

He sat up. "As long as we've got the beer, what do you say we open two of them?"

"By all means. It's Saturday."

Reaching for the package, he asked, "What does Saturday have to do with it?"

"It's my beer night."

"Beer night," he repeated, thinking she was the most perplexing woman he'd ever known. Shaking his head, Tom looked hard at Edwina, trying to see through the multiple layers. Her tidy exterior presented modesty and reservation. But get past that and there was a bit of playfulness. From there, she sometimes broke down and became daring to a degree—as she had with the tree swing. That was usually as much of herself as she'd show him, although there had been those few times when she'd gone beyond that and he really got to the bare bones, to where she became uninhibited, like the night they'd danced ragtime together. He preferred that Edwina best.

"Do you have scissors?" Her question threw him from his thoughts. She gestured at the package in his lap.

"Don't need one." A strong tug pulled the string binding free and a few tears rent the paper from the box. Written across the sides in cursive red lettering was *O'Linn Brewery, Chicago, Illinois.* "I've never heard of O'Linn."

"It's bottled in a brewery off of Lake Michigan. It was popular where I went to school. They served it in the clubs."

"You drank in public?"

"Of course." Frowning at the bottle she said, "We don't have an opener."

Tom took the beer from her and swiped the cap across the side of a fireplace brick. The metal piece flipped off and suds began to foam from the bottle's mouth. Handing the O'Linn to her, he observed, "You just don't seem the type of woman to drink in a bar. Much less *be* in a bar, Ed."

She took a sip, then lowered the bottle to her lap. "We didn't call it a bar. The Peacherine was a dancing club. It was acceptable to have liquor while the band played."

Opening a beer for himself, he drank a long swallow. The liquid was slightly cool. He'd kept it with his horse tack in the local stable until an hour before, when he'd picked up the package.

For a moment, he tried to picture Edwina Huntington in a wild dancing club drinking beer and doing the crazy bones with a bunch of college men. The image unsettled him. He could see her laughing, cheeks flushed from exertion, sitting at a table with that Abbie and casting coy glances around the room, being herself, or who she might have been before that bastard snuffed the spirit from her.

Tom felt cheated. He would have liked to know Edwina when she'd been a carefree young girl. He wished she would be like that now—for always—because what snippets she sparingly showed him, he loved.

Loved. That part of Edwina, he could truly say he did love.

"Ed, why did you have to change so much?" The question came out before he could catch himself. But since he'd spoken his thoughts, he didn't stop. "Why can't you be yourself again?"

Disquiet surfaced in her expression. Her chin lowered, and her voice became whisper soft. "Being myself got me into a situation."

She didn't have to say it. He knew who she was thinking about.

"What was his name?"

Not looking up, she murmured, "Why do you want to know?"

"So I can quit calling him bastard."

Her smile had little humor in it when she gazed at him. "Ludlow. Ludlow Ogden Rutledge."

"Hell's aces," Tom swore. "He was a pompous blood."

"No. He was my college professor."

"Oh, Jesus. Even worse."

Tom lost any appetite he had. Gone was the care he'd taken in the past not to pressure Edwina to tell him anything about—Ludlow. *Ludlow Ogden Rutledge.* The name sounded like it belonged to a man in a book shelved on a dusty bookcase. A swell who wrote miserable novels of pain and suffering, yet hadn't a clue as to what pain and suffering was.

"How old was he?"

Edwina sighed, sat a little straighter, then gazed directly at him. "Twenty-six."

Tom took a lengthy drink of his beer, uncertain he wanted to know anything more, yet unable to quit when she was apparently willing to talk about it. "How did you meet?"

"I would think that's obvious." Leaning to her left, she tossed the cheese wax into the fireplace. The curls of red smoked and sizzled, their consumption by flames a statement about the room's change in atmosphere— from warm to heated, hot with tension, sparked.

"Yeah, I guess it would be." Jealousy overtook him, thorough and devouring. He had never felt it before. He didn't like being in its clutches now. It meant he was one step closer to falling completely in love with her.

Edwina grew mesmerized by the fire, her words faint and distant. "I never thought I'd want to talk about it. But I believe I want to tell you. Everything. So you won't judge me poorly."

Guilt fanned across him. "I never judged you wrong, Edwina."

"Perhaps not, but I think you've wondered. And not knowing has made you dream up what you can't imagine. Better that you know what happened so you can forget about it . . . like I have."

He didn't think she had forgotten about it. She never would. Maybe in time the memories would fade. But they would always be there.

"I did meet Ludlow in one of my classes. He taught advanced accounting and mathematics. Abbie took the class with me. I convinced her to in my third year, for her own benefit. She hadn't gone to Gillette's with me when I entered. Her social calendar had been more important. But when the parties began to dull for her, she agreed spending time on a college campus would be far more preferable than doing nothing at all.

"When Ludlow came in dressed in a long black gown, all the girls were agog over him. He was young, handsome, and available."

Tom took another pull of O'Linn, letting the beer slide down his throat slowly in an effort to keep his pulse even.

"We soon found out Professor Rutledge was easygoing and not at all as severe as our other professors. He took an interest in Abbie first. She was—is—very lovely and charming. He asked her to go to the Peacherine, and she told him she wouldn't go unless I went with them. So I did. That was the beginning. I had no idea that he would like me better. Or that I . . . would like him."

Edwina moved her gaze from the flames and leveled it on Tom. "Ludie did ask me to marry him, and I'd accepted before we . . . before anything . . ." She licked her lips. "We were to be married. I never would have if that promise hadn't been between us."

"Why didn't you marry?"

"His family didn't approve of me. Ludie didn't need the money from teaching. The Rutledges were quite well off. His father threatened to cut him off financially if he married me. Ludie had to choose between me and his family."

Tom's voice was cold when he ground out through clenched teeth, "More like between you and money, the greedy son of a bitch."

"Yes. That is the truth." Swallowing a small sip of beer, she said, "For a long time after I came home, I denied that truth. Nothing between Ludie and me was ever really resolved. He broke off the engagement the same week I received a letter from my mother telling me I had to come home and take care of her. I tried to rationalize what had happened and blamed myself for not being . . . better. For not being more like Abigail.

When I pressed Ludie for details, he conceded that his family thought me unsuitable because I didn't have connections or a social name."

"Who the hell cares about that?"

"Apparently, the Rutledges."

"Then they missed out. They could have had you for their daughter-in-law."

The snaps and pops from the fire, sending sparks up the flue, filled the void in their conversation as Tom digested all she'd told him. Things fell into place. Now he knew the reasons why Edwina tamped down her lighter emotions and whimsical feelings, why she didn't like to show her fun side unless goaded into surrendering her mask of propriety. That fun side had been hurt. Better to lock it up and forget it existed, show only the buttoned-up version—the façade that couldn't be cracked to allow the slight chance of being abused once more.

No wonder she'd fallen into an affair with him rather than holding out for a proposal. Edwina considered herself a fallen woman, unworthy of love because she was, in her mind, flawed from a past relationship. Her way of thinking was foolish. Maybe it would matter to some men—more than a few—but it didn't matter to Tom.

Before, he'd thought that it did . . . a little. The uncompromising male in him had been acting like an imbecile, as was his way every once in a while. But now that he knew the entire story, he felt ashamed for ever thinking, even for a moment, that it bothered him.

"If you don't marry, Ed," Tom said, "then you've let him win."

Taking a nibble of cheese, she waved her hand. "This isn't a game. Nobody wins. Nobody loses. It's my choice not to marry and I've told you why."

"I think this thing about aspirations is a front. First off, few women have them. Prune-faced schoolmarms, maybe—and they've got no choice because they aren't marriage material."

"It's not a front." Indignance filtered through her

voice. "I really would like to do something that counts.
I've found that I like teaching school more than I ever
thought I would. If I can't get a job using my accounting
certificate, I'll continue to teach. You don't think what
I do is admirable?"

"I never said that. What you do is all right for a
woman of your status. Okay, I'll admit you should be
proud of yourself. Should I concede it's of benefit to the
girls to teach them how to land men when the teacher
herself isn't ever going to?"

"Well, thank you for that little piece of cheese, Mr.
Cat."

"If you had a husband, you wouldn't have to work.
He'd take care of you."

"I don't want a husband."

"All women do."

"I'm not all women."

"Damned if you're not."

They stared off at each other in charged silence; then
Tom reached inside his shirt pocket for his pack of Richmonds. Not in a mood to ask if she minded, he fumbled
for a matchstick and lit one. But he did exhale smoke
toward the fireplace so as not to offend her. Rather than
letting up, he ran head on into the subjects. "You've
got a lot to offer a man. You're superior in the brain
department, which is more than can be said about a lot
of girls. I'm thinking of that Hildegarde Plunkett. Saw
her walk into a tree trunk once while she was gawking
at Calhoon's daughter and that Addison kid who works
at the feed and seed.

"You're pretty." He held hands up to show unbiased-
ness. "Not that a man looks only at a face. Or figure,"
he added with a lopsided smile. "You've done well, judging by the way you live—you've got a nice house and
stuff inside it. I noticed all that china and delicate-looking
glass junk in that curio cabinet. You must have a level
head on your shoulders about money, because you do
well financially, from the looks of things. The only fault
I can find is your compulsion to buy fad cures—I

couldn't help reading the return addresses on your mail one time. Okay, a couple of times." Taking a draw on his smoke, he said after exhaling, "You've never seemed sickly to me—so what the hell do I know? Maybe that crap works."

Her melodious laughter filled the room, her eyes bright as new leaves. "Oh, Tom. I never thought I'd confess this. Least of all to you." Forcing an expression of seriousness, she conceded, "I'm dead broke."

Gazing through narrowed eyes, he balked. "No."

With a sigh, she said, "Deplorably and miserably and always a step away from giving over my house to the mortgage company. That's why I'm teaching finishing school. At least it's one of the reasons. The others are legitimate. I do believe my girls should better their lives and be taught everything they can about being self-supporting."

"What happened to all your money? If you don't mind my asking. I mean, well, damn . . . you live in the north-end of town."

"So? That has nothing to do with anything." She re-arranged her legs so that she sat like him: Indian style. Black-stockinged toes peeked from the edges of the gar-net silk. "I inherited a lot of bills from my parents. They bought all the elixirs, the fad cures, and books on home therapy. My father had a small life insurance policy, but my mother went through the money in less than three years and didn't think about what she was going to do when it ran out. With the bills coming in—and I'm still uncertain how they managed to buy all of this on credit—she put a second mortgage on the house. I have two monthly payments to make. And believe me, it isn't easy."

Tom was momentarily speechless with surprise. When the severity of what she'd just said sunk in, he whispered in amazement, "Jesus . . . I should have paid you more than the five bucks I did for doing my books."

"You paid me just fine. I told you I charged fifty cents an hour, which was a very high-end rate—certainly not what I'd make working for someone else. The five dollars just about covered Marvel-Anne's wages for the month." She took a bite of cracker. After chewing, she added, "A teacher makes only about twenty-five cents an hour. I know it for a fact that Miss Gimble at the normal school is on a salary of thirty dollars a month, eight months of every year. Quite sufficient money for a woman in this day and age."

"I had no idea women got stuck like that. I don't keep up with that kind of stuff." He flicked his cigarette butt into the fire and picked up a cracker for himself. "I made fifty dollars last week when I took those six Connecticut lawyers out for the day. I'm not telling you to brag about it—just telling you so you'll know you're not charging enough for your services. I should have known that."

"No one is going to pay me more than fifty cents an hour. To think otherwise is an absurdity."

Eating the cracker, then washing it down with a swill of beer, Tom observed, "Well, it stinks."

"Oh, you should talk. You're the biggest disbeliever of all. You think women are inferior to men. Don't deny it."

He swelled his chest and showed his brawn, proving her point. "Sort of. But I think you could make me come around—only because I like your logic. And your mouth." Leaning forward, he gave her a kiss.

She tasted like buttery crumbs. He lightly traced the corners of her lips with his tongue, then met her mouth solidly once more. Nowhere did they touch but their lips. Harmoniously. Her part moan, part sigh, part laugh made him smile through the kiss.

"What?" he murmured.

"You."

Disengaging from her mouth and pulling slightly back, he said, "What about me?"

"Only you can discuss women's equality and their body parts in the same breath and get away with it. You're a toad."

He gave her a quick kiss, then straightened. "But you like me anyway."

"Too much for my own good."

Grinning, he declared, "I grow on people."

"So do warts."

"Then maybe I am a toad."

Their laughter mingled while they ate the crackers and cheese, then opened two more beers. Tom unscrewed the pickle and olive jars, taking pleasure in feeding food to Edwina, his belly knotting when she wrapped her lips about his fingertip. She spoke about a variety of things while she sometimes lifted a pickle to his mouth or a slice of cheese. He listened, but not really, instead watching her facial features as she changed them, depending on what she said. He took in her gestures, the way she said certain words, and how she absently stroked the fur on the rug. For every minute that went by, he grew more and more enamored of her.

"Oh! I didn't tell you." Her hand reached out to rest intimately on his wrist as she declared enthusiastically, "We're getting our own dentist! Dr. Teeter. He's moving his practice to Harmony."

She went on, babbling in a way that he thought cute, while rearranging the cheese cubes into a perfect pyramid. "I found out he's been writing to Johannah Treber, not Hildegarde Plunkett, whom he seemed interested in after he rescued her from the apple—or rather, Mrs. Plunkett was interested in *him*. Even though the outcome of the whole thing has benefitted us, the ladies are still blaming Mrs. Brooks for the mix-up because she told them doctors had made the reservations. But how was she to know they were dentists?

"We all should have known. Thirteen. It's an unlucky number. Especially on Halloween." Her fingers stopped their fiddling and she locked her gaze with his. He had been intently observing her every move. "What?" Her baffled grin brought out the beauty in her face. "You're staring at me."

He shook his head with a partial smile. "God, Edwina . . . I love you." Though he'd spoken it lightly and with amusement, he feared he really meant it.

Edwina laid contentedly on her side with her cheek on Tom's bare chest and her hand resting lightly over the thrum of his heartbeat. They had remained on the bearskin rug and, after finishing their picnic dinner, had made love—slow and mesmerizing and new, as if they'd never been together at her house. He'd done things to her body she'd never imagined, kissed her in places that were shocking. But she was shameless in wanting him to . . . and she in turn had touched him, explored him— everywhere. The experience had been draining, utterly satisfying, like no other pleasure she had known. The bed's counterpane now covered them with its warmth as they cuddled, legs still entwined.

In the quiet of the room, she listened to Tom breathing to the music of the fire in the hearth. Outside, the skies had darkened; Tom had drawn the shades. They hadn't lit any lamps in the room; the flames from the fireplace bathed the pale walls in a cozy amber hue.

Closing her eyes, Edwina's thoughts drifted. . . .

Edwina . . . I love you.

The significance of Tom's words had momentarily stalled her pulse, until she'd read through them and gleaned that the sentiment had been spoken good-naturedly, as one would speak to a younger brother or sister—not as a man to a woman, truly meaning everything the endearment could represent.

Though the realization had made her ache when she recognized the truth, she was thankful he didn't really love her. He couldn't possibly. Not when she'd told him she would never marry. And if he did . . . for some reason . . . fall in love with her . . . well, she wouldn't let him. She just couldn't.

But what about her? What if she accidentally fell in love with him? It would be horrible, damning everything she was working toward—self-sufficiency, her independence, her life as she'd mapped it out after Ludlow. Oh, she hated to think about the consequences of loving Tom Wolcott. Adamantly, she fought against even the thread of a notion that maybe she could—was.

"Are there any more of those lemon snaps left?" Tom's deep voice rumbled in her ear.

"Maybe a few. You dug into them fairly good before. I believe you had some thirty—or more."

"Counting, were you?"

"No . . . just thinking you must not get sweets very often." She propped herself onto her elbow. "Just where do you eat all the time? At the restaurant?"

He gazed at her, blue eyes hooded and relaxed. The smile on his mouth was a little boyish-looking to her. She reached over and stroked a lock of hair from his brow. "Mostly, I eat at the restaurant. This winter, I've cooked a few things in my room on the heater plate. I never did in the summer, though. It's hot as hell up there, so I'm not about to stoke up a fire."

Edwina had never really thought about meals and how they were always a ready item in her life. It was a given that Marvel-Anne had her dinner ready at six o'clock. Sometimes Edwina would help. She enjoyed cooking. Other times, she was grateful for Marvel-Anne's reliability, as she could get caught up in gardening, schoolbooks, and lesson planning.

The desire to fix Tom a nice home-cooked meal was an appealing one. From where the want to take care of him had come, she couldn't figure. Her students' mothers would go on about how rewarding it was to do for a man. But their husbands could sometimes be unappreciative, and that would get them started on what nuisances most of their mates could be. Edwina had merely listened to them go on, thinking it somewhat of a relief she wasn't in the same situation.

But with Tom . . . she . . . well, Tom would be a different kind of husband. She was sure. She felt sorry for him that he didn't have a loving wife and food on his table. But she didn't feel sorry in a way that was pity—it was more as if he were an orphaned little kitty she was compelled to take in and give a bowl of milk and affection. Not that Tom would drink milk. And the loving wife she was picturing was none other than—Heaven help her—herself. Really, such a thought about kittens, a wife, and Tom was rather stupid. Yet, looking upon his face, seeing the lines of laughter at the corners of his eyes, his strong forehead, his brooding mouth and square jaw—the whole of which was not helpless or in any way weak—she couldn't help wanting to do for him. Because he didn't ask for anything, she wanted to give him something. It was the most unexpected feeling, a dizzy lightheadedness . . . and a pang that hit her in her ribs, leaving her shaky and rattled.

She really should plan another social party for the girls . . . focus on one of them finding a beau instead of mulling over the empty possibilities of having one for herself. She could do something in conjunction with the New Year's Eve ball. She'd have to ask Mrs. Brooks if any large groups had reservations. Or she could ask Tom right now and get an answer, only she didn't want him knowing what she was up to. He might try to talk her out of it.

Since anything having to do with cooking Tom a meal or . . . performing any other kind of domestic duty . . . was purely fantasy, the least she could say was, "I'll get you the cookies."

Reaching behind her, she grabbed the box and handed them to him. Tom put his arm over his head and fumbled for a short pile of newspapers she'd seen stacked on the hearth bricks earlier. She'd assumed they had been left by the management as kindling. Not so. Tom opened the *Montana Herald*.

"You ever read the funny papers, Ed?"

"Good heavens, no."

Tom readjusted his position to lie on his side, the top of the bedspread sliding down to his waist. The newspaper crinkled as he opened it, then he neatly folded the pages so the funnies were compressed into a rectangle. He flipped the cracker box lid up, stuck his hand inside, and lifted a lemon snap to her. "Have one."

She took it, then tucked the counterpane beneath her arms and reclined on her side. The bearskin felt deliciously sensual against her naked skin. She'd never thought she'd ever lie on one, much less in the nude. She almost giggled, but she could see Tom's expression had turned expectant as he waited for her to settle in. She did so, snuggling in and nibbling on her cookie.

" 'Katzenjammer Kids,' " he said and pointed to the strip of three boxes. "Listen to this: 'It would be a shame to give dear teacher all this for her birthday.' "

She tilted her head, trying to follow along with him upside down. He moved on. She didn't pay close attention to the next box and she lost him. " '. . . could stand their digestion.' "

Tom's laugh was rich. "That's funny."

"Hmm. Yes." Though she didn't find humor in what little she'd heard.

He continued. " 'Here comes Paddy . . .' " She watched how his mouth moved when he read and smiled at the same time. His lips were firm and wide; the edges of his teeth where white. At his jaw, a muscle flicked, giving him a dimple she'd never noticed before. " '. . . Hello dar, fellers.' "

He gazed eagerly at her for a reaction, but she had to disappoint him. "Sorry," she murmured. "I still think it's scatterbrained and silly." *About as silly as a zebra's behind for a clock.* But, of course, she didn't make that comparison aloud.

A scowl overtook his features. "You're not getting it. See, Paddy, he's this kid—they're all kids—German immigrants. That's how come they talk the way they do. They have these accents and . . ." Again, she paid more attention to his lips than the words coming out of them. If she could have those lips anytime she wanted, she would be in Heaven. Blissfully. Eternally.

Unbidden, a smile crept over her mouth. It caused Tom to stop his narration and quit pointing at the pictures in the paper, frame by frame. "Is it funny now?"

"I'm chuckling with wild enthusiasm," she retorted, trying to force a laugh in her tone. Then she added a few ha-ha's for good measure.

Tom grabbed the paper and hurled it aside, then scooped her into his arms so that she lay on top of him. Her unbound hair fanned over both their shoulders in a cascade of firelit brown. The press of their bodies together got Edwina's full attention and brought to life waves of tingling across her skin.

In a voice thick with warning—and she sensed, seduction—Tom said, "You aren't laughing at the funnies. You're laughing at me."

"Not I. No, never. I wouldn't do that to you—certainly not. 'Katzenjammer Kids'—funny stuff. Yes, I love them." Keeping her giggle at bay wasn't so easy. It filtered through every sentence until at the end, she laughed thoroughly in earnest.

He grinned as he declared, "You're a liar."

"Absolutely . . . yes. What are you going to do about it?"

His eyes darkened, and he cupped the back of her head to bring it down for a kiss. He smothered her with a mastery that brought her to a fiery arousal within a single instant. The taste of lemon snap cookies melted against her lips and was sweet as her tongue entered his mouth. Her hips moved over his, wiggling immodestly as he slipped inside her.

Breaking the kiss, she braced both hands on either side of him. His hands came up to fondle her breasts, teasing the nipples and coaxing a moan from her. She wanted to move, but she refused to let the moment go by quickly. She wanted this to last all night. It felt too good to end.

Slowly, he began the rhythm of sex and her unraveling. She'd known he had that affect on her since that day in the lawyer's office. One gaze from him and she was undone. But she had him now and he could unwind her as long as he wanted until tomorrow.

She mumbled in a low and barely coherent voice, "Go slow . . ."

"I can go slow or fast. If you want slow, I'll give you slow." His smile reached his eyes. She saw confidence. To put that confidence to the test, she met his tempo with one of her own, a leisurely wiggle in her hips that made him swear and brought a mist of sweat to his brow.

"What are you trying to do? You said slow. If you move like that, it's not going to be slow."

Leaning forward so her breasts grazed against his chest, she purred, "But you said you could do slow. You're the dominant male. What you say is law."

His eyes snapped with self-control. "One times one is one. One times two is two—"

"What are you doing?"

"Distraction," he said through a half growl. "Multiplication. One times three is three. . . ."

Brushing a kiss along the side of his neck, she whispered, "You think you're so smart."

"Damn right." He kissed her ear, causing her to shiver. "I know my nines now, too. . . . Three times one is three. . . ."

His voice faded, and she let the pleasure ride through her body. She thought he'd reached his sixes . . . but she couldn't be certain. All she could focus on was the delightful spiral filling her with every move.

Edwina began to break down when he started on sevens, and she surrendered, pleading for him to stop his eights tables. He went through half of them, then his voice trailed. She never heard the promised nines. And, frankly, she didn't care. Tom drew her into a complete and shuddering ecstasy that left them both shattered.

As she collapsed onto his chest, her spent breath mingling with his, she smiled to herself and wondered if he'd ever manage to get to division.

Chapter

❧ *16* ❧

My Dear Miss Huntington:

    I received your reply and have to regretfully respect your decision to remain in Montana. Let me please say that if you should ever desire to come to our fair city, you would be quite welcome. If I cannot accommodate you, I have connections with other women in business who would be enthusiastic about interviewing you. You have my card listing my address, and I can also be reached by telephone now! Ring the operator. A modern woman I am!

              Yours,
              Madame Janette DeVille
              House of DeVille Bridal Salon

Edwina had read the letter twice. She set the parchment in her lap and stared across the parlor in thought.

The odds of finding a position in Denver were good. Probably better than good. She should have been elated, thrilled beyond words. But she was not. The letter meant freedom. Escape. And suddenly, escaping Harmony didn't seem so critical anymore.

With this letter, she had a way out. She hadn't thought

such a means would come so quickly . . . or so easily. When she'd first told Madame DeVille she'd been unavailable, Edwina had assumed that was the end of things. For a while, anyway—until she got her affairs in order. And afterward, she would be free to resume her search for bookkeeping opportunities, to make her mark using the education she'd fought her mother so valiantly for.

But lately . . . being a businesswoman seemed a little tunneled, a little less broadening, and a little too defined. Those old pangs of wanting marriage for herself, those old dreams of finding a true love and settling into a nest, were surfacing. She hadn't felt them since Ludlow. This was awful.

She'd wanted to go to school partly to get away from her parents' influence and partly to learn something of the world outside of Harmony. In both, she had succeeded. She hadn't known how well having a business degree would help her until Ludlow broke their engagement. Since she'd no longer be a suitable bride, she could at least fall back on something to support herself.

Edwina glanced at the letter once more. If only she hadn't met Tom. How would she feel about Madame's words then? Most likely, jubilant, on a cloud of hope and enthusiasm. Why couldn't she feel that way now?

Heaven help her, she was falling in love with him, the last thing she needed to do. Complexities—loving him would bring such complexities into her life, yet it would change nothing. She still meant what she said about never marrying. And she still stood by her convictions that a woman should bring something good into a marriage instead of debt and worry—and a lack of purity.

Edwina was of the old school in some ways. It would always matter to a man that the woman he wed belong only to him on their wedding night. She and Tom had had nights together that were not sanctioned by a church. They had gone against what society deemed appropriate. She hadn't cared. She still didn't care. But that didn't make the inevitable easier to swallow.

Eventually, their relationship would have to come to an end. They couldn't go on like this indefinitely. Losing Tom would be like losing her only friend. . . . Quiet reflection brought her to that realization. Tom Wolcott was her friend. She had many lady friends, but not a one to whom she could speak openly on almost any topic.

Once, she might have felt this way about Abbie, but they'd grown apart since Edwina had returned home. Abbie hadn't written much in the past seven months, only very brief notes with little information of a private nature. Just mundane, safe subjects—the weather, how she wasn't pursing any kind of vocation with the two-year degree she'd earned from Gillette's. Abbie didn't need the money; her parents provided quite nicely for her. She had an affluent family; going to Gillette's had been nothing more than a diversion from the humdrum.

Edwina wondered if Abbie ever saw Ludlow. Nobody had known about their engagement—Ludie had made Edwina promise to keep it a secret until he could talk to his parents about them. Abbie had known she and Ludie were close—after all, they had gone most places together, but never anything that could be misconstrued as other than a professor and a gang of students having a good time. Although with his being a teacher and they, members of his class, they had gone somewhat over the line socially by fraternizing at the dancing parlors. And there had been the times they'd gone to the ice-cream parlor, or the Midway Plaisance. But there were also those times when she and Ludie had gone off alone. . . .

The fancy black walnut Monarch clock on the mantel gonged the hour: six-thirty. At seven, she was to be at the Stykem house on Crescencia's request. She had a suspicion what the evening would entail.

Marvel-Anne lumbered from the dining room into the parlor. She'd taken her apron off and had looped her pocketbook handles on the bend in her elbow.

"I've put the bread dough in the icebox for tomorrow. It's a new recipe from Mrs. Kirby. I don't know how yeast can live in the cold, but she claims the lower temperature does something to its composition. We shall see." Her buxom bosom thrust forward on a tired sigh.

"Thank you, Marvel-Anne. I'm sure the bread will be wonderful."

"We shall see," she repeated. "I'll be going home now, Miss Edwina."

"Certainly."

Edwina rose and went to the vestibule with the housekeeper as the woman took up her hat and coat from the tree. She placed the unadorned felt bonnet on her salt-and-pepper hair, jamming the pin home in the back. Then she buttoned up to her throat and smoothed gloves down her fingers.

"It's icy out there tonight," she commented. "I've ashed the walkway, but you mind your step when you visit Miss Stykem. Especially on the sidewalks. The city streets aren't taken care of the way they should be. Those holes on Sugar Maple are a downright menace."

"I'll be careful." Edwina held the door open for her and stood next to the jamb. "You be careful, too."

"I always am."

Edwina stayed a moment and watched as the gruff housekeeper took mincing steps down the walkway.

A thought came to Edwina . . . quite sad and distressing. When she went to Denver, what would happen to dear Marvel-Anne?

Tom and Shay moved around the interior of Hess's Livery. Lamplight from above threw off soft yellow on the walls, the saddle racks, the row of stalls, and tack hanging on doors. From the rafters, several whitetail antler chandeliers hung with kerosene lamps fit inside the network of tines. The cross-braced doors had been closed in an effort to keep the inside heated for the animals as they unloaded gear. The outfitters who'd just returned had gone up to the Brooks House Hotel.

"You got a watch on you?" Shay asked, undoing a double diamond–hitched knot on a chestnut pack horse.

"No. But I suspect it's close to six-thirty."

Shay walked to the horse's other side and loosened the knots there until the canvas-wrapped pack slipped free of the animal's back. "We've got to be at Cressie's at seven. It's really important. I'm going to have to leave you in five minutes. I want to clean up first. Shave and all."

"You can leave now, if you want. I can finish this." Tom removed a set of elk antlers that had been skull-side up and set them in the corner with a front quarter of meat.

"You've got to be there on time, too. I'll just get Winchester ready for a brush-down. There's only one more horse to do after you're finished with Ned."

Tom pulled a bowline knot free and removed the other front quarter of elk. "Is there anything you can tell me about tonight before I get there?"

Shay cut the distance between them with a side glance. "Not really. Cressie and I want things just right. We've had this planned for five days." Returning to the bay and beginning to unlatch the cinches, he spoke in a reminiscent tone from the underside of Winchester's belly. "Me and you, we go back a ways."

"We do."

"And I never thought about the future and all that. It was just me and you and seeing what we could of the country. I've always thought I was a wandering man. That was until I got here."

"Felt that way myself. Nice town."

"Nice women," Shay added while straightening. "Cressie, now, she's not real smart. And I'm not saying that in any kind of disrespectful way. It's just that she had a hard time with schooling and it just takes her a little longer than most to figure out things. So me and her, we have this common bond, you know? I left school at sixteen and she stuck it out but still struggled. She knows how it is."

"That's good."

"Oh—she did tell me she got the typewriter mastered. She'd never changed a ribbon on it until that day you came into the office. She wanted me to mention that to you so she wouldn't look bad."

Tom went around to Ned's bridle and unbuckled the ear strap. "No need. I never thought worse of her for it."

"She didn't want you thinking she was inept. She isn't. Cressie, she tries to better herself. That's why she's going to Miss Huntington's school."

"An admirable thing for a woman to do." Tom began to have a feeling where all this was leading. And it really was no surprise. "Women who can understand and respect a man's past and present are good women to love."

"Yes, I surely love Crescencia."

"I figured you did."

"What about you and Miss Huntington?"

Tom went still a moment, then continued working. He hadn't told Shay, and never would, about him and Edwina meeting. Even though he and Shay had few, if any, secrets from one another, this one would go to Tom's grave.

Coiling the ropes into loops, Tom said, "There's nothing about me and Miss Huntington."

"I was thinking there might be some hope for you that night we took the girls out for dinner. I saw the way she looked at you, Tom. I may not be the smartest of men, but I know a look of pining when I see one."

"Well, friend, I think you read the message wrong. Miss Huntington said she isn't interested in marriage."

"Every woman is."

"That's what I told her. She said otherwise."

"Damn shame. She's a handsome woman."

"More than that," Tom murmured, bending down to snag a curry brush he'd made out of a piece of hand-sized wood and Coke bottle caps; it worked better than a brush, in his estimate, to get the mud off the horse's hocks.

"Maybe you could make her come around. Show her your charm."

"She's immune to charm."

"Sounds like she's a tough nut to crack."

Tom gave a low laugh. "Worse than a walnut."

"If she's what you want, she's worth going after, no matter how long it takes to make her come around to your way of thinking."

"But a man can go only so far without nicking his pride to hell and back."

"What's pride when love's at stake?" Shay's expression sobered. "Tom, me and you have caroused with our share of women. I think when you find someone you know you can live with for the rest of your life, you shouldn't let her get away. That doesn't mean making an ass out of yourself. It just means having patience."

"My patience only goes so far."

"Then stretch it—if Miss Huntington is worth it. Is she?"

Tom mulled over the question, absently removing his hat and running a hand through his hair. "Yes. But the Edwina I want isn't someone she's willing to share with the world."

"I don't follow you."

"She's got a few sides to her that are different from the woman you see when you look at her."

Shay nodded, all-knowing. "Likes to let her hair down, huh, but doesn't want anybody to know?"

"You could say that."

"That's a tough one. All I can say is, tell her it's all right to let it down."

"Tried that and she got into a little trouble."

"That tree swing you told me about."

"Yeah."

"Well," Shay said, musing, "if the old birds in this town want to peck, let them."

"What are you getting at?"

"Make Miss Huntington realize you're the better choice. Put her in your life."

Tom settled his Stetson back on his head and narrowed his eyes in thought. "Like how?"

"Hell," Shay said with a laugh, "that's for you to decide. I gave you the idea."

They went back to work in silence a short while, then as Tom rounded Ned's backside, he noticed Shay had completely stripped the bay of gear.

Shay stilled his hands on the top of the horse's sweating back; steam rose from the damp hide. Then he absently ran a palm through the whorls in Winchester's coat. "You are going to stay in town, aren't you, Tom? No more moving on—right? That's what you said. We've talked about it—you and me. Right here."

Tom ran the makeshift curry down Ned's back knee. "Of course I'm staying here." Then his brows knit together. "Why? Are you thinking about moving on?"

"Hell, no. I've got a good job." He gave Tom a half smile. "I hope business is as good forever as it is now."

"I don't plan on it changing. As long as there's game to be had, there will be men who want to go after it."

"That's a comfort to hear."

Tom laid his elbow on Ned's back and stared at Shay. "You've done a hell of a job with the outfitters, Shay. I couldn't run the business without you. I want you to take all the money from today's job."

Resting arms on his own horse, Shay groused, "That's not our agreement."

"I don't give a damn what the agreement is. You're taking all the money."

"It's not a good habit to get into, Tom. We're partners. We split the runs down the line. I don't feel right taking more than my share."

Tom shot him a smile. "Then consider it a wedding present."

Shay looked appropriately nonplused, going as far as shaking his head in a negative way. "But there isn't going to be a—" Then he broke into a grin. "Well, hell, Wolcott, I never could pull one over on you."

Tom laughed with him. "I'll still act surprised when you and Miss Stykem make the big announcement."

Edwina sat erectly in the Stykems' parlor chair, her hands folded in her lap. Crescencia, along with her father, occupied the brocade settee beside her. On the divan at the opposite side of the room, Mr. Dufresne and Tom took up plum-colored wing chairs. Both men were hatless and polished. Hair wetted back, clean shirts and pants. Mr. Dufresne had shaved. Edwina could tell Tom hadn't. But he didn't look any less well attired for not. In fact, she thought she'd never seen him more handsome in a dark tan sweater with lacing at the throat and jean trousers that were a little faded. On him, the worn blue didn't look unkempt at all.

Nobody had said much of anything since Tom and Mr. Dufresne had shown up, several minutes behind Edwina. Offers for tea and moonlight cake were made by Crescencia, but all declined.

Finally Mr. Dufresne stood and cleared his throat. "Since none of us are going to dig into that delicious-looking cake Crescencia baked, I'd like to say what has to be said so we can get on with the evening and do it up proper." He went to Crescencia, took her hand in his, then bent down on one knee.

Rather than gazing at her, he caught Mr. Stykem's attention. "Mr. Stykem, I already asked this of Cressie, but I wanted to ask again with you present." Only after he had the elder man's undivided attention did he then focus entirely on the woman whose hand he held within his own.

Edwina felt tears flood her eyes. She had suspected that this was what the evening was about, so she shouldn't cry. But as Crescencia sat on the edge of her seat, smile wavering on her mouth and her father reaching into his trouser pocket for a handkerchief, Edwina could barely contain her emotions.

"Cressie . . ." Mr. Dufresne began. Edwina's eyes never left the couple. "I know we haven't known each other for all that long." Crescencia nodded, her red-orange hair gleaming and neatly in place. "But sometimes a man and woman just know it's meant to be." Mr. Dufresne gave her hand a slight squeeze and Edwina held her breath, trying to keep calm. "I've got an honest job. And I've got some money saved up so that I can rent us a house." Crescencia smiled, Mr. Dufresne's reflection caught for a moment in the glass of her wire spectacles. "You wouldn't want for anything. I'll take care of you." A tear slipped down Crescencia's pale cheek. "Miss Crescencia Louise Stykem, will you marry me?"

Before she could give her answer, Mr. Stykem honked his nose loudly in his handkerchief. Edwina dared a glance at Tom, who stared unblinking at her, as if it had been him waiting for *her* answer. Quickly looking away, her cheeks hot and her stomach churning with raw emotions, Edwina gazed at her lap and fought off tears.

"Yes, Mr. Dufresne, I will marry you," came Crescencia's soft-spoken reply.

Mr. Stykem sounded the horn of his nose once more, then dabbed at his eyes before speaking. "If only your mother were here to witness this."

Crescencia, still holding Mr. Dufresne's hand, looked at her father. "Then you approve, Papa?"

"Approve? Why, my dear, I'm delighted! I never thought the day would come. Forgive me for my past pessimism, but you have blossomed into a beautiful woman." Mr. Stykem stood and so did Mr. Dufresne; then the two men were pumping each other's hands and laughing jovially. "Welcome to the family, my boy."

Crescencia rose as well. Edwina remained still, feeling awkward and out of place. Such an intimate moment to be a part of . . . she felt like an intruder when she should have been flattered she'd been included in this special announcement.

Tom went to his feet and broke up Mr. Dufresne and Mr. Stykem. He refused the hand Mr. Dufresne held out; instead, he took the man in a big bear of a hug and lifted him off the rug. "Congratulations, brother." Then he set Mr. Dufresne down and Mr. Dufresne slapped Tom on the back, quite heartily. Edwina guessed it was one of those sacred male moments in which physicality was required so they could keep their masculine façades in place. Apparently, Mr. Stykem had left that ritual behind, for he still snorted into his handkerchief and blatantly rubbed at his eyes.

Edwina stood and offered Crescencia her hand. "Best wishes to you, Cressie. I couldn't be happier for you."

Crescencia's face was bright, her eyes sparkling. Joy became her; she seemed so much more pretty and confident. "I owe a lot of it to you, Miss Edwina. You gave me some faith in myself—and Mr. Dufresne . . ."—she cast a shy glance at him—"he gave me love."

Biting the inside of her lip, Edwina smiled and embraced the young woman. "You had the faith all along; it just took a while to develop."

Edwina pulled back and made a conscious effort to keep her wits about her. It would serve no purpose but to utterly embarrass her if she fell into a puddle of tears. This was harder for her than she imagined it could be. She'd known she would go to weddings and christenings and sit on the sidelines. She'd thought she would be able to handle the situations as they arose. But because she was close to Crescencia's age, this was harder to live through: because Cressie was twenty-two, her chances for a husband had been considerably dim; because Edwina was twenty-four, hers were nonexistent.

Old maid . . . spinster . . . auntie . . .

Edwina shuddered. The words society would apply to her were not easy. But worse yet were the ones she'd called herself: unworthy, ruined, hopeless.

Bucking up her spirits, Edwina managed to smile with the others, only to find Tom's gaze riding on her. Her lips softened, and she looked away. She couldn't let him see her hurt. She wanted no pity from him. She'd made her own mistakes, and she had to live by them.

"We want you to stand up for us," Crescencia said. "Our dearest friends, Mr. Wolcott and Miss Edwina."

"And I'll be there to give the bride away." Mr. Stykem laughed, his voice still wobbly with excitement.

"Me and Cressie," Mr. Dufresne began, slipping his arm comfortably about Crescencia's waist, "we thought

a Christmas Eve wedding would be nice. I know it
doesn't leave us much time to plan, but we're both too
anxious to wait longer."

"I never envisioned myself as a winter bride," Crescencia said, blushing as she looked Mr. Dufresne.
"Or . . . for that matter . . . a bride at all. I'd hoped I
could one day wear Mama's gown, but I was afraid to
hope too much."

Mr. Stykem opened the liquor cabinet and produced
a bottle of sherry. "This occasion calls for a toast. Crescencia, if you would be so good as to get your mother's
cut stem glasses that go with Grandmother Frederick's
English crystal service."

"Yes, Papa." She went into the dining room and
opened the hutch.

Edwina knit her fingers together and stared a hole
into the vine and grape leaf carpet pattern. Mr. Dufresne's and Mr. Stykem's voices surrounded her, but
she didn't hear the words. Lost in her own silence, she
needed to collect herself.

She felt Tom draw up behind her. Slowly, she turned
her head and met his eyes.

"Good news about Shay and Miss Stykem," he remarked. His tone was quiet and guarded, as if he knew
how affected she was by Crescencia and Mr. Dufresne's
marriage plans.

"Yes. Isn't it." She refused to lower her gaze from
his. "I'm quite happy for them, and I'll be honored to
stand up for Crescencia."

"Can you stand up there and accept that you'll never
have a turn?"

"Of course I can," she half snapped. "I'm a mature
woman. I know my place."

He leaned closer and lowered his voice, saying for
her ears alone, "I don't think you know anything of the
kind, Ed."

"Sherry, everyone!" Mr. Stykem exclaimed through
the frost enveloping Tom and Edwina. He began to pass
out the glasses, giving one to Edwina and winking. "My

dear, I hope you aren't one of those women who've taken the solemn pledge. A little splash won't damage your sensibilities."

She readily took the glass. "I'm certain it shan't."

Soon everyone had a drink in hand and Mr. Stykem stood proudly, his chest puffed like a robin's. "This moment is one of special meaning not only for my daughter, but for me. And for her mother." He blinked his eyes, then fumbled inside his trouser pocket and came out with his handkerchief. "I wish my Louise could be with us to toast her girl and her intended. Because she is not, let me say that we are both giving you our blessings." Then to Cressie, with a gleam of mischief in his gaze, "I suppose this means I'll have to find another secretary to run the office."

Crescencia gaily laughed through the tears shimmering in her eyes. "Yes, it does."

Her father came forward to kiss both of her cheeks. He raised his glass. "To Crescencia and Mr. Dufresne."

"Shay," Mr. Dufresne said, correcting him.

Edwina's glass rose to the toast, then mechanically, she brought it to her lips. The first dry sip exploded on her tongue, then warmed and burned a trail down her throat as she let the sherry slip into her mouth. She would have drained the glass in one quick swallow if she thought she could get away with it.

"Shall I cut some cake now for anyone?" Crescencia asked, cheeks rosy.

"I'll take the biggest slice you can manage to fit on my plate," Shay replied with a broad grin.

Laughter abounded, Edwina's included, only hers felt wooden and hollow. She hated herself for being so weak. Crescencia deserved her utmost enthusiasm right now, and anything less was simply selfishness. Edwina knew she should behave better. So she put her misgivings about her own unwedded future behind her and truly partook in the rest of the evening, sitting in the parlor eating cake and drinking tea—there was more sherry for the men—and listening to Mr. Stykem reminisce about Crescencia when she was a girl.

At nine o'clock, the gathering broke up when Mr. Stykem said he was going to retire. Mr. Dufresne and Crescencia announced they were going to stay in the dining room for a while to write the invitations and make plans for the wedding. They saw Tom and Edwina to the door, Crescencia giving Edwina a parting hug. Then once outside, Edwina pulled the cold night air into her lungs. Tom held the gate open for her and they walked side by side up the block to her house.

A slender moon's glow reflected off the wheel-packed snow in the street and off the snowmen and snow families children had put up in yards, eerily making the night as light as dawn. The sidewalk and houses were clearly in view, their stark landscape bare and dormant for the winter. House lights offered cheery beacons in windows. Some families had left bay window draperies parted; in the openings, Christmas trees were covered with ornaments and trimmings. Curls of wood smoke from brick chimneys gave the air a festive scent.

"Did you know what Shay and Miss Stykem were going to say tonight?" Tom asked, both hands shoved into the pockets of his coat.

"I suspected." She glanced at him. "Did you know?"

"I guessed."

The sound of snow compacting beneath their shoes was the only conversation between them until they reached Edwina's gate. Pausing, Edwina put her hand on the latch. "I'll be seeing you." She made a move to undo the hinge, but he stopped her with a hand over hers.

"I'll be seeing you?" he repeated, the pitch of his voice causing her to look up into his face. "You're upset about this, Edwina. I saw you. You were shaking."

Turning away so he couldn't see the lie in her eyes, she countered, "I wasn't."

"You were."

His warm fingers caught her chin and made her look

into his eyes. "Her getting married has made you jealous. You wished it was you."

When he stared at her in such a forthright way that went right to all she felt inside, she couldn't evade the issue. "I can wish about it all I want, but it's not going to happen."

"Because you won't let it."

"And you know why." She threw the words at him, disgusted with herself for ever letting Tom Wolcott come within a fraction of her heart.

They eyed each other, the tension closing in on them thicker than a blanket of fog. Before Edwina could protest, Tom pulled her flush against his chest and held her tightly in his arms. His mouth came down and covered her lips in a demanding kiss that left her reeling, then paralyzed. She hadn't been prepared, so she hadn't made him stop. The thrill of the kiss made her lose reason. She didn't want him to stop now. His tongue slipped inside her mouth and she allowed it—she encouraged him. Her gloved hands rose to his shoulders in an attempt to keep him close rather than push him away. Desire prompted her to be careless. She let him take full command of her mouth. But this was crazy. Stupid. She knew it.

This is crazy! The words echoed in her mind, giving her the will to break from Tom's mouth and gasp, "We can't do this here. Somebody might see us."

Surprise darted through her when he swore, "I don't give a damn. I *want* somebody—the whole town—to see us."

"Why?" she cried. "So I can be made a laughing-stock?"

He moaned. "Jesus, Edwina. You don't get it. I'm not ashamed of what we have. But you are."

She furiously shook her head, her hands balling into fists on his shoulders. "I'm not ashamed. I just know I can't flaunt a relationship with you. If I did . . . why, I'd be called horrible things. I'd never be able to show my face in town."

Tom swore at her. "But you sure as hell were able to after Rutledge."

The words cut. They drew painful blood, made her feel jilted all over again.

"Ed . . ." Tom's hands lifted to cradle her cheeks. "Ed, I'm sorry. I didn't mean it."

She could barely breathe. She didn't even know if she could walk, much less do so with any kind of dignity. "I'm going inside now."

"Edwina." Evidence of his remorse for the hurt he'd caused shone in his eyes. She believed he was truly sorry. She'd pushed him into saying something that she had known all along. She'd been able to go on after Ludlow only because she had come back to a place where nobody knew her secrets. And the only way to go on after Tom was to leave here—run away, hide.

"I'm going inside," she repeated, fighting tears and the sickness gnawing in her stomach.

Then before he could say another word, she slipped away from him and ran up the walkway to the safety of her house, where a cat was more forgiving than any human being ever could be—Edwina included.

Thursday, Tom stayed away from Edwina. And he let more than half of Friday go by before reaching a decision on how to proceed. He'd avoided her not because he wanted to, but because he thought that she needed to have time to herself, time to understand that he wasn't a heartless bastard who was just using the situation for physical gratification and nothing more. He didn't really think she saw him that way, but after what he'd said about Ludlow Rutledge, he wouldn't blame her if she told him to go to Hell.

He hadn't meant to open her old wounds like that. It had been reprehensible of him. Resentment over that son of a bitch Rutledge had prodded him into becoming an insensitive ass. All Tom had intended was to make Edwina realize that she had pulled herself together after that college professor broke their engagement. She was strong. She'd survived. Why couldn't she continue to survive with him? Here in Harmony.

Put her into your life.

Shay's words drifted back to Tom. Edwina wouldn't let them go about together openly in her world, so he'd have to bring her around to his side of it. To his life and what he could give her.

A plan had been forming in his head that morning while he worked in the store. He was worried about her. She said she was barely making ends meet. So he had this idea how she could make some cash.

And now that there was a break between customers, he glanced at the pocket watch he'd hung on the wall in lieu of the beaver clock. The hands read 2:12. Perfect timing. Edwina let her girls out at two.

Tom reached beneath the counter, felt his way in an old lure box of knickknacks, and grabbed the metal object inside. He went through the storeroom, knocked once on the back of the closet door, then let himself into the schoolroom.

Edwina sat behind the desk. She looked tired to him. Her eyes seemed puffy, as if she hadn't been sleeping enough. Her face was pale, no pink to her cheeks. Several tendrils of her russet hair, pulled up in a high knot, dragged down her nape. The vaguest notion of a curve at one side of her mouth was enough to make him proceed. He would have liked more than anything to take her into his arms, but he refrained.

"Hey, Ed," he began and found his voice uncharacteristically taut and hoarse. The strain over not seeing her for nearly forty-eight hours had gotten to him more than he'd imagined it would.

"Hello, Tom," she murmured quietly.

Good sign. She didn't tell me to get the hell out.

He figured he'd better just come out with it and give her no room to refuse. "I came by to ask you a favor." Several steps had him directly at the desk's side; then he started talking again without giving her a chance to say anything. "I've got to take some old friends from

Seattle up to Baskin Falls tomorrow for the whole day. Shay, he's out on a run already and won't be back until Sunday some time, depending on how lucky his party is. Normally I'd just close the store, but I'm expecting a guy from Butte to come in and pick up a couple of bottles of Good Sense-Deer Scent—I'm the only one around here who's got it. Then I could have somebody drop in from Waverly to look over some new rattle-its and dig-its—your assortment lures. The real fishing season gets underway in March and a sportsman can never be too early filling his tackle box. So I really need to be open tomorrow." He laid the key that he held on the desktop in front of Edwina. She stared at it, then at him. "I appreciate your doing this for me, Ed. I'll pay you your fifty cents an hour. Open the place up at nine. You won't have any trouble at all. You'll have to look for prices on the items, but they're there, and the customers usually know what they want. Half the time they know where it's at, too. The goods are pretty much labeled. I'll be back right around five and I can lock up." Backing from the desk, he nodded. "You're a lifesaver, Ed. If I can return the favor, just ask."

Then he hightailed it out of there before she could tell him no.

Chapter

❧ 17 ❧

Edwina stood behind the counter of Wolcott's Sporting Goods and Excursions at precisely nine o'clock. How had she been talked into this? Tom had spoken so quickly, without giving her an opportunity to say something like "I don't think so." Then he'd backed out of the schoolroom in a rush before she could so much as sneeze—if she'd had to sneeze, which she hadn't. And then when she'd stared at the brass key on her desk . . . the plans seemed so final. So undoable. She hadn't wanted to bring the key back to him and refuse—not to mention that she could use the money.

Actually, she felt like she owed him the favor. She'd been stunned the night they'd last spoken, and not at all herself. She hadn't given him a chance to explain the hurtful words he'd said. She understood why he'd say such a thing. At the time, she hadn't wanted to. Now she did. And she couldn't be mad at him. She was mad at herself . . . for . . . for falling for him. She was mad at herself for not being stronger. She didn't want to accept that she was . . . *in love* with him. Admitting it, even to herself, changed nothing. It only made things worse.

For two days, Edwina had felt sorry for herself, damning her fate, damning Ludlow for not marrying her. But she was infinitely glad that he hadn't. She could see now that she hadn't ever really loved him, loved him in a way that was all-consuming and forever. Infatuation, quite acute, was more like it. He had been her professor. A man about town. The ideal of marriage, the institution itself, had fueled her love for him. But now that she was beginning to see what real love could be . . . and understood what marriage could mean, she couldn't have it with Tom.

It was the grossest of all ironies.

Edwina sighed and fingered tiny rubber fishy things in a tray, mindlessly separating them by size and color.

Well, maybe she could have Tom as her husband. If she'd let herself be the kind of woman he wanted. But she felt too much guilt and remorse over the past. Besides, Tom hadn't declared any feelings of love for her—well, at least not so he meant it. Nor had she for him. Those important words were left unspoken between them. Neither of them dared to confess such a thing to the other for fear of the repercussions.

Edwina knew that was how she felt about the situation. . . . She should tell him. But she was afraid of what the avowal would do to them. To her. She could be only so reckless with her heart. It had been broken once. Mending it again would take a long time . . . years. . . .

But could she ever forget Tom? No . . . sadly, no. Never.

The store's door opened and Mr. Healy from Granite Home and Farm Realty came inside.

"Miss Huntington," he said in surprise, bushy brows raising beneath the brim of his derby. "Didn't expect to see you minding the shop. Where's Mr. Wolcott?"

"He's had to go out for the day." She dumped some pink rubber fish in a pile next to some orange rubber fish. "Is there anything I can help you with?"

"I was going to give him these papers to sign." The agent stuck his hand into his worsted coat and produced a narrow sealed manila envelope. "Tell him all I need is his John Hancock and I can proceed in whatever manner he likes."

Edwina took the document. "I'll make sure that he gets them." She tucked the envelope neatly beneath the cashbox. "While you're here, you might care to browse around. Mr. Wolcott has these for sale." She pointed to the colorful fish. "Fishing season starts in just a few short months."

Mr. Healy leaned in for a better look. "Hmm . . . walleyes. I could always use a few more. How much for the marabou jigs?"

"Um . . ." Edwina lifted the tray and read the price written on the bottom tag. "Ten cents."

"I'll take two."

Edwina smiled. She'd just made her first sale. Twenty cents' worth. Coins exchanged hands, then Mr. Healy doffed his hat. "Good day."

Left alone, Edwina continued to sort through the now identifiable walleyes until she had them in tidy piles. She found some chewing tobacco tins in which to put the various colors, then she clearly marked the prices on the front. After that, she placed her hands on her hips and took a good look at the store. The shelves needed dusting, the merchandise could use straightening out, and the hunting clothes had to be refolded more crisply.

Tsking her disapproval, she went into the shared closet and collected her dust pan, broom, polishing rags, lemon oil, feather duster, and her apron. She walked as she tied the bow in back, then decided to tackle beneath the counter first. She'd already noted the rubbish of nut shells. Walnuts. All over. Tom didn't keep them in a container, just left them loose. She quickly rectified that by plunking all the uneaten walnuts in a clean bucket. Then she used the side of her hand to get rid of the hulls.

Next came the disposal of empty blue-and-white cigarette packages. She put all his matches back in boxes. Papers littered the various shelves. Plucking them one by one, she neatened the stack and vaguely glanced at the writing. Invoices, old and new, for an assortment of merchandise. No wonder he couldn't tally a proper cash flow.

As she continued, she came up with an amber-glass beer bottle. She shook it and heard something rattle in the bottom. The beaver's teeth. She grimaced at the reminder. In the front of the shelf, near the ledge, lay a revolver with its barrel missing. She recalled that Tom had used the butt to smash the nuts.

A pair of men's heavy cable-knit socks turned up below. A tall canister for ground pepper was full of chalk remnants, fishing hooks, lead balls, bullets, and other trinkets that left her clueless. Sitting on the floor, she let it all fall into a jumbled mess, then proceeded to put each object with its match until there were over a dozen piles. Having run out of chewing tobacco tins, she rose and went to the storeroom to get the jelly jars she and the girls had been decorating. There had been extra ones, so Edwina had been able to spare some. They'd been decorating the jars—floral fabric on top with a puff of batting for plumpness and a grosgrain ribbon around the circumference to keep it all in place—for the Ladies' Aid charity.

Standing back after a few swishes of the feather duster, Edwina surveyed her handiwork: neat as a pin, row after row—plenty of colorful, pretty jars. The ribbons were a nice touch. And all the other odds and ends had been cleaned and lined up to rank-and-file precision.

The door opened and a gentleman she didn't recognize came in.

"Ma'am." He doffed a Western hat as he strode toward her; his spurs made a jingle against the floor. "I was wondering if ya'll carry bullet molders."

Edwina worried her lip. "I'm certain we do." She tapped her fingernail on the counter and tried to think: if she were a bullet molder, where would she be? With the guns, of course. "This way, please." Walking to the aisle that had a glass case of pistols, shotguns, and revolvers inside, she stared, looking for something other than a gun. She couldn't find anything.

The cowboy had held back, and his voice came to her. "Ma'am. They're right here."

Turning, she frowned when she saw him at the table with gadgets that were more like those she used in her kitchen. Some looked to be mashers, egg beaters, or can openers. This wouldn't do. Bullet things should be with bullets and guns. She could see now that the whole store had to be revamped.

Edwina helped the man with his purchase, and as soon as he departed, she dug right into the rest of the merchandise, logging it all by theme rather than the haphazard way Tom had set it up. While she did this, customers came and went. She'd rung up nearly ten dollars in sales by noon when she paused to eat a light lunch, then go right back to work. She came to a table that had bottles on it. Good Sense-Deer Scent. She knew what that was. The man from Butte was coming in to buy some.

Picking up the ounce-sized bottle, Edwina unscrewed the cap and lightly sniffed the contents. Musky smelling. Not altogether unpleasant, but not exactly fragrant, either. Kind of mildewlike. The label touted it as being deer scent. She had no idea how a deer smelled. She'd never been that close to one.

As she was about to screw the cap in place, she sneezed. Some of the cloudy liquid splashed onto her skirt in tiny droplets.

"Oh, bother it!"

Quickly securing the bottle cap and placing the container back on the table, she swatted at the spots. She'd have to tell Marvel-Anne to put solvent on them before the skirt went into the wash water.

Heaving a great sigh, she went through the room and came to clothing of all sorts. Hunter's jackets, pants, shirts, vests, hats, and silly-looking elastic things thrown into an open carton directly beside a box of dog muzzles. Peering sideways, she read the manufacturer's red label: SPALDING ATHLETIC SUPPORTERS. Taking one out, she tried to make sense of the three elastic straps and the white cup of cotton in the middle. After examining the item many ways, she deduced it was an elbow support for rifle shooting.

Feeling rather tickled by her revelation, she tried one on by putting the wide strap of elastic over her neck and sliding it to her waist, and the other strap on her shoulder. There! The cotton cup fit perfectly over the bend of her elbow, although her forearm felt hung up—her wrist dangled from the support. But if one was going to hold a rifle steady, this was the sportsman's gimmick to have. Her trigger hand remained perfectly motionless as she pretended to hold a shotgun—not that she ever had.

While she took aim at the monstrous grizzly bear, the door opened behind her. Whirling to the sound, she saw Mr. Calhoon with a package in his hand too big for the mailbox.

"Oh . . . hello, Mr. Calhoon." Edwina relaxed her stance but made no effort to remove the elbow support. And as a matter of fact, she got a brilliant idea. Tom had a bunch of the Spalding athletic supporters and they didn't seem to be selling. Not that she knew anything about elbow supports, but this model was rather tight and seemed quite sound.

Mr. Calhoon gave her an appraising stare with wide eyes, and she figured she must have dust smudged on her nose. "That's nice of you to bring the package in. I'll make sure Mr. Wolcott gets it. I'm minding the store for him." She walked toward him with an extra supporter in her hand. "I'm glad you've come over. I wanted to bring this to your attention."

"W-what?" He gazed hard at the Spalding, as if perplexed by it. Apparently Tom hadn't demonstrated them. She had this absolutely wonderful idea to sell all of them before Tom got back—just to show him her business acumen despite not knowing all the merchandise.

"This is the latest in elbow supporters, Mr. Calhoon. As you can see, anyone can wear it." She touched the wide elastic on her waist and even snapped it. "It's very comfortable. Doesn't bind. And the cup on the elbow is soft cotton. They're only forty-two cents. Quite a bargain, and I'm certain it will help you with your aim. So how many can I write up for you?"

"N-none."

"Come now, Mr. Calhoon. I know you're a hunter. You need one of these."

"M-maybe if I played on Kennison's baseball team," he muttered.

"I don't know why the team would need elbow supports." Frowning, she said, "All I'm asking is that you give one a try. I know you'll be pleased." She waved it in front of him. "Fine balbriggan cotton that can be washed in warm water. I read the label."

Backing away from the supporter she dangled in front of his nose, he stuttered, "Uh . . . I-I'll take one."

"One? Two might come in handy."

"B-but you can only wear one at a time."

"True. However, the prepared hunter has spares."

He looked away, unable to give the supporter his attention. "I'll t-take two."

"Very well." She rounded the corner and wrote up the order. She found her hand very steady indeed as she took up the pencil.

Mr. Calhoon dashed out the door with his paper-wrapped parcel. He hadn't even let her tie string around it. Odd . . . she'd never noticed that nervous tick at the corner of his right eye before. . . .

The afternoon wore on quickly. Business picked up and a steady flow came in and out. The gentleman from Butte came and bought the deer scent and four of the supporters. She sold one to a man from Waverly—along with the rattle-its and dig-its. Three of the Spaldings went to Chief Officer Algie Conlin and two to Deputy Pike Faragher. Mr. Hess picked up one. So did Mr. Elward. Also Mr. Zipp from the barbershop, who claimed he didn't hunt but only fished—she'd been able to talk him into one. Throughout the transactions, she kept her supporter on, and it was amazing the sales it brought just by wearing and describing how the apparatus worked. She couldn't wait to tell Tom.

Between customers, she organized the entire store. As the hour came close to five, she hurried to finish tying the drab curtains back with bright periwinkle bows. Then she gave all the dead animals a dusting. The antlers on the moose looked much better with lemon polish giving them a shiny glow. And the grizzly bear was much improved with the dried flowers in its grasp. The pastel colors of the petals livened up the stiff old thing.

She surveyed the new and improved look and her heart fluttered while she admired her handiwork. The store's conversion had been a complete success.

She pulled the tie on her apron, then put it away with all her cleaning wares. Next, she took the rubbish can outside to dump its contents in the bin on the side of the building. As she rounded the corner, she startled Mr. Higgins's Airedale terrier sniffing at the seams of the bin. The dog lifted its wet black nose, locked onto some scent, and came right at her. Even though its teeth weren't bared, she'd never been attacked in such a way. She backed up, but the Airedale continued to charge until reaching her skirt. Then it did the most peculiar thing: it rubbed against her. It stuck its nose to the fabric, then rubbed its face all over the folds of her skirt.

Before Edwina knew what was happening, Mrs. Kirby's schnauzer and the Labrador retriever that resided at Dutch's poolroom had stampeded in and were trying to rub their faces on her skirt as well. Throwing the rubbish can at them, she ran back into the store and closed the door.

She peered out the window to see the three dogs jumping up and down, trying to get inside.

"My Heavens! They've gone berserk." Flipping the OPEN sign over to CLOSED, she yanked down all the shades to block the dogs from her view. Then she proceeded to the counter to add up the day's take.

Edwina had just finished the columns, smiling as she

wrote the figure down, when Tom came through the door.

"You're back," she said with an air of excitement in her tone. "Wait until I tell you."

Her gaze whisked across him. She took in his height and the breadth of his shoulders, the way his hair curled at his collar. The cut of his coat, snug in the arms. His boots that made him even taller. The features of his face, lean and chiseled. Eyes so blue they seemed surreal, and a mouth wide and tempting for kissing.

"How come there's three dogs outside trying to get in?"

"Oh, them." She shook her head. "I don't know. But they like me all of a sudden."

As Tom stepped farther into the store, his gaze locked on the counter. In less than a few seconds, he noticed the tobacco tins of individually colored fishes, the potted plant she'd taken from her own desk, and the bright, bold merchandise price signs she'd penned. Then he made a slow pivot and drank everything in like a wide panoramic photograph in a stereoscope.

He didn't say a word.

She knew he was happily stunned. "Well?" She hung on his next words . . . but her cheery smile faded when she read the expression in his eyes as he faced her. . . .

"You don't like it . . . ?"

Not liking it wasn't how Tom would have described how he felt. It was more like a sock in the gut that left him with a sour stomach, like a jab to his jaw that made his teeth ache.

What in hell had she done? And in only eight hours. The place was too sanitized. Too tidy. Too feminine. What was with the flowers in his grizz's paw? And the price tags clearly marked on everything? And the bows pulling the curtains back.

Tom strode cautiously to the counter and went behind it, his eyes lowering to the shelves: jars and ribbons, neat rows, his walnuts put in a bucket. How was he supposed to sift through them to find the empties and the wholes? His gun—it was right there in front, not thrown on top of the invoices where he liked it. And the bills of sale were all stacked up. How could he figure out who he'd gotten what from? A left pitch meant the stuff had come in; a right pitch had meant the stuff was still on order. And his empty beer bottles—the one he used for putting cigarettes out sometimes and the one he kept the beaver teeth in. The amber bottles were in a row like soldiers, not in the different spots he kept them in so he knew which one had the teeth and which one had the butts.

"Jesus . . ." he managed to say when his voice came back. "What in the hell did you do this for?"

Too late, he realized Edwina had meant to do well by the changes. The light in her eyes clouded and she looked ready to cry. He didn't mean to hurt her feelings, but she had to know that his store was the way he liked his store. Maybe to the average guy it looked disorganized, but it was very organized to Tom.

"I thought I'd improve things," she said crisply. "I spent the whole day fixing the place up. Putting everything where it should go."

"But everything already was where it should go." Tom leaned over the many tins of walleyes, all sorted by color, and scowled.

"No, it wasn't," Edwina said in her defense, getting her dander up slightly. Yet she still looked wounded. "The bullet molders weren't with the guns. Now they are. And the can openers are now with the other can openers."

"I don't sell can openers."

"Those things." She pointed, and he swore silently.

"They're shell recappers."

"Whatever. They have to do with guns, don't they?"

"Yeah, but—"

"Guns, rifles, and all that relates to weaponry is now in the glass case. And the merchandise is all clearly marked with its proper price." She left the counter and walked down the aisle, pointing left and right. "You didn't have prices showing on anything. I had to find them under the boxes or the backs of things."

He walked around the counter and stood in front of it, propping his elbow onto its edge. "And there's a damn good reason why."

Turning, she glared at him. Her green eyes dimmed; her mouth went sullen. "I don't understand."

"A guy who wants a spool of fishing line is more apt to pick up two or three if they aren't marked. Then when he brings them to the counter and I tell him how much they are, he won't put those back that he didn't really need."

"Why not?"

"Because he'd look like an ass if he did. Once something is in a man's hands, he won't set it back down, because that's not how men shop." Tom nudged some of the walleyes out of his way, then jumped onto the countertop to sit down; his long legs dangled over the side. "I don't know how it is with you women when you shop, so ya'll can rearrange your hat shops and such however you see fit."

"Well, we women look at the price."

"And chances are you don't buy half of what you see."

"It depends. Frugality is a concern."

"*Frugality* isn't in a man's vocabulary. He does everything big. Big dogs, big guns, big horses and rigs. Showing him the price is only going to remind him that his wife or his wallet told him he had less to spend." Tom gazed at the leafy greens of an ivy in a pot and slid it behind him out of view. "You see, Ed, there's a knack in selling retail."

Not to be deterred, Edwina folded her arms beneath her breasts and tapped her toe. "You had dog muzzles by the hunting clothes. That didn't make sense."

"Sure it did. A hunter brings his dog with him. And dogs who have trouble staying quiet need a muzzle. Seeing them there by the vests reminds the hunter he needs a muzzle, too."

"Then explain why you have the elbow supporters by the muzzles and pants." She reached into the Spalding box and came out with a jockey strap, then walked to him. "Only one left." A sharp single nod of her head told him she'd been enterprising somehow; only he didn't know how . . . or why she was calling them elbow supporters. "I told every man how much they were before he even held one, and I sold all the supporters in that box but this one. And the only reason I didn't sell this one was because I was wearing it."

Tom's shoulder sockets cracked from the jolt they received when he abruptly straightened from his lax posture. "What do you mean you were wearing it?"

"I was demonstrating," she replied with assertiveness. "And after a couple of hours, I got used to the feel of one around my waist."

"Christ almighty, Edwina! Don't tell me you really wore one! In front of the customers!"

"Of course I did. The cup actually does keep everything nice and snug." She examined the jockey strap and stretched the elastic between her hands. "I may even get one for myself for when I'm sewing and—"

Tom shot off the counter and grabbed the Spalding out of her fingers. "Give me that!" He jammed the cotton band into his jeans pocket. "Don't ever touch one of those again. Jesus! The cup keeps everything 'nice and snug,'" he mimicked. "Ed, don't you know that nothing down there even hangs on you! Don't tell me you put it under your skirt."

Edwina's brows puckered. "Heavens, no. Over my shoulder and actually, if you must know, one breast. It just rides like that on me."

"Oh . . . God . . ." Tom massaged his temples. How was he going to tell her? "Ed . . . Ed . . . Ed . . ."

Misgiving marred the curve of her mouth. "What?"

"Ed . . . come here." He held his hand out for her to take, beckoning with it when she didn't readily come. She finally did, and he guided her to the counter. Placing both hands on her waist, he lifted her onto the top and

331

blocked her in with arms on either side of her. Better to keep her still once she found out.

Gazing into her waiting eyes, he inhaled deeply to get his thoughts together. That's when he smelled the scent. One sniff. Then two. Just to make sure. "Did you open a bottle of Good Sense, Edwina?"

"Only out of curiosity."

"Some spilled, huh?"

"Not enough that you couldn't sell the bottle as full."

Tom lowered his chin to his chest, fought back a grimacing smile, then lifted his head. "Those dogs outside, they tried to rub on your skirt, didn't they?"

"Why, yes. How did you know?"

He shook his head. "Let's take one thing at a time." Raising his hands to her shoulders to keep her steady, he held her gaze with his. "Edwina."

"Tom?"

"Edwina . . ."

"What . . . ?"

"Spalding makes athletic equipment. Do you know what athletic is?"

"I'm not stupid," she snapped back.

"Wasn't implying that you were. Just wanted to make sure you and I were talking the same language here before I went on. Do you remember last summer when Kennison's baseball team played the Helena Hornets?"

"I wasn't there. I don't like sports."

Tom unblinkingly stared at her, his method of explanation—using the story of why Dewey Broderick had crumpled in the outfield from that missed ball smacking into his groin—just shot to hell. Tom would have liked to light a smoke because he really needed one just then.

"What is it? Just tell me. I'm a mature woman. How many times do I have to make that clear? I can handle anything. I'm a—"

"What you had on wasn't an elbow supporter. It was a jockey strap. A piece of cotton and elastic equipment that a man wears on his privates when he's running after balls, birds, or big game or being in any situation in which he aims not to be flying around in his drawers."

Edwina choked, her eyes watering and her breath coming in little gasps. "You have to be kidding with me. Aren't you?" Then in a high squeak, "Aren't you!"

"No, sweetheart, I'm not."

Her lower lip quivered. "Really?"

"Really."

"Dammit all!" she sobbed, hiding her face in her hands. "I—I—I sold sixteen of them!"

"I appreciate the sales effort, Ed, but that's an item that sells itself out of necessity."

She wailed all the louder and began to genuinely cry. He didn't want to have to tell her about the deer scent when she was well on her way to major waterworks, but she paused midsob and considered him through spiky, wet lashes. "Why are those dogs after me? What's in that deer scent? Some kind of venison smell?" She hiccuped, looking hopeful.

Ruefully, he shook his head. "No, it's estrus." Her being a female, he figured she would know what that meant so he wouldn't have to explain.

"What's that?"

Damn. "A scent a female deer gives off when she's . . ." Tom muttered the rest. "And it's . . ." More muttering. ". . . her water."

"Water?"

Tom fumbled for his cigarettes, needing the comfort of the pack against his fingers. He didn't bring them out—just kept his hand in his pocket for a second before saying: "Urine."

Edwina's face paled. "You mean to tell me you sell deer urine in that bottle and I've got it on my skirt?"

"That's the long and short of it."

Crestfallen, she started in with the crying again.

Tom nudged her legs apart so he could pull her into his arms and hold her close while she sat on the counter. "Sweetheart . . . you didn't know."

"W-what kind of a man w-would buy a b-bottle of . . .

d-deer urine?" she asked in a sobbing voice that was muffled in the collar of his shirt.

Stroking her quivering back and keeping her near his chest, he replied, "A man who wants a buck to think he's a doe, ready and willing."

"Th-that's—th-that's . . . d-disgusting."

"Yeah, well, it has been proven to work, and a hunter who wants a six-pointer bad enough will try anything. And for some reason, dogs can smell it a mile away. Barkly must be on the other side of the creek or he would've come running to stick his nose in it. Can't exactly say why dogs like it so much."

Willowy arms had draped carelessly over his shoulders. Her full breasts softly convulsed against his chest. Warm tears wet the side of his neck. The bleakness of her distress went straight to his heart. He wanted to protect her, make her feel better—love her, kiss her.

"Edwina . . ." He tried to get her to look at him. She wouldn't. She started in with her babbling. She sometimes did that when she was upset.

". . . I got a letter from Denver. This kind of thing doesn't happen in a big city." She hiccuped once more and shuddered through tears. Her cheeks rested next to his jaw. "In Denver, they don't bottle deer . . . you know. It's not natural. I don't like this sort of thing. It makes me . . . makes me . . . cry!"

"Ed, it's okay."

"It's not okay!" she railed, her hysteria increasing. "I had a man's . . . p-private thing on my elbow!" Her shoulders racked and hot tears spilled fresh on his collar, thoroughly wetting it. "Oh . . . help me. How am I going to face Mr. Calhoon . . . ? Mr. Hess? And Chief Officer Conlin . . . and Deputy Faragher . . . and . . . Mr. Elward . . . Mr. Zipp . . . and all the others?"

Even Tom winced at the list. She'd sold them to half the men in the damn town. "Well, honeybaby," he crooned into the shell of her ear, "if anyone of them says any different than it being an elbow supporter, I'll punch him in the nose."

"Oh don't go making stupid threats just to save me. It's silly."

Tom glowered. *Stupid threats? Silly?* He meant it. He'd go after any man who so much as made a single joke on account of Edwina's blunder. He would do anything to protect her because he . . . loved her.

"Denver doesn't have deer. They don't even have sporting goods stores, I'm certain. And if they did," she complained, "they wouldn't sell bottled deer. They would have the normal things like balls and bats and lawn tennis and hammocks and the round things . . ."

Round things?

". . . and boxing gloves and bicycles and bicycle bells and . . ."

Her words lost all meaning to his ears. *I love her.* She didn't want his love, but she had it nonetheless. He'd never been in love before. He had no clue as to how it would feel or when or what it would feel like when he did have a woman in mind to love. He couldn't explain the way he suddenly felt. Just that in his mind and body . . . and soul, Edwina had just snuggled in without her being aware of how profoundly she affected him.

The helplessness she displayed had set it off, had made him know. He'd had a sense that he was falling in love with her. That desire to be with her every waking hour had been with him for days . . . weeks. But did that mean love? He had nothing to go by. Nothing with which to compare.

But the more she prattled and cried and plied her soft body against his, he let himself get used to the idea.

He loved her.

Telling her would be out of the question. Not yet. Not now. She wouldn't be receptive to the idea. She would tell him he was mistaken. He wasn't. He knew it. This was that real and guarded thing that few men readily spoke about among themselves. Tom felt like shouting it.

He loved Edwina Huntington.

But she didn't love him.

That was a dismal fact. . . . He wanted to change her

mind. Edwina did things in her own way and time. If he pushed, she would run. So he would hold the thought in his head. For now.

". . . Mr. Healy," she continued, in no apparent connection to anything he'd heard. "And those papers of yours for you to . . . do something. Sign? I don't know. They're under your cashbox and . . . at least I didn't sell him a jockey strap." Tears came anew, just when he thought she might be dried out.

Tom held her at arm's length. "Edwina." He gave her a very slight shake. "Pull yourself together."

Dismally, she gazed at him, her eyes red and her lips full and moist. "I sold sixteen Spaldings."

"Yes, I know. So what?"

"So . . . I'm ruined."

"Dammit, you've said that before. Buck up."

She sniffed, rubbing the underside of her nose with her forefinger. "I don't want to buck up yet. Give me five more minutes."

"I'll give you five seconds."

Then Tom moved in and kissed the mouth that looked so sweet. She tasted of salt and spent dejection. At first she just sat there. Then he built the kiss into one more of passion than comfort. He couldn't help himself. She aroused him like no other woman had. After long minutes of kissing, her arms came around his neck and he settled in between her legs.

Their mouths joined. Her breasts pressed against his chest. The mood changed completely, from gentleness to fervor. She held him with her thighs, entwining her legs around him.

The kiss turned frantic, ardent. Their hands made urgent explorations. He filled his palms with her breasts. She grazed her fingernails across his shirt back, bringing his skin alive with pleasurable tingles beneath the fabric. Kissing wasn't enough. Their clothing had to be rearranged. Her shirtwaist came untucked; his hands roamed over the fullness of her breasts pushing up from the lace edge of her corset. His own shirt hem came loose from his pants at her eager tug. Her fingers trembling played over his chest, bringing forth a moan from his throat. Tom bunched her skirt and petticoats and brought them to her waist. She undid his buckle; denim and cotton dropped to his ankles. Then her fancy drawers slid down her silky legs.

Their lips fused and their breath mingled as their bodies came together as one.

Edwina hung onto him. Her backside felt like satin against his hands as he cupped her and brought her close for a deep and consuming thrust. She wound her legs around his waist as he pushed into her, over and over. The rhythm took over as they rode on a wave of euphoria.

Tom felt the building tension inside her. He waited for her to come to completion, and then he let his own hot abandon take over. He plunged one last time. In that flash of pure desire, he gave way to his own shuddering release.

Panting and spent, he kissed her mouth. She kissed him back, lightly, a brief meeting of lips and breath. Then he kissed the curve of her neck. Her arms came around his shoulder, and she pressed her cheek next to his. He felt her heartbeat thrumming against his, the climactic tempos matching.

They clung together, arms wrapped tightly. Tom held onto Edwina like he never wanted to let her go. And he didn't.

Tomorrow he'd have to make her face reality. This affair wasn't going to work. Because it wasn't enough for him.

Chapter

❖ 18 ❖

Edwina stoked the heater in the school, stood back, and held out her hands to the warmth that poured from the grate. The cold lingered in the air, and the windowpanes dripped condensation. In less than ten minutes, the students would arrive. If Edwina hadn't overslept, the classroom would have been heated and very pleasant for the beginning of lessons. But she had come in late. . . .

For most of the night, Edwina had lain awake. Thoughts of Tom had prevented sleep from taking her even though a full day had passed since they had seen one another. Sundays were difficult to be together; yesterday had been no different. The Ladies' Aid Society had had a meeting after services that she and the girls had had to attend to present the decorated jelly jars. By the time she'd returned home, any chance for an encounter with Tom had been nonexistent.

So she had eaten her dinner and gone to bed. She had recalled her tears in the store and the way Tom had comforted her, the way they'd made love. On the counter. It was unfathomable that she had done such a thing. But she had—shamelessly.

There was only one explanation. Only one reason why

338

she would risk being with him in such a way. And without precautions . . .

She was in love with him.

Hopelessly and utterly, madly and mindlessly in love. The feelings hadn't crept up on her. She'd suspected for a while. But last night had proven that she wasn't so guarded with her heart. She'd let him in. She'd taken him in completely.

But what to do about it?

Could she—should she—tell him? What purpose would it serve? He'd made no serious declarations that he loved her. Why would he? She'd told him not to, told him that she was her own woman and would make her own way through life without him. What kind of man would love her in spite of that?

Few. None.

If she told him how she felt . . . maybe . . .

Edwina shook her head and turned her back to the heater to warm her backside. Gazing at the high ceiling, she tried to think. People in love could, if they had to, work around their differences, their financial difficulties. It happened. But was it fair to bring that sort of trouble into a marriage? And who was talking marriage?

Biting her lip, Edwina walked toward her desk, but she stopped short when the closet door opened and Tom came into the schoolroom.

"Morning, Edwina."

A blush heated her face and neck. In the light of morning, and having gotten over the horror she'd felt at having sold those athletic supporters, she felt embarrassed by Saturday's wanton behavior.

"Tom." His name felt soft on her lips.

Neither said anything further. They stood staring at one another, as if each had something to say but dared not say it. The crackle of the heater's fire took over the room in place of their unspoken words.

Then Tom shoved his hands into his pockets and took on an exaggerated pose of relaxation. "About the other night," he began, and she got the strange feeling that her world was about to fall in around her. "I don't think what happened on the counter should be repeated."

Chills prickled Edwina's skin. "What do you mean? That we shouldn't make love anymore? Or just not on the counter?"

"I mean that this isn't working out." His gaze was deadly serious.

Edwina's blood began to pound in her head. Her stomach churned. It was as if she'd lived this already . . . another time . . . another place. No, that wasn't fair. This was different. She'd been in control. Hadn't she? Why, then, did it hurt so badly? "If you want to see other women . . ."

"Oh, hell, Edwina, it's nothing like that. I want—"

But he couldn't say the rest because Hildegarde Plunkett and Ruth Edward came through the door.

"Good morning, Miss Edwina," Hildegarde said.

Ruth followed suit with distinct enunciation. "Good morning, Miss Edwina."

"Good morning, girls," she replied, torn between her duties to her students and the unfinished conversation hanging between her and Tom.

Tom brought his voice down to a whisper. "We'll take care of this this afternoon after two."

She nodded, then he left through the front door just as Johannah Treber came in, stomping snow from her shoes on the mat at the threshold.

The rest of the morning and the afternoon traveled as slowly as a snail through a garden. Edwina could barely concentrate on the lessons. She repeated them, she spoke, she read, but she couldn't remember doing any of it. At last, when the small clock on her desk chimed the hour twice, she dismissed the girls and then waited for Tom to return. She took up scissors and began making paper snowflakes to put up in the windows, needing to occupy her hands lest she rise from her chair, fling the door to the store open, throw herself in Tom's arms, and tell him she was mistaken in her casual attitude on this relationship. Tell him to give her one more chance.

That nothing in the world meant anything unless he could share it with her.

With her head down, she snipped and clipped little pieces and slashes in the folded paper. When the door opened, she started, looked up with a smile of relief that he had finally come . . . then froze. Froze as if she had seen a ghost, a remnant from Halloween . . . but in reality, a remnant from her past.

He stood there, as dashing and dapper as she recalled him to be, his blond hair combed over his ears and neatly styled beneath a smart, square-crowned hat, the same tidy mustache, distinctive jaw, and golden brows. His strong face was unchanged except for the faint lines at the corners of his chocolate-brown eyes. The glossy fur on his calf-length seal coat gleamed from the sunlight that streamed in through the windows. Rich leather gloves encased his lean fingers.

Edwina went speechless and still. He stepped forward, and she had the strangest urge to run—run to Tom. . . .

"Hello, Edwina." His voice, low and silvery, sounded too honeyed to her. She was used to a resonant baritone.

Swallowing the shock that had lodged in her throat, she said, "Hello, Ludie."

"The woman who works at the restaurant said I'd find you here." He doffed his hat and tucked it beneath his arm.

Chaotic emotions ran rampant through Edwina. She had a dozen questions to ask him, namely what are you doing here? She'd never thought she'd see him again, have to relive the humiliation of his telling her he could no longer see her. The pain had faded, but the wound, she quickly found out, was still there. It had scarred, but it ached nonetheless, reminding her of the pain she had endured.

In the midst of the tumult of her thoughts, one unknown rose above the rest: had Ludlow come to reclaim her?

Last summer, she would have gone to his arms and taken him back. But today . . . she was different. She didn't have the same passionate feelings for him as she'd had when she'd been in college. There *were* feelings inside her . . . but they were ones of caution and unease—tread lightly, be wary, don't trust.

"What brings you to Montana?" she ventured to say after the lapse of deadly quiet that surrounded them seemed to go on for an eternity.

"Just passing through." Then he motioned to the ladder-back chair beside her desk. "May I?"

"Oh . . ." She flushed, then fumbled with the snowflake trimmings that sat in a pile before her. He meant to stay a while. Did she want him to? No . . . yes, in a way. She hadn't seen him in so long. There had been times she'd imagined that he came back into her life and she'd treated him as shabbily as he'd treated her. But she couldn't do it to him now. His casting her off had been his mother's idea; still, he should have been man enough to make up his own mind. "Certainly."

He pulled the chair out and reclined his modest frame, setting his hat on her desk beside the book on matrimony. Her glance bounced briefly between the two, thinking it a queer irony.

Brown eyes, the ones she had once lost herself in, pulled at her attention and she gazed at him. He gave her an obvious perusal while smiling fondly. "You look lovely, Edwina. Never more so. It must agree with you to be home."

Being home had nothing to do with how she looked. If there was an air of beauty about her, Tom had put it there.

"So . . . you're a teacher now." He glanced over his padded coat shoulder out the window. "The sign says this is a finishing school. How grand. But I'd hoped you would use your accounting degree."

"I will be when I . . ." She didn't complete the thought. *When I go to Denver.* But she didn't want to go anymore. "There aren't many—if any—careers for female accounting clerks in Harmony."

"A shame. You were so bright."

"I still am," she replied, keeping her gaze locked on his. She'd never been a boastful or vain woman. But the way he said it, as if she were no longer smart enough to be whatever she desired, made her defensive.

Ludlow crossed his legs at the knees and folded his arms over his chest. "I have missed your wit, Edwina." Then more quietly, "I have missed you."

"I'm sure you've gotten along quite well." Before he could reply, she went on. "How are your parents?"

The mention of that subject brought a wince. His eyes clouded; the snappiness of his waxed mustache seemed to soften. "They are the same."

They are the same. Meaning their opinion of her hadn't changed. Well, bully for them. For some reason, it disturbed her. She'd hoped they would have told him they had made a big mistake in judging her by the value of her bank account or her lack of social standing.

One thing became utterly clear, however, with Ludie's words. Either he had decided to be his own man and would now go against them and ask for her hand or he had come just to satisfy his curiosity, to see what he had given up and to reinforce his belief that he had done the right thing. No matter which was his reason, both unsettled her. Neither could make her change her mind about him.

She no longer loved him.

"And you, Edwina? How have you been getting on without your mother? I had heard through Abigail that she passed away."

"I'm doing well." She didn't want his sympathy, so she inquired, "How is Abbie? Do you see her?"

A flicker of . . . nervousness, perhaps . . . came into his eyes. "Do you remember the time we all went to the Peacherine and Haley and his Fish Tail band had just opened there? It was the first time we danced the ditty bob walk. You accidentally hit me in the chin with your foot. I had a bruise for days."

She let his reminiscent mood go unchecked. Old memories came to her, and with them, an unconscious smile.

"It was the band's fault. They went from a four-time to a two-time beat. I was still trying to keep up with the music when they switched syncopation—new rag, or so they called it."

"Grand times." Ludlow laughed, warm and full of reverie. Reaching into his coat, he pulled out two cigars. "Remember these? The Midway Plaisance after you knocked down all the ten pins."

The Carl Upmann Red brand cigars hadn't been just for the Midway. After that day, the three of them had puffed away in the dancing club, Abigail turning green and sick at first, right alongside Edwina. But Edwina had gotten used to them and did enjoy the bouquet of a good cigar. It had been a long time since she'd indulged. . . .

"Eh, Edwina? For old times' sake." Ludie handed her one of the cigars. She took it, more automatically than with any conscious thought. A matchstick flared, and she hesitated a moment before putting the cigar to her lips to be lit.

Ludlow put the flame to his own, waved out the match, then leaned back and puffed. "I wonder whatever happened to the Fish Tails. . . ."

The blood in her veins slowed. "You don't go to the Peacherine anymore?"

His gaze locked on hers. "No, Edwina. I haven't been since the last time we three went."

Edwina lowered her cigar, its burning end curling smoke in a spiral toward the ceiling. This wasn't right. She shouldn't be sitting here with him. How would she explain him to . . .

"Ludie, why have you come to see me?"

But Ludlow had no opportunity to speak. The door behind her creaked open. Ludlow shot to his feet—either out of some exaggerated politeness or owing to the fact that a man had appeared through what had seemed to be a closet door.

Guilt brought Edwina to attention; in a split second, she had opened her desk drawer and thrown the smoldering cigar inside. She turned her head toward Tom and tried to pin an innocent expression on her face. But she *was* innocent . . . why did she think she needed to pretend?

"Sir, have you been in there long?" Ludlow bellowed at Tom, then said to Edwina with his cigar clamped between his teeth, "Has he been in there the whole time?"

Edwina glanced at Tom. His features were hard set. His blue eyes looked distrustful—not of her, but of Ludlow. His mouth was set grimly. The stance of his muscled physique was imposing, strong, dominant.

"I don't believe he has," she replied at length.

Tom came farther into the room, his boot heels sounding the power coiled in his body, hard and tense. "I own the store next door. The storeroom connects the two businesses."

Ludlow's edgy laugh went around the smoke wafting from the cigar tip. "It's a rather odd way of paying Miss Huntington a visit. Why didn't you use the front door?"

Edwina rose, not liking the tone in Ludlow's voice. He was being boorish and trying to assert his superiority—making no effort to hide his disdainful scrutiny of Tom's less-than-affluent apparel. She hadn't noticed until now how obnoxious Ludie's better-than-you-are demeanor could be. Had his stuffiness been there all along and she had merely looked the other way?

"I don't have to use the front door," Tom shot back, his eyes glaring. He gave her a fast glance, then resumed scowling at Ludlow.

Her heart slammed against her ribs. There was no indication that Tom could know who Ludlow was. She'd never described him, never spoken about anything beyond the vague generalities of their relationship. She hadn't dreamed she'd ever have to introduce the two men to each other.

Ludlow's blond brows rose. He removed the cigar from his mouth with his left hand, then extended his kid-gloved right. "Whatever you say. You are quite obviously Mr. Wolcott, proprietor of the sporting goods store."

Tom slowly lifted his hand toward Ludie's, once again glancing at Edwina—as if by her gaze, she could send him a private message. There was too much to be said with her eyes alone. How could she sum up everything in a look? She couldn't. She didn't even attempt to. Cowardly, she looked down, then up. Her expression was one of helplessness.

Just as the men grasped hands, Ludlow shattered the fragile tension in the room by giving his name. "Ludlow Rutledge," he stated with that proud intonation that in Chicago caused heads to nod with recognition.

Tom's reaction was the opposite—deadly hatred filled his face; his nostrils flared. But he said nothing derogatory, and she loved him all the more for his blessed silence. If he had called Ludlow out, Ludie would know she'd told Tom about him. Ludie would have a lot of questions. Why would she have reason to tell Tom about the intimacies of her past—unless she was intimately involved with Tom in the present?

Pulling his hand away, Tom raked his fingers through his hair to comb the tension from his forehead. He did so with straining biceps and taut cords at his neck. She watched the pulse jump at the hollow of his throat.

Ludlow reached for his hat. Even he had the good sense to see that Tom Wolcott wasn't in the mood for socializing. "Miss Huntington," he said to her, "it has been a pleasure. I'm certain our paths will cross again soon."

Then he left—no word about why he'd come, where he was going; no hint of why he'd said their paths would cross again—soon.

Distress caused her legs to weaken. She lowered herself onto her chair and took in a deep breath to still her racing heart. Then when she felt able to look at Tom, she lifted her eyes to his. What they had left unspoken between them before had been pushed away by the immediate problem: how could she explain to Tom about Ludie's showing up on her doorstep when she couldn't explain it to herself?

"Tom . . . I had no idea he'd come here."

Sinewy thighs strained against his trousers as he rested his weight on one foot. "What did he want?"

"I don't know. He didn't tell me."

Nodding with tight control, Tom hooked his thumbs into his belt loops. The waistband of his pants dipped, his belly flat behind the tucked-in ends of a red-and-black plaid shirt. "Were you glad to see him?"

She could barely think with the pounding of her heartbeat in her ears. "I was surprised."

"Glad?"

"Surprised," she repeated firmly.

"He smokes two-for-a-dollar cigars—those fancy Havana red bands." The observation seemed completely out of the blue—until he added without inflection, "Your drawer's smoking."

She quickly yanked the drawer open and smashed the glowing cigar tip with the doily that had been beneath the ivy plant now on Tom's counter. When the smoldering assortment of papers whose edges had begun to blacken were put out, she looked up.

Only to find Tom no longer there.

For the first time since Wolcott's Sporting Goods and Excursions had opened, Tom closed up in the middle of the day for no good reason other than he felt like it. He'd gone back to the store through the closet, snagged his tackle and pole, flipped the sign on the door, and locked the place up.

Standing on the bank of Evergreen Creek, up to his ankles in snow, he had smoked one cigarette after another until the pack was empty. So was his hook—as it had been for the past three hours. But he didn't give a damn about that. He hadn't come here to fish.

He'd come to try to get rid of the image of Edwina and Ludlow Rutledge in her classroom smoking cigars together. She'd fallen into a habit with him. He had known the minute he saw her guiltily slamming her drawer closed on the evidence that she'd done this before with him—smoked cigars. He didn't care that she smoked. That wasn't the point. It was the familiarity with Rutledge that her doing so implied. And she'd smoked again with him—now—after all the man had put her through. Jealousy had made Tom leave rather than confront her. He hadn't been able to trust his own voice not to rise. He wouldn't have been bullying her but rather Rutledge—even though the man had left.

He believed Edwina when she said she had no idea as to why he'd come. But he'd come just the same. Why? Did he want her back? Would she go back to him?

Tom had gone to see Edwina for the sole purpose of telling her that their set of circumstances—this affair—wasn't working out. He wanted more. He'd intended to bring up marriage to her again to see how she would react. He would have told her that he loved her to prove his point that marrying was the right thing to do. It was true—he did love her enough to spend the rest of his life with her.

The slowly trickling water, tumbling icily over rock beds and the frozen bank, kept Tom company when he should have been with Edwina instead.

But the distance he'd put between them had given him much-needed time to come to a conclusion. The fact that her old . . . friend . . . had come to town didn't matter one way or another. She obviously wasn't in love with the man anymore, or else she would have been rapturously in his arms—instead of smoking expensive Havanas—when Tom had come into the classroom.

Dusk had fallen, the trampled snow aglow from a pink cloud sunset. Tom gathered his gear and walked back to the store. He took only a minute to set his things on the counter before leaving once more and heading straight to Edwina's house.

Walking directly up the front walkway, he cranked the bell. The door opened and the housekeeper answered. Her face gave away her surprise at seeing him standing there. At least he remembered his manners and put fingers to his hat.

"Ma'am, I'd like to speak with Miss Huntington."

Marvel-Anne stood like an unyielding ox when she informed him, "She's not at home."

Tom kept his best courtesies in place. "Might you be able to tell me where she's gone?"

Weariness crept into her gaze, but when he kept an affable smile glued on his mouth, she gave in. "Minister Stoll's house."

"Church business?"

"No. She's visiting with friends from the Gillette College. Miss Crane and Mr. Rutledge. I don't expect her back until after I've gone home. Shall I leave a note that you called?"

"No." Tom tipped his hat in parting.

He went through the gate and let it slam behind him. In minutes, he was back at the store standing inside the dark interior. He lit a lamp on the wall, then stared at Edwina's handiwork. He hadn't changed anything since Saturday. All was exactly how she'd "fixed" it. It hadn't been in his heart to alter what she had done with good intentions . . . and love. Whether or not she was in love with him, he saw her decorations as tokens of that emotion. But maybe it was more like affection and friendliness; he didn't want to accept that. Right then, he wasn't sure what to think.

He wasn't sure of anything.

Walking to the counter, he reached behind the ledge, and snatched the bowl of small balls. He proceeded down the center aisle, stopped, and set the bowl down in the empty box of athletic supporters. Gripping one tiny sphere, he tossed it once and caught it in his palm, his lips pressed hard together. He coiled his arm and leg back and let the ball fly straight into Buttkiss's teeth. It made him feel somewhat better. He grabbed another ball and let it soar across the room. Then another. And another . . . until the bowl was empty and his forehead had broken out in a sweat from the effort.

*   *   *

When Edwina had returned home from the school after waiting over an hour for Tom to come back, she'd found a note and a calling card on her vestibule table from Abbie. She'd written that she had just come into town and was staying at her uncle's house. She wanted Edwina to come by at six for an impromptu get-together with her and Ludlow, where they could catch up on each other's lives. She'd dotted the *I* in *Abbie* with two eyes and a smile—the same way she had shown Edwina how to do for the *I* in *her* name. Edwina hadn't written it that way in . . . a long time.

Edwina had lowered the note and gazed at her reflection in the hall mirror. Had Abigail and Ludie traveled together? What were they doing in Harmony?

Telling Marvel-Anne she wouldn't be eating dinner, Edwina had gone up to her room and sat, trancelike, on the bed. So many things were happening in such a short space of time. . . . Tom was most important, but he'd made himself unavailable. She could try to track him down . . . but a lady didn't gad about after dark without having a proper destination. Tom Wolcott's apartment wasn't a proper destination. And she had the feeling he didn't want to be found at the moment—or he would have come back to the store before she'd gone home for the day.

Two hours later, Edwina had been admitted into the Stoll home. Now she sat in the quaint cherrywood-framed divan by the fire sipping a glass of Madeira Abbie had insisted on serving before dinner. It was a very awkward moment. Ludie resided in the oversize chair, his feet on an ottoman, and Abbie . . . she didn't sit. She flitted about the parlor, chattering on about Chicago. Minister Stoll had retreated into his study to leave the "young people" to their talk while Mrs. Stoll helped the cook in the kitchen.

Abigail, in physical appearance, looked like the old Abigail from college, only more refined, cultured. She talked differently. She sounded like . . . Ludie. Her deep titian hair was swept up on the crown of her head in an intricate and fashionable pompadour. Her eyes, brown and almond-shaped, seemed to tilt at the corners more . . . giving the impression of elusiveness, sauciness. She wore face powder, a fine and translucent cosmetic. And lip rouge—just a touch to emphasize her mouth. Earrings dangled from the lobes of her ears. Edwina could swear they were real diamonds.

But what was most startling was the large emerald-cut ruby on her fourth finger. Each time she moved about the room, the gem caught bits of light and gave off sparkling brilliance. Edwina couldn't stop sneaking looks at it. The ring was valuable. It meant something. Had Ludie given it to her? Were the two of them engaged?

"Ludlow," Abbie said in her husky tone, "be a dearling and go outside for a cigar so that I can talk with Edwina alone."

Ludlow, who had sat silently in the chair, his gaze alternating between Abbie and Edwina, rose. Edwina had been immensely uncomfortable for the past quarter-hour—ever since she'd been ushered into the parlor. Abbie obviously didn't know Ludlow had come to see her. Edwina still was uncertain why they were here. She'd asked once and Ludlow had been about to say something, but Abigail had cut him off with an airy remembrance of the time they'd all gone to Gowan's soda fountain. He had not uttered one word since.

And he still did not as he took his leave through the open pocket doors and wide grillwork entrance to the parlor. He disappeared into the dark vestibule, and a moment later, the front door clicked closed.

Abigail breathed in, the neckline of her stylishly cut ivory chiffon silk bodice pushing against the cleavage it revealed. She came to Edwina and sat beside her, taking Edwina's hands into one of hers. Edwina could barely hold onto the wineglass. She set it on a side table, swallowed, and gazed at Abigail.

"It's so good to see you gain, Edwina." She gave Edwina's fingers a squeeze. "I should have written more often."

"So should I," Edwina conceded. "It seems as if a lifetime has passed since we last saw one another."

"Yes, it does. But it really hasn't been, you goose." In her eyes, a glimmer of the old Abbie shone through. "I remember you living with us just like it was yesterday. Do you recall," she said, her voice lowered in conspiracy, "the time we took our skirts off right down to our shimmies and we climbed that old elm in my yard—straight up to my room so we wouldn't be discovered for having snuck out of the house?"

Edwina laughed softly. "I think I still have the bruises on my knees."

"Oh, what a pair of hoydens we made."

"Yes . . ." Edwina's smile dimmed somewhat, as did Abigail's.

"I'm sorry about your mother, Edwina. Truly I am. I should have done more. Something . . . when she departed."

"There was nothing you could do, Abbie. You were in Chicago. I was here."

"Yes, here." She sighed. "Quaint little Harmony. I don't recall it being so . . . so rustic from my visits when I was a child. How do you like it?"

"I like it well enough," Edwina replied with guardedness.

"Oh, I suppose you do—if this is all you have to choose from. But, you goose, you've got an accounting certificate, which is more than can be said about many of our sex these days."

Edwina hadn't been listening with her full attention. Preoccupation over the reasons why Abigail and Ludie were here prevented her from reliving the past with the same enthusiasm as Abbie.

She slipped her hand from Abbie's, clutched her hands together in her lap, then stared at her friend. "Abbie, are you engaged to Ludlow?" The question came out before Edwina realized she'd been wanting to ask it the moment she'd seen the ring on Abigail's finger.

Abigail sat primly, back stiff, ankles delicately crossed

and knees together. "I didn't want to tell you anything in a letter. It seemed so . . . cold. Especially knowing how you and Ludie used to feel about one another. He told me everything."

Cold seeped into Edwina's bones. "Told you . . . everything?"

"Your secret engagement and his breaking it."

Relief flooded Edwina. At least he'd kept quiet about their physical romance.

"That last week before you left, he took me into his confidence. I was hurt that you didn't tell me yourself. Why didn't you?"

"Ludie asked me not to tell anyone."

"I wasn't anyone, Edwina. I was your friend. It deeply wounded me. I felt quite betrayed."

"I'm sorry. . . ." In hindsight, Edwina could see that she should have told Abbie that she was engaged. But she had been trying to be true to Ludlow by keeping her silence.

Abbie went on as if she hadn't heard Edwina's apology. "It didn't surprise me that his family didn't approve of you. The Rutledges are old money, you know." She settled into the cushion a little. "Remember, Edwina, it was me he liked first. But I wouldn't step out with him unless you came, too. Then he decided he liked you better."

"I didn't mean for that to happen. . . . It just did."

"Yes, I know. Then it undid. I would have accepted your marriage if it had taken place. I know you loved him. But since he broke things off with you . . . well . . . a lot has happened since you left Chicago. I haven't been getting along with my mother." Her full lips went into a spoiled pout. "She thought she could tell me what to do. Well, she couldn't. So I made up my own mind. And . . ." She shrugged her bare shoulders. "I'm not exactly engaged to Ludlow."

The implication—one of scandalous proportions—sent Edwina reeling. The two of them were together and traveling without being married? That was . . . was worse than Edwina's affair. At least she didn't expose her indiscretion!

She hushed her friend. "Abbie . . . what do your aunt and uncle say? What do your parents say? My goodness, I knew you always wanted to be modern, but Abbie, this is *too* modern—even for you."

"They don't say anything. How can they? Everything's perfectly legitimate." Her gaze grew defensive. "I mean it's all legal."

"I don't understand . . . your calling card. It read Miss Abigail Crane."

Abbie waved her hand. "Oh, that. I just haven't had time to have new ones printed. Everything happened rather . . . suddenly." Then with a vivid flush on her cheeks, she hotly said, "Why, you goose, you didn't think— Well, never in all my born days! Edwina Huntington. I would never have an affair with a man. What kind of a woman do you take me for? I have morals and principles. I may be a free thinker, but I do believe in the vows between a man and woman before they're . . . undressed in front of one another and doing loathsome things in a bedroom."

Edwina grew horrified. She put trembling fingers to her lips and fought back tears. "I'm sorry . . ."

"As well you should be," she said sternly.

"Then what are you and Ludie to one another?" Edwina whispered.

"Why, you goose, I thought for sure you would have guessed by now." She held her left hand out and flashed the ruby ring for Edwina's close inspection. "We're married."

Chapter

❧ 19 ❧

Edwina walked onto the veranda, Ludie behind her. She had managed to get through the dinner, but with few words. Abbie's news had stunned her into almost complete silence while Abbie monopolized the table talk. She said they were visiting Harmony on their way to the West Coast for a California honeymoon. They'd been married less than two weeks, and, according to Abbie, they were blissfully happy and madly in love.

Having finished her dinner obligation, Edwina had sought escape after the dessert plates had been cleared. Good-byes spoken, she went out the front door, eager to leave. The shock of hearing such things during the meal still hadn't worn off, and all Edwina wanted to do was go home, crawl into bed, and snuggle with her cat. Pets came in handy in times of woe. Loyal to the end, they loved their owners unconditionally and made good listeners, giving back never an unkind word or admonishment—just purrs and happy kitty sounds.

"Edwina," Ludie called from behind.

Disconcerted she'd been followed, Edwina stopped at the porch post and laid a hand on it. "I said my thank-yous. I have to be going home now."

"Edwina . . ." His scholarly fingers, with their well-groomed nails, curled around her forearm, now covered by her coat. Her eyes lowered to the place he touched. She went still; her heart wedged against her ribs. "I wanted to tell you before Abigail did. That's why I came by the school this afternoon."

"You didn't owe me anything."

"Yes, I did."

The smell of his cologne seemed too pungent—too citrusy. She didn't like it . . . not when compared to . . . another's.

"Edwina, look at me."

She didn't want to, but unable to help herself, she did. "I don't love her. I married her only because my parents pressured me to wed. My father said my still living at home and not being settled in my own life didn't make for a good appearance. I've put in for dean, and being established can help me get the position. Abigail was convenient. But my heart, Edwina . . . it belongs to you."

"I don't want to hear this," she whispered. "I have to go home."

"Wait." His hand held her wrist so that she couldn't move. "Edwina, believe me when I say I love you. I never stopped. Abigail . . . she's not you. She's what my parents wanted for me."

"But you're married to her," Edwina snapped. "How can you talk about your wife in such a way?"

"How can you defend her?" Ludie's mustache hid his mouth and she couldn't tell whether he was smiling. She finally detected that he was, but the smile was not one of amusement. "The entire trip down here, she anticipated the moment when she could tell you of our marriage. She's jealous of you. I told her to write, but she said she wanted to see the look on your face when you found out. She said you betrayed her."

Tears burned the backs of Edwina's eyelids. Now it was Edwina who felt betrayed. Pulling her hand away from Ludie's hold, she gained her composure and said, "You could have written me just as easily. Don't blame this entirely on your . . . wife."

"Would you have read a letter from me, Edwina? The last time we spoke . . . on that night . . . you said you never wanted to speak to me again."

"But here I am, doing just that."

"Edwina . . ."

She backed away from him. "There's nothing more to say. You're married—to a woman your parents approve of. I always knew Abbie was better than me in that regard. She was affluent and she had a place in society."

"But I don't care about that."

"Well, you should. You're married to her, for better or for worse. You should commit yourself to the marriage. It's lifelong."

"Lifelong hell," he swore. "She's not like she used to be. Not when we three went out together. Back then, she was . . . whimsical and warm and a good time." His brown eyes became resentful. "Now she's just like my mother, caring about her standing in the community, going to this charity function and that, turning herself into a copy of the matrons she's ensconced herself with."

"There's nothing I can do about that. You've made up your mind. You did so the night you told me you couldn't marry me."

"I was pressured to give you up. I shouldn't have."

"But you did." Edwina grew outraged. "How dare you talk to me about this? I don't want to hear it. Do you expect me to feel sorry for you? If you do, you're sadly mistaken."

"Edwina . . . I love you."

She shook her head. "Stop saying that."

"I can't stop telling you the truth. I need to know . . . Would you take me back if I wasn't married?" He attempted to bring her into an embrace, but she sidestepped him. "I could get a divorce—"

"Don't. You've made your choice. You have to live with it."

"Living without you isn't living."

"You have a wife now. Love her."

"I can't."

Edwina mindlessly headed down the porch steps, thankful the patchy ice had melted under the afternoon sun. Extreme upset roiled inside her. She wanted to go home, to get away.

"Edwina! Don't go yet." Ludlow had to keep his voice clipped and not shout her name or the entire house would have heard.

She made no reply. Her fast walk turned into a run after she exited the gate. She didn't look back. If she had, she would have seen a slender woman's silhouette in the parlor window, a trembling hand on the side frame, then the lace curtains dropping back in place.

Tom went inside Plunkett's Mercantile, his coat collar turned up to his neck to ward off the softly falling snow that had been coming down since dawn. The store was warm and fragrant, the scent of cloth dye and spices and leather goods giving the place a homey feel. Aisles were always neat and orderly; merchandise was always stocked well and the service was top-notch. Plunkett ran a nice outfit, which was good—he had the only mercantile in town.

Beside the cracker barrel, cups of hot cider in their hands and the pot-bellied stove at their backs, stood Roger Elward, Pike Faragher, and Moses Zipp. They guffawed in unison about something Tom didn't catch. He acknowledged them with a tip of his hat, then continued toward the counter.

"Mr. Wolcott," Plunkett said, a feather duster in hand. "What can I do for you?" He wasn't of the same proportions as his wife; as a matter of fact, quite the opposite. Hy Plunkett was as thin as a broom handle.

"Two packs of Richmonds." Tom dug into his back pocket for his billfold and laid money on the counter. Behind him, the laughter rose again. This time he was able to make out their words.

"So she says to me," Deputy Faragher embellished with a chuckle, "you've got to buy one of these elbow supporters if you want to hold your rifle steady."

Snickering.

Then Moses Zipp spoke. "I said, 'I don't even rifle hunt.' She goes and stretches the elastic and says, 'Why not try it for fishing, then—it'll improve your cast.'"

More hilarity.

Tom gazed at his right hand, noticing the veins on top were straining as he slid the packs of cigarettes toward him, putting one in his coat breast pocket and unwrapping the other. "Obliged, Plunkett."

Turning, he struck a match and lit his smoke while walking to the men at the cracker barrel. He waved the flame out while Elward proceeded to say, "Did you get a look at how she had one on?"

Choking laughter.

"Good night, sister!" Faragher snorted. "I had to keep a straight face, but as soon as me and Algie left the store, we just busted our bladders from laughing so hard."

"You wouldn't happen to be talking about Miss Huntington?" Tom asked in a voice level and emotionless.

With watery eyes, Faragher blew his nose into a handkerchief then stuffed it back into his trousers pocket. "Yes, Wolcott, as a matter of fact, we were. What in the hell possessed you to let her operate your store? A woman doesn't know squat about hunting gear."

"Yep." Roger grinned. "Sold us jockey straps as elbow supporters."

Zipp rolled the toothpick in his mouth to the corner. "If it wasn't so damned funny, I'd be mad as a hornet I spent forty-two cents on something I didn't need for supporting my 'elbow.'"

Pokes in the ribs. Pats on the backs.

Tom felt every muscle in his body go hard and taut and coiled. He wanted to hit something, somebody—some*bodies*. He checked himself, then he kept his voice down as low as he could manage and still be heard. "You're mistaken about those Spaldings. They *are* elbow supporters. Miss Huntington was right. And she wore one correctly, too."

Wide eyes stared at him.

"Any one of you who says different is a liar. I will call you out and make it my personal business to set you straight. For your sakes, I hope like hell I don't ever hear you—or anyone else who bought an elbow supporter—discussing this again. Because if I do, whoever is joking about Miss Huntington's sales effort is offending me. And in a town where there's only one sporting goods store to cater to your year-round needs, I'd suggest you remember that." Then he put fingers to the brim of his hat and barely nodded. "The spring fishing season will be getting underway in a couple of months. Now's the time to get your tackle boxes in order."

Tom left the stone-silent store and stepped onto the boardwalk. He tugged his hat band low over his brow and inhaled deeply on his cigarette before letting the smoke be caught on the light breeze. Walking to the opposite side of town, he made his mind go blank. But he could do so only for seconds before Edwina filled his head.

This morning, she hadn't held classes at the finishing school. That boxy lady who worked for her had come by and met the girls, telling them that Miss Edwina wasn't feeling well enough to lead classes. She'd sent them all home, giving him a sideways glance when he'd popped his head out his store's door just as she locked up the school; then she'd gone on her way.

Tom hadn't had any plans for speaking with Edwina— going through the storeroom or any other way. With Ludlow Rutledge in town, she had to come to terms with her past and then come to him. He had his pride, dammit. He'd gone to her last night, only to find she was with the professor and Miss Crane—Abbie—at Minister Stoll's. Having her old college chum in town along with the man who'd left Edwina in the lurch was enough for her to contend with. Tom wasn't going to put any more emotional pressures on her.

Riding things out didn't make him feel any more comfortable about the entire affair. With Rutledge here . . .

and that Abbie . . . what if Edwina wanted to go back to Chicago? What if that son of a bitch asked her to marry him again and really meant it this time? Would Edwina have him?

Tom damned himself for not being able to tell Edwina how he felt about her before Rutledge came to town. Doing so now would seem almost . . . desperate—as if he didn't want another man to have her, so he'd declare his own love to keep her for himself.

The timing of everything couldn't have been worse. Just when Tom had been able to secure a house for Edwina—for them. Not exactly the kind he would have liked to buy for her, but a decent three-bedroom plan—and even with a bathroom on the second floor, the total cost, including a cellar under the whole house and two attic rooms, was two thousand. It was sturdy, from the looks of the architectural drawings that Healy had shown him.

A few days ago, Healy had come and told him about a lot off of Hackberry Way, somewhat out of town—a half mile. But it was north of the tracks. Tom had put in for the loan after riding out to see it, and had been approved—which made him want to run and tell Edwina, but he'd kept his silence. He'd wanted to show her the title as a surprise. It was one hell of a thing that Healy had brought the papers by and handed them to Edwina, but she didn't suspect a thing.

If only he could tell her. But until Edwina came to him and told him what Rutledge was doing in town and if his visit affected them, Tom wasn't going to go chasing after things he might not be able to have.

Reaching the town square, he sought Healy's real estate office and let himself inside after pitching his cigarette into the street. Melodic ladies' voices drifted from the agent's office, most of them recognizable, but one was not.

"Well," said one after a breathy sigh, "I didn't think you'd have anything to my liking, but I thought since we were in town for a few days, I might as well get some ideas for our house."

"I imagine what you're looking for will be better presented in Chicago," Healy replied.

"Oh, Chicago," came Mrs. Plunkett's lament. "It's so wicked, but such a place as I'll never see—but I do so want to one day. I wouldn't tell my Hy—Heavens, no. He'd think the hoi polloi of this town wasn't good enough anymore. He'd want to move there, I'm certain."

Tom held back and pretended to be interested in the architectural drawings on the wall. What a liar that Plunkett lady was. She talked down big cities every chance she got.

"Well, my dears." Mrs. Treber's nasal tone was distinctive. "Since we don't have anything nearly as grand as Chicago, we'll have to take Mrs. Rutledge to our fair ladies' boutique. Not as elegant or regal as I'm sure you're used to, but the proprietress does stock some very high-quality gloves."

Mrs. Rutledge?

"Please, ladies, call me Abigail. I'm not of the old school."

Feminine giggles abounded.

"Well, you're certainly younger than us." Mrs. Calhoon remarked.

Mrs. Elward chimed in. "Nineteen would be my guess."

"Ladies, you're too kind!" That unfamiliar voice again. "I'm twenty-three, but not a minute older."

The chatter came close and Tom tucked himself behind a gallery wall as the ladies entered the foyer to the office. They began talking once more, rapidly, without giving Mrs. Rutledge time to reply.

"Your husband is such a dashing young man."

"So very handsome."

"Oh, quite."

"A college professor."

"How noble a profession."

"Very. Educating young people with eager minds."

"Miss Huntington operates our finishing school and does so splendidly—oh, but you must know that."

"My, yes, Miss Huntington brought Crescencia Stykem out of her shyness. She's to be married Christmas Eve."

"You'd have to know Miss Stykem, Mrs. R—Abigail. Quite a timid creature. But she's blossomed."

"Yes! Like a rose."

"Because of Miss Huntington."

"Charming woman."

"Pretty, too."

Amidst the praise came Abigail Rutledge's huff of indignance. Tom tried to get a look at her without being seen. All he could catch was a glimpse of a hat and a shoulder. *Abigail Rutledge*. So she was married to the bastard.

"I certainly don't like to be the one to tell you. It's horrid to be put in a position of having to say this about . . . about Miss Huntington."

"What?"

"Tell!"

"Do!"

"Please!"

Drawing out the suspense before spilling her dirty news, she primped, straightening her collar and delicately patting her coiffure where it swept up beneath a garish hat. "As you know, she stayed in my home while going to Gillette's. I was raised with the values that a girl doesn't . . ."

Hat-covered heads came in closer so their owners wouldn't miss a word.

". . . a good girl doesn't go out on her own and make a . . . well . . ." She brought a lacy handkerchief to her nose. Tom could make out only her profile.

"What?!" the ladies cried together.

Abigail took the cue and stated bluntly, "A good girl doesn't go out and make a spectacle of herself dancing in clubs to—ragtime!"

There were loud gasps, hands on bosoms, furtive glances.

"Mind you, I went once only because she begged me to. It was awful. They served alcoholic refreshments and men held women too closely and they smoked. The women, that is. Of course, I was scandalized and told her I wanted to leave immediately, but she refused."

"Why . . . this doesn't sound like Edwina." Grayce Kennison had spoken up for the first time.

"No, it doesn't . . ." mumbled Mrs. Plunkett. "Dancing . . . to ragtime." She shook her head, then locked eyes with Mrs. Treber.

Abigail dabbed the underside of her nose with her hankie before replacing it in the pocket of her coat. "I didn't like having to tell you, but I felt it my duty to let you know. Your daughters are in her care, after all. A woman of her reckless and abandoned nature can be a bad influence on their tender minds."

With a smarmy little smile, she straightened her shoulders as if what she had just disclosed was nothing at all. But Tom knew that in the close-knit world of these women, it was a hell of a big deal. He could have come to Edwina's aid and told them all the woman was a hypocrite, that she had wanted to go to the dancing clubs just as much as Edwina—and that going to them had been her idea to begin with.

But to do so would reveal that he and Edwina were on confidential grounds. What reason would Miss Edwina Huntington have for telling Tom Wolcott of her college escapades? His speaking up would definitely fuel more questions. Saving her reputation would only damage it more.

The women, deep in thought, left the office. The frigid cold they'd let in on their departure remained with Tom as he stepped out of the gallery.

Edwina strode purposefully through the foyer, buttoning her day gloves as she went toward the front door. Passing the mirror, she didn't bother to check if her hat was still straight or her hair in neat order. She had to find Tom. But she barely had touched the doorknob when the bell cranked and a group of shadows loomed at the other side of the stained-glass oval.

Dread worked its way up Edwina's spine. The last thing she needed was company.

Drawing in a breath, she opened the door to find her students' mothers on the stoop. All six of them.

"My dear," Mrs. Brooks began, "you shouldn't be dressed and out of bed. We were told you were ill today."

Edwina worried the inside of her bottom lip. "Just this morning. A terrible headache. I lay down for a while and now I feel much better." In a rush, she added, "As a matter of fact, I have an errand that I can't be detained from. So if it's nothing pressing, can we arrange another meeting?"

Mrs. Plunkett forged her way to the front of the ranks. "Miss Huntington, we do indeed have something quite urgent that we need to take up with you."

Mrs. Elward seconded her companion. "Yes, quite."

Deflated, Edwina stepped aside and bade them enter. She had no clue as to what had brought them here— together—seemingly very intent on discussing a topic of urgency. *Oh, help.* What had she done that she didn't know about?

Ushering them into the parlor, Edwina waited for them to be seated, then she sat on the organ bench facing them. After enduring a few seconds of contemplative gazes at her person and noting that the women's eyes frequently met in some unspoken conversation, she became resigned to the fact she would be there a while. She removed her gloves and set them on her lap.

Marvel-Anne, who must have heard the ladies' entrance as they filed in, came from the kitchen through the dining room, wrung her hands dry on her apron, and asked if anything was to be served. Edwina asked for tea—and the rest of the macaroons, which brought an anticipatory smile to Mrs. Plunkett's face.

"Ladies," Edwina hesitantly began, "is there something wrong?" She looked to Grayce Kennison, who could always be counted on for her forthrightness and decent candor.

Grayce, subtly beautiful in a Brussels lace waist and nine-gore skirt, sat up a little taller. "We've spent the morning with Mrs. Rutledge."

Edwina's courage in the face of opposition slipped just a notch. Abbie could divulge things about Edwina. But would she? Could she be that . . . that cold and unfeeling?

"Yes, Mrs. Rutledge," Mrs. Treber crooned. "From Chicago, you know. Quite the posh-posh."

"Definitely," agreed Mrs. Calhoon.

Mrs. Brooks took over. "We were extolling your accolades as a teacher, Miss Huntington, and she . . . well, she informed us of something about your . . ."

". . . about your days in college," Mrs. Treber finished, gazing dead on at Edwina.

Edwina wanted to squirm out of her seat and take her leave, but Marvel-Anne came in with the tray of cookies and as soon as they were taken politely by the guests, she left and returned with the tea. She filled all the cups, then took a moment to add sugar and cream. The effort bought Edwina time, time she needed to think. Whatever it was, could she talk her way out of it? Could she still sound respectable? What could Abbie have said? There were so many things she'd done that could be deemed disgraceful . . . but the worst, Abbie didn't know about. And even if she did, these ladies would not be sitting here sipping patiently on tea and nibbling macaroons if they'd found out about her relationship with Ludlow Rutledge. They would have taken her to task right there on the stoop.

"Miss Huntington," Mrs. Kennison said in a soft tone. "When they are young and impetuous, both boys and girls can do things of a nature that might not be found agreeable by those with more mature and wiser minds."

"Well said, Grayce." Mrs. Plunkett nodded after thoughtfully swilling down a sip of tea.

Mrs. Elward took over. "As Grayce said, both boys and girls. But as you know, it is a girl who is least-forgiven for her behavior."

Edwina's stomach twisted in a knot. She pulled on the fingers of her gloves, needing to spend her energies or else she'd bolt from the bench and right out that front door.

"I never had the opportunity to go to college," Mrs. Brooks said, placing her half-eaten cookie back on her tea dish. "Had I, I'm certain I'd be the better for it. I don't begrudge those girls who can go. Why, I'd like for my Margaret, but she'd such a willful thing . . . I'd be afraid . . ." She let the thought trail off. "Well, never mind about that. What I'm trying to say—what we're all trying to say—is what Mrs. Rutledge told us was a great surprise."

Lulu Calhoon nodded. "A great surprise."

"Imagine, all this time, and we didn't know." Mrs. Treber set her saucer aside. "We could have been taking advantage of the situation."

"Very much so." Grayce's posture was flawless as she knit her thin fingers and laid them on her lap. "We want to make it clear we hold you in no ill regard. A young girl can get carried away."

Edwina was going to scream if they didn't tell her what she'd done! "Ladies, you have me quaking inside," she confessed, then immediately wished she hadn't been so open with her feelings. Never let your opponent know your true feelings—or so her father had told her when he'd taught her to play checkers.

"We don't mean to upset you, dear," Grayce said soothingly.

Mrs. Brooks shook her head. "Not at all."

"On the contrary." Mrs. Plunkett took a bite of her macaroon. "We have just reconciled ourselves to the news and don't know how to proceed. Right, ladies?"

"Just ask her," Grayce said to Prudence.

"We should." Mrs. Calhoon looked to Mrs. Elward. "Fanny, you say it."

Fanny Elward, nervous by nature to begin with, set her teacup on the side table. Its base clattered against the saucer as she did so. Then she stared so long at Edwina that Edwina began to feel dizzy and lightheaded. She might have dropped into a supreme faint had it not been for Fanny's finally speaking up in that next second. "Miss Huntington, is it true you know how to dance to ragtime music?"

Edwina felt as if the breath had been punched from her lungs. The shock left her immobile. *Oh, Abbie, you told them! That!* She foundered for a reply, sensing the maelstrom of trouble that Abbie had released with that confession. And how had Abbie managed to tell them without implicating herself? None of the ladies had mentioned that Abigail Crane had been a ragger herself.

What to say? What to do? How to recover?

Expectant faces waited. When she tried to speak, her voice wavered. "I . . . in my defense . . . I . . ." There was no way to lie. She couldn't get out of it. Reduced to a quiet defeat, she could at least hold her chin high when confessing. "Yes, I did dance to ragtime when I was in college."

Grayce Kennison was the first to react. "Oh, thank Heaven!"

"It *is* true!" Mrs. Plunkett smiled broadly.

Mrs. Elward glanced first at Mrs. Plunkett, then at Edwina. "We weren't certain from the way Mrs. Rutledge told us. She had a gleam in her eye."

"I saw the gleam before any of you," Mrs. Treber said.

Mrs. Brooks tsked. "Yes, but I was the one who dared say that if Miss Huntington *had* danced ragtime, our fondest hopes would come true."

"Our fondest hopes and our *most secret* hopes," Mrs. Calhoon added.

Edwina didn't understand. None of it. Weren't they mad at her? Weren't they going to tell her she couldn't teach their girls anymore because she was a disgrace? A bad influence?

"Ladies . . . I . . ." Complete confusion ran through her.

"Don't worry, my dear." Grayce's mouth curved upward. "We've known you since you were a child. We know what kind of girl you are. Dancing to music isn't something new. Why, no—I danced the waltz way too close with my James. That's how it is when you're young and impetuous. Ragtime is no different than what we tried to get away with in our generation."

"True, Grayce." Mrs. Plunkett dabbed her mouth. "My Hildegarde would say I'm an old fuddy-duddy, but truth be told, I was a lot more spry in my younger days and Mr. Plunkett and I did trip the light fantastic ourselves. I, for one, would like to say Mrs. Rutledge did us a favor when she told."

"But she thought she was being nasty," Mrs. Calhoon said, prompted by Mrs. Plunkett.

"Very nasty," Mrs. Treber said, condemning Abbie as well. "We don't know her the way we know you."

Edwina grew overwhelmed. Putting a hand to her collar, she blinked back the tears that had gathered in her eyes. Such loyalty . . . such faith. She didn't know what to say. "Then you aren't upset that I know how to dance ragtime?"

"No," they replied in unison.

Then Grayce Kennison's blue eyes lit. "My dear, don't you know why we're here?"

She slowly shook her head.

"Ladies, allow me," Mrs. Plunkett cut in, cheeks ruddy. She was given nods of approval, then said with a flourish, "Miss Huntington, we want you to teach us and our girls how to do the crazy bones!"

The ladies had left a scant fifteen minutes ago after two hours of continuous talk about music and ragtime and its variety of steps. As much as Edwina had enjoyed conversing with them about it, she was glad when they said they had to get home to cook dinners for their husbands.

Only after four o'clock had Edwina been able to get away and seek Tom. She left the house and walked down the sidewalks that had been cleared of snow. They hadn't had any new fall since Sunday and it made navigating easier for Edwina—especially in her haste. She walked on Sugar Maple, gazing absently at the bare trees and thinking how it seemed that it was just yesterday when she'd been crushing brittle leaves beneath her shoes and cursing her luck at Murphy Magee's having sold the warehouse twice. She now lifted her eyes skyward a moment and sent him a heavenly thank-you.

Taking Birch Avenue, she gathered her thoughts. How would she tell Tom? Just come right out and blurt out her feelings? Or wait until he said something? He had, after all, been going to tell her something yesterday when he'd come in on her and Ludie. But what he'd been about to say . . . was it good or bad? And he'd gotten only part of it out before her students had arrived when he'd first tried to tell her. . . .

This isn't working out . . .

If you want to see other women. . . .

It's nothing like that . . .

What was it, then?

Edwina rounded Old Oak Road and took the shoveled walk to Wolcott's store. The door opened and a customer departed just as she went inside. Both Tom and Mr. Dufresne were at the counter. She hadn't counted on Mr. Dufresne's being there. He usually was gone most of the week.

Tom's gaze lifted when she went toward them. She smiled at him. He smiled at her in return. Her heart warmed. "Hello, Mr. Wolcott."

"Miss Huntington."

Mr. Dufresne lounged against the countertop while sitting on the stool. "It's good to see you, Miss Huntington."

"Likewise, Mr. Dufresne."

She was at the counter now—and suddenly remembered the last time she'd been . . . on it. A blush that must have made her face redder than a geranium took hold of her cheeks, because Mr. Dufresne straightened and asked, "Are you all right, Miss Huntington?"

"Oh . . . fine." Then to Tom, she sent a message with her gaze. He read it clearly.

Walking to the coat tree, he collected his jacket and hat. "Shay, I'm stepping out for a while. Watch the place."

"Got it covered."

Tom held the door open for her and they exited together. She wasn't sure where to go, so she stopped as soon as she reached the sidewalk. Coming up behind her, Tom quit walking as well.

She turned to face him. He slid his hands in his pockets and appeared casual and relaxed, while she was in turmoil. "How are you doing, Edwina?"

"Good." Then, "Not good. Not really. We need to talk."

"Yeah, we do."

"Where do you want to go?"

"Let's take a walk out back."

She nodded. He took her arm through his and guided her to the grove. She viewed its white wintry façade, thinking back to when she fell out of the tree and onto Tom. It hadn't been funny at the time, but now, reminiscing made her smile. And the tree swing. The rope still hung from the oak Tom had tied it to. A lot of memories were here . . . all fond for Edwina. Even Barkly's pranks could be viewed with some slight affection.

Tom came to the area where he'd had his Flightmaster set up in the fall. All that remained—and would remain until spring, when the weather turned—were the stumps he'd used as chairs. Brushing two off, he offered her a seat. She took it, folding her gloved hands in her lap, and keeping her gaze forward.

"Has anybody been giving you a hard time today?" Tom's question threw her, and she looked at him.

"Why do you ask?"

"Just wondering."

"No . . . nobody has. As a matter of fact . . . well, I'll tell you later. First, can we talk about what you were going to say to me yesterday?"

It was his turn to stare ahead. "Did you know Rutledge was married?"

"Yes . . . I found out last night."

"How'd you feel about it when you found out?"

Edwina set her gaze with his. It would seem they were both interested in the beauty of the trees, but she was certain that neither of them cared at all about them. Telling Tom the truth could . . . probably would . . . hurt him. But if there was to be a future for them she wouldn't base it on falsifications or watered-down versions of how she really felt. Loving a person meant total and complete honesty. There was no other way.

Slowly, she formed the words in her mind, then spoke them as quietly as snow drifting down from a gray sky. "When I found out . . . I felt deceived."

Then she dared chance a glance at him; she saw his jaw had set, his eyes had narrowed.

Oh, God . . . she'd just made the biggest mistake of her life.

Chapter

❧ 20 ❧

Deceived.

Tom stared at the network of bare branches, then reached into his pocket and retrieved his Richmonds. With an easy gesture, he placed the cigarette so it rested on his lips. Striking a matchstick against the tree's trunk side, he lit the end. He quietly smoked and thought about what Edwina said. That she felt deceived meant emotional connections were still there.

"She was my dearest and only close friend for a long time. Although I never came out and said it, she had to know that I'd been in love with Ludie. He told her about our engagement when he broke it. She was angry with me for not confiding in her. She told me that I'd hurt her feelings. I never meant to. That she would marry him *wanting* to . . . get back at me makes me angry. I'm sorry, Tom. I had to be honest."

He nodded.

"But he doesn't mean anything to me anymore. It's silly, really, to feel this way."

Tom took a drag on his cigarette. "If it's how you feel, it's not silly."

"They don't matter to us, Tom. I accept their marriage. I hope for their sakes they can be happy. But if they aren't, that's their own affair. I've moved on with my life." He watched as she squeezed gloved hands together in her lap. "I have to know what it is you were going to say to me yesterday. It's important."

He believed her about Rutledge. Rutledge and she had been through for a long time. Tom had known this from the way she looked at him when they were together at the schoolroom or store, the way she had touched him and let herself be cuddled in his arms. If she'd been in love with someone else, she wasn't so good at disguising her feelings that he wouldn't know, so there was no point in discussing the former college professor anymore—that was finished.

What needed to be settled now was the relationship he and Edwina had, or were going to have if she would agree. He leaned forward to rest his elbows on his thighs. "I was going to tell you that the way our relationship is at present isn't working out for me."

"Oh . . ."

The meek, wounded tone of her voice made him continue on rapidly.

"I don't want to stop seeing you, Edwina. I want things on a permanent basis from now on. No more sneaking around." He turned his head to look at her. "This means an open commitment, Ed."

"What kind of open commitment?"

"Meaning we go places together in public. We hold hands if we want. We share a kiss if we want. Attend dances and parties if we get invited. Not that I'm any good at these kinds of things with the people you know. But I'd try. Just like I'd want you to try to do some of the things I like—fishing and camping, going out for the day on a horse. You know. Stuff like that. You made me see that it's no fun doing it by myself or with Shay. I want you with me."

"As if we were a couple," Edwina said softly.

"That's right. One plus one equals two: me and you—a pair. Can you?"

The smile that fluttered at the corners of her mouth

was tender sweet to him. "Are you asking me to marry you?"

"I believe I just did."

"But you didn't say the words."

"If I say them, will you answer yes?"

Her green eyes shone like summer grass. "Try me."

Tom sat up straight, pitched his cigarette into the snow, then took her hand in his. "Edwina Huntington, will you marry me?"

In the span of time that seemed like an eternity, she gazed slowly at his face, looking at his eyes and mouth, then his nose, his jaw. She was reading him. Or doing something like memorizing him.

Worry getting the best of him, he couldn't help asking, "What are you doing?"

"I'm imprinting you in my mind so I'll always remember how you looked when you asked me." Then a short moment later, she replied, "I never thought I would *want* to hear those words after resigning himself to being alone. After talking myself into living like a spinster because I thought it was best. Tom . . . you made me see that it's all right to be . . . imperfect and be in love. For that, I will always cherish you—how special you've made me feel." She brought her hand to his check. "Of course I will marry you."

"Well . . . hell, Ed." Then he took her into his arms and sealed the vow with a kiss on the mouth. *Edwina Huntington said she'd be my wife*. He wanted to shout it. The series of light and warm kisses he gave spoke of his love for her, of how he worshiped her and would cherish her. He had to tell her about the house. She'd be surprised. He couldn't wait to see her reaction.

Breaking their kissing, he said, "I'll make you happy, Edwina."

"You already do." She leaned back and smiled at him. "Even though you got to Ab Trussel and took that extra foot."

Joining in her playfulness, Tom laughed. "What are you calling an extra foot? It was my foot to begin with."

"I've got to give you credit—you know how to make a good bribe. What would you do if you ever had to bribe a woman? You couldn't get her to take your side with froggies."

"Never had to bribe a woman."

"Maybe not," she said with a grin, "but you've used your share of trickery with me, that's for sure. You knew all along that line was off and you had the nerve to eat all those cookies."

"You shoved them at me, as I recall."

"I was trying to distract you." She toyed with the hair on his nape, the action of her fingers raising gooseflesh on his arms. "Just like you were trying to distract me wearing that holey old shirt you sleep in when I came to your door."

"How was I supposed to know it was you?" He grazed her lips with a kiss.

"I don't know . . . you just should have." Her eyes narrowed a little. "When I think how you painted your side red just to get back at me . . . Tom Wolcott, don't you ever do a thing like that again."

"From now on, I won't paint a thing unless you approve."

"I should hope so."

They kissed once more, smiling as their warm mouths joined, teased, nibbled and lingered. As they sat on the stumps with their arms draped over each other's shoulders, Edwina gazed into Tom's eyes. "You do make me very happy, Tom. I never thought I could be so happy."

"Likewise, Edwina. I can't imagine what my life would be like without you in it."

"I don't want you to try to imagine."

"Me neither." He gave her another gentle kiss. Her lips were soft and full and would be his forever. Stroking his thumb across the nape of her neck, he felt the satiny texture of her perfumed skin. As a way of leading into his surprise about the property he'd bought, Tom murmured against her damp mouth, "We'll have to tell Calhoon to start sorting our mail and putting it in the same place."

"Mail." The *m* vibrated on his mouth. "That reminds me. I got a letter from Denver a few days back." She kissed him once, then pulled far enough back so he could see her face. "It was from Madame DeVille. She owns a bridal salon in Denver. She said she could help me find a position. But I don't need her to do that now, because obviously I won't be going. I'll be working here."

Tom creased his forehead. "You mean the school?"

"Well, of course I would continue the finishing school. I do so enjoy it." Her eyes sparkled in an enthusiastic way. "And the most amazing thing happened to me this afternoon. The ladies—the girls' mothers—they came by to see me, and you'll never guess why. I suppose I should thank Abbie for gossiping about me."

Tom recalled the vindictive woman's words in Healy's. That's why he'd asked Edwina if anyone had treated her ill. He'd assumed those old bats would have come down hard on her for the dancing.

"What did they say?"

"Abbie told them about my dancing to ragtime and after an agonizingly long moment, they asked me if I'd teach them and their daughters to do the crazy bones! Imagine that. I thought for sure they'd scorn my past visits to the clubs, but they weren't in the least. They even defended me against Abbie. I couldn't believe it. So I'm going to be adding dancing to the curriculum at Huntington's Finishing School."

"That's good, Ed, but once we're married, I don't want you to teach school anymore."

The animation left her face. "What do you mean you don't want me to teach school?"

"I don't want you employed. It's as simple as that."

"Teaching isn't working. It's educating."

"You're getting paid for it. That's employment."

"I told you I'm in financial straights right now. I have to work."

"Not after we're married. I'll take care of your debts."

Fire lit her gaze and a thin chill fell into her words. "You will do no such thing. It's my responsibility. I'm not foisting it off on you."

"You aren't 'foisting' it off on me. I'm telling you that once we're married, you and all you have will be for me to take care of."

Edwina ducked out of his arms. "If that isn't the most archaic thinking I've ever heard. You've said pigheaded things in the past about women, but I never thought you'd lump me into your idiotic ideals about them. I thought I was special to you . . . that you thought my running the school was commendable."

"And I do think that, Edwina. But that was before— when you weren't going to be my wife. Now you will be. How the hell would I look if my wife kept a job after we were married? I'd look like one sorry son of a bitch who couldn't take care of her. That's what." He dug for his smokes, then swore and gave up on finding one.

"Well, I should give a you-know-what what people think about my marriage. It's none of their business."

"Sweetheart, in this town, everything everyone does is everyone's business."

They stared at each other for precious seconds, then she put her hands on her hips and said in an exasperated tone, "What a ninny I was. I thought you were coming around and were going to stop all this superior manhood folderol."

"Edwina, thanks to your reasoning, I don't have a problem with a woman making her own way. But when she's got a man, she doesn't have to."

"That shouldn't be an issue. Having to and wanting to are different." She glared at him. "You really mean it—I can't continue to teach finishing school?"

"I'm sorry, Ed. . . . It just goes against my way."

She abruptly stood. "You're a Neanderthal."

Not knowing what a Neanderthal was put him in the precarious position of not knowing how to defend himself. So he faked his way through the taunt. "I'm not a Neanderthal. I'm a realist."

"Realist schmealist. I don't care. Tom Wolcott, you're infuriating. You ask me to be your wife, then you make plans to take over my life. It was a very difficult decision for me to come to. You don't know how hard I fought off the idea of marriage because I thought I wasn't good enough for the institution. When I did reconcile myself to it, I thought I'd be blissfully happy. I'd have a husband and I'd have the school—two things I never thought I'd have. I scraped the money together to open Huntington's Finishing School. I persevered through a time when my sisters might have fallen into a fit of weeping. You said I should be proud of myself. Well, I am. I may not be able to use my accounting certificate, but I've accomplished something just as good. I'd rather have no husband than a husband who thinks like you. I won't be one of the ladies in this town with no outside interests other than darning your holey socks or worrying about what to prepare you for dinner."

"What are you saying, Ed?" He ground the words out between his locked teeth.

"I'm saying . . ." her voice faltered, then her eyes grew misty. "I'm saying that I can't marry you after all."

He tried to bring her into his arms, but she backed away. "Edwina, you don't mean it."

"I do mean it," she exclaimed, a tear rolling down her cheek. "I won't turn into my mother. I watched her wither away through twenty-five years of marital monotony doing for my father. She had no outside interests, no money, no nothing. That will *never* happen to me."

Tom could settle this right now. He had the means. All he had to say was she could keep the school and start up this dancing thing.

But he had his own memories, and they weren't ones he wanted repeated for his wife. Curling his fingers into fists, then straightening them, he relived the anguish of his childhood, of how he'd seen his parents grow estranged. "My ma, she worked every damn day of her married life washing clothes for other people. She died at the age of thirty-two because of working. Hell, I'm thirty-two. I'm not ready to go to my reward yet. I've got a lot of living left, and I wanted to do that living with you. I will not have any wife of mine go out and make her own way. I've seen how it wears a woman down. I won't watch you do it to yourself, Edwina."

"There's a big difference between physical work and mental work."

"Not to me. Work is work." Combing his hands through the hair that rested above his ears beneath the brim of his hat, he added, "You won't find Crescencia Stykem going out to earn a paycheck after she marries Shay."

"Crescencia doesn't want to earn a paycheck. She's perfectly happy to stay in the house and take care of it. That may be fine for some women, Tom Wolcott, but I'm not some women."

"Don't I know that."

Edwina swiped at the tears rolling from her eyes. "Well . . ." she managed in a tone that was more brittle than ice, "we seem not to have anything further to say."

He didn't want to let her go, but he could not compromise his convictions.

She held back a sob, her shoulders quaking. With the pride and dignity only Edwina could gather in such a moment, she walked away. Tom watched her go, a painful knot forming in his chest. He had his pride, too.

Mr. Alastair Stykem
requests your presence at the marriage of his daughter,
Miss Crescencia Louise Stykem,
to
Mr. Shay Martin Dufresne,
on Monday, December 24th, at 4 o'clock,
Harmony General Assembly Church,
Hackberry Way.

The young girls inside Crescencia Stykem's parlor giggled while the bride-to-be received and opened small tokens of their affection and accepted good wishes for her Christmas Eve wedding, just days away. Edwina sat with a smile frozen on her mouth until her cheeks began to hurt and she felt like crying once more.

Abigail and Ludlow Rutledge had boarded a train out of Harmony three days after they had arrived. Edwina had begged off further invitations, and once Abbie realized she couldn't reduce Edwina to bitterness about her choice of husband, she'd stopped sending messages to her. Ludie hadn't come to see her again, nor had he tried to get in touch with her in any way.

It saddened Edwina that the two people she'd thought the most of in Chicago she now thought the least of in Montana. Both had become self-centered and were arrogant in thinking she would be withered by despair at their news. But Edwina couldn't spend time thinking about a couple who had moved on; she had something more pressing on her mind: Tom.

The past week had been the worst she'd ever had to cope with. She cried, then was angry, then cried again. She hadn't wanted to face it. Tom didn't love her enough to see her reasoning. At the age of twenty-four, she had been left at the altar twice before even coming close to it. This was the end for her. Never again would she allow herself to think for even a second that she would marry.

With Tom, she'd given herself hope. After she'd told him about Ludie and he hadn't walked out the door, she'd thought there was a chance . . . albeit one of her own making. She shouldn't have let herself think about marriage. But the walls she had put up had begun to crumble. She'd fallen deeply and madly in love with him, and she had pushed better judgment and past experience aside.

She hadn't spoken with Tom since that day in the grove. She'd seen him pass by her window on occasion with Mr. Dufresne, but he never stopped, never came inside to see her and tell her he'd rethought his views. And she had not gone to him. She couldn't. Her aspirations and beliefs held steady; this was no whim.

At least she hadn't seen him in four days, so her chronic upset over catching glimpses of him had faded some, but her heart still longed for him. The school had closed last Friday for the holiday break and Edwina had yet to tell the girls of her plans.

Huntington's Finishing School would not be opening again. In a way, Tom had won. She wouldn't be teaching anymore.

Swallowing the lump in her throat, she observed the merriment around her, but her thoughts were not on the day Crescencia would wed. They were on the last few days, during which her world had careened, jostling her into facing the facts.

She could not remain in Harmony without Tom in her life. It was too painful. She couldn't—wouldn't—do it.

She'd spoken to the telegraph office on Tuesday and asked Mr. Beady to send a wire to Helena's telegraph office, asking the telegraph operator there to put in a phone call to DeVille's Bridal Salon to say she would be leaving Montana Christmas Day and making her way to Denver. Then she'd gone to the bank and spoken to Mr. Fletcher about her loan with Equity Mortgage in San Francisco. She'd asked him the best way to handle her default on the second mortgage, as well as the first. There was no way she could continue to pay both. He'd told her he'd have to foreclose on the property. His words had pained her like nothing else had, but she could not see that she had another choice in the matter.

Staying in Harmony would have eventually meant being debt free, but how could she start over in Denver with ties to Montana? With new employment, she'd have to pay for housing. Rent on an apartment would be high in the city. Not to mention that without Marvel-Anne, she'd have to take care of her own wardrobe. That would mean sending out to laundries. More costs. She simply could not afford to keep up residences in two places.

Foreclosing on the Sycamore Drive home that had been in the Huntington family for two generations would have Edwina's mother turning over in her grave. All she could hope for was celestial forgiveness.

"Look!" Cressie beamed, lifting a quaint gift. It was a diary from Meg Brooks.

Meg gave Crescencia a smile. "So you can write all your feelings in it about marriage." Then with a conspiring grin, she added, "And share them with us!"

The others laughed; Crescencia blushed to the roots of her hair.

Someone handed another present to Cressie, and Edwina sipped her punch while gazing out the window. Snow fell in tiny specks. The pine trees in the yard looked like green spires with white icing. Her mind wandering once more, Edwina recalled her conversation with Mr. Fletcher. She'd asked him, quite adamantly, to please auction off her things in Waverly or Alder. She couldn't bear having her friends buy her belongings. She would take with her what was practical . . . but the rest, the furnishings and other household items, would have to be sold so she could try to pay off those bills that remained.

Wistful and feeling utterly alone and lonely, Edwina brought her attention back to the party. A wan smile remained on her face until the last of the presents had been unwrapped and Crescencia sat with a pile of tiny treasures at her feet. When Edwina had come, she'd forgotten to place hers on the center table with the others, so now she opened her pocketbook to take out the small gift wrapped in a white handkerchief and tied at the top with pink ribbon.

"I'm sorry . . . it slipped my mind to put mine with the others." Edwina rose and handed the present to Crescencia. Then she returned to her seat.

Cressie pulled the bow free, then gazed inside. "Oh . . . my, Miss Edwina."

"Let's see!"

"Show!"

"What is it?"

The girls were all curious. Crescencia lifted out the rolled gold bracelet, hand engraved and enameled. Oohs and aahs resounded as the bride-to-be tried it on. The band gleamed prettily from her wrist when the light reflected off it.

"Why, Miss Edwina . . . it's just lovely." She fingered the handkerchief that had been its wrapping, lifted its soft cambric to her eyes to dab the tears that had gathered, then paused to examine the teaberry-threaded monogram on one of the corners. "C. L. D. Crescencia Louise Dufresne."

"It will be one of many handkerchiefs which will bear your new initials," Edwina explained.

"But I'll cherish this one most because it's the first."

With the room having gone from cheerful to sentimental, Edwina hated to have to break her news. But the time had come.

"Girls . . . I have something to tell you."

"What is it, Miss Edwina?" Ruth Elward asked, sitting with ankles crossed on the settee beside Hildegarde Plunkett.

With all the expectant eyes on her, Edwina had to hold onto her courage. "I'm afraid I won't be able to continue the school after Christmas."

Camille cried, "What?"

"No . . ." Johannah brought her hands together at her waist. "I'm not ready to graduate."

Lucy murmured, "That can't be."

"You have to." Meg's hands slid down the arms of the chair in which she sat.

"Miss Edwina . . . no." Crescencia laid the handkerchief on her lap.

"My mother said good manners will land me a husband." Hildegarde frowned. "How can I ever hope to get one if there's no school?"

Edwina felt as if her emotions were fine bone china.

If she said the wrong words, she would splinter and break. "I'm sorry girls . . . I'm moving to Denver to take another position."

"But what about us?" Johannah stood and rung her hands. "Dr. Teeter may be close to asking for my hand. He's told me I have teeth like the Mona Lisa—only she never showed hers. But he can tell by the composition of my lips when my mouth is closed. He told me to bite down and I did, and he was very complimentary. I nearly swooned. If he asks me to marry him, what'll I do? What'll I say?"

Edwina smiled softly. "You'll say whatever's in your heart. If you love him, you'll tell him yes." Only Edwina knew it wasn't as simple as that.

"I suppose. . . . He did go on about my bicuspids the other night. Right in front of my parents, too."

"What's a bicuspid?" Ruth asked.

"It's the teeth behind your incisors," Camille explained.

Ruth folded her arms over her small breasts. "I don't know what an incisor is either."

"They're these teeth, you boob." Hildegarde opened her mouth and pointed. "I get brittle candy stuck in my bicuspids."

"Oh, who cares!" Meg cried. "Miss Edwina is moving to Denver and we won't have a school anymore. This is awful."

"No, it's not, girls." Edwina gave them all a hopeful gaze. "You've come so far since September. What you've learned will get you through life."

"But what about the dancing?" Camille asked.

Lucy seconded her. "Yes, the dancing."

Johannah nodded. "The ragtime."

"Well . . . perhaps your mothers can find another teacher qualified to give you the lessons."

"But she won't be you, Miss Edwina," Crescencia said quietly.

"It's what I have to do." Edwina was having a hard

time battling the tears in her eyes. "I'm sorry . . . I just have to leave."

Crescencia rose, went to Edwina, and stood beside the chair. "Girls, we have to stand by Miss Edwina. If she wants to go to Denver, we have to be happy for her. Let's not make her feel guilty about it. We'll get along."

"I suppose."

"If we have to."

"My mother says getting along in life isn't easy."

"I was so looking forward to the ragtime."

"We can . . . I guess."

"Of course. We'll try."

Edwina gathered her mettle and gave them her best and most ardent smile of encouragement . . . but inside, she wept over the loss of these dear, dear girls.

The inside of the church smelled of hot beeswax and ladies' perfume. At the organ, some woman played "Oh, Promise Me," the notes wafting to the wood-pitched rafters of Harmony's General Assembly. Tom stood at the altar beside Shay, gazing toward the double doors that Crescencia would come through with her father. The pews had been done up with swaths of some kind of sheer fabric that reminded Tom of curtains. At the center of each pew side, a cluster of holly leaves and bright red bows decorated the aisle; the aisle itself had been covered with a runner of white cloth that nobody had been allowed to step on. Clovis Lester, a seven-year-old kid who, for the first time in Tom's recollection, was out of overalls and wearing a suit, had made an attempt at walking on the runner but had gotten a yank on his ear by his mother.

The church fell quiet; coughing and sniffing and sneezing and all those noises that people seem compelled to make in a church all stopped as the organist went from the sentimental ballad to the wedding march. Attendees rose, gazing at the double doors when they opened. The first out was Edwina. Tom's pulse thundered in his head. She was so incredibly beautiful, he ached to hold her.

The silk and lace trimmings of her dress fit her as if they had been made to be a second skin, hugging every luscious curve of her body. Her hair—that combination of reddish brown and dark brown—had been left down in a cascade of curls, some of it pulled back with a peach-colored ribbon that rested behind her ears. The creamy softness of her pale complexion seemed translucent and ethereal. She held a sprig of greenery, more ribbons tied around the stems. Her eyes downcast as she walked, she kept observing her slippered feet as if worried she might step on something wrong.

Watching her, desiring her, and wanting her in his arms, Tom was torn by the conflicting emotions that clenched hard in his gut. Should he just love her for the way she was and not inflict his ideals of marriage on her? But if he did, he'd compromise himself, his values. Not that he had a whole hell of a lot of them.

In his mind, women, once married, did not hold a position of employment. If they did, it looked as if their husbands could not support them. That was what he believed. That was how things were. He didn't want to defuse any of the success Edwina had had with her school, but once she was his wife, she'd be a wife in the true sense—domestic. Not a teacher. Not a dancing instructor. Not a bookkeeper.

Didn't she realize he wanted to give her the best kind of life? One in which she had no worries, having only to make her house the way she wanted it and visit with her lady friends—the things his mother hadn't been able to do.

As Edwina came closer in a slow march, her chin lifted and their gazes briefly caught. Tom felt as if he should be stepping forward to claim her . . . that this was their wedding instead of Shay's. Two more steps and she would be within his reach. One more. He could smell the fragrance of rose petals . . . almost feel the silk of her dress beneath his caress. But as soon as he could have held his hand out to her, she went in the other direction, just the way they had gone for real.

She turned, her head held high and her gaze fixed on the open doorway that filled with Crescencia and her father. Forcing his attention from Edwina, Tom did his best-man duty by giving his all to the bride as she walked down the center aisle. She did look very pretty in her wedding dress, with her hair piled high on her head and a multitude of red curls fanning her face. She'd removed her glasses, and she had to squint as she traversed the white runway. Once, she stumbled, and Stykem had to grip her arm tighter; but her expression remained full of smiles and plain-as-day adoration for Shay Dufresne. Tom was glad for his friend. Really. If ever there was a man who deserved to have a loving wife beside him, it was Shay.

Once at the altar, Stykem placed Crescencia's hand in Shay's, mumbled a few words Tom couldn't make out, then fumbled for his handkerchief to loudly blow his nose while walking to his seat in the front pew. A few of the schoolboys snickered and were rewarded with reproachful looks from their mothers.

The ceremony began and Tom kept his head bowed for most of it. As the words of love and commitment were spoken by the Reverend Stoll, he felt like a bull elk out in the open and in the rifle sight of every man in the church. Although they couldn't know about the affair he and Edwina had had, he sensed they knew from the language in his body that he was ready to tell Shay to step aside so he could claim his girl. But since he didn't make a move, they were probably sitting there and muttering to one another, *"Wolcott could have had himself a good woman, but he let her go. What a jackass."*

From the corner of his eye, he watched Shay place a gold circlet on his bride's finger. Then Stoll proclaimed that the ring was confirmation of their marriage promise. Tom absently lifted his hand to his coat pocket to get his cigarettes, then reminded himself where he was. If ever he could have used a smoke, it was now. When the hell would it be over? He was suffocating.

With another glance at Edwina, he viewed her profile. So lovely. Her lashes were longer than those of any woman he knew. Her nose . . . just pert enough not to be saucy. Her mouth . . . ripe and pink. Perfect.

How was he supposed to get through the reception at the Stykem house? The Harmony Odd Fellows orchestra, sorry as it was, had been engaged to play for as long as the guests wanted to dance. Tom didn't want to step to music with anyone but Edwina. But it was unlikely she'd ever put herself in his arms again.

Not soon enough for Tom, the couple was pronounced man and wife. With fingers entwined, they turned and faced those present as Stoll introduced them as Mr. and Mrs. Shay Dufresne. Applause and a few whistles sounded, then they went down the aisle together. Edwina walked from the altar next, then Tom.

Once in the narthex, Tom drew up close behind her, breathing in the fresh sweet smell of her perfume.

"Congratulations, my dear." Edwina leaned forward and gave the bride a soft hug. "You look radiant."

"Thank you." The blush on her cheeks could be attributed to nothing but an awe-filled love for her husband. Even Tom could decipher that.

Edwina then expressed her good wishes to Shay, who had no trouble bringing her into a bearlike hug, even going as far as kissing her cheek. "Thanks for standing up for my Cressie."

Tom followed suit by extending his hand to his longtime friend. "Well done, Shay. Stay happy."

Shay, with his warm and frank eyes crinkled at the corners, gripped Tom's hand hard. "No problem, Wolcott. Never been more happy in my life."

Then to Crescencia, Tom expressed his sentiments. "You're a fine woman, Mrs. Dufresne. I can see you've put the spark of love in this man's eyes."

"And he in mine."

The narthex began filling with guests and Tom held back. As witnesses, he and Edwina were supposed to sign the license the minister had. The crush of glad tiding givers had Tom taking Edwina's hand in his and guiding her back through the church and down the aisle. Taking such a sacred walk, even if it wasn't for real, gripped Tom in a profound and solemn quiet. Was Edwina thinking the same thing?

He had no opportunity to read her expression when Stoll, who'd remained at the altar, dipped a quill in ink and greeted them.

"Ah, the witnesses. If I can have your signatures here." He pointed to the legal document. "And here."

Rounding the lectern, Tom allowed Edwina to take the pen first, noting how she wrote her name in fluid motions with exact heights on all her lowercase letters. Then he took the quill from her; their fingers brushed for a second, sending a jolt to his heart. He wrote his own name in the haphazard why he'd always done: barely discernible, but Tom Wolcott just the same.

That completed, Tom remembered to give the minister the envelope from his coat pocket that had the five-dollar wedding fee in it. "Thanks, there . . . ah, Stoll. Good job."

"Weddings and baptisms are my favorites." The man of the cloth beamed, then capped the ink. "I think it's time to adjourn to the festivities." Then he left, and Edwina and Tom remained together at the altar.

She began to turn away, but he touched her hand.

"Ed . . . you've never looked more beautiful."

Her eyes rose to his, lashes casting soft shadows on her high cheeks as the candles sputtering above them cast her in silhouette.

"I've never seen you in a suit," she commented. Safe subject. He could tell she was nervous.

"Yeah . . ." Tom gazed down at the funeral suit Shay had made him buy for the occasion. He'd never had any call to wear a gray coat and trousers—worse yet, a white shirt—with a tie, no less. "It's a suit, all right."

"Well . . . I should go see if Crescencia needs my help . . ."

Tom didn't want to let her go yet. He felt that if he

let her walk away this time, he'd never get the chance again to talk with her . . . watch her kissable lips when she spoke, see the different hues of green in her eyes. "Ed . . . let's not end things the way we did. I want to be with you. I want to marry you. This wedding made me see how much I need you in my life."

He couldn't read her thoughts. She'd closed off the emotion from her face. He wished he knew what she was thinking. For the faintest of moments, she gave him hope when the dimness in her gaze lightened, flickered, bringing a degree of warmth. And maybe love?

"Have you changed your mind about my continuing teaching?"

Damn and double damn, he didn't want to talk about that. The subject would sour her on the idea of marriage. But at the same time, he couldn't ignore her question because the school was still the issue that stood between them.

"Edwina . . ." He tried to put her hands in his, but she shied away. "You have to understand that I want what's best for us . . . for you. I'm thinking about you."

The hue of her eyes went from light to fiery. "You're thinking of yourself, you mean. You just have no idea how it is for women. No concept. No clue. I could be my own woman and be married—I'm already half there with the school started. If you can't see that, if you can't try to put yourself in my shoes, give a minute over to my dreams and ideals, then we have nothing to talk about. Ever again, Mr. Wolcott."

That tone again. *Mr. Wolcott.* That teacher one that drove him up a wall. It didn't suit her. She wasn't a shriveled matron. She was all vinegar when she got like this. Inasmuch as he loved her, dammit all to hell and back, he could not tell her what she wanted to hear just to win her over. It wouldn't be fair to either of them.

"Regardless of our personal feelings for one another"—Tom went for his Richmonds, but remembered he shouldn't light one up in church—"we're going to have to put on a front while at that reception."

"I'm not going."

"What do you mean, you're not going?"

"Crescencia understands. As does Mr. Dufresne. I explained it all to them. I have to go home and pack."

Placing the cigarette on his lips anyway, Tom said, "What for?"

"I'm surprised your friend didn't tell you. I'm leaving town. First thing in the morning."

Chapter

❧ 21 ❧

Edwina stood on the depot's snow-edged platform with Honey Tiger's basket looped through her arm. The No. 84 had come in and would leave in less than two minutes for the Cheyenne junction, hooking up with the outbound No. 101 to routes south of the Wyoming border. Puffs of vaporous steam hissed from the pistons on Harmony's only Christmas Day train. Marvel-Anne waited beside her while the porter took her baggage to the car.

"Now, you be certain to write, Miss Edwina," Marvel-Anne admonished, her hair pulled back in a severe bun.

"I'll write, I promise." Edwina's hands quivered from nervous energy. This was a monumental step, a big change—worse than when she'd gone to Chicago, because then, she had known she was coming back home. To Harmony . . . a place that didn't seem so ordinary and plain anymore. This trip would take her to a city, far away from comfortable things and family—namely Marvel-Anne, who was the only mother figure she had. Away from the people she knew and . . . yes, loved—still—in spite of how it had ended. Familiarity would be traded for newness.

"I'm sorry, Marvel-Anne," Edwina blurted out. "I

wish I could have given you more than a fifty-dollar compensation check."

"Oh, pish, Miss Edwina. I told you it wasn't necessary at all." Marvel-Anne's stiff straw hat covered her hair like a helmet. "All these years, your father kept me on and paid me a decent wage. Your mother treated me like one of the Huntingtons from the start. I never had any need to buy anything other than something to clothe myself with or pay any bills besides the small rent at Mrs. June's. I've got enough in my bank account to live on until I die, with plenty left over for a right grand funeral."

"Don't talk about funerals," Edwina ordered with a fond smile.

"We've all got to go one day."

Edwina took in a shaky breath, anxious to be off because she feared she'd make a spectacle of herself by breaking down and weeping. Yet at the same time, she was so afraid to get on that train, she wasn't certain her feet could take her onboard.

Motion caught Edwina's attention and caused her to gaze across Old Oak Road to the town square. Dashing past the gazebo, Camille, Johannah, Lucy, Meg, Ruth, and Hildegarde ran toward the station in a most unladylike flutter of skirts and petticoats.

The girls tromped up the depot steps, breathless and rosy-cheeked.

"We didn't think we'd make it!" Camille exclaimed.

Ruth added, panting, "No, we didn't!"

"My mother told me the present was supposed to be here yesterday. She even telegraphed to find out what happened. The order didn't make the train; it came in the mail, and we just now tracked down Mr. Calhoon so we could get it."

"We just wrapped it at my house," Meg said.

"All of us." Johannah now held the small gift and presented it to Edwina.

"We hope you like it." Lucy's hands were stuffed in a fur muffler.

So touched she was speechless, Edwina could only silently unwrap the present, Marvel-Anne taking the paper from her. The case itself was a gift, long and narrow and made from mother-of-pearl. She undid the latchhook on the side and lifted the tiny hinged lid. Inside, on a bed of morocco satin, lay a pen and pencil of fine gold plate.

"Oh . . . girls. They're lovely."

"Look on the pen, Miss Edwina," Camille said, standing on tiptoes to peer into the case.

Edwina did so and held the pen to the light. On the delicate cylinder, letters were engraved in slanted script. *From your students with love.*

Tears fell freely down her cheeks when she gazed at them, committing every one of their faces to memory. "I shall treasure it always."

The train's whistle blew and the porter called, "All aboard."

Without warning, Marvel-Anne pulled Edwina into her stocky arms and gave her a crushing hug. In a voice gravelly with emotion, she bade her to be careful. "Mind where you go in the city, Miss Edwina. Don't carry too much money in your pocketbook."

Laying her cheek on the elder woman's shoulder for a moment, Edwina said, "I won't."

Then pulling away, she gave her best smile to the girls—which wasn't easy, because she found it difficult to lift the corners of her mouth. "You girls fooled me. We said our good-byes yesterday with your mothers at Mrs. Kennison's house. So I won't say them again today."

Hildegarde rubbed the bottom of her nose with fingers encased in woolen knit gloves. "I can't say good-bye again or I'll start crying. My mother said I don't look delicate when I cry."

"Last call!" came the porter's cry.

Edwina braced herself, gave them a parting look, then turned and boarded the train. She went quickly to a seat, placed Honey Tiger beside her, and gazed out the damp window. Using the heel of her wrist, she made a circle out of which to see. Spying the girls and Marvel-Anne still on the platform, she waved.

Then the engine lurched forward and wheezed, then began to chug up to speed. Edwina craned her neck to keep them in her view as long as she could, but soon the train was gaining too much ground. As the train went around the curve and clattered over the small span of bridge across Evergreen Creek, she spied Barkly baying up a tree. Behind the hound . . . Tom stood with hands in his pants pockets, a red plaid jacket spanning his chest. She put a hand to the glass as if to touch him.

Her gaze sadly clung to him, and for a moment, she thought he saw her in the small clearing in the cloudy window. But when her car went past, he kept on looking as if searching for her. If he'd come to stop her from leaving . . . to tell her he'd had a change of heart . . . he did nothing to show her.

Edwina lowered her hand and faced forward. Reality had to reign. Being with Tom had been the best time of her life. It had been a lovely affair; now it was over. She tried to blink back the hot rush of tears that swam in her vision. But she was quite unsuccessful.

Tom Wolcott had gone to hell in less than a month. He hadn't had a haircut in longer than he could remember, and he hadn't eaten a meal that had agreed with him since before Shay's wedding. He'd been an insomniac for weeks and lived only on what he could manage to talk himself into believing was appealing to his stomach—mostly beer. The empty bottles beneath the store's counter had been adding up, but he didn't give a damn.

Actually, he didn't give a damn about much.

Shay rode his tail a lot, telling him he needed to see a barber. But Tom had gotten used to the beard and mustache that concealed part of his upper lip. He just licked the beer foam off it when the bristles got in the way.

Standing between the aisle of clothing . . . elbow

supporters . . . and camping gear, he reeled his arm back and threw a ball at Buttkiss for the hell of it. The clown's teeth clunked inward. The store was empty; it was nearly five—almost time to go home. Alone. Sit around. Feel like crap.

But who did he have to blame? Himself. He was stupid, stupid, stupid—a real horse's ass.

Tom threw a dozen or so balls, then went to the counter and sat and stared at the store. He hadn't changed a thing since Edwina had doctored it up. The dried posies were still poked into the grizz's paw. Ribbons held the curtains back. On the countertop itself, all the walleyes remained sorted by colors, neat and tidy— a woman's touch. The only touch he'd ever get from a woman again . . .

Sometimes he went into Edwina's side of the warehouse and just stood in the middle of it, trying to smell roses hanging in the cold air. He'd close his eyes and see her sitting at her desk, with a shared dinner in a hamper, then standing, with a hoop around her waist.

Rather than selling her half of the building, she'd given it to him. *Given it to him.* He'd read the document that Fletcher from the bank had dropped by the day after Christmas. Edwina had legally relinquished all claim to the property known as lot four, block two. Why had she done it? Given him something this valuable under the circumstances? He'd pay her for it, come hell or high water. The whole damn transaction didn't sit well with him and made his stomach feel worse. Tom couldn't bring himself to use it. The contents remained how she'd left them.

Drumming his fingernails on the counter, he gazed at the accounting sheet in front of him—blank, of course. It had been blank for days—weeks. He might have sought another bookkeeper, but the hell he knew if Harmony had one. The owners of businesses that he had talked with all said they muddled through the ledgers and tallies themselves.

Tom shoved the paper and books to the side, in turn

knocking over a round canister of Powell's candied walnuts. Shay had given them to him for a Christmas present and Tom had yet to crack open the seal. He slid them toward him, pulled the key off the top, and began to unwind the rim of metal keeping the lid on. As soon as the top snapped, the scent of maple sugar and nuts filled his nose. He ate one, not really tasting it.

The door to the store opened and Mrs. Shay Dufresne came in with a purpose to her eyes that he had never seen before. Since marrying Shay, she'd come out of her shell quite a bit. She'd had him over to dinner a couple of times at their modest house off of Birch. She was a good cook, a tidy housekeeper, and could be, to Tom's amazement, a real chatterbox.

In her hand was a handkerchief balled into a white wad, and inside her fist, a tiny bottle.

"M-Mr. W-Wolcott," she began in a tone that said badger all over it.

He hadn't heard her stutter in longer than he remembered. Something had gotten her fired up but good.

"Yeah, Mrs. Dufresne?"

"You are an a-a-abomination. The l-lowest of the l-low . . ." Her vocal cords failed her and she popped the cork off that bottle and waved it beneath her nose. It gave her stamina, whatever it was, and she glared at him head-on. He felt as if she were ripping him a new . . . well . . . new way of thinking about her.

"What did I do?" He didn't want to admit to himself that he was a tad bit on the concerned side with her dander up a mile high. So he tried to make himself look casual and ate another nut.

"You know perfectly well w-what you did to my d-dearest . . . my most . . ."—her eyes watered behind her glasses—". . . precious friend in all the w-world. You *cad!*" She spat out that last word.

Tom grimaced.

After another quick sniff of the bottle, she proceeded to take him down a notch. "I finally got my Shay to confess what happened between you and Miss Edwina.

I caught him in a weak moment." In spite of the verve in her tone, her face went red as a holly berry, giving Tom a good idea what the moment was. "He told me that you asked Miss Edwina to marry you but you wouldn't let her keep her school if she did. Your actions are r-reprehensible. Any other m-man would have seen what a good woman he had and been p-proud of her being such an asset to the community! Shame on you, Mr. W-Wolcott! Shame on you!"

Sitting back on the stool, Tom felt as if she'd just slapped him, but there had been no physical blow.

"A woman has the right to be industrious and educated. If she enters m-marriage unprepared, and if p-perchance by some misfortune she is thrown p-penniless upon the world with no means of obtaining a livelihood, she'll not have a single way to survive. Miss Edwina was l-lucky in that regard, having gotten her education and used it in a v-vocation that did a great service to the young girls of Harmony. And you . . . you n-nincompoop . . ." She lifted the bottle to her nostrils, gasping a little. "You were too blind to see what a wonderful woman she was. *Is.* She loved you. I should have seen just how much. I was too enamored of Shay that I wasn't a compassionate enough friend. But you! You hurt her! You . . . you . . . m-man, you!"

At least they agreed on that. Tom fingered a walnut, not wanting it at all but needing to have something to hold on to; his belly ached from the words and the maple sugar.

Crescencia slammed a pamphlet on the counter, then closed the latch on her purse. "Read that, M-Mr. W-Wolcott—if you dare!"

Tom's gaze skimmed the title "Women Vocations: Voices of the New Century."

Without thought, Tom put the plump walnut in his mouth, then was left with having to chew it. Slowly, he did so. As his mouth worked the nut, Crescencia got a keen look in her eyes, a knowing kind of glare—like she had him over a barrel, or something worse.

"A woman makes those walnuts you're eating, only men like you keep her from using her first name on the top of the can!" Then after one last inhalation from the bottle, which by now he'd deduced was smelling salts, she jammed the cork home and as a parting shot, shouted, "Put that in your typewriter and ink it, Mr. Wolcott!"

Then she stormed out the store and Tom choked down the mass of crushed nut that had lodged in his throat. Reaching for the open beer he had under the counter, he took a long drink while raising the canister of nuts to inspect it. The lid read POWELL'S CANDIED WALNUTS, but once he had the tin high enough to look at the writing on the bottom, he saw that it said: MRS. ESTELLINE POWELL, LAGRANGE, OREGON.

Lowering the walnuts, Tom mulled over the information. It did seem like a sorry thing that she didn't put her name on the lid as well. He'd never given any thought to the possibility that nuts were packaged by a woman. If he'd analyzed the label, he'd have assumed Powell was a factory owner. And a man.

The pamphlet, its cover stark black with bold white ink, drew his attention. He picked it up, turned to the first page, and began to read.

In this country, women should cultivate a spirit of independence. They should acquire a knowledge of how business is transacted, of the relation between the butcher and the banker. As housekeepers, they would then be saved from many annoyances and mistakes. If they are unwed or widows without possessing the monetary means for support, they will suffer many losses and vexatious experiences by not knowing how to take care of themselves.

This literature is about the women who have made great strides for their sisters. But without the support of their fathers, husbands, or brothers, none of them would be where they are today.

Tom took another sip of warm beer, settled onto the stool, then turned to the next page.

Edwina held her arms from her sides while Madame DeVille basted the seam underneath. The bride who was to wear the suit had been afflicted with a fever and couldn't make her fitting. Since Edwina was closest to her size, Madame had asked her to put the gown on to check for secondary alterations.

The DeVille Salon's Winter Bride, as the creation was named, could only be described as stunning. Its white brocade and plain satin had been cut in the most flattering of styles. The skirt front was brocade; there was a full train of plain satin, five yards long, puffed in back. The waist came to a point in front and had lace and flower trim.

Wearing the lush bridal gown made Edwina sentimental and yearning, but she quickly forced the melancholy from her thoughts. She'd been in Denver nearly a month and so far, she'd gotten on as well as could be expected. The loss of her students and their mothers was a constant source of longing. She was sad that she wouldn't be teaching them ragtime. And there were days still when she couldn't get Tom from her mind, when she thought she'd go crazy from missing him so. But then she reminded herself that it was her own fault for falling in love with him. If she had never allowed him into her heart, it wouldn't be aching for him now. She had to be strong. She had to get him out of her head.

Madame rose from her crouch, stood back, and smiled. "Your figure is made for this style, Edwina. I'll have one sewn for you when you marry."

"I told you, Madame, I will never marry."

Madame DeVille, who was somewhere in her fiftieth year but very beautiful and elegant, merely nodded. "I have lost more women to marriages than I care to count. There is something about working in a bridal salon that makes them . . . get married," she ended with a wave of her hand, a card of pins with fancy heads in her grasp.

Madame moved to the window, paused to gaze out the third-story pane, then observed, "It's stopped raining."

Edwina had rather liked the steady rain that had been drizzling for the past week. It matched her mood—gray, weepy, damp.

"My, my, my." The woman's older tone was speculative. "There's a handsome man on the street staring at the building. Probably to see the stockbroker on the second floor, although he doesn't look like the investor type." Madame had done this often, trying to bring Edwina out of her reserve. Madame DeVille was a hopeless flirt, but resigned not to marry herself for reasons she hadn't divulged to Edwina. She said she'd married hundreds of times already—each time a woman wore one of her dresses on her wedding day.

Edwina didn't care if there was a man on the street—handsome or not. In her heart . . . there was only one, and he wasn't on a Denver street.

"May I put my arms down now?" Edwina asked.

"Certainly. You're basted. I've removed the pins," Madame said as she left the window, then walked through the spacious fitting booth and out the parted curtains to the workroom with its myriad sewing machines, long tables with bolts and bolts of white cloth, baskets of trimmings, silk roses, and a variety of other notions.

The circular pedestal on which Edwina stood faced three mirrors in different angles. Left alone, she gazed at her reflection.

This was the first time she'd ever worn one of the gowns. Her duties were to keep the seamstresses' hours and account for their wages. Then every other Friday, she wrote the checks from the bank drafts. Madame had a bookkeeper, a very pleasant young woman—a widow—so Edwina could not have that position. Grateful she had employment, she didn't mind.

She'd rented a small furnished apartment on Rocky Mountain Avenue, a half dozen blocks from the salon. She could walk to work each day without having to pay for a hansom cab. Honey Tiger didn't like being alone all day; the kitty had shown her dissatisfaction by shearing the curtains with her claws the first day Edwina had left her. For all her cat years, Honey Tiger had had company present. Even if the kitty slept most of the time, she must have known the thumping in the house was Marvel-Anne in the kitchen kneading bread, or Mrs. Crane's housemaid making up the beds. Kitty would just have to get used to it. Edwina had plenty to get used to herself.

The room had a small heating stove with a plate for cooking. Most times, Edwina ate dinner with Madame in the restaurant on the corner. On the weekends, she did for herself. Although she was tired from the week, she cleaned her room and took her washing to the Chinese laundry for washing and pressing. It cost plenty, but Edwina had no choice.

Gazing at her image again, she sighed. Her face was pale . . . her eyes were a little sunken. She brought hands to her cheeks and pinched them for some color. Then she wet her lips. She fused with a curl that had come down to cuddle her neck. If she didn't look so forlorn, she would have been a pretty . . . bride.

She'd had the wedding dream again last night. When she woke up alone and crying softly, she told herself it was because she was working at DeVille's and it was only natural to think about bridal gowns. But when she relived the dream, she knew she was missing Tom . . . and that's why she'd filled her mind and heart with him in her sleep.

They were always in the grove, the fall trees their golden cathedral. They stood by an arch of white lattice woven through with a multitude of white roses. The perfect setting for them to exchange vows. She'd tell him she loved him, and he would declare the same toward her. Then Tom would kiss her after they were pronounced man and wife. His bride.

But she wasn't. Not now or ever. It was a dream never to be.

With a wistful sigh, she gathered the front of the skirt, her serviceable black shoes peeking out from the pristine gown. Just about to hop down to the carpet, she froze as an image formed in the mirror. From the corner of her eye she viewed a man's shoulder, broad, wearing a heavy blue flannel coat. Then hair—just the side— freshly cut locks of brown. A half jaw and cheek. Lowering her hands, she straightened fully and saw the man's reflection in whole, behind her and to her side.

Tom Wolcott.

In Denver . . .

Edwina blinked, fearing her mind played tricks on her. She'd conjured him, pathetically . . . hopelessly . . . because she longed for him. But when she focused once more, he was still there. Real. Solid.

Turning slowly, she faced him and stared. She drank in his features, the serious slash of his brows; the haunting blue of eyes that had delved into her soul on more than one occasion; his nose, straight and with nostrils slightly flared; the shape of his mouth . . . set and firm.

He was more handsome than she remembered.

Despite the utter bedlam of her thoughts in which she was drowning, she forced an air of aloofness that she knew she didn't feel. She would not speak first. He had come eight hundred miles; let him explain why. In the mirror, she affixed her gaze to his, and what she saw there startled her.

Misgiving. Faltering hope. Regret.

"Edwina . . . you're getting married."

His statement confused her until she remembered what she wore. Gazing down at the smooth white bodice with its scooped lace neckline, she then lifted her eyes to his again. "I'm wearing this for someone. She couldn't make her fitting." Why was she explaining this? It was *he* who should be explaining his being here.

Relief flooded his face, his mouth relaxing and even turning up a hint at the corners. "You still look beautiful in it, no matter who it belongs to."

Edwina's patience was crumbling. She wanted to remain emotionally distant and remote, but he had a way of filling her with his presence, of making her aware of only him. She should have been more nonchalant, breezy, uncaring. Her breath had caught in her throat, and her legs were numb. Even if she had the inclination, she couldn't run away from him.

Still holding onto her silent avowal not to ask him what he was doing here, she got hold of her disorganized feelings and stepped off the pedestal. Walking around to the other curtained partition where she'd left her serviceable skirt and shirtwaist, she stopped midway to the draperies. She couldn't slip out of the bridal gown unless Madame gave her assistance. Turning, she clasped her hands together and tamped down the helplessness rising within her chest.

Tom unbuttoned his coat, as if he were going to stay awhile, then fumbled inside his shirt's breast pocket and produced a much-handled piece of paper. To her amazement, it had been folded in twelfths, and she watched as he undid each square so the paper became whole. The edges were worn, as if the paper had been referred to quite a bit.

Gazing over the paper's top margin, he said, "I wanted to tell you something, Ed."

Perplexed by his nervousness and the way he kept shuffling his weight from one foot to the other, she was somewhat on the defense. If he'd come here to try to change her mind about marrying him, still wanting her to give up her school—which was a moot point at this stage because she had done so already—she didn't want to hear anything he had to say. That might mean she was uncompromising, but she couldn't go through another argument about it, not without utterly breaking down and sobbing through every hankie she owned—which she had already done, too.

"Tom, you could have saved yourself the trip. Crescencia knows the telephone number of the salon."

"Yeah . . . well. . . . Crescencia, I don't think she

would have given it to me. She's not speaking to me after the riot act she read me." His next words were mumbled and she couldn't be sure, but she thought he'd said "And I deserved it."

"Really? That doesn't sound like Crescencia. She's nonconfrontational."

"Not anymore." Tom gazed at the paper, then at Edwina. "I haven't gotten it all memorized yet, but I'm working on it. I've gotten from Susan B. Anthony to Fanny . . . um . . . something with an *E*. I'll get it, though."

"What are you talking about?" She lifted her arms to tuck them beneath her breasts as she waited.

"Crescencia . . . she gave me this book to read. It's about women in vocations. Jobs and stuff." Hesitation marked his brows as he scanned his paper, then looked at her. "Did you know Powell's candied walnuts are manufactured by a woman?"

"Certainly."

"How come you didn't tell me that?"

"Would you have been interested?"

"No."

"That's why."

"But I'm interested now." Back to the paper, he began to recite. "Susan B. Anthony . . . well, she's this woman who's in charge of some club called the National American Woman Suffrage Association." Glancing at her, he conceded, "I had to look up *suffrage*. I thought it meant hurting—you know, suffering. I guess that it does mean that in a way. This Anthony woman, she's okay. But she doesn't like booze—which, what the hell, I gave it up last week so she'd be square with me if I ever met her. Not that I won't have a beer every now and then."

Edwina grew increasingly puzzled. What on earth had possessed Tom "The Hunter's Best Friend" Wolcott to see the reason in the suffrage movement? And had Cressie really berated him?

"Then there's this woman lawyer in Utah. And this

other woman in Indiana who's organizing textile workers." Tugging on the sleeve of his shirt, he shrugged. "The women workers in her factory could have woven this. I'd never thought about that before."

He proceeded, gazing at his list, then at her. "I'm not particularly a church man, so I wouldn't have ever found this out—but did you know there's a woman preacher in New York?"

"Yes."

"I didn't." Then to the notes again. "This Elizabeth Blackwell is a doctor at the Cornell University Medical Center. It never occurred to me that a woman could save my life."

"A woman gave you life," she said in a whisper-soft voice—no condescension, no patronizing—just a quiet fact.

"You're right."

"I'm not trying to be right."

"I know that." Then with an intake of breath, he read on. "A woman in London—some rich one who didn't have to or need to work—she aided aborigines. That was another word I had to look up. Anyway, she was honored with a peerage for public achievement. Had to look up *peerage,* too." He lowered the paper. "It's come to my attention my reading is just about as bad as my mathematics."

"Your mathematics aren't bad."

"Mediocre," he countered. "Whoever the skirt—um . . . woman—was who wrote 'Women Vocations' had a dictionary on her lap she did."

Edwina merely stared, still uncertain where all this was leading.

"The last one I know by heart is that Fanny, the ballet woman. She makes a lot of money in Austria. More than me."

In spite of herself, Edwina laughed.

Tom folded the paper, stuffed it into his pocket, removed his hat, and tucked it beneath his arm. She didn't know what to think. His expression had sobered to a degree she'd never seen. It . . . frightened her. The intensity was bone chilling. She felt like she had to sit down. The stays in her corset, which had been laced a half inch tighter than she usually wore it to make her waist as small as that of the woman for whom she wore the gown, pinched her to sudden lightheadedness. But she refused to falter. Whatever Tom wanted to say to her and the reason why he'd recited the names of some of the women from the pamphlet must be very important for him to have come all this way.

"Edwina, I don't admit I'm wrong very much. Hell, I don't think I ever have." His gaze fixed on her and held her immobile. "But I can see now I was wrong to tell you not to teach at the school after we married. It shouldn't matter a hill of beans what my wife does. Anyone who sees that differently is . . . well, I'd say jackass, but I don't want to offend you."

"You just said it," she pointed out, then paused before adding, "and, Tom . . . you *were* a jackass."

He snorted and looked to the tips of his boots, then at her with a rueful smile. "I was hoping you wouldn't agree."

It was her turn to reluctantly smile.

A brief moment of silence fell on them.

Tom looked around the room, through the curtains, then placed his hat back on his head. "I came down here because I wanted to let you know that I'm proud of you, Edwina; glad that you have a chance to use your education. You seem to be doing all right."

Words couldn't begin to express how she felt with his admission. A jumble of emotions played through her. In succeeding, she'd lost him, but gained his respect. Why couldn't he have seen this in Harmony?

"Are you happy here?"

His question barely registered. "I'm adjusting," she said after a moment. She had to tell herself to stay on safe topics. "How are things back home?" *Home.* Why had she said that? This was her home now.

"Fine. Shay is doing good. Crescencia . . . well, I

haven't gotten close enough to her since last week to ask. My guess is she's fine."

"And the store?"

"All right. Gearing up for spring . . . the fly fishing tournament and all." His hands were stuffed into his pockets in a gesture that said he was being a red-blooded man who didn't permit himself to be softened by women . . . or words. But she could tell right now that it was an act. He *had* turned softer, more gentle. On the outside, he still looked like Tom. But on the inside, he'd been discovering that a man could be broad-minded and still be a man.

Love for him swelled in her heart.

"Tom . . ." she said, licking her lips and hoping she was making the right choice in telling him. "I'm not a suffragette or a woman who preaches suffrage to men. I don't think the women in Harmony should apologize for wanting to be housekeepers, any more than they should have to defend earning a wage. All I ever wanted was to do what I enjoyed. At first that meant accounting. Then the school came into being and my educating women about their capabilities was important to me. I knew when I went to Gillette's there wouldn't be a slew of business jobs waiting—probably none. But I accepted that. Because when I got my certificate, it meant I had done something very few women had."

"I see that now, Ed." More gazing at his boots. He'd never done so much of it, in her recollection. It was sort of . . . funny—Tom Wolcott acting sheepish, the boob. Why couldn't he have been this way before she'd left? Why couldn't he . . . ? They . . . ? Oh . . . dammit all, anyway.

"You know, Edwina, if you're happy here, I'm happy for you. But if you were to say . . . that you feel you wanted to come back to Harmony . . . I wouldn't make it hard for you. I'd leave you alone . . . if that's what you wanted. You could still have the school. Hell, Ed," he said as he gazed at her, "why'd you give it to me?"

"Because you were entitled."

"I'm not entitled to take what you worked so hard at. It's yours. It always will be." More hedging. "If you want it. Like I said . . . it's there for you, Edwina." Another gaze at his boots; she had to bite her lip from smiling. "Do you want to come home . . . maybe . . . for some reason . . . just because . . . ?" He gave her no room to reply. "People miss you. Those girls . . . they've been up to no good. I saw that one—Hildegarde—at it again, spying on the redhead—what's her name?"

"Lucille."

"Yeah, Lucille. You need to refine Hildegarde a little more. She needs some deportment lessons or something on looking where she's going. And that other one . . . Meg . . . her folks run the hotel. I saw her riding down Birch Avenue to the bellman's cart. Not exactly ladylike behavior." His eyebrows pulled together. "That Camille. Pretty girl, but her head's in the clouds. Hasn't been doing much of anything while you were gone. She needs some kind of purpose. Maybe one of those ladies' projects—you know . . . that ladies do. . . . Ladies projects . . ." his voice trailed off.

Edwina dared to hope, but her heart was already pounding. "What about you, Tom?"

"Me . . . what?"

"Do you want me to come home?"

His eyes came to study her face, looking for her reaction. She didn't want to reveal anything. Not if they weren't thinking the same thing. "If you want to come home, Ed, I'd . . . like it."

"That's all?"

"Edwina . . . I wouldn't blame you if you didn't want to." He was mumbling. "But I want you to. If you want to. Do you?"

Now she did smile. Very broadly. Her mirth caused him to scowl. "Quit all the apologizing and backpedaling. I like you better when you're puffing out your chest and telling ridiculous male anecdotes. You oaf."

A grin hooked the corner of his mouth. "That's vermilion oaf to you, Ed." He came forward and tentatively reached for her but stopped shy of her hands. "I've never said this to anyone, and I should have said it to you before." A sincerity filled his eyes, holding her captive. "I love you, Edwina." Placing his palm on his chest, he curled his fingers a little into the flannel. "With all my heart. I love you for you. Don't change. Ever."

A tear slipped past her lower lashes. "I love you, too, Tom. I should have said so myself."

Then he took her into his arms and she readily went inside them, laying her cheek on his shoulder and breathing him in. He felt so good—strong and hard and . . . hers. She gazed up at him, and he kissed her gently. Feeling his mouth on hers was like a homecoming. She'd missed the touch of his lips, the way he kissed her. The way he could make her melt inside and become warm and dazed with passion.

Speaking against her lips, he said, "I would be honored if you married me, Edwina. I was a fool once. I won't be twice. Will you?"

He pulled slightly back to see her eyes when she replied.

"And I'd be a fool to say no. Yes, for the last time you'll ask . . . I'll marry you."

Their lips met once more, ardently. The caress of his lips on her mouth and his arms around her waist set her aflame. A dreaminess enveloped her. She could kiss him this way forever. And she would.

"There's one condition." Tom's voice tickled over her mouth. She lifted her head and gazed at him while he held up his hand. "Actually four." He showed her his fingers and brought them down in turn. "One, you reopen the school. Two, the money you earn is yours to use however you please—I wouldn't decline for-no-good-reason-other-than-you-want-to presents of any kind . . . your buffalo-head knives with turquoise inlay in the handles wrap up nice."

She broke into a smile. "Turquoise inlay on the handles, hmm?"

"With a lifelike carved buffalo head at the base of the

blade. I've gotten rid of almost all my manly pride. But there're still some parts that are staying exactly how they are—if you get my meaning."

"I get your meaning. What's three?"

"Three, you'll do the accounting for my store for pay." He dipped his head and dropped a kiss on her mouth. "And four, you keep this dress on. We're going to use it right now."

❧ Epilogue ❧

They had walked from Harmony's train depot, Edwina blindfolded and feeling foolish as Tom guided her over the snow-packed sidewalk. Honey Tiger gave little meows from her beribboned basket, detecting the hound trailing them as Tom held onto the precious cargo for her. She had said she could carry her kitty, but Tom told her Honey Tiger was just as much his cat now, too. Barkly kept up behind; she could hear him dart into someone's yard every now and then to run after birds if a gate had been left open.

She couldn't get her bearings after they turned at corners from east to west, north to south. When at last the latch of a gate clicked, she was ushered onto what had to be a walkway and up a set of steps to a porch. Only after she was told to stop did Tom remove the handkerchief.

Blinking several times, she stared at the stained-glass panels on either side of her old front door. She turned her head to Tom. "But . . . ? This isn't my house anymore. I told you I had to let the bank foreclose."

"And I'm the man who bought it."

"You did?"

"The price was . . ." He shrugged. "I don't want to

belittle the house, Ed, but it was sold below market value. I got it for an affordable amount. You'll be happier here than in a new place farther out of town. I couldn't pass it up."

"What do you mean farther out of town?"

"I had bought another property for us, but I had Fletcher buy it back when you . . ." his words trailed.

Ruefully, she finished for him. "When I left town."

"Your house came on the market and there weren't any fast takers. I don't think your friends felt comfortable taking it from you. I applied for the loan. It's a done deal. It's yours again, Edwina. Just like your side of the warehouse. I had the deeds drawn up in your name—a wedding present."

"Oh, Tom . . ."

"Don't get teary again." His mouth came close to her ear and he gave her a light kiss. "Let's go inside, Mrs. Wolcott."

She smiled at him as he unlocked the door, then slipped the key in his pocket. Handing her the kitty basket, he scooped her into his arms and carried her over the threshold. Barkly tried to squeeze in, too, but Tom kicked the door closed after he said, "Barkly. Out. You can't come in until I figure out how to make you like cats."

Tom proceeded to take Edwina through the vestibule, then the parlor, where he sat her down. The room looked huge. There was no furniture in it except for a few little personal items that had once belonged to her.

She rested Honey Tiger's basket on the floor and let the cat out. The tabby shook off, then meandered to the parlor window and stared out at Barkly, who was staring in. Edwina walked slowly through the room. Bare. It seemed so bare. But her curtains were still here. And . . .

"Tom, you got the Victrola." She smiled at the phonograph sitting in the corner.

"Records, too. The Joplins."

Turning, she swept her gaze at the fireplace. A cozy fire burned within and she could only guess that Tom had had Shay come over earlier and get it started. At the hearth sat a box of lemon snaps, water-speckled bottles of cold beer, and the funny papers beside them. The bearskin rug was stretched out in front. On the mantel— *oh my!* She placed her hand to her throat, her pulse knocking. It was that zebra clock. The one made of the animal's white- and black-striped behind. The hair-tufted end of the tail tick-tocked back and forth over its haunches . . . cheeks. It was . . . she swallowed. She wouldn't think it. Not today, when she was so happy. Tomorrow, she'd give herself permission to call it what she really thought. But only to herself. Never to Tom.

"I tried to fix the place up some, Ed. I couldn't afford to buy the furniture and pay for that grim-faced housekeeper of yours as well. I hired her back on; I hope you don't mind. I figured with you out of the house most of the day, you wouldn't have time to do things. Do you mind that I hired her for you?"

"Mind?" she repeated emotionally. "Thank you, Tom . . . for understanding."

"I did move in my bed from the livery and my clothes. I have a dresser we can use temporarily. It's not as big as you need, though. Women . . . you know, they have a lot of white stuff that goes in drawers." He took his hat off and hung it on a wall peg next to the clock. She'd never had a wall peg there before. "I know it's not what you're accustomed to, but we'll get it back to how you like it. There's a box in the kitchen. Some of the plates and doodads from that China cabinet you had. I bought the ones I thought you would want to keep."

"Oh . . . Tom. I'm sure they're just the ones I wanted, too . . ." A glass jelly jar rested on the mantel with a crumpled bill inside. "What's that?"

Tom glanced to the jar. "That's five dollars for the furniture fund. Do you remember me telling you I had a brother—John?"

"Of course."

"Well . . . the funniest thing happened. He sent me a letter after Christmas. He wrote that he had gotten married and fully intended to pay me back every penny he ever borrowed."

"Really?"

"Yeah, kind of odd for him. He's never owned up to responsibility before. Must be the love of a good woman that changed him. I know it changed me."

Touched beyond words, she went to him and kissed him tenderly on the lips. "I love you."

He cradled her cheeks with his big hands. "I love you, too."

"You were awfully confident I'd marry you," she said, teasing him. "You had to have done all this before you left for Denver." She touched his mouth with her fingertip. "You're hopeless."

"No, sweetheart, I was hopeful."

Their mouths came together for a brief and searing kiss. When they parted, she gazed adoringly at him. "I've got something else to show you." He left her and walked to the bay window, where three long planks of wood lay facedown on the floor. He lifted the first. It was a crisply painted sign in . . . of all colors . . . vermillion. It read: EDWINA WOLCOTT'S FINISHING SCHOOL.

Then he lifted the next: EDWINA WOLCOTT'S DANCING ACADEMY.

The last said: EDWINA WOLCOTT'S ACCOUNTING SERVICE.

"The guy in Alder couldn't fit them all on one sign. But they'll get the word out for you. You already have two clients for the accounting service. I talked with Max Hess over at the livery and he's got need of your expertise. So does Otto Healy at the real estate office. They said they'd come by your place as soon as you got settled."

"I don't know whether to cry or kiss you," Edwina declared through a weak smile that was giving way to tears.

"Don't you cry, Ed." Tom took her hand and pulled her into his arms. "If you're crying, how can a ragger dance with his girl?"

Laughing unsteadily, she shook her head. "Are you asking?"

"I'm asking. Put that recording on, honeybaby, and let's see what you've got."

Edwina walked to the Victrola, smiled when she saw Joplin's "Maple Leaf Rag" on the turntable, then cranked the handle. Music drifted from the trumpet and she went back to her husband's waiting arms.

Oblivious to the rest of the world, they danced to the tempo, swaying and hopping, smiling and laughing while the tick of a zebra tail kept time to the music.

Dear Reader:

I hope you enjoyed reading *Harmony*. Inevitably, into each book I write, I put some of my own observations and use them for the characters and plot. In most cases, no one is the wiser for my experiments; however, I was given no choice but to live out the jockstrap scene. One afternoon when I was alone in the house, I rummaged through my better half's underwear drawer. I tried the jockstrap on the way I wanted Edwina to, and thank goodness, it did fit. My wrist dangled, but to Edwina's mind, this was a good thing—more elbow support. So that's how I know about elbow supporters.

As for Barkly . . . he's a figment of my imagination based on my dog, Molly. Molly is a beagle hound and she has her own method of sniffing in a rhythm I gave to Barkly. I don't know why she sniffs this way. She just does, and it's riotously funny to watch. Molly is a soap eater, too. We have found we cannot put the small left-over pieces of bar soap in the trash can any longer because Molly ferrets them out and eats them. You can always tell she's been into soap because she has the evidence on her face—and she burps. Although she'll eat any kind, she does prefer Lever 2000 over Irish Spring.

Barkly's trick repertoire was partially my imagination and partially reality. I was hypothesizing about his teeth chattering in imitation of a squirrel. It's doubtful Barkly could truly imitate one, but when Molly's after a good itch on her leg, those choppers of hers really chatter over her fur. The salute Barkly made is an actuality. My Auntie Jerri trained her dog, Mugs, to salute. Her son went into the navy, and while he was gone, she taught the dog the trick. She put a little sailor hat on him with elastic, and he sat on his behind; when she said, "Salute!" the dog raised his paw to his nose and really saluted.

Tom's struggle with mathematics came from my nine-year-old daughter's tries at understanding her math facts.

The teacher told us that sometimes a person will never grasp the concept and must memorize the times tables. Tom's feelings of complete failure are, sadly, exactly those one has when unable to solve math equations. My daughter is lucky to have a kind and patient teacher; she's improving. Another thing Tom struggled with was procrastination. He meant to do those accounting books, and his roundabout way of getting to work—by staying in the vicinity of his ledgers—is, and I admit this sheepishly, mine. I figure if I'm within twenty feet of the computer, I'm still working. Perhaps it's a warped rationale, but I've written eleven books on this principle.

Edwina's method of raking is my own. I cannot say why, exactly, but I must rake leaves in a certain pattern. Also, raking leaves was how I brought much of this story to fruition. Raking is an extremely effective mental stimulator for me. Too bad leaves fall only once a year . . .

The items Tom sold in his store are authentic. The deer urine is a bottled product sold locally—I bought a bottle. And the froggies, super raspies, double-clucks, Ugly Butt targets, coyote howlers, and other such things truly exist. I went through the store with a clipboard and paper, in awe that men really fall for this stuff and spend big bucks on it. I found a lot of it—just in name alone—too humorous to pass up. I tried out that deer estrus on Molly. I put a drop in the backyard on the lawn when she wasn't looking. Then we let her outside. For a few seconds, she was her usual old self. Then she picked up on the scent and went berserk. Sniffing, nose to the grass, she found the spot and proceeded to roll and rub herself into it as if she couldn't get enough. Go figure. . . .

Well, I'm off to write the second book in the Brides for All Seasons series, which will also be set in Harmony, Montana. *Hooked* is Meg Brooks's story and is about the hotel her parents operate and the twelfth annual fly fishing tournament. She meets the man of her dreams, who introduces himself as Vernon Wilberforce, but he's not. He's really Matthew Gage, a San Francisco stunt reporter, and he's come to town to uncover a fishy plot. When the real Mrs. Wilberforce shows up and Meg is forced to wear a wig and mustache and take on the identity of Mr. Arliss Bascomb, agent for the Department of the Treasury, hilarity and mistaken identities abound.

And in case you missed it, Tom's bother, John Wolcott, has his story in the *Upon a Midnight Clear* Christmas anthology. My novella is titled *Jolly Holly*.

I hope you'll watch for *Hooked*. Following this letter is a short excerpt from it.

As always, I enjoy hearing from my readers. You can chat with me about books and writing on my message board at Painted Rock Writers and Readers Colony at:

http://www.paintedrock.com/message/7/pubmess.htm

You can get the latest news and release information about my books on my home page at:

http://www.paintedrock.com/authors/holm.htm

I still appreciate snail mail, too. Drop me a note if you can. A self-addressed, stamped envelope is appreciated for a prompt response.

Best,

Stef Ann Holm
PO Box 121
Meridian, ID 83680-0121

An All-New Collection of
Heartwarming Holiday Stories

UPON A
*M*IDNIGHT CLEAR

*J*ude
*D*everaux

*L*inda
*H*oward

MARGARET ALLISON
STEF ANN HOLM
MARIAH STEWART

Available in Hardcover
From Pocket Books

POCKET
B O O K S

1405-01

POCKET BOOKS
PROUDLY PRESENTS
Book Two in the
"Brides for All Seasons"
Series

HOOKED

STEF ANN HOLM

Coming Soon
from Pocket Books

The following is a preview of
Hooked. . . .

"Margaret, why must you insist on displaying your petticoat?"

Meg Brooks stood at the side of the Brooks House Hotel's registration counter and gazed down at her feet. The insteps of her silk vesting top shoes barely showed because, indeed, lace flounce fell a half inch below her skirt hem. Raising her eyes, she replied to her grandmother, "I read in *Cosmopolitan* that a flirt of underskirt is considered vogue and can do wonders in catching the attention of the opposite sex."

Grandma Nettie didn't bat an eye. The word "sex" didn't suck the breath out of her as it would have done Meg's mother. "If it takes a peek of petticoat to catch a man these days, then you're better off without a husband." The elderly woman sitting in back of the desk laid her needlework in an open sewing basket. "I never remarried after Grandpa died, and I can honestly say I haven't missed a thing."

"I *want* to get married. I've tried to land a man all the usual ways, but none of them see my wit and charm. Which, I might add, has been much improved since attending Miss Huntington's—or rather, Mrs. Wolcott's—Finishing School." With a little sway, she moved her hips from side to side to view her efforts. This was her Sunday best petticoat, its bottom ruffle a fine quality torchon. "As a much needed new effort, I let down the waistbands of all my petticoats."

"You're going to trip on the hem."

"No I won't. I'll walk with my skirt lifted."

"You'll forget yourself and trip."

"I'll be careful."

"You'd best take every last waistband back up before your mother returns from her anniversary tour. You'll give her a conniption fit." Grandma Nettie rose from the plush tapestry chair. Spry for her age of seventy-two, she rearranged the two-foot-length of bicycle chain, with self-locking shackles and bronze metal lock, in a long spill across the front of the counter—smack next to the registry book. "Honestly, Margaret, I don't recall your being this rambunctious. Where do you get it from? Certainly not your father. My George is quite levelheaded. Now Iris, she's of a different cake. Don't get me wrong, I love your mother as if she were my own daughter, but she can be a tad . . . too delicate."

Meg threw her hands up in exasperation. "A tad? She's a good deal more than that. Mama calls a chicken breast a bosom because she won't say breast at the dinner table, or anyplace else for that matter. And she calls the leg the limb. She'll say to Papa, 'Papa, slice me the bosom.' Confound it all, it's just not . . ." Meg searched for the right word, the only one coming to mind her newly formed favorite, because it covered any topic of importance to her ". . . not vogue."

Grandma Nettie's parchmentlike fingers fussed and primped over the chain until its links were perfectly straight. Meg watched, her heart sinking. Even though her grandmother had told her she was going to put the bicycle lock on exhibit, Meg had wished feverishly she wouldn't. The humiliation of it left a suffocating sensation in Meg's throat, especially because Grandma told her she was going to tell every guest exactly what it was for. And she had done just that so far.

"Grandma . . . really. Do you *have* to set *that* out?" She'd done so for the past two weeks, and each time Meg's embarrassment returned tenfold.

Wizened smoky blue eyes lifted to view Meg over the

narrow lenses of her bifocals. "I most surely do. This chain represents the militant movement that I intend to personally bring to President McKinley's attention. That is, as soon as your parents get back from Niagara Falls."

Groaning, Meg lamented, "But do you *have* to chain yourself to the White House in order to make him notice you?"

"My fellow sisters and I plan to convene on the steps June the fourteenth at noon sharp. We have it on good authority that's the hour the President takes his lunch on the State Floor in the northwest dining room. Our intentions are to ruin his meal by locking ourselves to the ornamental iron fence along the north façade. Mrs. Gundy is even planning to swallow her key. I'm hiding mine down the front of my corset. Let it be said, that the man who dares to try and retrieve it will be sorry he ever laid a hand on my person. I know how to incapacitate a man with physical force. Have I told you how, Margaret?"

"Yes," she moaned.

"Good. Don't be afraid to do so if the need arises."

Meg's eyes closed for a moment, and she pretended her grandmother was a kindly old lady who smelled of sweet spices instead of printer's ink from the flyers that she made up to announce the time for women's freedom had come.

Slowly opening one eye first, Meg's illusions of her grandmother in gardening gloves, happily toiling over blue flags along the flower bed, instead of sewing a cloth flag with suffragettes climbing a mountain that resembled a man's head, were gone in an instant. Her other eye opened, and she couldn't dispel the image of rebellion. *Drat it anyway.*

Grandma Nettie's limber arm rose into a position much like the Statue of Liberty's. "We shall fight for equality and the right for all women to have the vote."

"I don't want to vote," Meg replied stubbornly.

"Margaret! Of course you want to vote."

"No, I don't."

"Why with your intelligence, you could be anything you wanted to be." With robust enthusiasm, she declared, "I think you'd make a fine first woman president."

Thoroughly mortified and feeling the heat of a blush work up her neck, Meg blurted out, "I don't want to be the first woman anything!"

"You have to aspire to something. What do you want to be?"

She thought for a moment, then corrected her posture and stared straight into her grandmother's waiting eyes. "I want to be irresistible to men."

Before Grandma Nettie could reply, the porter, Delbert Long, opened the hotel's double front doors and escorted a guest inside. Her grandmother walked from behind the desk to greet the new arrival.

In no mood to further battle wills with her grandmother, Meg turned to leave out the very same front doors. The thud of her shoes on the floorboards sounded childishly loud in her ears. She'd gotten no farther than five or so paces when she heard an ominous rip. Wide-eyed, she stopped dead in her tracks and slowly looked down. She could feel the damage before she could actually see it. A silky slippage of material passed her hips and thighs as the torn waistband began to make its descent. Her head awhirl with the consequences of walking home in such a state, she could barely think.

She felt through the fabric of her skirt, grabbed what she could, and sidled her way back to the counter. Reaching over the registry book, she fumbled for the room keys that were kept on individual hooks. She took the first one her fingers touched, then lifted herself on tiptoe to view the inside of Grandma Nettie's sewing basket. Spotting a safety pin, she stole that as well. With the loose gathers of her petticoat around her hips, and her skirt riding high above her calves, she shot up the stairs without a backward glance.

Knees knocking together, Meg half walked, half ran, across the runner of hall carpet. She glanced at the circular tag on the key ring. Room 32. In her haste, she hadn't noticed if two keys had been on the desk hook. One meant occupied and two meant vacant. The hotel would be full by this weekend when all the fly fishermen arrived in Harmony for the tournament. A few already had registered and were in residence now. Fortunately, none were in view.

Almost stumbling to keep her underskirt from falling below her knees, Meg started skimming the numbers on doors. Things like this didn't happen to Camille Kennison, the prettiest girl in town. And they didn't happen to Crescencia Stykem who was now Crescencia Dufresne. Although if they were to happen to somebody, Cressie was the likely candidate. Only she was married and underwear disasters didn't happen to married people.

Coming to the right door, she bunched her skirt in her left hand and inserted the key with her right. Before she turned the knob, she rapped twice on the door and waited to the count of fifteen. No answer. Letting her breath out, she slipped inside the room and shut the door behind her.

Meg made a cursory inspection of the furnishings. There wasn't a single piece of luggage or personal affect in sight. Spring sunshine spilled in through the window and made a cozy pattern on the floor that stretched to the closed bathroom door. *Thank goodness.* After tossing the key onto the bed, she relaxed and let her petticoat fall to her ankles. Opening the safety pin, she held it between her lips, then wadded her Manchester cloth skirt to her waist and bent to hoist the petticoat over her ankles and knees to her hips.

"This wouldn't have happened if Mama had a sewing machine," she muttered around the pin. "But no. She won't have one of those contraptions in her home." In a wiggle, Meg brought the torn waistband to its proper place.

Not the best seamstress, Meg realized after the fact that she had made her stitches too far apart. Tightness and neatness, Mama always said, when making a seam. Well, Meg was too impatient for that. She'd revamped all five of her petticoats in under a flat hour, and was rather proud of herself for her speed.

Just as she matched the raveled edges of the waistband and was about to take the pin from her lips, the bathroom door opened and Meg's head shot up. Shock flew through her as a man—half *naked*—stood in the doorway. The starched white muslin fell from her grasp, and the entire petticoat dropped in a pile around her feet. *Oh my goodness!*

He had a towel wrapped around his lean middle, and she couldn't help staring at his navel. A very light sprinkling of coarse brown hair swirled there, and against a belly so flat she could iron a shirtwaist on it and not have a single wrinkle. Upward . . . a chest like a washboard and shoulders wider than she'd ever noticed on a man.

He was tall and muscular, with wet hair that seemed more light brown than dark, a slight growth of beard, bushy brows tapered just enough to be utterly handsome, a set of eyes too dreamy a green to gaze into for longer than a few seconds . . . because she felt herself starting to swoon . . . and the nicest shaped mouth she'd ever had the pleasure of nearly fainting over.

"Where did you come from?" His voice, so manly and . . . deep, sent a delightful shiver through her body. Not to mention, his gaze ran over her hotter than her hair curler when she forgot about it on the lamp. She could almost feel the sizzle in the air, as he lowered his eyes to her legs—she, the big boob, not having had the foresight to have dropped her skirt. Now, all she could do was stand there, like a silly mouse, too stunned to do anything more than keep her lips together in an effort not to swallow the safety pin. So he really got his fill of her stockinged legs and drawers.

"Hello," she finally managed to mumble through the pin held in her teeth.

"Who are you?" Aside from his question and the furrow in his brow, the man seemed undaunted to find an uninvited female in his room. It must happen to him a lot, Meg concluded.

"I, ah . . . Mah-eg Bah-rooks." She spit the safety pin out, somehow managed to close it, and clutch the notion in her palm. "I'm Meg Brooks. My father owns the hotel."

He seemed to be in no self-conscious discomfort—being nearly nude in front of her, and all. She, on the other hand, felt the onset of dizziness. For all her talk about wanting a man to notice her, here she was face-to-face with one, and she had not a single worthwhile or intelligent thing to say.

His greenish-gold eyes narrowed . . . oh so very attractive with their blunt lashes. "What happened to you?"

Sighing as she struggled to keep a modicum of dignity, she feigned unconcern while dropping her skirt to cover herself. "Oh, I had an . . . accident. You see . . . my . . ." Her mother's stern warning came inside her head and she was told never to mention an article of clothing to a man—ever. Even if he was your husband. "I . . . that is my . . ." *Drat it.* Why couldn't she just say the word "petticoat" in front of him and explain what happened? Because she would be thoroughly flustered if pressed to do so.

Meg gazed at the layers of muslin that resembled ripples of untoasted meringue covering her shoes, then lifted her eyes. At length, she took the coward's way out and hoped he wouldn't notice she didn't give him a definitive answer. "Are you finding your accommodations here sufficient? Is there anything you require?"

He took a few steps, and she noted his stomach never flinched in the least. It stayed just as taut and hard when he moved. "Have you brought my bags?"

Guiltily flashing her gaze upward again, she said in a rush, "You have bags?" *Why hadn't he taken them up with him?*

"When I left the livery, I did. All I have with me are my saddlebags."

That explained it. A haphazard check-in. "Oh . . . then I'm certain Delbert will get them for you."

Think, Meg! She had to get out of here. If Grandma Nettie found her, Meg would be in hot water. Escape was the operative word here. But not until she could walk without tripping on her unmentionables. How did one make herself look a lot more at ease and calm pulling up her petticoat and pinning it while a man watched? She just couldn't . . .

Stepping out of her underskirt, she dipped down and bunched it in her fists. "I have to be going now." The stiff cloth pressed against her breasts as she cradled it with arms crossed over as much as she could to keep the petticoat snug and obscured. As if she could really hide the evidence!

"If you need anything . . . don't, ah, hesitate to ask the front desk." With a backward walk, she managed to get to the door and clutch the knob. Turning her body with what she hoped appeared to be a polished gracefulness, she opened the door. Checking first to see if the coast was clear, she didn't take a single step out of the room. *Gads!* Grandma Nettie was coming down the hallway escorting the new arrival to his room, while Delbert Long rolled the second-story bellman's cart right behind them *and* directly toward her!

Meg slammed the door and pressed her back against it, the petticoat still at her breast—only one-handed now. The other hand like a vise on the doorknob.

"Another accident?" the man queried. A single brow rose in a wry arch.

Panic welling in her throat, Meg couldn't reply.

The sharp reverberation against her shoulder blade as the wooden door panel was knocked on, made Meg jump away as if she'd been scorched.

More knocking. Then: "Porter, sir," came Delbert's announcement.

Standing in the middle of the room, looking helplessly from one end of its bed to the bureau and fireplace and bathroom door, she didn't know where to hide. And when the man proceeded toward her with that damp towel looking ready to fall off, she squeezed her eyes closed and took in a deep breath. Certainly no help for the situation, but if that towel unwrapped from his middle and exposed him, she didn't want to see. On the other hand, she could look through the fringe of her lashes, and he wouldn't be the wiser. It would satisfy her curiosity, even though the anatomy wouldn't be in clear focus.

Precariously close to her ear, and in a resonant-toned whisper so deliciously low and baritone it caused her to literally gasp, he bade, "Go into the bathroom and close the door."

Her bearings crashing in on her from the deepness of his voice, her eyes flew open. Through the repeated knock on the door, she said, "I can't hide in there. You don't know Delbert." Having no choice, she made a dash for the bed and scrambled down. She tucked herself beneath the mattress frame, making sure the full width of her skirt hem had been pulled in and hidden with her. Scooting into the middle, she roused the dust bunnies from the floor. The flying tufts of lint made her think she had to sneeze. She buried her nose in the wad of her petticoat and peered over the cloth.

She couldn't see the man's feet. He'd gone to the door. It opened and Delbert gave a hearty greeting.

"Good afternoon, sir. My apologies for the delay in fetching your luggage. As you can see, the matter has been rectified. I'll put them where you like."

The porter entered the room and came straight to the bed and stopped. She stared at his shoes. Lace-ups. Box calf bluchers. In need of polishing on the right heel.

"The bed will be fine," the man directed. She couldn't see him. He must have remained by the door.

Meg's nose itched. She rubbed it in the muslin.

Delbert walked away, then returned once more and set articles on the bed; it creaked some. The springs were slightly worn.

Two bare feet came close, then disappeared into the bathroom. He came back and stood by the bed once more. She studied the masculine toes. Nicely shaped. The nails clean with perfectly trimmed whites. Some dark hairs over the tops of his knuckles. Low arches. She thought they were very beautiful for being feet. Wait until she told her friends Ruth Elward and Hildegarde Plunkett.

"Thanks," the man said, as a jingle of coins exchanged hands.

She couldn't possibly be so lucky Delbert would leave without giving his full routine. Not him.

"Sir, allow me to show you the features of this room."

Meg's forehead lowered and bumped quietly on the floorboards. Nope. No luck for her.

"This is one of our better rooms. You'll notice the bed is quite comfortable, it being of the iron brass frame variety rather than solid oak, which can tend to warp and become creaky." Delbert walked on. His shoes were buffered by the large rug in front of the mantel. "We keep wood for the fireplace year round in case of a cold spell. With this being late March, one can never tell. The temperature drops quite considerably at night."

"I'll remember that. Thanks for telling me." Bare feet walked by the bed and toward the door once more. "If I need anything else, I'll call on the front desk."

"But I haven't shown you the bathroom features. Modern plumbing—just a year old. I can see you've tried out our shower bath. Was it acceptable?"

"Dandy."

Meg bit back a smile. He was being sarcastic and Delbert didn't realize it.

Thuds sounded as the porter walked to the bathroom, undaunted by the man's dismissal. Delbert Long was never put off. "This way, sir, and I'll demonstrate in case you overlooked anything."

The man must have sensed Delbert wouldn't leave until finished, so he went with him. Hot and cold water faucets turned on and off. Then the shower curtain slid on its hooks. The opening and closing of the cabinet. A flush from the toilet, or as her mother would say, the necessary.

At last, they exited the bathroom.

Meg turned her face to see if she could find a snippet of the porter's shoes. As she did so, she practically choked on a bouncing puff of linen fuzz. Her sneeze came through her nose before she could stop it.

"What was that?" Delbert asked.

"I didn't hear anything."

"It sounded like a sneeze."

"Somebody in the next room."

"Couldn't be. These walls are solid."

Meg held her breath as Delbert's shoes filled her view once more. She began inching her way farther back to the bed's headboard. As she did so, her pompadour caught on a coil and tugged. She bit her lip hard to keep from crying out as she got hung up, but a small squeak escaped her. Delbert would find her now. His hearing was impeccable.

"What's that I see on the floor?" the man demanded, his tone considerably irritable.

Delbert wasn't easily swayed. "I heard a noise again."

"There is no noise." Then angrily, "There's a safety pin on my floor."

"Indeed," Delbert conceded.

"The maid must have missed it." Before the porter could, the man crouched down on the balls of his feet and picked it up. His towel brushed the floor, his calf muscles straining for a moment while he moved. She gaped at the definition of his legs. "Here it is. I won't make a complaint about it. This kind of thing happens."

"Thank you for your understanding, sir."

"No problem." The man walked Delbert to the door and as Delbert wished him a pleasant stay, the door was closed midway through his oft-repeated sentence.

Meg did readily move. Her scalp throbbed where her hair had caught. If she could have, she would have lifted her arms to undo herself, but space didn't permit such a maneuver.

"You can come out now. He's gone."

"Ah . . . yes, I know. But I can't."

"What do you mean, you can't?"

"I've had a slight . . ." Dismal, she couldn't finish.

"Let me guess." He lowered again and stuck his head beneath the bed. She gave him her most bewitching smile, the one she practiced in the mirror after brushing her teeth. Unfortunately, it didn't have the affect on him she'd hoped. "You've had another accident."

Frowning her disappointment that he didn't find her divinely captivating, she mumbled, "Yes, I did. My hair is stuck and I can't get out. You have to get me free. My hands won't reach the springs."

She thought she heard him mutter an expletive as he stood. The towel fell on the floor in a clump, then more shuffling inside bags until a pair of worsted trousers came into sight and first one leg then the other slipped into the dark blue legs. He lowered onto his knees again, then laid on his belly and crawled in toward her.

This close to him, and in such a confining space, the scent of his bathing soap filled the air. *El Soudan*'s coconut oil. She'd know it anywhere. The traces smelled so good, she could . . . Meg swallowed . . . she could almost taste him. She got that fainthearted feeling again when he reached for her and his fingers tangled in her hair.

Explosions of tingles ran down her spine as he sifted through her hair and pulled out the pins in order to take down the high pile. Her gaze stayed fixed on the floor; she didn't dare risk looking at him. She didn't want him to know that she'd discovered paradise in his simple touch.

He was very gentle. A few more carefully orchestrated pulls that separated strands of hair, and she was free.

"All right, you can come out now." He backed away from her and extended his hand. It was big and square and inviting.

First a little hesitant, she relented and laid her fingers in his. He had a smooth palm with no callouses. His grip wasn't that of a loafer; she was acutely conscious of his impressive strength. She slid from under the bed, her petticoat still balled in her fist. He assisted her to her feet. As he did so, her hair tumbled into her eyes, around her shoulders, and down to her waist. She'd never liked the color. Copper. So . . . so vivid and . . . coppery. She'd stuck out like a sore thumb all through school. Well, maybe not only herself. Crescencia Stykem's hair was red-orange. Meg supposed copper was better, but not by much.

The man stared at the waves surrounding her as she pushed them aside so she could see him in return. He gave her a look over . . . but she couldn't tell what he thought of the copper color. Probably thought it was too . . . too much.

"Thank you . . . I have to go . . . but . . ." Now Meg had her hair to contend with as well as the petticoat. She couldn't face Grandma Nettie in the state she was in. She had to fix herself up before she left this room.

He reached for her and lifted her hand. At the base of her throat, she felt her pulse beat unevenly. Into her palm, he pressed her hairpins and the safety pin. Then in that husky voice of his told her to "Go into the bathroom and put yourself together."

If he hadn't nudged her with a light push of her shoulders, she doubted she could have moved. She'd been transfixed by the play of light from the window that reflected in his eyes.

Once she snapped out of her trance, she strode into

the bathroom and made short work out of repairing herself. In the process, she took in the items strewn on the floor. A pair of trail-dirty Levi's, a faded red shirt, a twist of white drawers, belt with holster . . . and gun. *My goodness.* And the avowed saddlebags. With a parting glance in the mirror, she poked the last hairpin home and told herself this would have to do.

Ready to face him once more, she threw herself into her most ladylike and gracious air of reserve as she stepped into the bedroom apartment once more.

The man had slipped into a shirt in her absence, although he hadn't buttoned it. A wedge of chest showed through the opening. That tantalizing glimpse of hair.

She paused at the bed, stared at the mound of luggage and fishing gear, then picked up the key she'd tossed. "My key," she explained. "It has to go back on the hook at the registration desk . . . or else . . . that is, my grandma. . . . It just has to go back."

His brows lifted slightly, but he said nothing.

"Well," she sighed, taking short steps to the door, "thank you for everything. I'm sorry for any inconvenience I might have caused you."

He made no comment.

She couldn't leave. Not yet. Not until she knew his name. She was halfway in love with him. She had to find out who he was.

"Well, thank you again . . . Mr. . . . ah . . . ?"

"Ga—" A heavy frown marked his forehead, as if he'd become quite annoyed about something. Then, "Wilberforce. Vernon Wilberforce."